The Propriety of Affection

R.M. Gardana

Published in the United States by

Hamilton Press

ISBN: 978-0-578-00655-0

Dedicated to my husband, Kristofer, for all his love
and support and to my good friend Tanya for
being the first to read this novel

CHAPTER ONE

Marian Amberly was the eldest of six children produced during the second marriage of Sir John Amberly. She was handsome, lively and free-spirited and was the daughter who most resembled the second Lady Amberly in her own youth. The one trait she did not inherit from her mother, however, was her mother's ambition to marry. Marian had a fortune of twenty thousand pounds from her parents and was rumored to be the prospective heiress of her maternal uncle's fortune. In spite of these material blessings, however, a season in London at eighteen and a season in Bath at nineteen failed to produce any acceptable suitors to bestow them upon. Now, at the age of twenty, at the beginning of a new season in London, Marian's heart remained untouched and her mother grew increasingly exasperated with her daughter's indifference.

Rachel, who was nineteen, was slightly more reserved than Marian. She and Marian could be, at times, very different, but the two sisters were very close. Marian consulted her in many things and was scarcely happy when Rachel was not at her side.

After the family was settled into their townhouse in the east side of London for the season, the first thing to be done after their arrival in town was for Lady Amberly to leave cards with all her acquaintances whom were already in London, including the Dowager Lady Beauregard, former Countess of—

Marian and Rachel were obliged to go on these errands with their mother, though Rachel was spared from attending large public parties until she was officially "out" the following week. After Lady Amberly had properly disposed of all her cards, she took the girls for a bit of shopping. The girls spoke about the Vauxhall Gardens, balls, the Derby and many other London diversions with great anticipation.

As she was following her mother and sister out of a bookshop, Marian was reading the titles of her books and almost walked into the street right as a carriage was passing at a rather fast pace. She was caught just in time by a handsome young man who happened to be standing near.

"Thank you," Marian breathed, as her eyes met those of the handsome stranger. Her heart was pounding in her chest as she realized the danger she had just escaped. "I—ought to have paid more attention to where I was going. You must think me very foolish."

"No," the stranger replied with a smile of amusement. "If I had been reading Pope, I would have been distracted as well." He had already picked up the books she had dropped and insisted on escorting her to her mother.

"I'm much obliged to you, sir," Marian said, blushing crimson when he had returned her to her mother and she was seated in the carriage.

"I'm delighted to be of service, Ma'am," he replied. Then with a bow he turned and continued on his way, leaving Marian none the wiser as to his identity.

"Who was that?" Lady Amberly demanded.

"He saved me from being run over. I almost walked into the street."

"You ought to pay more attention to your surroundings, Marian," Lady Amberly replied. "You can't always expect to be rescued by handsome strangers who won't introduce themselves. That young man *looks* genteel enough, though more and more trades-people are trying to pass themselves off as gentlemen nowadays."

"I think he's handsome," Rachel said. "There is something very gentlemanly about his manner. I wonder if we shall see him again."

"I hope so. I should like to know to whom I am obliged."

In the afternoon, Lady Beauregard, the Dowager Countess of— called on Lady Amberly and her daughters. The dowager was Lady Amberly's aunt as well as the mother of Sir John's first wife, Lady Marian Amberly and consequently, she was the grandmother of Sir John's four eldest children. It had taken the dowager more than a decade to forgive her niece for the scandal of marrying her late daughter's husband, but she was at last receptive to Lady Amberly's attempts at reconciliation for the sake of having a relationship with her grandchildren. And though Sir John's four eldest children were quite grown by this time, Lady Amberly was properly respectful of her aunt and therefore remained in tolerable good standing with the dowager.

The dowager was accompanied by her granddaughter, Lady Emily, a very elegant young lady with fair hair and features. Marian had never met Lady Emily, but she was not fond of the dowager, whom she had met a few times during a previous stay in London.

The dowager and Lady Emily stayed for half an hour engaging in light conversation dominated by the dowager. They spoke of the London season, presentation at court and suitable beaux for the young ladies. By the time the dowager had left, she told Rachel that her first dance at her coming out should be with the dowager's grandson, Lord Richard, who, her ladyship informed her, was among the most eligible bachelors in London.

The dowager then asked Rachel if she were attending Lady Beauregard's dinner party. Rachel begged her ladyship's pardon, but she had a previous agreement with a young lady whose acquaintance had been made in Bath the previous winter. Perhaps it was for the best, her Ladyship replied. After all, Miss Rachel had not yet come out in London and it would be proper to wait to dine in much company, as London was far different than the little country assemblies Miss Amberly and her sister were used to, she had no doubt.

"Can you believe the arrogance of that woman?" Marian said, the moment she and her sister were alone. "Oh, how kind of her to condescend to allow you the ultimate *honor* of dancing with her grandson! I am sorry for you, Rachel. Fortunately for me, Lord Richard did not happen to be in town when I came out, or I should have had to dance with him too."

"But have you actually met Lord Richard?" Rachel asked. "Have you any reason to think so ill of him?"

"I have met him once," Marian replied. "Do you remember when I went to stay with Sarah for two months? Well there was a Miss Henderson there for some weeks as well. She is a cousin of the count's on his mother's side, you know. Lord Richard happened to come for two weeks, on his way to London from visiting a school friend. I was not out at the time, of course, but I daresay he would have devoted more attention to me, had he known I was worth about twice as much as Miss Henderson. As it was, he hardly marked me at all, but spent much of his time walking about the park with her."

"Perhaps his lack of attention is the real reason for your dislike," Rachel suggested with a smile of amusement. "You resent that he paid more attention to a young lady of half your consequence. But as you were not out, is that not as it should be?"

"You misunderstand me, Rachel. I care not for his good opinion. I found him to be the most insupportable coxcomb I have ever seen. When Miss Henderson was at the pianoforte, nothing would please him but to go stand beside her while she played and induce her into singing duets."

"Was Miss Henderson as repulsed by Lord Richard as you profess to be?"

"Indeed no. In fact, she was quite charmed by him, it seemed. Naturally Lord Richard had no serious designs. Miss Henderson was simply a fair bit of amusement while he was in the house. Her father is not titled, nor is her fortune anything to speak of. That is, it is nothing to speak of for a son of the nobility. Only ten thousand pounds."

"And so you are to dine at Lord Beauregard's," Rachel said. "I should like to go. All this talk of Lord Richard has made me quite curious to see him."

"If I faced the prospect of spending the evening with Miss Perdue," Marian said, "I should prefer to go to Lord Beauregard's myself."

"You are very unkind," Rachel said reproachfully. "I don't know why you have such a dislike for Miss Perdue."

"She is no more fond of me, I daresay," Marian replied. "And I cannot bear false civility."

"You must tell me if Lord Richard remembers you as well as you remember him," Rachel said slyly. "For you seem to recollect a great many details about one encounter with someone you detest."

"I doubt he will remember me at all," Marian answered. "Take care not to fall in love with him, Rachel. He will break your heart in the end, if you do."

Sir John and Lady Amberly arrived at the residence of Lord Beauregard with John and Arthur, sons from Sir John's previous marriage, and Marian. John, the eldest, looked bored, as he usually did when he was not playing cards or riding in Hyde Park. He was generally not impressed by the daughters of the aristocracy and described them as painted dolls with no real substance. Arthur, Sir John's third eldest, took pleasure in the company of all young ladies and made himself agreeable to everyone. After they greeted the host and hostess, Marian searched the drawing-room for anyone of her acquaintance. The only person she knew in the room besides the dowager countess was Lady Emily, so she proceeded to her.

"Miss Amberly," Lady Emily said. "How good of you to come. Allow me to introduce my friend, Miss Sheffield. Miss Sheffield is the sister of Mr. Sheffield, of Aberdeen." All the girls curtseyed to one another.

"Do you go to Almack's, Miss Amberly?" Miss Sheffield asked.

"No," Marian said. "My father does not much care for Almack's."

"But Miss Amberly, that is where the most fashionable men in London are to be found. You must attend all the Almack's balls if you want to find a suitable husband."

"Miss Amberly is only joking," Lady Emily said. "Surely they will attend, as her sister is to be introduced into society next week."

"I assure you we will not," Marian said. "My father says it is the most insipid way to spend an evening and the refreshments are nothing remarkable. No, my mother is to throw a coming out ball for Rachel on Tuesday evening."

"Well I suppose it is acceptable for one's family to throw a ball," Miss Sheffield said reluctantly. "But only the most respectable people attend Almack's. And you know very few younger sons are allowed, so most of the men you meet will be *elder* sons."

"It is my experience that younger sons are often times more respectable, as the elder sons are brought up to be idle," Marian said "I should not like to marry a man who is like *my* eldest brother. Who wants to be married to a man with no morals or scruples, whether he has a title or not?"

"Oh how droll you are!" Miss Sheffield exclaimed. "You don't suppose that once a man marries you he concerns himself much about you afterwards, do you? Why, my parents hardly spent three hours a day in one another's presence. Father was always at Parliament or out on a hunting party, while Mother went visiting or entertained her guests at home. To be sure, Mother was exceedingly melancholy when Father died of consumption and died herself not half a year afterwards. The time my mother spent with my Father during his illness was probably more than the whole rest of their marriage put together. How dull it must have been!" Marian was quite repulsed by Miss Sheffield's unfeeling speech.

"What if one marries a man with a bad temper?" Marian asked. "Or a gamester or drunkard? Should not you take temperament into consideration when rejecting or accepting a man?"

"To be sure!" Miss Sheffield said. "I'm not saying you must choose the first man who asks you. But if his vices are only such as will not affect you, you needn't be too scrupulous. After all, there are very few elder sons who are not somewhat reckless."

"But Miss Sheffield," Lady Emily said. "Is not your own brother an exception? I have never heard anything unfavorable about him."

"Dear Edward! Well, certainly he is an exception. How I wish he were not! He can be so tiresome you know. He preaches at me constantly, but I never pay him any mind. However, he was destined for the church and inherited the estate because our eldest brother was killed in a drunken brawl and had no heirs. But Miss Amberly looks shocked. I daresay I have proved her point about eldest sons." Miss Sheffield laughed and Marian curtseyed and walked to another part of the room, for she could stand no more of Miss Sheffield's prattle.

"Miss Amberly," said the dowager. "Come here, my dear." Reluctantly, Marian walked to where her Ladyship was standing in conversation with a very handsome young gentleman who appeared to be about five and twenty. "I believe you have not met my grandson, Lord Richard."

"It is an honor to make your acquaintance," Lord Richard said, bowing. Marian curtseyed. She had forgotten how very handsome Lord Richard was and had not seen him in four years. However, she knew that he was a mere coxcomb and hardly worth bothering with, even if he was in line for a title.

"Miss Amberly has been out for two years, but the family did not come to town last winter. You were in Bath, were you not?"

"Yes ma'am," Marian said. "My father had ill health last year and wished to go to Bath instead. But m'lord," she said, turning to Lord Richard. "You have met me once before. Do you not remember?"

"Upon my honor, I do not remember when I've had that happy privilege."

"Perhaps you did not think it such a happy privilege then as you do now," Marian replied. "I believe you were quite taken up with another lady at the time."

"Upon my word, Miss Amberly, you cruelly arouse my curiosity."

"Oh yes, child," the dowager interjected. "Do tell us what you mean. I am sure if dear Richard were taken up with any young lady, he would be married now. For surely no woman in her senses would turn him down."

"Perhaps I am mistaken," Marian said. "Indeed, it may have been some other young man. Yes, come to think of it, I'm quite sure it was." Marian gave Lord Richard a taunting look that plainly told him she did in fact believe him to be the man she spoke of. However, Marian was in no humor to satisfy the busybody inquiries of the dowager and would not admit it in her presence. Her ladyship was satisfied with this reply, however, and soon walked away to some of her other acquaintance.

Marian curtseyed and was turning away when Lord Richard called her back.

"I do beg you to tell me what you meant just now," he said. "I know you did not persist in the presence of the dowager for reasons I can well understand. But do tell me where we've met before? For now I come to think I *have* seen you before."

"What a shame for you to speak so of your own grandmother," Marian said coyly. "Especially as she is so very fond of you. If you'll excuse me, sir, I must go speak to my brother, for I see he is all alone." With another curtsey she walked away to her eldest brother, happy for an excuse to get away.

"What do you think of this party, Mary?" John asked. "They all bow and smirk and talk behind one another's back."

"No doubt you paint a very accurate picture," Marian said. "But you would do well not to say it quite so loud. Someone may hear you, you know."

"Quite true," John replied. "You know there's nothing I like better than some young coxcombs and old gossips to laugh at."

"And some pretty girls to flirt with," Marian added. "Your cousin Lady Emily seems like she would just suit you!"

"A painted doll!" John protested. "I need a woman with more substance than that. She probably knows some pieces on the pianoforte and how to make a few primitive drawings and every dance there is. In short, everything necessary to catch a husband and bore him to death afterwards. No thank you. None of your spineless ladies for me."

"How you make me laugh! But my dear brother, are not all we marriageable young ladies how you describe us? Pretty showpieces on display?"

"Not you, Mary. You've more to you than that. These girls can't hold a candle to you. *You* won't allow yourself to be brow-beaten by any man, I'm sure. But see how many ladies set their cap at me! I must be always on the defense against relentless mothers and their pretty daughters."

"We daughters must be on the lookout too."

"Oh is the old dowager trying to play matchmaker?" John asked. "I heard her call you over to introduce Lord Richard. What do you say to that? Should you not like to be a countess?"

"Not if it means being married to Lord Richard. If I ever did, I should have to bid farewell to my senses."

"Upon my word, Lord Richard does seem struck with you," John said. "I do not believe he's looked away from you since you left him."

"Well I'm very glad my fortune is only twenty thousand, for with less than fifty thousand, I am in no danger of his serious pursuit. The eldest son of an earl, you know, must have a certain minimum he will accept before he sells the honor of being his wife. And if he means to toy with me, I shall have all the more pleasure of tormenting him."

"A challenge will make him pursue you all the more. If you want to be rid of him, your best strategy will be to make him believe he's made a conquest of you and leave him to congratulate himself and leave you alone."

"I don't want him to have the pleasure of thinking he's made a conquest of me."

"Well you must leave the poor boy something to console himself with," John said. "Perhaps you might drop a handkerchief when he's looking, and then walk away."

"John, how can you talk so?" Marian cried.

"I daresay he would pick it up," John said. "Why do not I ask him?"

"John, I absolutely forbid it." Despite his sister's protests, John called Lord Richard over to them. Marian quickly opened her fan and held it over her mouth and nose to hide her blushes and her vexation.

"Amberly," Lord Richard said. "How good of you to come. Your sister was just teasing me in the most cruel manner. She tells me we have met before but will not tell me where. Can you tell me what she means by it?"

"Indeed I cannot," John said. "Perhaps it was at a ball and you did not ask her to dance. You know young ladies seldom forget such an occurrence."

"Indeed it is quite impossible to ask every lady at a ball," Lord Richard replied. "For more often than not, there are far more ladies than dances and often more ladies than gentlemen at a ball. However, I assure you I shall never repeat such a mistake with Miss Amberly, if only she will come out from hiding behind her fan." Marian, sufficiently assured that her brother had only been teasing her, lowered her fan, closed it and gave Lord Richard a defiant look as if daring him to accuse her of coquetry. Marian held eye contact with Lord Richard, expressionless, and did not blush or look away—an effect his lordship was unaccustomed to, for he was quite caught by the fire in her eyes.

Lord Richard was awakened from his trance by the interruption of his mother, who had come to introduce to Marian her husband's nephew, Mr. George Wesley, who was to escort Marian down to dinner and to claim the other two young men to take their own place in the succession.

Marian was set between her brother, John, and Mr. George Wesley. George Wesley was the younger son of a baron and Lady Eleanor, who was the sister of Lord Beauregard and Lady Marian. Mr. Wesley was a tall, thin and quiet young man who looked barely of age and spent much of his time looking over at the young lady sitting next to Sir John, quite evidently wishing he was in Sir John's place. Marian looked across the table and after seeing that Lord Richard was almost directly opposite her and engaged in conversation with Lady Amberly, she determined not to look that direction anymore. She was not sure whether it would be proper to begin a conversation with Mr. Wesley and he said nothing, no doubt unsure of what to say.

"John, who is that young lady sitting by our father?" Marian asked John, who only had Arthur on his other side.

"I don't know," John replied. "No doubt just out in society."

"That is Miss Seldon." Mr. Wesley spoke unexpectedly. "She is a very accomplished young lady and the heiress to an estate in Surrey."

"Is that her father sitting by Lady Emily?" Marian asked, determined not to let her opportunity for conversation pass.

"Oh no," Mr. Wesley said with an amused smile. "That is Lord Thomas Billingsly. His father, the Marquis of—, is sitting beside Lady Beauregard. Miss Seldon's father is not titled, but he comes from a very old and respectable family. No doubt but Miss Seldon is worthy of any title fortune may give her." Mr. Wesley looked slightly embarrassed as he said this last part.

"Is her father here then?"

"Mr. Seldon is currently residing in Bath on account of his ill health," Mr. Wesley said. "Miss Seldon is in town visiting her cousins, Mr. Sheffield and his sister, and it is with them she came this evening."

"Are you very well acquainted with the Seldons, then? Is Miss Seldon just out?"

"I—I believe this is her first season in town." Mr. Wesley looked a little confused. "I've danced with her once or twice and have seen her at some parties. At one dinner I had the honor of escorting her down. She told me she is very fond of music and I believe she sings very well. But I am of no musical turn myself." Mr. George Wesley seemed to think very highly of Miss Seldon and Marian began to suspect that he was well on his way to being in love with her.

"I am very fond of music myself," Marian said, deciding to take the conversation another direction, seeing that Mr. Wesley was beginning to grow uncomfortable with conversation of Miss Seldon. "I am very fond of reading, too. Are you fond of reading, Mr. Wesley?"

"I do as little reading as I can get away with," Mr. Wesley said. "I have read the classics in school and some poetry. However, I much prefer art. I should like very much to be an architect. I also paint. My father says it is all right as long as I don't make it a profession. Painting is not a gentlemanly profession, he says."

"I have done some watercolors," Marian said. "I do like to draw, but my sister Rachel is decidedly the better painter. We are both fond of many of the same things. She is the better rider, I am the better musician. But we are both fond of horses and of music. Do you often ride into Hyde Park before dinner?"

"Sometimes I go with Lord Richard. He is very fond of riding in the Park. Particularly when there are ladies to impress. He's a very good horseman and musician."

"Oh yes. He has amused me exceedingly with his musical talents. Lord Richard is a very good musician, and I daresay he knows it and takes every opportunity of ensuring that everyone else knows it too." Mr. Wesley laughed at the illustration.

"Has my cousin been so unfortunate as to merit your ridicule? This is a very fine picture of him! One would think he was quite a dandy by your calculation. However I make no doubt but he would laugh very heartily at hearing himself described in such a way. For he has a very good sense of humor and knows when to laugh at himself."

"I would not have you repeat what I've said to his lordship," Marian said, alarmed that her censures should reach Lord Richard's ears. "I beg you not to think I would speak slightingly of him. I am not very well acquainted with Lord Richard, after all. I'm sure he's a very good sort of young man."

"Oh yes, by your account I'm sure you think him the very best kind of man. Come, come, you might as well say he's a coxcomb and a dandy, for it's plain you believe it to be so. And I could not say you would be very far off the mark. I do believe him to be a man of honor, however, and very condescending to his inferiors."

"Oh, yes. He was very condescending to me this evening. I believe he very nearly promised to dance with me at the next ball we meet at. I assure you, I feel the full force of the compliment. I don't know how I shall ever deserve the happiness of dancing with the future earl of—. After all, I am only a lowly baronet's daughter."

"Indeed I did not mean you were at all his inferior, nor would he say so himself. I only meant he was condescending to servants and working men, not to gentleman's daughters." This young man, who had started out very sober, was now vastly entertained with his dinner partner and thought her quite charming; and were his heart not already bestowed elsewhere, it might be gained with a little effort from Miss Amberly.

"Tell me, Mr. Wesley, is your cousin generally a forward kind of man? He does not strike me as easily intimidated."

"Lord Richard can be very forward if he chooses," Mr. Wesley said. "I've never seen him bashful or at a loss for words. The ladies in general seem very fond of his company. He has a terrible propensity to flirt, though he scarcely means anything by it. I should very much like to see him in love, just to see what effect it would have upon him."

"Are you fond of dancing, Mr. Wesley?" Marian was beginning to be afraid of lingering too much on Lord Richard and endeavored to change the subject.

"I do like dancing," Mr. Wesley said. "My brother is not so fond of it. Charles is a very sober fellow and all but the most somber dancing is a little too vivacious for his taste. He does enjoy the theater, however. And Vauxhall. Gaming tables he naturally avoids. Respectable card parties he's got no objection to, of course, but he doesn't play high. Indeed, he should have been the younger son, for he ought to be a clergyman."

"Are you to be a clergyman then? Or shall you be a great barrister?"

"No, I'm no orator. I suppose I must be a physician or join the army. I should not like to be in the army. I would rather be a great architect and a member of the Royal Academy. Father would disown me if I were to enter any profession which requires what he calls 'manual labor.'"

"Surely art can't be manual labor anymore than writing sermons or commanding troops. Especially if you like it."

"Perhaps not. But art is a profession that anyone from any class may undertake. It requires no particular education and one may never go to school and still produce a fine sculpture or painting. That, I believe, is where the principles of my father contradict it. Besides, artists are 'in trade,' and that would put me on the same level as a merchant or a surgeon. The associations, even more than the work itself, are objectionable to my father. It is not proper, he says, for a baron's son to be in trade, even if he is not the eldest."

"My mother's father was a banker and her mother was a merchant's daughter, but she was raised as genteel as anyone, though her fortune came from trade," Marian said, endeavoring to check her indignation. "I daresay my father thought her genteel enough to be a baronet's wife. I suppose your father doesn't know that your mother is my mother's first cousin? And consequently, descended from the same family?"

"Indeed—I believe—" Mr. Wesley was beginning to look rather awkward.

"Forgive me, Mr. Wesley," Marian said. "I have spoken out of turn. Your father is a man of importance and he ought to have the right to conceal any connections that might tarnish his good name. I beg you to believe me when I say I meant no disrespect to your family." Mr. Wesley, not knowing what to say, merely gave her a nod. Both were silent for a few moments. At length Mr. Wesley spoke.

"I am by no means angry at your frankness, Miss Amberly. Do not take my silence as a mark of displeasure, but a lack of anything to say. I have no excuse to make for my father's opinions. How can I, when it is his scruples which make it impossible to follow my own desires? My father is not a bad man, Miss Amberly, but he is proud. I daresay he would like me to marry Lady Emily and her fifty thousand pounds."

"But should you like it?"

"No, I think not. Lady Emily is a very accomplished young lady, to be sure. However, she is accustomed to a certain lifestyle which would not agree with the lifestyle of an officer or physician. Besides, it is not to be supposed she would marry a younger son with so many elder sons at her disposal."

"Would it suit you to marry an heiress, then?" Marian asked. Mr. Wesley looked slightly confused. "Or do you object to a marriage with any woman of means?"

"I should not object to marriage with any woman," Mr. Wesley replied. "If only the marriage were for the right reason."

"You don't approve of mercenary marriages then?"

"Indeed no. It is a profanation of the holy state of matrimony instituted at the beginning of history. However, I shan't judge anyone for doing as they choose."

"Perhaps you really had better be a clergyman, Mr. Wesley. You said that so eloquently just now. You should take a parish and hire a curate to do all the work, except performing marriages, which will, of course, be your lot." Mr. Wesley merely smiled.

"I would never have thought I should be a clergyman, Miss Amberly. 'Tis a sad world we're coming to if one must be a clergyman to have morals."

"Perhaps you are right. How vexing to have one's self corrected! Well I daresay being the younger son you'll not be pursued by young ladies with mercenary motives. But I hope you'll forgive my impertinence."

"Indeed, Madam, there's nothing to forgive. Frankness is a quality resented only by those who wish to do as they please and never have anyone contradict them, for fear they must cease doing something which gives them pleasure."

Soon after this conversation, the ladies retired to the drawing room. Lady Amberly, Lady Beauregard and the dowager engaged themselves in conversation on one side of the room and Miss Sheffield endeavored to entertain the other young ladies on the other side.

"Have you met my cousin, Miss Amberly?" Miss Sheffield asked, gesturing toward Miss Seldon. "Allow me to introduce Louisa to you. Oh, I beg your pardon. *Miss Seldon.*" Miss Seldon looked a little awkward as she curtseyed to Marian. "My cousin is very proper, you see, Miss Amberly," Miss Sheffield went on. "I may address her by her Christian name, because of our relationship, but I should not introduce her so. I find it more simple to refer to her as *my cousin* when in public, for it irritates *her* if I call her Louisa and it irritates *me* to call her Miss Seldon. You shall marry a lord, Louisa, for then I may simply call you your *ladyship.*"

"I suppose you think yourself very witty, Catherine," Miss Seldon said finally. "But you will find the world is full of vulgar and ill-mannered people who also fancy themselves so. Do not think that incurring the world's censure is a mark of cleverness." Miss Seldon coldly inclined her head and walked away to the pianoforte, where she began looking through some songbooks.

"You have offended her, Miss Sheffield," Lady Emily said. "Perhaps you ought to the let the poor girl alone. What has she done to offend you?"

"She has offended me with her company these three weeks," Miss Sheffield replied haughtily. "And she is likely to offend me with it for another month. She lectures me nearly every day. She is the dullest creature on earth! She would make a capital wife for my brother. Between the two of them my life is perfectly tedious. My only consolation is that we are not in the country. For without balls and parties to go to every day, I should be driven to distraction. It's almost enough to make one wish to get married." Marian excused herself and went after Miss Seldon. She picked up a collection of Purcell's music and began looking over it. Miss Seldon looked up.

"Are you fond of music, Miss Amberly?" she asked after a few moments.

"Oh, yes," Marian said, looking up. "But you are very fond of music too, are you not, Miss Seldon? I hear you are quite accomplished on the pianoforte."

"Indeed, I don't know who should praise me so. I am very fond of music, but I believe I do not practice as much as I ought."

"I would request you to play a piece now, if I did not fear Lady Beauregard would take it amiss. But it would be impolite to open the instrument ourselves. However, I make no doubt we shall have our opportunity after we are joined by the men."

"I would not make such an imposition, to be sure," Miss Seldon replied. "Besides, Lady Emily is said to have an exquisite singing voice and I am quite curious to hear her. And how beautiful she is! Golden hair, just like Catherine's. I wish I had beautiful hair like theirs. Or even yours, though it is dark."

"My dear Miss Seldon," Marian said, "You must not think of yourself so meanly. You have many first-rate qualities, I'm sure, which certain silly and frivolous girls do not. You have good sense and decorum and certainly more patience than I would display when confronted with such remarks as Miss Sheffield chooses to make."

"Oh yes. She is sometimes entertaining, but almost always thoughtless. A thoughtless girl of fortune is no good thing, for she may be led by some fortune hunter to believe herself in love. And she has a fairly large one. Thirty five thousand, I believe."

"Her brother, Mr. Sheffield, of whom she speaks of so disparagingly—is he here this evening?" Marian asked.

"Oh yes," Miss Seldon replied. "I shall point him out to you when he comes into the room. But for now, you must give me your opinion on Italian concertos."

Lord Richard was the first of the gentlemen to come into the drawing room, and he naturally gravitated to the pianoforte where sat the young lady who, for this evening, was of most interest to him.

"I admire your taste, Miss Amberly," he said presently. "And yours, Miss Seldon, for desiring the company of the pianoforte over that of rattling young ladies, as I know is the inclination of some." He looked over to where Lady Emily and Miss Sheffield were sitting.

"Indeed, my lord," was all the reply Marian could force herself to make to such an ill-bred comment before turning back to Miss Seldon.

"Mother," Lord Richard said suddenly so that nearly all the room could hear him. "Why have you not opened the pianoforte? Did you not see these young ladies wished to play?" Marian, feeling herself turning very red, stood up and stepped away from the instrument. Miss Seldon immediately followed suit. The rest of the gentlemen began entering the room.

"By all means, it should be opened," Lady Beauregard said. "Emily, will you play for us?" Lady Emily walked toward the pianoforte and Lord Richard spoke again.

"Nay, Mother. I have heard my sister perform, as she does well enough. I wish to hear Miss Amberly sing." Lady Beauregard looked mortified at being thus spoken to and Marian felt hardly less so.

"My lord, I beg you," Marian said, as low as she could and still be heard by Lord Richard. "Do not subject me to such humiliation. I assure you I have no desire to usurp your sister's right to play first. Besides," she added, "Miss Seldon and I have a great desire to hear her ourselves."

"Very well," Lord Richard said. "Go on, Emily. Miss Amberly wishes to hear you play." Lady Emily obediently sat down at the instrument and began to play, and Lord Richard stepped closer to Marian. "I will hear you play, Miss Amberly. You won't escape me." Marian gave him a cold curtsey and walked to her brothers were sitting.

"Lord Richard is the most impudent young man I have ever met!" Marian told John indignantly. "He speaks to me in a most familiar manner and he hardly knows me!"

"Well, when a man is bewitched by a woman," John replied, smiling, "He must be forgiven for acting under that spell."

"What nonsense you talk, John," Marian said. "Bewitched indeed. I think it more likely he likes to have all attention on him."

"I quite agree with you, Mary," Arthur said. "He is nothing more than a rascal who is to inherit a title. I hear he has broken many female hearts, leaving his own untouched."

"Well, he is the son of a lord," Marian said, "So he may do as he chooses."

"Well our mother was his father's sister," Arthur said. "So he need not think himself so very far above us."

"Our cousin is a very good sort of lad, Arthur," John told his brother. "Perhaps he is a little over-fond of ladies' society, but his behavior here is not very far from your own at our country balls at Shelby." Arthur flushed. "I could name off more than one lady who has fallen in love with you in that little country village. Remember the shopkeeper's pretty little daughter? She was so enchanted that the son of a baronet should ask her to dance that I do believe she surrendered her heart to you at once."

"Hush John," Marian said. "You mustn't tease poor Arthur. And you really ought to find another subject for your raillery."

"Would you rather I teased you?" John asked.

"I would rather you not tease at all. It is a pastime for Henry's age, and perhaps Reggie's, but you are two and thirty and ought to be a better example to your brothers."

"I assure you no one else has any notion that I am not the most proper and genteel of men," John said. "And no one should believe you if you told them otherwise."

"I think you should marry Miss Sheffield, John," Marian said. "At first I thought she and Lord Richard might make a good a match, but I think she would do better for you. Then you could tease each others' hearts out and leave the rest of the world be." After Lady Emily finished her piece, Miss Seldon sang an Irish melody. Miss Seldon played well, but her voice was not distinct. *Mr. George Wesley must surely be in love with her,* Marian thought to herself. *Otherwise he could not think her singing so very extraordinary.* Marian did acknowledge to herself, however, that Miss Seldon seemed a very good-natured girl and reflected she should not be sorry to become better acquainted with her. While Miss Seldon was playing her piece, Lord Richard walked to where Marian was sitting and informed her that she should be called on next to take her place behind the pianoforte.

"For I have allowed you to escape it long enough," he said.

"Why all this ado, my lord?" Marian asked. "Why are you so determined to hear me? I assure you, it is nothing extraordinary. I am afraid I will disappoint you after all this prelude."

"I declare that to be impossible, Miss Amberly," Lord Richard replied. "However, it is perhaps the novelty that intrigues me so. I am very fond of mystery, Miss Amberly."

"Well I am very open, my lord," Marian said. "And not very mysterious at all.

Therefore, I suppose we are fated to be enemies."

"I certainly hope not, Miss Amberly," Lord Richard said. "I am sure we should never be enemies. I have no enemies, and I'm sure you could have none either." Miss Seldon finished her piece. "Come now, Miss Amberly. It is your turn. I daresay you won't disappoint us all." With a brief inclination of the head, Marian allowed herself to be led to the pianoforte while John told Arthur in a low voice that he should not be sorry to see his sister the next countess of—and Arthur replied that he *should* be sorry to see her marry such a coxcomb and had a far better faith in her sense.

Marian sang "Fairest Isle" and the effect was most charming. She did not have the strong, rich voice that Lady Emily had, but she had a softness of tone that made her pleasant to listen to when singing a slow song. Furthermore, she *looked* very charming with her dark hair and fair skin. So charming, in fact, that Lord Richard thought it would be very pleasant to have her fall in love with him.

When Marian finished her song, she noticed among Lady Beauregard's guests the young man who had rescued her and he was looking intently at her. She stood up and would have gone to acknowledge him, but Lord Richard was again at her side.

"You played that song so beautifully, Miss Amberly," Lord Richard said. "I knew I would not be disappointed."

"Are you fond of music, Lord Richard?"

"Oh yes. I should very much like to play a duet with you, Miss Amberly, but I'm afraid it would not be proper for me to perform in front of all this company. Only ladies, you know, are allowed to exhibit in large parties. But if ever we are in a more private party, I shall be happy to perform for you." Marian, at a loss how to reply to such a shocking comment, would deign no reply, but after leading her back to her seat, Lord Richard seemed ready to sit beside her.

"Should you not invite Miss Sheffield to perform?" she asked him. "All the other ladies have performed and after making such ceremony of escorting me to the pianoforte, she might take it as a slight." Lord Richard looked confused, but bowed and told her she was quite right and walked away to Miss Sheffield.

"What a charming master of ceremonies he makes!" John said. "He tells everyone when to perform. Very gallant indeed!"

"I'm very glad you put him in his place, Mary," Arthur said. Miss Seldon soon joined them with the young man who had been watching her.

"Miss Amberly," Miss Seldon said. "Please allow me to introduce my cousin, Mr. Sheffield."

"I thought I should never see you again," Mr. Sheffield said. "I'm glad to discover your name at last."

"I'm glad to finally know to whom I am obliged," Marian replied. "Allow me to thank you again, sir, for your kind service."

"Tis a pleasure to be of service to a lady," Mr. Sheffield replied. "I assure you, it was nothing. Think no more of it, I beg you." Lord Richard returned to his assiduous attentions and Mr. Sheffield stepped back to make way for his more loquacious rival.

CHAPTER TWO

After breakfast the next morning, Lady Amberly and her daughters sat in the sitting room while Sir John and his eldest son went to White's and Arthur and Reggie went riding in Hyde Park, much to the dismay of Rachel, who wished very much to go and Reggie, who wished very much not to go. When Rachel begged her mother to let her go with her brothers, Lady Amberly replied that it was their day to be at home, should any of their acquaintance decide to call. So, the two sisters were obliged to entertain themselves by decorating a tea caddy with rolled paper, until someone should happen to call.

"I think Lord Richard is an extremely agreeable young man," Lady Amberly told her daughters. "I was set next to him last night and he was very pleasant indeed."

"All the more pleasant because of his title," Marian said in a low voice to her sister, who tittered.

"He seemed very struck with you, Marian," Lady Amberly went on. "He was very subtle with his inquiries, but not subtle enough for a mother to not see what he was about. However, I do not mind, for I should like it very much if you were to become a countess."

"I'm sure he has no such view, Mother," Marian replied. "He means to entertain himself with me until something better comes along. Take my word for it—he is a man of the town, as the saying goes."

"So you think you know better than your own mother, do you? No, I am certain that unless you are very foolish, you shall be the future Countess of— I told him you were fond of music, reading and riding and he said those were just his tastes."

"Of course he said that, Mother. A gentleman must agree with everything a lady says and pretend it is the most delightful thing he's ever heard. I suppose you told him on which days I go to Hyde Park so they he may endeavor to meet me there and what songs I like so that he may profess to like the same ones."

"He's rich, young, handsome and he's a lord," Lady Amberly said. "What else could you possibly want in a husband?"

"I want a husband to love and respect me. Someone who shares my tastes. Not someone who will grow bored with me after a month of marriage and have a kept mistress."

"Marian! What a shocking thing for a young lady to say! What has a young girl like you to do with kept mistresses?"

"Nothing, Mother. And it shall stay that way so long as I don't marry a man who's a libertine just because he has a title."

"How dare you say such a thing about Lord Richard! He is a most respectable young man, I assure you!"

"I didn't say Lord Richard, Mother. As of now I don't know whether he is one of those men or not. But I certainly shall not marry anyone before I find out such a thing. And perhaps Lord Richard is very good sort of man, but he is too free in his speech. He said one or two things last night that were quite shocking. Especially to a lady so little known to him. He was far too familiar in his addresses."

"Even so." Lady Amberly said, unable to utter any other reply. "Rachel, dear, how was your visit with Miss Perdue?"

"Oh yes," said Marian, who was not over-fond of the said Miss Perdue, "Is she set to marry Captain Jennings? He seemed to like her very well. Well enough to stand up with her after he had asked me for the same two dances. But that was before she met that young lawyer, who was much better worth her time and her seventy-five thousand pounds."

"Oh you're not still fretting over that ridiculous officer, are you?" Lady Amberly demanded. "Why should you, when you're destined to marry a lord?"

"Was she agreeable?" Marian asked Rachel, not wanting to enter again upon the subject of Lord Richard. "I hope being in town hasn't lessened her affection."

"I believe she was pleased to see me," Rachel said. "But you must not blame her for Captain Jennings' foolish judgment. I'm sure she did not know he had engaged you."

"I'm sure she did not. Was anyone else there?"

"No, it was only a small family party. Only her father and younger sister. She is to come to my ball next week with Mr. Sheffield and his sister. I did not know Mother even knew the Sheffield family. But Miss Perdue went to school with Miss Sheffield."

"Oh! I nearly forgot!" Marian said. "Mr. Sheffield was the young man at the bookshop on Monday. He was at Lady Beauregard's last night."

"Well he seems to be a very agreeable young man. But even Mama did not recognize him the other day."

"I daresay he is very agreeable," Marian said. "However, I had not much opportunity to converse with him, as there was another young man who commanded most of my attention after dinner." This last part was spoken in a lower voice with a meaning look at her sister. Then in a louder voice, "But you know Mother gave the dowager leave to add whom she pleased to the guest list. We must keep on good terms, you know."

"Yes, Mama's guest list makes me quite dizzy, there are so many. Well, Mary, you must dance with Mr. Sheffield at my ball, or I shall be quite put out."

"I should like very much to dance with Mr. Sheffield," Marian replied. "He seems so gentlemanly in his address and I like his eyes. A very pretty shade of blue."

"Such a good observation for a short acquaintance," Rachel said with a smile.

"Mr. Sheffield is a very good sort of young man, I'm sure," Lady Amberly said. "But why settle for a mere gentleman when you could have a lord?"

"You give Lord Richard's idle compliments too much credit, Mama," Marian said. "He's the sort of insincere man that can make himself agreeable to any woman. I assure you, he means nothing by it but to carry on a flirtation, and I shall not give in to it."

"Well if he should make an offer after all, it would be very foolish of you not to accept it," Lady Amberly replied. "You would be a countess one day."

"Yes, Mother, but I hope you would like me to marry a man of integrity and who has more to recommend him than a title and a pretty address. Such things do not guarantee an agreeable life companion."

"Dearest, I am only looking out for your interest. Nothing would please me more than to see you elevated. And all my daughters. Mr. Wesley might do very well for Rachel, except I think perhaps the dowager wants him to marry Lady Emily. However, Mr. Wesley will be only a baron and Lord Richard shall be an earl."

"I don't care what rank my husband is," said Rachel. "So long as he's handsome and likes horses and music."

"Well all three characteristics leave less than a quarter of the gentlemen in London," Marian replied. "Leave out the first and last and that leaves nearly all of them. 'Tis better to set your standards now. It will help you when you have to make a decision between a somewhat handsome man who likes horses but not music, a plain man who likes both horses *and* music and a very handsome man who likes horses at the races and music when he is the one performing it. If you prefer the last, Lord Richard would do very well for you." Rachel laughed at this speech, and before her mother could reply, a servant came in and announced that Mrs. Forrester and her daughters had come to call.

"I suppose we must see them," Lady Amberly said. "Though Heaven knows I don't want them constantly hanging upon us to gain some consequence."

Sir John's sister had married a Mr. Charles Forrester who was the rector of the living on Sir John's estate and the younger brother of a gentleman of a neighboring estate. The sickly elder brother of Mr. Charles Forrester had married a woman some fifteen years younger than himself with twenty thousand pounds and when he died, left behind three children, the youngest of which was now a sickly boy of sixteen. Unfortunately for Mrs. Forrester and her two daughters, Mr. Forrester's estate was entailed so that if young Frederick were to die without heirs, as seemed very likely, the estate would pass to Mr. Charles Forrester. A very natural consequence of this was that Mrs. Forrester and her eldest daughter were very desirous that Miss Forrester should marry Charles Forrester's son, William, who was quite healthy, as well as handsome, and would no doubt live to be the next heir of Merton Abbey.

When Mrs. Forrester and her daughters entered the room, there were many insincere expressions of regard passed around, regret at having missed one another at home so many times and compliments on one another's daughters and how beautiful they had all grown!

Mrs. Forrester was a not-quite-middle-aged woman who had not yet lost *all* her bloom. She had a brother with a house in town, where she and her daughters also resided when in London. Her object in London was the same as that of many other mothers with daughters to dispose of. Her eldest daughter, of course, was to marry William Forrester if she could. However, if a more eligible offer presented itself, she should of course take it, for dear Frederick might live to produce an heir after all. In which case, William would be left to the younger daughter. Naturally, William himself was not consulted on these matters, as prospective husbands seldom are.

Miss Forrester was nineteen, haughty and beautiful and imagined herself to be of much more consequence than she really was. She knew how to perform four or five songs on the pianoforte, dance all the latest dances and knew enough French to fancy herself quite in style. Her clothes were all made in the style most becoming to her figure and she was quite an accomplished coquette. She was shallow, vain and insincere and liked very much to parade around with young ladies of less consequence than she, so that she might appear to better advantage.

Miss Diana was seventeen, not as handsome as her sister, but much more intelligent and agreeable. She was more well-read than Miss Forrester, but had not much talent for music. She was very gifted with water-colors, however, and had made several presents of her work to the Amberly girls.

"How is your brother, Miss Forrester?" Marian asked. "Is he in London?"

"La, no!" Miss Forrester exclaimed. "What should he have to do in London? The air would make him quite ill. No, he is at home in the country. But he and Mr. Turner are to meet us in Bath in May. William and Laura are to come to London and attend us there. Poor Laura! She doesn't have many opportunities to get out, you know. I should have liked to have her come with us to London, but we can't invite others to our uncle's house. It's quite crowded as it is. If she stays hidden away in the country so long, she'll never do any better than a country clergyman. Diana and I are quite determined we shall get her married off to a handsome sea-officer in Bath, are we not, Diana?"

"I don't believe she desires any such thing, Julia," Miss Diana replied. "She should like to visit a public place, I think, but I don't think she intends to find a husband."

"Well what else does one go to public places for?" Miss Forrester retorted. "Why do you suppose Mother brought us to London? You don't suppose it's to visit all the fancy bookshops, do you?"

"I am not husband-hunting," Marian said. "Though I believe our mother is doing our hunting for us. She already has me married to a young lord."

"A lord!" Miss Forrester exclaimed. "Well of course you must get him if you can. Who is he? Perhaps I know him."

"Lord Richard Beauregard," Marian said. "His father is the earl of—"

"Oh him!" Miss Forrester said. "I danced with him at a ball last week and thought he was very agreeable. And vastly handsome! But why should your mother think you would marry him?"

"Because he paid me some pretty compliments at a dinner party last night and my mother fancies that means he is in love. But I daresay he's not, so if you want him, you may have him." Miss Forrester thanked her, but had trouble disguising her sarcastic tone, which Marian still caught and was amused rather than offended.

"Where are your brothers?" Miss Diana asked Rachel, to change the subject. "Have they gone to the clubs?"

"Our eldest brother has," Rachel said, "as has our father. Arthur and Reggie are riding in Hyde Park, however." The conversation continued for the rest of the visit on Hyde Park, Vauxhall and Court Presentation, which Miss Diana was quite interested in, and Miss Forrester was not interested in at all, being an event in which she could never take part.

At eight o' clock Tuesday evening, Lady Amberly's drawing room having been converted into a ballroom, Sir John's library into a cloak room and the sitting room into a card-room with a table for refreshments, Lady Amberly and her daughters were ready to receive their guests, which gradually began to fill up the place. When Lord Richard arrived with his sister, parents and grandmother, the superfluous civilities which Marian half-expected from Lord Richard did not come. He made one or two civil comments and continued into the room after his parents and sister.

Not quite knowing what to think, Marian followed him with her eyes and saw him addressing himself to a pretty, coquettish-looking girl and felt her cheeks grow hot.

"You were right, Marian," Rachel whispered. "Lord Richard is extremely handsome. Is he really to open the dance with me?"

"So old Lady Beauregard says," Marian replied. "However if he does not ask you before someone else does, I trust you cannot be expected to reserve what he has not requested. You must open the dance and of course you must have a partner with whom to open it." However, Rachel was spared from having to make such an awkward decision by being claimed by Lord Richard for the first two dances.

Marian had the honor to dance the first two dances with Mr. George Wesley, for he could not dance with Miss Seldon, as Miss Seldon was not on Lady Amberly's guest list by fault of not being a man, having a brother or being the daughter of any particularly illustrious person.

"Did you not go into Hyde Park yesterday?" Mr. Wesley asked her after they had joined the set. "My cousin said he supposed you would, by something your mother said. He quite insisted upon my riding with him in the park."

"Your cousin seems to me a very capricious young man," Marian replied coldly. "He is too warm one evening and another he is too cold. I want nothing to do with that sort of person. Anyone who is not straightforward has no chance of improving my opinion of him."

"Do you mean to say he has neglected you this evening?"

"I have no claim on his attentions," Marian replied. "And I do not aspire to that sort of intimacy which you seem to imply. However, let us not talk of him anymore. The subject sickens me and if we linger anymore upon it, it shall put me quite out of humor, which I won't take kind at all, as it is only the first dance and we are at a ball." Mr. Wesley smiled.

"Shall we discuss the weather, then?"

"What a droll subject for a ball!" Marian exclaimed. "Come now, Mr. Wesley, cannot you do better than that?"

"What do you say to Napoleon?"

"Worse and worse! We are at a ball and must discuss pleasant subjects. Vauxhall, perhaps, or Bath, or the theatre."

"If you wish to talk about Bath, I shall tell you that my grandmother is planning an expedition there shortly," Mr. Wesley said. "She wishes to go in June, just before the London Season ends."

"Bath is a charming place. We were there last winter for some months. We did not come to town at all, because my father was too ill. And we were in Ramsgate for the early part of the summer. My eldest sister lives some miles outside of Ramsgate, by the sea."

"Has she an estate there?"

"Her husband does. It's been nearly a year since I saw Sarah at all and even longer since I've been to visit her at Fort de Mar."

"Should you like to visit again?"

"Oh, I should like it very much," Marian replied. "Fort de Mar has a very fine view of the sea and even a miniature cascade. Not as grand as the one at Vauxhall, of course. But my brother-in-law has a boat, which can fit ten people."

"You make me very curious to see it."

"I suppose her ladyship means to take Lady Emily with her to Bath?"

"We are all going to Bath, Miss Amberly. That is, my brother and my cousins Lord Richard and Lady Emily. My grandmother has offered to convey Miss Seldon as well, whose father currently resides in Bath for his health. Her ladyship declared that my brother and I and Lady Emily are to accompany her. I doubt not she has some scheme planned. She hopes the waters will be conducive to courtship."

"And do you think this plan will be successful?" Marian asked, looking at Mr. Wesley suspiciously, to see if he would blush. He merely smiled at her.

"Perhaps. One never can tell about these things."

As Mr. Wesley led her back to her seat, Marian noticed that Mr. Sheffield was just coming from the dance with Miss Perdue, which somehow piqued her. More vexing still, Miss Perdue introduced Mr. Sheffield to Rachel—an office she had expected to perform herself. Marian was going to approach them when she was stopped by Arthur, who wished to introduce one of his friends to her—a Mr. Billingsly, who immediately asked her to dance, if she were not otherwise engaged. Not knowing how else to reply, Marian accepted and allowed her partner to lead her to the dance.

Mr. Billingsly was an awkward dancer and a less-than-articulate conversationalist and it required nearly all of Marian's patience to maintain her composure through the dance, especially when her sister, who was dancing with Mr. Sheffield, and Miss Perdue, who was dancing with George Wesley, had much more agreeable partners. Then, what was almost enough to overcome her present distress was her joy at her elder sister, Sarah, entering the room with her husband, Count De Roche and followed by her cousins, William and Laura Forrester.

Great was her relief when she escaped Mr. Billingsly and made her way to the newly arrived party. Hardly knowing who to greet first, she kissed Sarah, then Laura. To William she held out her hand, which he gallantly kissed and to her brother-in-law, whom she had not known quite so long as the others, she curtseyed. Count De Roche gave her a civil greeting, then retreated into the card-room.

"What a fine joke for you to come all this way and not tell any of us!" Marian said, once she was comfortably nestled in a corner with Sarah and Laura. "I wonder what Mama will say!"

"Oh she already knows," Sarah replied. "I could hardly come without informing her first. But I do believe she was quite delighted. She thought it would be a nice surprise for you and Rachel. But I daresay Rachel is occupied at present." Across the room, Rachel was chatting gaily with both Lord Richard and Mr. George Wesley at once.

"Yes, she is Lord Richard's target for gallantry this evening," Marian said coldly. "No doubt he is paying her frivolous and insincere compliments."

"And so it is Lord Richard!" Sarah said. "I am always amazed at what a fine young man he is grown into. I daresay our grandmother would have liked us to make a match of it, but he was considered too young to marry, for we are the same age, you know. He had to make his trip to the continent first. I like Philippe very well, but he has been very withdrawn of late. I worry about his health. But he must go to the West Indies at the end of the week. He has business there. Now Marian you must excuse me, for I must go and speak to my father, for I have not yet seen him." When they were left by themselves, Marian asked Laura how they all came to be there.

"Oh, well Sarah wrote to my mother to say if she could spare us—I mean William and me—for two or three weeks, she would be very much obliged. Mama put up no fuss about it for she was very glad we might have some opportunity to see the world. So William and I went to Fort de Mar and were there for a week, and now we are just arrived in London this morning. Count de Roche must leave at the end of the week for the West Indies and William is to escort Sarah back home. I might perhaps go back with them. That is—yes I suppose I must. I shall not mind, for I would like very much to go sea-bathing. Though I am told the water is very cold this time of year." Marian could hardly refrain from smiling at her cousin's attempts to hide the fact that she wished to remain in London.

"Of course you must stay some weeks with Rachel and me," Marian told her. "Come now, Laura, you know you are quite like our sister. You need not stand on ceremony with us." Laura smiled at this interpretation of her thoughts. "You must write your mother tomorrow morning and tell her we intend to keep you for at least a month. But if you did indeed pack only for two weeks she must send you more clothes." Laura made a blushing acknowledgement that she had indeed come prepared for such an invitation.

Their little tete a tete was interrupted by Marian's younger brother Reginald coming to request Laura as a dancing partner, and John came to take Laura's place by Marian's side.

"What a good joke!" John said. "I told Reginald it would be quite a breach of decorum if he did not ask our cousin to dance. Naturally he was reluctant and I'm quite surprised he believed me at all. I should have asked her soon myself, you know, if he had not. It would be forgivable in Reggie, for he's so awkward, but I am her eldest cousin and ought to protect her from the vultures of society. And I do believe I shall still give her the honor of being the first lady I dance with tonight, for I assure you, I have not danced with any other."

"Have you been playing cards, then?" Marian demanded. "If you are not going to dance, you had better play cards rather than idling about."

"Oh but it is much more fun to pique young ladies by saying something civil to them, listen to them make not-so-subtle hints about dancing, bow and walk away on some pretense. Besides, you know I don't play cards at these sort of parties. They never play high and it's no fun otherwise. No, I assure you I am much more entertained in the ballroom."

"You ought not to play high at all, John," Marian said. "It is a very bad habit. And I think you are quite wrong to imply you wish to dance with a young lady then not ask her. That shows very bad manners, when you know ladies have very little control over their dancing partners."

"Oh but they have too *much* over their partners, if once they can get them as partners," John replied. "If only it were not improper, I should dance with you, for it is quite unacceptable that my sister should be sitting out for two dances. And, if it is quite all right with you, I shall defy decorum and dance with you anyway."

"No doubt *you*, as the eldest son, would get very little censure for such a trick. But *I* should not be so fortunate."

"Oh yes, scandalous tongues will talk," John replied. "My dear sister, you know I could never put you in the way of censure. And here comes Arthur. He already got you one partner tonight, so I can do no less."

"I desire you will do no such thing," Marian told him. "I'm sitting out two dances because I wish to. I wanted to talk to Sarah and Laura."

"Not to worry, I will get you a better partner than Arthur got you. Come Arthur, I will show you who better deserves the honor of dancing with Marian than that clumsy fellow you obliged her to dance with."

"What is he rattling on about now?" Arthur asked, as John scanned the room. "He's done nothing but idle about the room in the most insufferable manner."

"Oh ho! Lord Richard!" John called out to Lord Richard, who happened to be passing. Lord Richard stopped and bowed to them. "Lord Richard, did you not promise to dance with my sister at the next ball you met at?" Marian colored deeply and looked away from Lord Richard.

"Of course," Lord Richard replied with a slight bow. "I am engaged to Miss Carter for these next two dances, but I shall be very happy to fulfill my obligation to Miss Amberly for the two following."

"Thank you, your lordship," Marian said, indignantly turning to look at him. "But I should not like to have my company imposed on any young man who shows himself desirous of avoiding it. And as to obligations, you have none, as far as I am concerned."

"If I have offended you in some way, Miss Amberly, I am truly sorry," he replied. "It would be a great honor if you would stand up with me for the two dances following these."

"Thank you, sir, but I am engaged. The dance is about to start. You had better go claim your partner." Lord Richard bowed and walked away in some confusion.

"What a green-girl you are!" John exclaimed, though much amused. "Whining because Lord Richard has not paid you much attention this evening then refusing to dance with him."

"I think she did very well not to dance with him," Arthur said. "Lord Richard is far too arrogant. But Marian, are you really engaged for those two dances?"

"No," Marian admitted. "But I could not bear to agree to dance with him because he was obliged to ask me. Perhaps you could speak to William? If he knew my situation, I'm sure he would oblige. I've known him all my life and we are cousins, so perhaps it would not be too out of place."

"Perhaps not," Arthur said. "But he is already engaged to Rachel for those two dances. But here he comes now. You can ask him yourself." William Forrester was tall and fair with a pleasing countenance, and much of the gallantry of Lord Richard, without the self-assurance.

"William!" John said. "Just in time. Arthur and I were just trying to find out a suitable dance partner for Marian. Would you lend us your assistance?"

"Indeed I will. In fact, I will save you the trouble altogether, by dancing with her myself, if she will consent to be my partner." He held out his hand and Marian gratefully took it, not wishing to sit out four dances altogether.

The two dances with her cousin passed by in pleasant conversation about the country, public places and William's paternal cousins.

Lady Amberly was of course obliged to invite her neighbors from the country to the ball, knowing they were in town, but they sent their regrets, informing her that they were already engaged elsewhere, but if only Lady Amberly had sent her invitation a day sooner, it should have been quite different. Marian had no doubt that had Mrs. Forrester known that William was to be present, her other engagement might be very easily postponed. As it was, however, Mrs. Forrester had no desire to take her daughters to a ball held in another young lady's honor, where they might be outshone.

After William led her back to her seat, Marian spent a few awkward moments wondering how she was to get herself out of her situation. Mr. Sheffield, seeing her disengaged, approached her.

"Miss Amberly," he said. "I'm very sorry I have not had an opportunity of speaking with you this evening. I made an attempt once or twice, but you were otherwise engaged and I did not wish to disturb you." Marian smiled graciously at this little speech. "However, as I now find you alone, I would be honored if you would dance the next two dances with me." This Marian readily assented to, for it was just what she had been hoping for all evening, and had the additional benefit of helping her out of her awkward situation. Therefore, after a few more minutes of polite conversation while waiting for the music to start, Mr. Sheffield led the way to the dance.

"I see Miss Perdue has been so kind as to introduce you to my sister," Marian said, after a few minutes of silence. "Have you known Miss Perdue long?"

"Miss Perdue and my sister went to the same seminary," Mr. Sheffield replied. "And Miss Perdue has spent more than one summer at Sheffield Park. This is her first season in London, I believe. But she was in Bath last year."

"Oh yes. Bath is a charming place. Perhaps there are not quite so many diversions there as in London. After all, it is supposed to be a resort for invalids. There is Sydney Gardens, of course. And the Pump Room. And the hot baths, obviously."

"Invalids?" Mr. Sheffield said with a smile. "When I went, I think not half of the inhabitants of Bath were invalids. The hours of the entertainments are earlier, to be sure, but I believe that for many, it is simply an extension of the London Season, and for others, a substitute."

"Perhaps it is. But there are some of us who love dancing and the theatre so well so as not to wish to give it up before it is absolutely necessary."

"True. But such entertainments would not be suitable for true invalids. There are those who fancy themselves ill, but they seem well enough when they make their appearance at the assembly rooms. If I were ill, I think I would much rather go to bed."

"One does not need to be an invalid to go to Bath. In fact it is much better not to be, for if one is ill, they are obliged to drink the waters. I drank some last year, just to try it, and I assure you, it's quite horrid." A movement of the dance now required them to separate, and Marian found herself facing Lord Richard.

"I told you we would dance this dance," Lord Richard said, taking her hand. "Even if only for a moment."

"Well you may congratulate yourself that you have fulfilled your supposed obligation of dancing with me," Marian replied. "After all, why should you waste your compliments on the daughter of a humble baronet, when you can dance with a diamond of the first water, such as Miss Carter?" The dance then separating them again, Marian was soon back with Mr. Sheffield, and Lord Richard was with his partner, but quite out of humor.

After their two dances were over, Mr. Sheffield led Marian back to her seat and went to fetch a glass of lemonade for her. Marian looked around the room and saw her sister with William and Laura. She would have liked to join them, but dared not leave her seat, lest Mr. Sheffield should not be able to find her. She was not alone for long, however, for Lord Richard appeared suddenly before her.

"Miss Amberly," he said. "I find you alone at last."

"Why, Lord Richard," Marian replied, opening her fan. "I must confess myself shocked at your seeking me of your own free will. I had supposed you devoted to another lady for the evening."

"Miss Amberly," Lord Richard said, sitting beside her. "I beg you to tell me how I have offended you? You have been very cold all evening, though I have been as civil as I could. Nay, you seem almost offended that I have been paying you no *particular* attention, yet last week you seemed to think I was paying you *too much*. What shall I do to procure your favor? I beg you to tell me, and I shall do it." Marian saw that Mr. Sheffield was returning and she did not wish him to see Lord Richard addressing her in this familiar way.

"I beg you to return to your own party," she replied. "Mr. Sheffield is returning and I am sure you have slighted your own partner to come to me in this fashion. You are by no means required to pay me any particular attention. You are quite right in supposing me not to wish for such idle compliments. Do enjoy your evening and assure yourself that you have quite done your duty by me." She then rose from her seat and Lord Richard followed suit. Lord Richard bowed to Marian and inclined his head to Mr. Sheffield and walked away.

"He is an odd fellow," Mr. Sheffield said. "I suppose he thinks his title entitles him to behave as he chooses. Are you very well acquainted with him?"

"Not very well. He is a relation of mine, however. My mother is his father's cousin and my elder sister and brothers are his first cousins. I have spent very little time in his company. He behaves in a way far too familiar for our degree of acquaintance." They were interrupted by the arrival of Miss Sheffield and Miss Perdue.

Miss Perdue was a young woman who was neither very handsome nor very plain, was a rather accomplished singer, spoke Italian somewhat well and was not very accomplished in anything else. She had the appearance of having a very healthy appetite, pretty eyes and a decent complexion. The height of her attractions, however, was her seventy-five thousand pounds, which she could take possession of in two months, when she reached her majority.

"Edward," Miss Sheffield said, "You must allow me to steal Miss Amberly from you for a few moments. You keep Georgiana company." Miss Sheffield took Marian by the arm.

"Miss Amberly, you must tell me about your dance partner for the dance before this one. You know, the tall, handsome one? Miss Perdue says she believes he is your cousin and quite like your own brother. Pray tell me, what is his situation?"

"I am afraid what I must tell you will lower him in your estimation, Miss Sheffield, for William is but the son of a clergyman. It is true, his mother is my father's sister and his father holds the living on my father's estate. He and his sister Laura were educated with my brothers and sisters and me by the same governess."

"Oh how delightful!" Miss Sheffield said. "Well, you may tell him, whenever you happen to be alone, that I have thirty-five thousand pounds. For you know, Miss Amberly, I have quite reconciled myself to marrying a fortune hunter, but I might as well find as many prospects as I can, so I might choose the most handsome and agreeable of all." Marian tried to disguise her shock at such a speech, made with very little ceremony to nearly a complete stranger.

"I assure you, Miss Sheffield, my cousin is no fortune hunter," Marian said coldly. "He is perfectly willing to enter a profession, if need be. Indeed, he may very well take orders in another year or two." Marian did not see fit to inform Miss Sheffield that there was a very fair likelihood of William eventually getting his own estate, as she did not see Miss Sheffield as a proper companion for a sensible, modest young man such as William.

Miss Sheffield, however, was by no means discouraged by this reply and continued to talk on until supper was announced, after which eight more dances were danced and Marian managed to escape dancing with Lord Richard at all.

CHAPTER THREE

No sooner was breakfast over the next morning than Marian and Rachel began begging their mother to call on Sarah and Laura. This Lady Amberly readily assented to, as being the proper thing to do. Eager as they were to be Sarah's first callers, however, they were not quite quick enough, for having discovered that their beloved Laura was with her, and, more importantly, Laura's brother, Mrs. Forrester and her daughters were already waiting upon the countess.

When Lady Amberly and her daughters arrived at Sarah's lodgings, therefore, they found them all comfortably arranged in pairs. Perhaps the most comfortable pair, however—on the lady's side at least—was William and Miss Forrester. Marian would have liked very much for Rachel to join them, especially as she suspected a certain partiality on William's side, but Rachel would go to Laura and Miss Diana to talk about the ball. Determined that someone must disrupt the alleged lovers, however, Marian made her way to them. For nothing pleased her more than to vex Miss Forrester and give relief to her cousin.

"Oh Miss Forrester," Marian said, sitting beside her. "Such a pity you had to miss our ball! I suppose it could not be helped, however, as you had a previous engagement. But I do hope your evening was quite charming, nevertheless."

"Yes, thank you," Miss Forrester said, endeavoring to be as cold and uninviting to their new companion as possible.

"Pray, where is it you went again? I hope it was worth it, for Lord Richard was there, and you might have danced with him, as he made himself quite agreeable to all the ladies in the room." William could not help letting a smile escape at this comment.

"We were at the theater with some acquaintance of ours," Miss Forrester replied. "I believe they are cousins of your brother-in-law's. Mr. James Henderson and his sister."

"Oh, are they in town? Pity they were not there—Miss Henderson might have availed herself of his lordship's attention as well. She has done so before, you know."

"Do you know," Miss Forrester said, "Diana and Laura were having a very lively conversation about your ball earlier? I daresay you will find their conversation much more entertaining than such dull subjects as we are discussing, since that is what you wish to discuss." Marian chose not to take the hint.

"Oh! I do not mind dull subjects. William knows I do not. Is that not so, William?"

"Indeed it is," William replied, quite amused. "Miss Amberly is far more adept at carrying on dull conversations than I am. And I must no longer be remiss, for I have not yet spoken to your sister."

"Aye, you must do so at once."

"I declare, Miss Amberly," Miss Forrester said after William walked away, "I think William must be in love with your sister. Else there must be something very odd about her appearance, for he has not ceased to glance at her ever since you came here."

"I am sure Rachel would be very grieved to think that she had given you any uneasiness."

"Oh, you needn't be concerned on *my* account, I'm sure," said Miss Forrester. "I could not be more indifferent myself. I quite wish them joy." Marian chose not to reply to this remark. "La, how bored I am! Mama, why do we not all go to the Exeter Exchange? Susan tells me there are the most exotic animals there. She had quite a laugh at the ostrich, for she said it reminded her vastly of Lord Hornby."

"Oh, yes Mother!" Rachel exclaimed. "May we go too?"

"You and Marian may go if William and Sarah choose to chaperone you all," Lady Amberly replied. "But I have some calls to pay this morning."

"And I have promised my sister-in-law that I would assist her in choosing a muslin for her daughter's portrait next week," Mrs. Forrester said. "She is to sit for Sir Thomas Lawrence next Friday. And my sister Parker so depends on my taste—it would be quite cruel to disappoint her."

Quite the contrary, Marian thought, *I should think it a blessing, whether Mrs. Parker knows it or not.*

"Of course I shall attend them if they all wish to go," Sarah said. "After all, Laura must see as much of the world as she can, while she has the opportunity." Laura hurried to prepare herself for a walk, attended by Rachel and Miss Diana.

"Well, it's all settled then," Mrs. Forrester said. "My dear William, may I count on you to see my girls safely home?"

"Of course, Madam," William replied with a bow. A servant came into the room and announced that a young gentleman and lady were here to call on Lady Amberly and her daughters. Sarah told her to call them up while Marian wondered who would call on her mother here. Mr. Sheffield and his sister came into the room, and after paying his respects to all the ladies in the room, Mr. Sheffield began to explain how he had come to the lodgings of Madame De Roche.

"Forgive the intrusion, Madame," he said to Sarah, "But we went to call on Lady Amberly and her daughters this morning and found they were not at home. But upon learning they were here, I decided I might as well pay my duties to all the ladies at once, with whom I had the pleasure of dancing last night." William was struggling to keep his countenance and Miss Forrester was earnestly examining the handsome newcomer and his sister, who, amazingly enough, had not yet opened her mouth. Lady Amberly introduced Mr. Sheffield and his sister to Mrs. Forrester and her eldest daughter and Sarah invited them to sit down. Laura and her cousins presently returned to the parlor.

"We're forming a party to go to the Exeter Exchange, Mr. Sheffield," Marian said. "Would you and Miss Sheffield care to join us?" Mr. Sheffield replied that he would be delighted and Marian saw the prospect of society more entertaining than Miss Forrester and Rachel vying for William's attention.

Marian walked with Sarah, who mainly talked about her children, their nurses and their progress. Marian was very fond of her elder sister, but as Sarah was married and she was not, they differed very much in which subjects composed an interesting conversation.

Marian would much rather talk about the faults of her dancing partners than little Jacque's progress in his alphabet.

Miss Sheffield, being considerably more bold than even Miss Forrester, had usurped Miss Forrester's place by William's side and was now dominating the conversation. Laura held on her brother's other arm, and Rachel held onto Laura's. Therefore, the only thing Miss Forrester could possibly do was to join her sister and Mr. Sheffield, who was politely attending Miss Diana.

"Dear me, how dreadful it smells in here!" Miss Forrester exclaimed. "It smells like a stable!"

"What did you expect?" Marian asked her. "They are animals. I don't suppose you expected it to smell like a rose garden?"

"How was I to know an elephant smelled like a horse? Or worse. I think I shall faint."

"It's not so bad," Rachel said. "I don't mean to say it smells *good*, but I don't think it would make one faint."

"But Rachel," William said, "You forget that Miss Forrester has not your love of horses. I think she has not set foot in a stable since she—decided she was not a horsewoman seven years ago."

"I suppose you mean the time she fell into the mud while she was riding Starlight," Marian said. "Her mama was so vexed she ruined her new pelisse."

"No, I am no horsewoman, I'm afraid," Miss Forrester replied, quite piqued. "I've dedicated my time to something that entertains many, instead of just myself."

"These poor creatures!" Laura exclaimed. "They have hardly any room to move about in their cages. What a change that must be from roaming the plains of Africa. Do you suppose this is what Noah's ark looked like inside?"

"Certainly," William said. "Except without all the people and the shops."

"What a funny little creature your cousin is!" Miss Sheffield exclaimed, putting her arm into Marian's as they stepped away from the others.

"Do you mean William?"

"No, I mean Miss Laura Forrester of course," Miss Sheffield said. "I don't see how anyone could laugh at *Mr.* Forrester. He's very handsome but very solemn. I'm not sure I could marry a man like that."

"Well then it is fortunate you are not engaged to him," Marian replied. "It would be a pity to discover such a fault so far into the relationship."

"Well, he may court me if he chooses and I shall make up my mind by and by. But one thing I'm not quite sure I understand. Are not those other young ladies cousins to your cousin?"

"Yes."

"Well then why does Mr. Forrester call them 'Miss' and you and your sister by your Christian names? Are not you all the same relation?"

"Yes, but you see William and Laura were raised with us and we all had the same governess. We are quite like sisters to them."

"And Miss Forrester—she does not consider her cousin as her brother, does she? She seems to view him quite as her property."

"Miss Sheffield," Marian said, "I hardly know you well enough to discuss inner-workings of my family with you. I hope you'll forgive me, but this conversation has gone as far as is proper."

"Indeed," Miss Sheffield replied, a little coolly. "I did not know you were as sensitive as some people. I shall try to be more guarded." Marian curtseyed and returned to the rest of the party.

When the party sat down to tea, the conversation turned to Vauxhall Gardens. Those who had seen them declared it was a sight not to be missed and those who had not declared that they should not be happy till they had.

"We are to go tomorrow night with our aunt and cousins," Miss Forrester told William. "And Mama has instructed me to beg that you and Laura will accompany us, for we need another man to escort us all. Indeed, you must go, for there are to be fireworks tomorrow."

"If Laura wishes to go I have no objection. We shall be very happy to oblige you I'm sure."

"And of course you must go with us too, Rachel," Miss Forrester said. "Then our party shall be just right."

"Oh yes!" Rachel exclaimed. "I should like it very much! I'm sure Mama won't mind."

"Do you mean to say you invite one sister and not the other, and in her presence?" William asked Miss Forrester. "Especially when the one excluded is the *elder* sister?" Miss Forrester grew quite red.

"I did not mean to offend Miss Amberly, I'm sure," Miss Forrester said. "But if we are more than ten, we shall not be able to fit in two wherries or in one supper-box. And as Rachel is my particular friend, I'm sure her sister would not take it ill."

"Well, she may have my place then," William replied.

"But you must go, for we must have another man in the party. My cousin George is rather dim-witted, is he not, Diana? He cannot escort nine ladies alone."

"I cannot think it is right," William said. "It is not fair to Marian."

"Do not be uneasy about me, William," Marian said, amused at Miss Forrester's thinly veiled tactics to exclude her. "I can find my own amusement."

"Yes, you may come spend the evening with Catharine and Miss Seldon," Mr. Sheffield said. "My cousin Miss Seldon has expressed a wish of getting better acquainted with you."

"Thank you," Marian said, not quite knowing what to say. "I—I think I would like that."

"Good, that's settled then," Mr. Sheffield said. "We shall send our carriage for you at seven o' clock." Miss Forrester was quite at a loss for words.

Mr. Sheffield and his sister took Marian and Rachel home in their carriage and Lady Amberly was waiting for them when they arrived. She informed then that they had missed Lord Richard and Mr. George Wesley who had been to call while they were away.

"I don't care a fig about Lord Richard," Marian said. "But I am sorry I missed Mr. Wesley. He seems such a good young man. It's a pity he must always be in company with Lord Richard."

"Hold your tongue, child!" Lady Amberly exclaimed. "I'll not have you snubbing his lordship! I understand he asked you to dance last night and you refused."

"John was having a bit of fun and told Lord Richard he had promised to dance with me. I merely told him he was under no such obligation."

"Dearest child," Lady Amberly said. "You know I have only your best interest at heart. I want to see you distinguished. You're such a clever, handsome girl—it would be a pity if you were to dwindle away in the country."

"Miss Forrester invited me to Vauxhall tomorrow night, Mama," Rachel said. "William and Laura are to go as well. There are to be fireworks."

"And are you to go too, Marian?"

"No, Mama," Marian replied. "Miss Forrester did not think there would be room. I am to spend the evening with the Sheffields."

"Those Forresters think themselves so high!" Lady Amberly said indignantly. "They suppose they may slight anyone and get away with it! However, it is all very well, since you are to spend the evening with Mr. Sheffield and his sister. I understand Mr. Sheffield has twelve thousand a year and two good livings on his estate."

"I confess that had no influence on my accepting their invitation," Marian replied. "But John and William are to call at four and I must get into my riding clothes. You know how cross John gets if he's kept waiting." Rachel followed Marian up to change into their riding clothes, for John and William had promised to take them to Hyde Park.

As was to be expected, after getting to the park John soon deserted them for "Rotten Row" and William and Rachel, who had not noticed John's desertion, were riding together. Marian began to trot her horse back and forth, careful not to stray too far from Rachel and William. As she was trotting behind them, two horses appeared on either side of her. Slightly startled, she looked to her right and discovered that one horseman was Lord Richard and the other was Lady Emily.

"Miss Amberly," Lord Richard said. "You were out when I called with George earlier today. We were very sorry to miss you."

"Thank you, Lord Richard. We went to call on my sister. She is only in town for a few days, you know. Then Mr. Sheffield and his sister called and we all went to the Exeter Exchange."

"Indeed? And how did you find the noise?"

"Oh, it reminded me very much of a gentleman paying empty compliments," Marian replied. "It all sounds the same to me." Lady Emily laughed.

"How cruel you are to the men," she said. "I'm afraid my brother shall not be able to compete with your cutting remarks."

"Miss Amberly," Lord Richard said. "How is your sister? I was quite enchanted with her at the ball last night. She was very polite and did not seem to take any of my compliments amiss."

"She is very well. Did you not see her? She and William are only a few paces ahead of us." But when Marian looked, William and Rachel were farther ahead, for they had continued riding when she had stopped. They had, however, finally noticed she was behind, and were riding back to meet her.

"And where are your brothers?"

"John was with us, but he found some friends going to 'Rotten Row' and went with them. I do not know where the others are."

"Are you going to Vauxhall tomorrow night?"

"No, I'm not going, but Rachel is. She was invited by some friends from Essex, but there was not room for me."

"How frightfully rude that is!" Lady Emily said. "Well, you shall go with us, if you please. We have plenty of room in our shallot, do we not Richard?"

"Of course," Lord Richard said. "Miss Amberly is always welcome and I am sure will be a creditable addition to our party." Marian blushed at what her own rudeness toward Lord Richard had been in the past.

"I wish I could," she replied. "But I have already agreed to spend the evening with the Sheffields. Perhaps another night."

"Good afternoon, Lord Richard," William said. "I see you have been looking after my charge. But Marian, was not John with you?"

"John found a better means of entertainment," Marian said. "And you deserted me."

"I would never dream of it," William said. "But Rachel and I were just having some very good sport looking at all these people here."

"Oh yes," Marian said. "I daresay we may imagine ourselves back in the Exchange without much effort. But how could you indulge in such a diversion without me?"

"With great difficulty, I assure you. We missed your wit sadly."

After they had finished riding, Lord Richard and Lady Emily took Marian and Rachel home while William went to inform John that they had gone. When William returned after an unsuccessful search for his cousin, he found that Lady Amberly had invited Lord Richard and Lady Emily to dinner and had been graciously accepted.

Dinner was hardly begun when a note came for Miss Amberly from Miss Sheffield:

My dear Miss Amberly, I hope you will forgive me, but we have just remembered a previous engagement for tomorrow evening. It had slipped our minds at the moment we engaged your company for tomorrow evening and my brother sends his deepest regrets that it must be postponed till some other time. Till then, I remain,

Respectfully Yours,

Catherine Sheffield

Marian read the letter aloud with evident disappointment in her voice.

"But of course that means you must come with us now!" Lady Emily said. "Lady Amberly, she may come with us to Vauxhall tomorrow night, may she not? I think it would be very sad to miss out on the fireworks." Marian finally agreed to accompany Lady Emily, not altogether displeased with the thought of seeing Vauxhall, of which she had heard so much.

"What do you think of Miss Amberly, Richard?" his sister asked him on the ride home.

"She's a fiery little vixen," he replied. "But I shall tame her."

"Shall you indeed? And what, pray, shall you do? I would not have you be too hard on her. She's a very nice girl. A bit green, perhaps, but enough time in town shall cure her of that."

"I shall make her fall in love with me," Lord Richard said. "She is not like other girls who play the coquette with me for the sake of my money. She is pure, untamed passion and clearly determined to have nothing to do with me. I look at it as a great challenge, therefore, to win her heart."

"And what do you plan to do once you have gained her heart, brother?" Lady Emily asked. "Not break it I hope? And do try to remember she is a baronet's daughter, not one of your tavern girls."

"Perhaps I shall take her to the Dark Walks tomorrow," Lord Richard replied with a smile.

"Upon my word, you shall not!" Emily laughed. "How can you talk in so shocking a way? No wonder she takes your compliments so ill. She's not such a simpleton as you may think her."

"With her wit? Surely I do not think her a simpleton. That is the charm. A stupid girl would be too easy. She seems determined not to fall in love with me and I am determined she shall."

"Well, we shall see."

Next morning, Marian wrote a short note to Miss Sheffield expressing her regret at the change and thanking her for advance notice, upon the receipt of which Miss Sheffield announced at breakfast that Miss Amberly was unwell and unequal to coming to them in the evening, much to the disappointment of Mr. Sheffield and Miss Seldon. Miss Sheffield, however, could talk of nothing but the delights of Vauxhall Gardens and the charms of her dear friend, Miss Perdue.

CHAPTER FOUR

Lord Beauregard's coach came for Marian at exactly six o' clock, and after charging her sister to inform Miss Forrester whose party Marian was joining and how she was conveyed to the gardens, Marian was taken to Park Lane.

She was received with all readiness by Lady Emily, insipid civility from Lady Beauregard, patronizing condescension by the dowager and warm civility by Lord Richard. Lord Beauregard was in his study and chose not to disturb himself. She was much relieved by the arrival of Sarah and her husband, the count, and Marian would have gone instantly to her sister, except Lord Richard placed himself by her side and gave every indication he would not let her escape.

"Miss Amberly," He said. "You seem rather out of spirits this evening. Do you find the company of Mr. Sheffield and his sister so superior to that of my sister and me?"

"By no means," Marian replied. "I like Lady Emily very well. I find Miss Sheffield's manners rather abrasive."

"O lady with the razor-edged tongue," Lord Richard said. "Dare ye criticize another for the same?"

"Oh but it is not the same, Lord Richard. You see, there is a vast deal of difference between asking personal questions of someone with whom you have only a short acquaintance and responding to such inquiries in such a way as to dissuade anymore impertinent questions."

"Are you referring to me or Miss Sheffield?"

"Indeed, I find you and Miss Sheffield have rather a lot in common in that respect. You must see it as well, for you recognized my description of Miss Sheffield as a portrayal of your own character."

"You are very hard on us both. I know Miss Sheffield very well, and I must say I have never heard her speak in an untoward way."

"Perhaps she reserves it for members of her own sex, in which case I must give her credit, for it is far more forgivable in a member of one's own sex than in that of the opposite."

"You seem always to have an answer for whatever I say."

"London is a harsh place, your lordship. A lady may either conform and be insipid and be crushed into nothingness by society, or artful and be friends to one's face and enemies behind one's back, or one may prepare herself to face the lions without fear and let them see her for what she is, with no arts to hide her true self. I do not look down on any person, and I do not wish any to look down on me." Lord Richard looked at her earnestly. She was right—she was different from any girl he knew. Artless, yet clever— qualities all but too seldom found together.

"Indeed no one can look down on you, Miss Amberly. You have no superior. You are passionate, but do not hide your feelings. You are fearless, yet I sense you have a gentle spirit. You have a way with words that puts me to shame." Marian looked at Lord

Richard, and for once she did not have a sharp reply. Indeed, she could think of no reply at all. She could feel her heart beating and her cheeks blushing under his gaze.

"Excuse me, my lord," she said at last. "I really must speak to my sister." Lord Richard smiled as she walked away, convinced that he had at last begun to penetrate her heart.

At dinner Marian sat beside Sarah and Lord Richard took the place on Marian's other side, careful not to be too profuse in his compliments, since he knew it would be disagreeable to her. Sarah then directly began talking of the public assembly they were to attend the next evening.

"Oh and Mr. and Miss Henderson called this morning. They are Philippe's cousins, so I suppose we must invite them to be of our party as well. Lord Richard, you remember Miss Henderson, do you not? She was staying with us when you came to visit four years ago."

"Yes, Lord Richard," Marian said, regaining some of her vigor at the mention of Miss Henderson. "You remember Miss Henderson, I'm sure. The two of you entertained us with some very fine duets."

"Us?" Lord Richard looked at Marian.

"Oh yes, Marian was there too," Sarah said. "Do you not remember? But she would not play for an audience then, and spent much of her time in a corner with a book or in the garden with the children. Miss Henderson is handsome enough, but she is nothing to Marian."

"I have seen Miss Henderson at some assemblies during the winter. I understand that her brother has a house in Bath?"

"Yes, he has one both in Bath and in London and his sister lives with him," Sarah said. "They generally come to London before Christmas and return to Bath in June."

"In this mode they fancy they may keep up with the fashion without actually owning a house in the country," Marian said. "As long as they can leave London before it becomes unfashionable to remain any longer, they may pass themselves off as the *haut ton*. It is really quite clever, for then they have more to spend on elegant parties and fashionable clothes." Lord Richard smiled.

"I am glad to see Miss Amberly's sarcasm has found another target. And I am grateful to you, Madame De Roche, for helping me to solve a mystery that has been perplexing me since my first meeting with her in London, for she claimed we have met before but would not tell me when."

"You must be careful what you say to Marian," Sarah said. "For she has an excellent memory."

"Lord Richard," Marian interrupted, "Is not your cousin, Mr. George Wesley, coming tonight? I had expected to see him here, for I seldom see you without him."

"George is indeed going to Vauxhall," Lord Richard replied. "But not with us. He dined with the Sheffields last night and they formed a party to go." Marian grew pale at this information. "He's in love with their cousin, Miss Seldon, you know. I should not be surprised if there were a wedding by the end of the spring. It is a capital match. Miss Seldon is to inherit her father's estate and George has none. It is a fine thing for a younger son to find an heiress—especially if he should happen to like her." As Lord Richard continued in this vein, Marian found herself less and less able to attend to him, and her appetite soon left her.

Lord Beauregard and his mother stayed at home, but Lord Richard saw to it that the party was properly escorted to his father's shallot. Marian had never been on a shallot before, but she was rather too distracted to enjoy it properly. Sarah finally asked her what the matter was.

"I just don't understand why Mr. Sheffield would invite me to spend the evening with his sister, then make other plans," Marian told her sister. "It hurt far less when I thought they had previous plans. It is now evident they did not. Even so, why could not I have gone with them, if they truly desired my company? I suppose they thought I would not find out."

"My dear, it does not do to dwell on such matters. You must try to take pleasure in what is before you, not what is out of your reach."

"Perhaps you are right. I must console myself with the notion that, should Miss Forrester see me, I shall be in company with the son of a lord."

When the boat landed, Lord Richard and Count De Roche handed the ladies down and they all proceeded to the garden. The orchestra was playing a selection of Haydn, and upon entering the gardens, one of the first sights to be seen was a large statue of Handel. The Grand Walk was lined with trees and crowded with people, and though the sight was very grand and picturesque, Marian did not think it looked very much like a garden.

"Are there no rosebushes?" she asked. "I had expected to see some flowers." Lord Richard laughed.

"What, you did not expect Vauxhall to look like a country garden, did you? If you want hedges and flower-gardens, you had best go to a country estate. Besides, there's much more to see here besides flowers. The cascade, for example."

"But if there are no gardens, it should not be called Vauxhall *Gardens*," Marian insisted. "They should call it Vauxhall Park, perhaps."

"It is too bad that the owner of the garden, park, or whatever you want to call it, did not seek your advice when naming it," Lord Richard replied.

"I always fancy it to be rather a garden of people," Lady Emily said. "All the ladies have brightly colored dresses and everyone looks so different."

"Hurry up, ladies," Lord Richard said. "Or we shall miss the cascade."

"Nonsense brother," Lady Emily said. "The bell has not even rung yet. You will find that my brother is forever in the utmost haste, Miss Amberly. He fancies he must be the first to arrive wherever he goes."

"Now Emily," Lord Richard said, "You know I only want Miss Amberly to see all the wonders of Vauxhall, as she has never been." There was a loud clanging noise and Lord Richard smiled. "You see? There is the signal for the cascade." The party made their way to the miller's house, where a crowd was gathering. Among the spectators,

Marian noticed Mr. Sheffield and his sister who were in the company of Mr. George Wesley, Miss Seldon and, whom she did not expect to be of the party—Miss Perdue. Mr. Sheffield himself happened to look over almost the same moment. There was a look of surprise on his face at seeing her and he gave her a rather stiff bow, which she returned with an equally awkward curtsey.

Mr. Sheffield continued to look at Marian with an odd, almost resentful expression on his face as Lord Richard leaned close to her to inform her that the cascade was starting and took her hand to lead her to a better view. What must Mr. Sheffield infer from such a mark of familiarity? It was almost too much to bear, and Marian could derive but little pleasure from the cascade, pretty as it was, when her spirits were in such turmoil.

Though they did not know what had lowered her spirits so dramatically, Lord Richard and Lady Emily tried their utmost to raise them again by taking her down the South walk to show her the ruins of Palmyra. They laughed at her discovery that the ruins were only a painting and assured her she was not the first to suppose they were real. Marian saw their attempts to divert her, was grateful for it and endeavored to appear in good spirits. Indeed, after some time, she was able to derive some amusement from the evening, not the least of which was giving Miss Forrester a look of triumph as Lord Richard handed her into the supper-box and took a place beside her, as Mrs. Forrester's party happened to be passing by to take the box two places down. William, Rachel and Laura stopped to speak to Marian as the rest of their party went on.

"I see you managed to get to Vauxhall after all, cousin," William said with a smile. "And how do you like it?"

"Don't ask her that," Lord Richard said merrily, "For then you will get a lecture about how it ought to be called Vauxhall Park instead of Gardens." Lady Emily reached over and hit her brother on the arm with her fan.

"Don't tease our poor guest, Richard. She has just begun to be cheerful again."

"I am sure Miss Amberly, wise as she is, knows better than to take a rattle like me seriously. An impertinent fellow like myself can hardly be expected to say anything worthwhile, after all." Marian could not help but smile at this. "At last," he went on, "I find the way I can speak without offending Miss Amberly is to insult myself. And I can think of no worthier object to whom I might sacrifice my pride."

"I trust your lordship is keeping the ladies sufficiently entertained," William said. "This place is quite a novelty to me, for I must admit I have never been."

"Never been to Vauxhall? Where can you have been?"

"Living a retired life in the country, I must admit. The son of a clergyman doesn't always have access to such luxuries."

"I think it's lovely," Laura said. "The cascade was delightful, was it not, Marian?"

"Oh, yes," replied Marian, who could hardly remember the cascade at all.

"I am very glad you are here," Rachel said. "I should have been quite miserable if you missed out. Miss Forrester is a sweet girl in her own way, but I rather fancy she feels threatened by you. I don't know why. I am only sorry you cannot be in our box. I'm afraid we will be dreadfully crowded as it is, for we are to fit ten of us in at once."

"Well you may join us for we are only six," Lady Emily said. "You've no objection, have you Mother?" Lady Beauregard replied with a curt nod.

"Thank you, your ladyship," Rachel replied. "But I fear that Miss Forrester will take it very unkindly. I should not like to slight her."

"Ay, we must go to them now," William said. "For I have left poor George to entertain the other ladies by himself." With a bow, he led Rachel and Laura away.

Marian thought the portions astonishingly small and frightfully dear, yet Lord Richard was determined to impress the whole party and the table was adorned with ten chickens which were so small that Marian thought must have been barely hatched when they were cooked, nearly transparent slices of ham, cheesecakes, strawberries, grapes and biscuits. There was a glass of wine for each lady and a quart of arrack punch for the gentlemen. However, knowing that he was there to impress, Lord Richard chose to refrain from it, being well aware of the effects. Thus Count De Roche was left to drink it by himself, which he seemed to find no difficulty in doing. When he was beginning his third glass, his wife endeavored to check him.

"Don't try to restrain me, woman!" he said loudly, after her gentle remonstrance. "I shall do as I very well please. Don't fancy I'll allow myself to be browbeaten by any woman!"

"You are going to make yourself ill," Sarah protested. "And we are in a public place. I beg you not to draw attention to yourself."

"Oh hang the public!" Count De Roche said. "They may gawk all they like. They are none of them much better themselves!"

"For Heaven's sake, Philippe," Sarah said. "Lower your voice! What will Lady Beauregard think of us?"

"She may think what she pleases! And I warrant she knows how to respect her husband!"

"I assure you we all hold you in the highest respect, Count," Lord Richard said. "But I must beg you to spare my mother any unnecessary humiliation. She has a delicate constitution and such speeches might be trying to her spirits." Count De Roche sullenly dropped into his seat and was silent, for even he did not dare affront Lord Richard. Marian was grateful to Lord Richard for sparing her sister any more unnecessary embarrassment and resolved to behave more kindly toward him.

Sometime during supper, the garden was illuminated in a moment by what seemed to Marian like a million lamps all lit at exactly the same time. The effect was quite charming and really seemed almost like magic. After supper, John and one or two other young men whom Marian did not know, came to take Count De Roche away from them. Deciding that John's party would be better suited to his spirits, the count went with him, declaring he would go home in John's carriage and leave his lordship to tend to the ladies.

"Ay," John said, laughing loudly. "I have served Arthur the same way. He must tend to the ladies by himself, but he is so much better suited to it than I." Sarah looked extremely vexed at her husband's desertion, but perhaps it was for the best, as she would not have to listen to his vulgar ramblings anymore that evening.

"He is not always like that," Sarah told Marian. "But he is not himself when he has had too much to drink. It is the French blood in him, I suppose. I am only sorry he must behave in such a manner in front of my aunt and cousins."

"Indeed I never knew him to behave so," Marian replied. "He seemed to me always respectful and attentive. Perhaps the Vauxhall punch is more potent than what he is used to."

"Yes. I suppose he fancies it is like any other wine and that he may drink as much as he chooses, with no effect." After they had exhausted the subject of the count's drinking habits, which did not take long, Marian asked Sarah what she thought of Mrs. Forrester and her daughters.

"Mrs. Forrester and her daughters seem genteel enough," Sarah replied. "Mrs. Forrester, perhaps, is a little cunning and her eldest daughter scarcely less so. But you can hardly blame them, for the girls have only ten or fifteen thousand pounds apiece and it is unlikely that young Forrester will live to majority."

"Oh yes, he always was a sickly boy," Marian said. "But then so was his father, I understand, and he lived to produce an heir."

"It was very attentive of them to call on me as soon as they heard I was in town."

"Oh yes, very attentive," Marian replied dryly. "I am sure their primary inducement was the fact that William is staying with you. They make a point to be anywhere he is to be. And Laura's presence gives them every excuse to be about him all the time."

"Well, and they are both their cousins, are they not? Should they not wish to call on them when the opportunity should present itself?"

"Indeed, but you must ask yourself if William were not so handsome or very likely to inherit their estate, would they be so eager to solicit his company? I am sure William and Miss Forrester have nothing in common."

"Well we must not go on in this manner anymore," Sarah said. "This talk might rightly be called gossip and gossiping is a mark of ill-breeding."

"By the number of fashionable ladies that practice it, I should think it was rather a mark of *good* breeding." Sarah and Marian were a little behind the others, but at this time the others came back to them.

"Come, Countess," Lord Richard said. "You cannot keep this charming young lady to yourself all night. Miss Amberly, you must come walk with Emily and me." Lord Richard began leading her away from Sarah. "We have just been talking of the theater. Have you been this season?"

"This season? No, I have not. I have not been to the theater since we were at Bath last year."

"'Tis a pity," Lord Richard said. "*The Rivals* is not playing anymore, but Emily and I were contemplating whether we should go to see *The Tempest* next Tuesday. What is your opinion?"

"I wonder that your lordship should seek my counsel on such a subject," Marian replied, rather surprised. "Surely you and your sister can reach such a decision by yourselves?"

"Of course, if we could but agree. Emily fancies the theater is too common, for any tradesperson may go as easy as anyone. I, however, happen to like variety. And there is nothing like a comedy to lift one's spirits."

"I think the opera much more refined," Lady Emily said. "But I shall likely go with Richard on Tuesday, if only he will promise to protect me from any impertinence."

"I shall do all in my power," Lord Richard replied. "However, I would be vastly obliged if Miss Amberly would consent to be of the party, as well. And, of course, Miss Rachel and John. I shall have George with me, and I'm sure we shall all make a very merry party."

"My cousin Laura is to stay with us some weeks after Sarah leaves town on Saturday," Marian said. "I would not think of leaving her alone."

"Well she may come too," Lady Emily said. "I daresay say she'll make a fine addition to our little party. But we must find ourselves a chaperone, for our parents shan't let us all go out together."

"Does not your grandmother intend to go with us?"

"Good Heavens, no!" Lord Richard replied. "We shall have a very dull evening if she does. She never takes her eyes off us whenever we are all out together. I beg you not to charge me with being insensitive, but she really does make me feel quite suffocated." Marian could not help smiling for Lord Richard's description of his grandmother quite coincided with her own opinion.

"If only Miss Smith were here, she might go," Marian said. "She is our governess, but she is in the country with my younger sisters."

"Well, I suppose I must ask Mrs. Camden," Lady Emily said. "She's a fearfully dull little creature, but I feel very sorry for her. She married a captain in the army, you know, and the way her husband carries on with the ladies is scandalous. However, he is never with her. She is only just our own age, perhaps a little older. But she is a married woman and may act as chaperone for us and she won't give us any trouble." There was a very loud explosion which made Marian start, for the fireworks had just begun. Marian had never seen such a spectacular sight. To be sure, it was quite loud, but the explosion of color that lit up the sky made the sight quite worth it. After the fireworks were over, the party stayed an hour more and returned to Lord Beauregard's house in Portman Square.

As Lord Richard's party was to come from the Gardens so late, Marian stayed the night at Portman Square. After breakfast, Lady Emily retired to her room and, in preference to attending a tete a tete between the dowager and Lady Beauregard, Marian felt it prudent to do the same. She had not been in her room more than half an hour before Elizabeth, Lady Emily's maid, came to inform her that a young man was waiting downstairs to see her.

Quite at a loss to guess who could be calling on her at Lord Beauregard's house, she instantly went to the drawing room where she was awaited by none other than Mr. Sheffield. Her astonishment at seeing him and the recollection of the previous night brought the color into her cheeks.

"You are surprised to see me," Mr. Sheffield said. "I hope it does not follow that you are angry at my presence?"

"Indeed, Sir, I have no reason to be angry," Marian replied, a little uncertainly. "But I confess I am quite at a loss to guess the purpose of your visit."

"I am here to enquire after your health. I hope you are well?" So unprepared for such a question, she could only nod her acknowledgement. "I know I must seem rather forward. I called first at your father's house and was directed here. Indeed, you seemed very well last night."

"Then I wonder you took the trouble of coming today," Marian said, a little peevishly. She relented, however, upon seeing the hurt expression on his face. "I beg your pardon, Sir. It is very kind of you to show me your concern."

"I would not wish to embarrass you," he said. "Only—I hope that you would still wish to continue an acquaintance with my sister and Miss Seldon?"

"I assure you, I never had any intention of giving it up." Marian was perplexed at his words and supposed it must be some ill-expressed apology for canceling their engagement with her. But if that were the case, why did not his sister come with him? "Rather, I had wondered whether you did not wish to drop my acquaintance."

"Drop your acquaintance?" Mr. Sheffield exclaimed, stepping toward her. "My dear Miss Amberly, how could you suppose such a thing? I had very much looked forward to being in your company last evening. And I was greatly concerned to hear that you were ill."

"I was not ill," Marian replied, not a little confused. "When did you hear that?" Then, much to Marian's annoyance, Lord Richard entered the room, at this inopportune time, followed by George Wesley.

"Why Sheffield!" Lord Richard exclaimed. "George and I were just riding in Hyde Park. We called at your house to invite you, but you were out. Well! I can't say I blame you, for who would want to go riding about with the men when he could be calling on the ladies?"

"I was out early this morning on business," Mr. Sheffield replied.

"And very urgent business it was, I see," Lord Richard said with a laugh. "No, never mind your protestations, for if I had such business to conduct, I would set out early too!"

"I assure you, I have not been here fifteen minutes," said Mr. Sheffield. "And this is the first call I have made this morning."

"Ay, and so fifteen minutes is all that is required. And you should not make many calls of this sort unless you had been at a ball the previous night."

"What sort of call do you suppose it is? I was only calling to enquire after Miss Amberly's health. I assure you, I had no other intention in mind."

"And I perhaps shall make a similar call on Miss Seldon," Mr. Wesley said. "If Mr. Sheffield does not object, I shall accompany him to his house, when he goes." Mr. Sheffield nodded his assent and Lord Richard continued his raillery.

"Of course we all know that George is *only* calling to enquire after Miss Seldon's *health*. He certainly has no *other intentions* in mind." Marian began to be embarrassed for Mr. Wesley and noticed also that Mr. Sheffield was looking rather uncomfortable and therefore she entreated Lord Richard to cease his raillery.

"If the lady defends you, I am indeed vanquished. I envy you your fair champion, Sheffield, for she is such a conqueror as to be quite impossible to overcome." Marian blushed at having such language directed toward her and Mr. Sheffield looked as if he did not know how to reply. At last Mr. Sheffield took his leave and Mr. Wesley followed him out.

"My lord, why must you speak with such indelicate expressions to your friends?" Marian asked when they were alone. "Perhaps Mr. Wesley is accustomed to your teasing, but I'm sure he does not wish to have his private affairs insinuated in front of others."

"And what, pray, do you fancy his private affairs to be?"

"Indeed, I know nothing for certain. But surely you were implying an attachment to Miss Seldon that I am certain Mr. Wesley would by no means wish to be made public."

"Mr. Sheffield is not the public, Miss Amberly. Miss Seldon is his cousin and surely he is as conscious as any of us about the matter."

"That, perhaps, makes the raillery all the more offensive," Marian replied. "I am sure Mr. Sheffield was quite shocked at your insinuations."

"Is your interest in my cousin or in Sheffield?" Lord Richard asked. "You seem to take an eager interest in the delicate feelings you attribute to them both."

"I am interested in them both, my lord. They both seem to me young men of feeling, conviction and a strong sense of propriety. Therefore I feel it is not right to make them feel awkward."

"A sense of propriety you feel is absent in me." It was rather a statement than a question and upon receiving no reply Lord Richard was convinced it was the truth. "I apologize if I have caused you any uneasiness, Miss Amberly. I am a man of high spirits and must learn to suppress them. I hope my folly, at least, has not injured me very much in your opinion." He took her hand and pressed it to his lips. "I would hate to lose your friendship so soon after gaining it." Just then it occurred to Marian what an odd appearance it must have to be alone with such a young man. She hastily removed her hand from his grasp and began to excuse herself.

"Before you go," Lord Richard said, "Will you at least do me the honor of reserving the first two dances for me at tonight's assembly?"

"I think—I believe—I'm not quite sure," were Marian's incoherent replies.

"After all, misfortune robbed me of that pleasure the last time we were both at a ball. I am the more eager, therefore, to prevent that accident from being repeated. Come, Miss Amberly. Will you not help me correct the situation?" Marian could not help being amused at this excessive gallantry, but accepted his request and retired to her room to make preparations for returning home.

Between the time Marian returned home and their arrival at the assembly, she and Rachel had very few opportunities for private discussion about the previous evening.

Marian had scarcely been home half an hour before the family sat down to dinner, and then the ladies were so busy with dressing for the ball that there was no time for talking of anything else. Once they were in the ballroom, however, they found sufficient leisure to relate their impressions to one another.

They shared their opinions concerning the various attractions of Vauxhall, and Marian related her perplexity at Mr. Sheffield's behavior and told of the count's inebriety. Rachel in her turn told a shocking tale of how she and Laura were led, unawares, by the Miss Parkers to the Dark Walk and were surrounded by five or six young men.

"I am sure we were quite afraid for our lives, and I do believe Laura was even more frightened than I, and the Miss Parkers were scarcely less so. But how much more shocked was I to discover than John and Count De Roche were with this party of rogues! When they saw who we were they of course saw us back to the Grand Cross Walk. But John was quite angry and scolded us, but when I demanded how it was any worse for us to walk there than for him to lie in wait for unprotected ladies, it quite silenced him.

"They saw us back to our party, and left, quite vexed, I believe, at being discovered. I believe Miss Forrester was vexed as well, for after that, William took me in one arm and Laura by the other and did not let us from his side the rest of the evening."

"I wonder that John can behave in so shameful a manner!" Marian exclaimed. "Has he no family pride, or sense of morality? He can be very kind, but sometimes I am quite ashamed to have such a brother. Never mind, I shall give him a talking to sometime. And so Miss Forrester no longer had William's undivided attention. I don't wonder that she was vexed."

"Well you see how it all came about," Rachel said, "was after supper when we went walking, William offered me his arm and Miss Forrester took the other, quite unasked. Laura looked a little dismayed and so I left William's side and took Laura's arm myself."

"No doubt Miss Forrester thought it much to her benefit," Marian replied.

"Indeed, I don't know. But then the Misses Parker came on either side of us and suggested we walk about. So we ended up in the Dark Walks. I daresay they did not mean any harm and only thought to have a bit of adventure. But I suppose they will never look for such an adventure again."

"I should imagine not." Just then the dancing commenced and Lord Richard came to claim Marian's hand before she could revoke her promise to dance with him.

After dancing two dances with Lord Richard, Marian went to Sarah and was introduced to Mr. Henderson, whom she had not yet met, and reacquainted with Miss Henderson. Lord Richard, who had followed her, paid his respects as well.

"Why Miss Amberly," Miss Henderson said. "It's been ages since I last saw you. I believe you were not out then? I must say, you have grown quite pretty these four years."

"Thank you, Miss Henderson. You're looking quite well yourself."

"And Lord Richard," Miss Henderson continued. "It has been some time since we were last in one another's company."

"I am more than willing to renew the acquaintance by soliciting the next two dances," Lord Richard said gallantly. Miss Henderson readily accepted and Marian watched them walk away with much vexation. Then Mr. Henderson spoke.

"If it's not too bold ma'am, I should be obliged if you would do me the honor of dancing with me." Marian knew not how to refuse him and supposed that perhaps they could stand up near his sister and Lord Richard, and so she accepted.

Mr. Henderson was neither handsome nor plain, not very tall, and had an air of awkwardness about him. His conversation was tedious, for it was all about him and his business. It was evident he fancied himself a real gentleman, for he had a house in London and in Bath. He dressed with more show than elegance and clearly thought himself quite good enough for a duke's daughter. In short, Marian was quite in ecstasy when the dances were over.

Next she danced with George Wesley and had the relief of some intelligent, lively conversation, then she danced with William who said he supposed he had enough cousins to occupy his whole evening and was determined to dance every dance to escape Miss Forrester's constant attendance, though he was, by common politeness, expected to dance with her at least once.

Mr. Sheffield, at last, asked her to dance. However, Marian did think him quite out of spirits and less eager to talk than usual.

"I hope, Mr. Sheffield, you do not intend to keep up this silence forever."

"I am very ready," he replied, "To speak on any subject you choose."

"Mr. Sheffield, why this coldness?" she asked. "After extending the hand of friendship, are you so ready to retract it?"

"No indeed, Miss Amberly. I hope we shall always be friends. There are many similarities between our minds, I believe, that will always make our company agreeable to one another. I only have some perplexities that weigh upon my mind."

"Well if they are business matters, those are best left outside the ballroom," Marian said gaily. "We ought to discuss only cheerful things here."

"I only hope—" Mr. Sheffield paused. "I hope that your intimacy with the Beauregard family will not affect your desire for our acquaintance. They are very fashionable to be sure, but I trust that my sister and I are not entirely deficient."

"No, indeed," Marian said. "Though I don't understand why you should say such a thing. Have I given you any reason to suppose I prefer their company over that of you and your sister? I rather thought it was the other way around."

"Certainly not," Mr. Sheffield said. "I was very sorry you were unable to join us last night."

"I am quite at a loss to understand your meaning, Mr. Sheffield. What is it you are talking of?"

"I hardly know myself. I have already said more than I intended. I pray you'll forgive me. As you say, these are not subjects for a ballroom."

"Have you a better one, then?" Marian asked.

"What do you say to a ball? My sister and I have been contemplating giving one in about two weeks. We shall of course issue a personal invitation when we decide on a date."

"That is very kind of you, Sir." The dance ended and Mr. Sheffield returned Marian to her party. He remained a few minutes more in attendance, but soon retired, eclipsed by Lord Richard's more pointed attentions.

After Mr. Sheffield had walked away, Lord Richard asked Marian for the next two dances. Suspecting that Mr. Sheffield had left them because of Lord Richard, she replied that she meant to sit out those two dances, for she was tired, after which, Lord Richard came upon the surest way of gaining a future compliance by asking Miss Henderson instead.

"And perhaps," he said, as he and Miss Henderson rose to go to the dance, "when these two dances are over, you will have rested enough to dance the next two with me." Marian agreed and afterward was vexed with herself for falling into such a trick.

"But you must go through with it, now you've agreed," Sarah told her. "But I must say I don't know what Lord Richard means by dancing more than once with more than one young lady. I'm not sure it is quite proper."

"Oh if it is improper I'm sure I must not," Marian said. "Surely it will not be considered impolite to avoid an action that will bring censure upon me. I fear already have spent too much time in Lord Richard's company, from a hint Mr. Sheffield dropped. He did not say so exactly, but from his language I might have guessed it."

"My dear, I am certain you could have done nothing to excite anybody's contempt. Only sometimes your tongue is a little sharp. But otherwise your conduct is most proper, I believe."

"I wonder what Lord Richard means by showing me such pointed attentions. I know he can mean nothing by them. But I wonder that his family should not cease to solicit my company, for surely they cannot but mark his behavior. I am sure they think me vastly too inferior to solicit me for a daughter-in-law. Not that I would wish to be married to such a man even if his family should wish it."

"Oh yes, a charming, handsome and titled man would make such a dreadful husband," Sarah replied with a smile. "Who would wish to be the next Lady Beauregard?"

"Mother has quite determined upon the match, but I assure you, I have not. I want a husband who loves me for myself, not one that will grow weary of me after he has won my heart. A husband like Lord Richard would be always provoking my jealousy by his flirtations."

"It seems to me he is already provoking your jealousy," Sarah replied. "Else you would not have been so ready to accept what you had only just refused because it was offered to another young lady."

"Indeed, Sarah, you make me feel like such a simpleton." Sarah only smiled at the girlish woes of her sister.

CHAPTER FIVE

The next morning, after breakfast, Laura was settled into Sir John's house, and Sarah and William came to take leave, Count De Roche having set out for the West Indies very early. William was to return to town in three days, where he would take Arthur's place in his lodgings, for Arthur was to go to Rosewood Manor to take care of some business for his father and would likely be gone until it was time for William and his sister to go to Bath with their cousins.

Among the first callers of the day was Mr. Henderson. He made no attempt whatsoever to disguise that Marian was the principle object of his attentions. He had much of the forwardness, and very likely more, of Lord Richard, though his compliments were less eloquent, and, consequently, more odious to listen to. So conspicuous were his attentions that even Laura began to be quite embarrassed for her cousin.

"What an odd young man he is!" Laura exclaimed after Mr. Henderson ended his visit, which had lasted nearly an hour. "And his manner is so familiar. How long have you known him?"

"He was introduced to me only last night," Marian replied. "I know little of him and have not much desire to know any more. I daresay, I don't know what he means by calling upon me in this familiar way. No doubt he and his sister fancy we are their way into higher society."

"He does seem to have taken a fancy to you, Marian," Lady Amberly said. "However, I would not give him too much encouragement. He does not seem very genteel and has no estate."

"He does not seem to want much encouragement, Mother. He is very much like Lord Richard in *that* respect. Though in all other respects, I must say Lord Richard is infinitely more preferable."

"Yes, I was very pleased to see you danced with him twice. I daresay he has improved on you."

"I only said he was preferable to Mr. Henderson, and that is not saying much."

"Marian is not the only lady who danced twice with the same partner," Rachel said. "I could not help but notice that Mr. Wesley danced twice with Laura." Laura said nothing, but looked down at her work as her cheeks grew red.

"Mr. George Wesley?" Marian asked.

"No, the *elder* Mr. Wesley," Rachel said. "And I had fancied the dowager had him singled out for Lady Emily, but I dare say he has different plans himself."

"I've only just met him," Laura protested. "I think him very agreeable, but there is no reason to suppose anything in it."

"Did he not call on you this morning?"

"Yes—that is, he called on all of us. It was not for me, however. And he only stayed half an hour. I—I believe he called mainly for Sarah."

"Half an hour is quite long for a proper call," Marian said. "You must not suppose the length of Mr. Henderson's visit to be within the boundaries of most calls."

"Speaking of visits," Lady Amberly said, "I must order a good dinner, for my brother has returned to London and of course he must dine with us."

"Oh yes," Marian said. "Last time he was here he talked about buying a small estate in the country. Has he found one yet?"

"I don't suppose so," Lady Amberly replied. "For I believe he has but just returned to England. He did say he was to go look at one this week. I hope for your sake it is a very pretty little estate."

"For my sake?"

"Of course. You know that he intends to leave most of his fortune to you."

"I know you have told me so," Marian replied. "But you have also told me Lord Richard intends to marry me, and I am by no means convinced of *that*."

"Well, I will advise him to get a house with a very pretty little garden and perhaps a summer-house or a classical temple. And to be sure, it must be in a respectable neighborhood, for the old earl may live some years yet and it will be very desirable for you to have a separate house."

"My Uncle Carlyle may live some years yet," Marian said dryly. "We can hardly throw him out of his own house. And who knows but he may live long enough to marry and produce an heir of his own?"

"Nonsense, child. My brother is over fifty years old and quite past the age of trying to find a wife. Not but what I hope he shall live a while longer yet." Marian deemed it prudent not to reply to her mother's assertions and Lady Amberly soon found other things to occupy her thoughts.

Lady Amberly's brother, Mr. Carlyle was a kindhearted old man with an appreciation for wit and learning. It was perhaps for this reason that Marian was his favorite of his sister's children and he determined upon making her his heiress. He had succeeded his father in the business of banking and investments and by now had a very comfortable income which enabled him to have a house in town and purchase a small estate. He very frequently went to the West Indies to look after his investments, not willing to trust anyone else to do it for him.

Lady Amberly planned a small family party with the additions of Miss Perdue, at Rachel's request, and Lord Richard who had happened to call earlier in the day. Lord Richard, ever eager in his attentions to Marian, was closely watched by Mr. Carlyle, for he had plans of his own for the disposal of his niece's hand. Whether Lord Richard would be an obstacle to his plans was not certain. Marian did not seem to dislike being the object of such gallantry, nor did she seem particularly enamored with Lord Richard.

Meanwhile, Reginald, whom no one had ever told that Marian was to be his uncle's primary heir, endeavored to ingratiate himself with Mr. Carlyle. Reginald was certainly not the brightest of his sister's children and had never learned his Greek and Latin very well, but he was very proficient in arithmetic, and Mr. Carlyle began to perceive that it might not be very difficult to teach him accounts. He therefore invited Reginald to stay with him while he was in London, and if circumstances proved favorable, perhaps even travel with him to the West Indies. This was readily agreed to and Sir John withheld not his consent, hoping that Reginald might learn something useful, which he had hitherto not done.

After dinner Mr. Carlyle took a seat next to Marian as Lord Richard was standing by Rachel, who was sitting at the pianoforte. After the common civilities of inquiring how Marian spent her time in London, Mr. Carlyle asked her what she thought of the young lord.

"I think him very handsome and charming," Marian replied. "He is very conscious of his charms and consequently, not very humble, but he has a far better address than another young man who called this morning who equals Lord Richard in self-importance, but not in consequence."

"My dear, let me caution you to beware of such young men. This Lord Richard, I understand, has quite a reputation with the ladies."

"To be sure he does," replied Marian, a little flustered. "But I'm sure that need not concern me, for I am quite indifferent to him, except as a source of diversion." At this time Lord Richard came over to them and stood behind Marian's seat. Mr. Carlyle, though not over-pleased with this attention, pretended not to notice his presence.

"I have found a very pretty little estate just south of Fulham," Mr. Carlyle told his niece. "I think it shall suit me very well, for it is a convenient distance to town. But my dear, I should like to have your opinion on it. Therefore I hope you will oblige me with your company next Thursday for an excursion to the place. Then you may tell me whether you like it."

"I shall be happy to oblige," Marian replied. "But I cannot imagine why my opinion should be so important."

"Because you may very well be mistress of it when I am gone. My godchildren, James and Eleanor, shall accompany us and make a nice little party."

"Frederick," Lady Amberly said. "Pray come help us make up our card party. Sir John and Albert are playing at backgammon." For Lady Amberly was as eager to leave Marian and Lord Richard in a corner by themselves as Mr. Carlyle was eager not to. Naturally, Lady Amberly won out in the end and Lord Richard took Mr. Carlyle's place.

"Miss Amberly, I'm afraid I never got your opinion of Vauxhall. How did you like it?"

"I liked it very well, for the most part. The behavior of some of the young men was quite shocking. But the walks and the fireworks were pleasant."

"Perhaps you would like Ranelagh better. It is generally believed to have a more genteel set. There are flower gardens there, the lack of which seemed to be a great source of vexation with you at Vauxhall." Marian smiled.

"I believe I got over it tolerably after two hours," she said. "The cascade and my brother-in-law's behavior at the supper-boxes were quite enough to drive flowers out of my mind."

Marian was beginning to grow quite confused about her own feelings toward Lord Richard. He was handsome and agreeable to be sure. There were times when he looked at her earnestly and her heart seemed to stop. He was passionate—but how long would his passion last? Of course, the triumph of catching one of the most eligible bachelors in London, to the extreme envy of nearly every other lady, had its merits. But had she really caught him, or was it all a passing flirtation? Could he possibly have any real intentions, as her mother insisted, or was he trying to make a conquest of her heart only to prove that he could? She had begun to get caught in the same snare she had warned her sister about only weeks before.

And then of course there was Mr. Sheffield. Mr. Sheffield had not the easy, over-gallant way that Lord Richard did, but he was handsome and charming and Marian did not doubt he would make a pleasant companion. There was more sincerity in his manner than in Lord Richard's. He displayed not the passion of Lord Richard, but his affection, once gained, would be a steady, long-lasting one. Lord Richard, however, called nearly every day and Mr. Sheffield hardly at all. Mr. Sheffield and his sister had cancelled their engagement with her and Lord Richard and Lady Emily solicited her company.

Mr. Sheffield was very civil, but showed her no particular regard, and Lord Richard was charming and attentive to every lady who came across his path. In short, Marian was not more sure of the regard of one than of the other.

On Monday, Mr. Sheffield called with his sister and Miss Seldon and extended a personal invitation to a ball to be held at his house on Thursday, May 27. This was of course readily accepted, and Marian was extremely vexed when this visit was interrupted by a less desirable one from Mr. Henderson. Careless of any other company in the room, he boldly requested her to go riding in Hyde Park with him.

"I beg your pardon, Sir," she said indignantly. "I have only been acquainted with you three days. You can hardly expect I would go anywhere alone with someone so little known to me."

"I assure you, Miss, there is no harm in it. If you are afraid of being alone with me, we shall take my sister, and I shall ask Lord Richard to accompany us."

"I beg you will do no such thing and I pray you'll excuse me if I decline. It would very improper." Upon his further pressing her, Mr. Sheffield spoke.

"You have the lady's answer, Sir," he said. "If she does not wish to go with you, I would advise you not to importune her further."

"I'm sure I shall have a right soon enough," Mr. Henderson mumbled. No one chose to reply to this enigmatic statement. Mr. Henderson moved to the side, but did not leave, apparently meaning to out-stay Mr. Sheffield. Mr. Sheffield, however, did not think it proper to leave such a character to impose upon the ladies of the house any longer.

"Have you not any other business to conduct this morning, Sir?" Mr. Sheffield asked him. "Or do you plan to keep these ladies from their business till dinner?"

"What have ladies to do with business?" was the reply. "I'm sure they have nothing to do except receive visitors and cover screens." Marian and Rachel looked at each other with extreme astonishment at such ill-breeding. "And you need not suppose I must conduct any business on my own, for I have a steward who does it all for me." Mr.

Sheffield, seeing he would not be able to reason with such a person, whispered something to his sister, who gave a curt nod. Mr. Sheffield walked over to Lady Amberly and said something inaudible.

"You are very kind," Lady Amberly said.

"Miss Amberly," Mr. Sheffield said, "I took the liberty of asking your mother if you may accompany us to Gunter's and she has granted her permission. We shall have you back for dinner."

"Well then, if you please, Sir," Mr. Henderson said, as Marian went to prepare to go out, "Set her off at her uncle's house by six. But I must say I don't take it very kind of you to take her away."

"Why should you be concerned about it?" Mr. Sheffield asked. "Have you not two other ladies to entertain?"

"Well, but I came on purpose to court the eldest," Mr. Henderson said. "Though I don't know that it's any concern of yours."

"Court her! After so short an acquaintance? Have you any reason to suppose she wishes for such attentions?"

"Well I do not know that the lady's inclination has much to do with it."

"Indeed! Well that's a very odd sort of attitude for a lover to have. And how do you suppose you'll succeed with such a tactic?"

"Her uncle favors the match."

"Her uncle!" said Mr. Sheffield and Lady Amberly at almost the same time. Then Lady Amberly asked, "Why which uncle do you mean, Sir?"

"Your brother, Ma'am," Mr. Henderson replied. "Mr. Carlyle. He's my godfather. He was very pleased to hear on Saturday that I had Miss Amberly's acquaintance."

"Was he indeed?" Lady Amberly said. "To be sure, my brother has some very odd humors." Marian returned, dressed to go out.

"Before you leave, Miss," Mr. Henderson said, "I should like to have your answer to Mr. Carlyle's invitation."

"Why, I don't believe you have made an invitation," Marian replied, rather surprised.

"He wishes to know if you," he nodded at Lady Amberly, "And your children would dine with him this evening. I should like to give him an answer as soon as may be."

"Very well," Lady Amberly said. "You may tell him we accept."

"I wish I had room enough in my carriage for your sister and cousin," Mr. Sheffield said when they were driving away. "But I feel certain that you were the main object of that gentleman's attendance and therefore he will not impose on them much longer."

"I cannot thank you enough for rescuing me from such a character," Marian said. "I don't know what he means by calling on me so often."

"He said he was courting you," Miss Sheffield said with a provoking smile. "I daresay you will have a very odious husband."

"I hardly know the man, and more I do know him, the less I wish to. I certainly shall not marry him." Mr. Sheffield ordered them all ices from Gunter's and the ladies carried on a polite, but restrained conversation on general topics. Miss Sheffield in particular seemed uncomfortable talking to her, though Marian could not imagine why. Perhaps it was because she had not called on them in due time. When Mr. Sheffield returned her home, therefore, Marian resolved that she would call on the ladies at her first opportunity.

The next morning the Dowager Lady Beauregard condescended to call on Lady Amberly and her daughters. So magnanimous was her ladyship that she even solicited the company of Marian for a few weeks in Bath, where she and several of her grandchildren were to go in June.

Marian was fond of Bath, but not particularly fond of her ladyship. However if Lady Emily and Mr. George Wesley were to go, she might have some worthwhile company. Even more pleased was she to hear that Miss Seldon was to go as well. Having gained her mother's blessing on the matter, it was settled.

While the dowager was still there, Mr. Henderson made his daily call. Lady Amberly was extremely vexed that her ladyship should see such an acquaintance and would have given orders not to admit him, except she was afraid it might vex her brother, as Mr. Carlyle seemed to be fond of the young man. There was nothing to do, therefore, except introduce him to her ladyship and hope he might make himself less ridiculous than usual.

The dowager gave a slight inclination of the head and continued her conversation with Lady Amberly. Mr. Henderson, however, took a seat beside Marian.

"So this is his lordship's grandmother, is it?" he whispered. "I shall have to tell my sister I have made her acquaintance."

"Sir, I beg you will not speak to me in so familiar a manner," Marian replied. This caught the attention of the dowager, who turned to look at them. Marian stood up and walked over to where Rachel and Laura were sitting.

"Well Miss," Mr. Henderson said, evidently not discouraged, "I have come here this morning on purpose to offer you a ticket to the theater tonight. My sister and I are going and would be much obliged if you would accompany us."

"I thank you, Sir," Marian said coldly, "But I cannot accept, for I am already going with Lord Richard and his sister, and they were so kind as to include my sister and cousin in the invitation."

"I should be very happy to invite Miss Rachel and Miss Forrester if it were in my power," Mr. Henderson said, looking a little uncomfortable. "But as it is, I only have one seat besides my sister's and Mr. Carlyle's, for there are others sharing the box with us. But your uncle desires very much that you should go with us."

"I'm much obliged, I'm sure," Marian said. "But I cannot suppose my uncle would wish me to be so ill-bred as to cancel a previous engagement to make another." Mr. Henderson could think of no reply to this.

"And I am very sorry my brother should appoint you as his messenger," Lady Amberly added. "He ought to come himself or send a servant. It is very improper that he should employ a gentleman to run about delivering his messages. I think I shall speak to him about it."

"I assure you ma'am, it is quite a pleasure," Mr. Henderson said. "I should be very sorry, indeed, to lose the commission." Here the Dowager took her leave and said she did not doubt that her grandson would soon send his carriage to collect Miss Amberly, Miss Rachel and Miss Forrester.

"Indeed, girls," Lady Amberly said. "It is past five o' clock. You had better go change into your gowns." All three of the young ladies, and especially Marian, were eager to get away from the obnoxious Mr. Henderson, and therefore had no trouble heeding Lady Amberly's suggestion.

Lord Richard and his party arrived at Drury-lane in due time. It was very crowded and very noisy. Laura, who had never been to the theater, was fascinated by everything and everybody. Rachel, who had only been to the theater in Bath, where the audience was considerably less disruptive to those who actually wanted to watch the play, was vexed that she missed every other word. Marian, who knew rather better what to expect, did as is proper for one to do at the theater—mainly look about for her acquaintance. Out of curiosity she looked for her uncle's party, and when she found it, she wished she had not, for Mr. Henderson was openly staring at her until she was quite put out of countenance. She hardly had time to notice that Mrs. Forrester and her daughters were of the party.

Mr. Wesley and Mr. George Wesley were both of the party and Marian observed for the first time that Mr. Wesley was in conversation with Laura, and much more animated than she had hitherto seen him. What a thing it would be, if Laura, the daughter of a country clergyman, should catch the eldest son and heir of a baron. The younger Mr. Wesley, meanwhile, continued to be engrossed with Miss Seldon, and there were open speculations about when an offer would be made.

During the intermission, Mr. George Wesley went over to Mr. Sheffield's box and Mr. Henderson came to Lord Richard's. He made a profound bow to everyone in the box, and Lady Emily and Mr. Wesley, who were not used to his assiduities, only stared. Mr. Henderson, however, was not to plague Marian as usual, for bold as he was, he was no match for Lord Richard, who would not suffer him to keep Marian to himself in a corner. He stood in very close proximity to Marian and had something to say upon every subject Mr. Henderson attempted. Lord Richard had just finished a speech about carriage horses when Mr. Henderson spoke.

"Speaking of carriages, your lordship," he said, "I meant to ask if you might go riding with Miss Amberly and my sister and I sometime. For I asked Miss Amberly here yesterday, but she would not go, on account she was afraid of being alone with me."

"Indeed!" Lord Richard said, scarcely able to contain his mirth. "Well then I should be very much delighted to be of your party. I have a curricle I feel certain would just suit Miss Amberly's taste. Something tells me she would rather enjoy a fast pace."

"I meant rather you should take my sister with you," Mr. Henderson said, "And I would take Miss Amberly myself."

"I have a still better combination," Lord Richard replied. "I shall drive you about the park and Miss Amberly may go with your sister, if she pleases." Everyone else in the box laughed and Mr. Henderson looked quite confused. "And since we're on the subject, I was just going to propose to Miss Amberly…" He paused and everyone looked as if they thought they had not quite heard him correctly, when he continued. "…that we all make an excursion to Box Hill on Saturday."

"What a charming idea!" Lady Emily said. "I long to go. I've not been this year and it is supposed to be quite pretty at this time."

"I think such frolics are a waste of time," Mr. Henderson said haughtily.

"Do you?" Lord Richard asked. "May I ask why an excursion to Box Hill is a waste of time more than a drive in Hyde Park? I daresay you accomplish no business in either and both are pleasurable. Nobody supposes them to be conducive to anything but pleasure."

"Driving in the park accomplishes the business of courting and to be seen," Mr. Henderson replied.

"Noble business indeed!" Lord Richard cried. "If that is business, then I am a most thorough and scrupulous business man!" The ladies all smiled. "However, Sir, since the excursion is so disagreeable to you, it is fortunate you are not required to go. I hope, at least, you will not try to deny us all the pleasure of going just because you don't like it yourself." Mr. Henderson, feeling he was in the presence of one who was superior to him in both wit and consequence, made his bows and walked away. "Miss Amberly, I was under the impression you did not know him before Friday?"

"Indeed, my lord, I never met him before in my life, to my recollection."

"Well he seems to think of you quite as his own, I daresay, though I don't know why. He does not behave so genteel as his sister."

"Oh yes. She is very refined and accomplished, to be sure." Mr. George Wesley returned to the box, leant toward Marian and said,

"Mr. Sheffield sends his compliments to you and your sister."

"Does he not come over himself, then?"

"No, he cannot get away from his guests. Miss Perdue, in particular, seems reluctant to let him out of her sight."

"I daresay she is," Marian replied. "And are the ladies well?"

"They seem very well," Mr. Wesley answered. "Miss Seldon said she had rather be here, for I do not believe she is over-fond of Miss Perdue."

"I like her better and better. But I think I have been negligent where she is concerned. I ought to have called long ago. I shall be remiss no longer and I am resolved to call upon her tomorrow."

CHAPTER SIX

As promised, the next day Marian went to call upon Miss Sheffield and Miss Seldon, but found Miss Seldon alone, as Miss Sheffield had gone shopping with Miss Perdue. Miss Seldon received her graciously, but seemed a little reserved. Marian apologized for not having called on her sooner, expressed her regret that Miss Sheffield was out and talked of general subjects for a while.

"I am very sorry if I offended you," Marian said. "I wished very much to call upon you sooner, but my time is not always my own. My mother can be very demanding."

"Perhaps it is I who offended you," Miss Seldon replied. "Otherwise—may I ask you a question, Miss Amberly? Or perhaps I had better not. That is, it is no business of mine. But I must say, I'm quite at a loss…"

"You may ask me what you please," Marian replied. "I shall do my best to answer."

"I had understood that last week you were to come spend the evening with us, were you not?" Miss Seldon asked.

"Indeed I did think so," Marian said, blushing at the recollection. "And I was eagerly looking forward to it, I assure you." Miss Seldon looked as if she did not quite comprehend her.

"Then why did you write and say you were ill?" she asked. "I was very sorry to hear you were ill, but when we saw you that night at Vauxhall, I confess we did not quite know what to think."

"Ill!" Marian exclaimed. "I never said such a thing! Miss Sheffield wrote to me the previous night and said she and her brother had just recollected a previous engagement. *I* was very much disappointed. If ever you call on me, I shall show you the letter."

"I can hardly believe Catharine would tell such a falsehood," Miss Seldon said. "I did not think she could be so wicked. And yet, she was very vexed when Edward said we would not go to Vauxhall because he had invited you to spend the evening here and was not sure you would like it. When Catherine takes anything into her head, she is determined to have her way."

"And what did Mr. Sheffield think about all this?" Marian asked. "For the other night when we were dancing, he alluded to my preferring the company of Lord Richard and Lady Emily to his and Miss Sheffield's."

"He was a little offended when he saw you at Vauxhall after hearing you were ill, but then he supposed Lord Richard must have induced you to do it."

"Indeed he did not! Lord Richard and his sister did try to persuade me to break my engagement with you, that I might go with them, but I would not. They were present when I got Miss Sheffield's note, however, so I agreed to go, for they renewed their invitation."

"I'm sure Edward will be very pleased to hear it. However, I cannot tell him now, for he has gone to Bristol to rescue his brother from some sort of trouble."

"Is he gone? I'm sorry to hear it. Will he be gone long?"

"I don't know. Perhaps one or two weeks," Miss Seldon said. "Surely he will be back for the ball."

"And so Mr. Sheffield has a brother, does he? What sort of man is he?"

"Oh! Well, I believe he is a very good young man at heart, but he does have a tendency to let others lead him into trouble. He is only three and twenty and a lieutenant in the army. It is to be hoped that time will improve him."

"Is he handsome?"

"Not so handsome as Edward, but he looks well enough."

"I believe you have not yet been introduced to my sister," Marian said. "I am sure she will be very glad to make your acquaintance, if you should happen to call."

"I should be very happy to meet her," Miss Seldon replied. "Mr. George Wesley assures me that you and your sisters are most agreeable young ladies. If I have an opportunity, I shall call on you tomorrow, if you please."

"Oh, but we shall not be at home tomorrow," Marian said. "My uncle wishes to take us all into Fulham, to see a house he wishes to purchase. I assure you, I would rather not go, for that odious Mr. Henderson is to attend us, and there is no one I am less inclined to favor with my company."

"He is a very persistent young man," Miss Seldon said, "And by no means discreet. He blatantly told us all he is courting you, though Catherine and I have never met him. Surely there can be no propriety in such a declaration. No delicacy!"

"But unfortunately my uncle is very fond of him and his sister and I begin to perceive that my uncle rather wishes me to marry Mr. Henderson. I should be diverted if I were not so vexed, for my mother has determined that I shall marry Lord Richard, and therefore she takes care that Lord Richard is present whenever Mr. Henderson is. For example, my mother has invited Lord Richard tomorrow in such a way that my uncle could not refuse without seeming very ill-bred. But I predict a great deal of discomfort for tomorrow."

"Which do you wish to marry?"

"Well, I'm not sure I should like to marry either of them. However, if I must choose between them, Lord Richard is infinitely superior in understanding, whereas Mr. Henderson has an unpolished, intrusive manner which makes him unattractive."

"So you prefer Lord Richard?"

"I hardly know my own mind on the matter," Marian said, with her eyes fixed upon her hands. "I am very certain I could never be induced to accept Mr. Henderson's hand, but Lord Richard—well he has charms, to be sure, but sometimes one must doubt his sincerity."

"I am sure *you* could never make an unwise choice for a partner in life. You have a sensible mind."

"But it is not always the mind that makes such decisions for us," Marian replied. "I can only hope my understanding will speak for me, as well as my heart."

The anxiety of what the following day would bring weighed heavily on Marian's mind, for if Mr. Henderson could begin a courtship after one day's acquaintance, surely it would not take him long to come to the point. Her anxiety had not done by breakfast the next morning, and Lady Amberly must have had apprehensions similar to her daughter's, for she contrived to procure Marian the seat next to Lord Richard in his curricle, which his lordship was only too eager to offer. So it happened that Marian and Lord Richard were settled into the curricle before Mr. Carlyle could collect his thoughts amidst the bustle and procure his niece as the companion of Mr. Henderson, who was to drive Mr. Carlyle's barouche.

At last it was settled that Miss Henderson should ride up front with her brother, for she had proclaimed a preference for riding outside when she supposed that the seat in Lord Richard's curricle might be hers. Laura had gone to visit her cousins for the day, for her brother had just returned from Ramsgate. That left Lady Amberly, her son, younger daughter and brother to sit inside the carriage. Thus the party set off in a manner satisfactory to some, not satisfactory to others.

Mr. Carlyle's prospective estate was a very pretty little one, sufficient for a man attempting to establish himself as a landed gentleman. The house had ten bedrooms, three drawing-rooms, one of which might be opened unto the music room to make room for dancing, a library and a dining room. The property contained a small park and a large pond, upon the bank of which was a summer house which might seat eight people comfortably.

"It's a pity we did not come prepared," Marian said. "We might have dined out here. As it is, we must stop at an inn for a cold luncheon."

"When we go to Box Hill on Saturday we shall have the very best of cold meats and fruits," Lord Richard replied. "My sister will arrange it charmingly, I'm sure."

"Well, and what do you think of the place, Marian?" Mr. Carlyle asked his niece. "It is charming, is it not?"

"It appears to be a very suitable house for a family of six or seven," Marian replied. "The grounds are very pretty. But is there a rectory on the property?"

"Ah, well, the estate is rather a small one and does not have its own living," Mr. Carlyle said. "But there is a boxed pew reserved for the occupants at the neighboring church. I do not suppose the lack of a living is of great importance, for none of my nephews intend to go into the church and surely no one in your husband's family will need such a situation." He beamed at Mr. Henderson.

"I hardly know anything about my husband's family," Marian replied, growing quite red. "For I have no husband in view."

"Ay, my dear," Mr. Carlyle said. "'Tis very well to be modest, so we'll say nothing of the matter for now." The party soon divided up to make its own exploration of the grounds, and Mr. Carlyle very cleverly managed to get Lord Richard paired off with Miss Henderson, leaving Marian free to be pursued by Mr. Henderson. Marian walked toward the house to examine the views from the windows, followed by Mr. Henderson.

"It's a very pleasant estate, is it not?" Mr. Henderson asked. Marian, vexed that he had followed her, merely replied that it was and continued to look out of the windows. Mr. Henderson went on. "You can be at no loss as to my purpose in following you here."

"Indeed, Sir," replied Marian, quite flushed, "I can conceive no reason a young man should follow about a young woman whom he has not known a week. Surely you can have no business with me, upon so short an acquaintance." Mr. Henderson was unsettled.

"Why surely, ma'am, I have not known you *personally* till very recently, but your uncle speaks so highly of you, I feel I have known you for some time now. And, if I may be so bold, from the first night I saw you, I felt I could be happy with no other woman."

"That is bold indeed, Mr. Henderson. You quite shock me. I must tell you I have never seen you in any light but as a relation of my sister's." She began to leave the room.

"Miss Amberly, you must hear me," Mr. Henderson said, stepping front of her. "I am come for the purpose of making a proposal of marriage."

"Well I am very sorry for it," Marian replied haughtily. "I cannot accept your proposals. I am sorry if it pains you, but I never intended to give any such encouragement. Now, Sir, I must beg you to let me pass, for it is hardly appropriate for us to be here alone." He moved aside but still walked beside her.

"But you must know your own uncle wishes for our union as much as I could," Mr. Henderson said. "And he was very encouraging."

"Well then my uncle has misled you. He ought not to have made assumptions with so little reference to myself, for it could not be plainer I have no desire for the match." Mr. Henderson colored deeply. Marian pitied him, but dared not express it, for fear it might be taken as encouragement. They soon caught up with the rest of the party, due to Marian's quickened pace.

With some artful contrivance, Miss Henderson was able to procure herself the seat in Lord Richard's curricle for the ride home. Marian, too fatigued and vexed to concern herself with it, made no objection. Mr. Carlyle, unaware of Mr. Henderson's declined proposals, attempted to press her to sit beside Mr. Henderson. Lady Amberly, ever attentive to her daughter's welfare, declared that Marian looked ill and was certain she ought to ride *inside* the carriage and Reggie could sit up there just as well.

Once they were all settled and on their way back into town, Mr. Carlyle plagued them all with more than one hint about a match between his godson and niece.

Marian was more vexed than surprised when the following morning Mr. Carlyle called and requested to speak to his niece privately. Lady Amberly replied that they might go into Sir John's study, for he was out and not likely to return for two or three hours. Marian quite nervously followed her uncle into her father's study, for she suspected what the nature of his discourse would be.

"My dear child," he began, "I was told something last night, which I must say has made me very uneasy."

"I am sorry to hear it," Marian replied.

"I understand that Mr. Henderson has paid his addresses to you. He informs me that his proposals were offered and promptly rejected. Am I correct?" Marian answered in the affirmative and he went on. "I assure you, it is a most desirable match, and I am quite determined upon it."

"I don't know why you should be determined on it," Marian replied. "Nor do I know why you should be surprised. I hardly know the man and the match has not the sanction of my parents, nor do I believe it will. My father, I am sure, will not force me into anything I do not wish to do and my mother has quite determined I shall marry Lord Richard."

"Lord Richard!" Mr. Carlyle said. "Mr. Henderson is a decent, honest man and Lord Richard is a coxcomb at best and a libertine at worst. You do not mean to say you suppose you will marry Lord Richard?"

"I do not have a wish as to who I *will* marry, at the present. I only know I will *not* marry Mr. Henderson. I find his manners repulsive and impertinent. Furthermore, I do not believe he has any respect for me."

"Posh! What has respect to do with it? He is a man of fashion, which would be recommendation enough for many young ladies of your age. He has a fair fortune himself and with the estate I am to purchase, you will want for nothing."

"I will want for love and respect for my husband," Marian said. "And I believe those to be of high importance in a marriage."

"Let me appeal to your compassion then. Mr. Henderson's father was a very great friend of mine and named me godfather of his two children. He died some years ago, but I feel obliged to do all I can for the family. Their mother, you see, has been very ill and resides in their house in Bath. I do not know how I shall face her with the knowledge that her children are not properly established."

"How can you say so, Sir?" Marian asked. "Did you not say that they have a decent fortune of their own? Why must they have yours and mine as well?"

"Well they will not be considered truly *genteel* by all classes until there is property in the family. I had it all planned very well, you see. You are to inherit the bulk of my fortune. The estate is to be settled on you immediately upon your marriage to Mr. Henderson and Mr. Henderson is to increase his sister's settlement by another ten thousand, so she might be better able to procure a suitable husband. Thus I would be able to provide for you all."

"I am sorry it grieves you, but I will not marry Mr. Henderson," Marian said. "I simply cannot endure the thought. His very presence arouses my disgust. You may leave your whole estate to Mr. and Miss Henderson, but please do not attempt to force me into a situation so abhorrent to every natural feeling."

"Those are very harsh words!" Mr. Carlyle exclaimed, greatly displeased. "But I cannot feel justified in giving away my money to those not related by blood when my own sister has six children of her own. By this means only was it to be thought of."

"Then divide it equally among us all," Marian said. "No one will question your right or your good intentions."

"I warn you, child," Mr. Carlyle said. "If you refuse this request, you will forfeit my favor. You shall not have the estate. Oh, I cannot cut you off completely, but you shall have no more than what I intended to give my other nieces and nephews."

"Your money is your own, Sir." Marian was red with agitation. "I shall not repine. I cannot be bought at a price! I am very sorry to be the cause of your anger, believe me, but I have other feelings I cannot ignore without being wretched the rest of my life. My mother will not lament the loss of your estate for me when she learns under what condition is to be gained. Not that it is what I wish for myself, but she has much larger estates in mind for me." The interview over, Marian went to her room with a headache and did not return downstairs until she was informed that Miss Seldon had come to call on her. She opened her writing desk and took out the note from Miss Sheffield, which she intended to hand over to Miss Seldon and went down to meet her friend.

"Catherine sends her apologies for not coming with me," Miss Seldon said. "She is engaged with Miss Perdue at the moment."

"I daresay she wishes to avoid me because is ashamed of her falsehoods," Marian replied. "But here is the letter she sent me. You may keep it. I have no use for it." Miss Seldon quickly read over the note.

"However, I did not need this proof," Miss Seldon said. "I asked her about it myself yesterday. She was very lighthearted about it. She simply laughed and told me I needn't mention it to Edward. I am quite ashamed for her, Miss Amberly."

"No matter. It is no reflection on your own character. I think we are all related to those whom we have reason to be ashamed of."

"Well, never mind all that," Miss Seldon said. "I have something far happier to tell you of. Mr. George Wesley has finally made me an offer of marriage. He is to speak to my father when we all go to Bath in three weeks."

"Well, then let me offer my congratulations," Marian said. "You'll be very happy together, I'm sure."

"It is not very public yet," Miss Seldon said. "Catherine knows, and I'm sure Mr. Wesley has told his brother. And perhaps Lord Richard."

"Oh! Lord Richard. I wonder what he will have to say on the subject. He was always a great advocate for the match."

"Oh, yes. Lord Richard is a very civil young man, I'm sure. He is a little too free in his compliments perhaps, but very civil."

"He and his sister have planned for an excursion to Box Hill tomorrow," Marian said. "Shall you be coming with us?"

"I believe so. I think I should like it. I have heard it is a very fine place to visit."

"I daresay we will need more than Mrs. Camden as a chaperone for such a large party of single young men and ladies," Marian said with a laugh. "There will be ten of us, at least. It is a pity that my elder sister is no longer in town."

Mrs. Camden was unable to attend the party to Box Hill, but fortunately the young people were still favored with languid and indulgent chaperons. Sir John, having been cooped up in town for some time was ready to take a trip to the country, be it only for a day. Mr. Carlyle was also prevailed on to keep his brother company, though he continued to be out of humor with Marian. Uncomfortable as Marian was with this loss of favor, she was relieved that Mr. Henderson had the good sense to have business elsewhere. She was further relieved that, though Catherine Sheffield was of the party, she did not bring Miss Perdue with her. Miss Henderson, however, did come, and seemed quite determined to dominate Lord Richard's attention. Lady Beauregard came and brought her maid with her, which Miss Sheffield told Marian she thought rather singular.

"But I daresay she keeps her maid at her side constantly. Is she not rather a sickly creature? I wonder she has survived so long."

"I don't think we ought to talk about such things," Marian replied.

"Oh Heavens! I had forgotten how very proper you are. You are very like my cousin Louisa. But pray, is not Lady Beauregard to be your mother-in-law?"

"No, Miss Sheffield, and I beg you will not go about spreading such a tale. I am not engaged to Lord Richard."

"Well I heard from somewhere it would likely happen very soon. But had you not better be introduced at Almack's first? It is the proper thing to do before entering the aristocratic circle."

"I am to go next Wednesday with Lady Emily," Marian replied, wearied of the subject. "But I am not to marry Lord Richard. He has not asked, nor do I think it likely."

"But he pays you such marked attentions."

"Miss Sheffield, as you have been exposed to the world more than I, you ought to know that attentions from a man like Lord Richard are not meant to be taken seriously. He means only to toy with my feelings, and I shall not give him the satisfaction of succeeding."

"Well that Mr. Henderson fellow—you can be in no doubt of *his* meaning. He declared to us all that he was courting you. I must say, I thought that very ill-bred, but people who are in love are not always sensible."

"Miss Sheffield, have you anything to talk of besides beaux, marriage and engagements?"

"Nothing so interesting. I adore music, but there is really not much to say about it. Horseback riding is an acceptable diversion, but unless one falls from one's horse, or something equally exciting happens, it makes for rather dull conversation."

After the party enjoyed their outdoor luncheon of cold meats, salads and fruits, Lady Emily invited Marian and Rachel to walk about the woods with her and her brother. Lady Emily took Rachel's arm and Lord Richard claimed Marian for himself.

"I thought of bringing a violinist so we could have a little outdoor ball," Lord Richard said, smiling. "But my mother said it was the most shocking thing she'd ever heard, and so it had to be given up entirely."

"Surely you would not really have thought of it?" Marian said. "I never heard of such a thing among well-bred persons."

"Do not you think we should have been a merry little party of elves and nymphs, dancing among the trees? No, I can see you would not. You are quite shocked." Lord Richard laughed. "Perhaps I would not have truly put the plan into execution, but you must admit the notion is rather charming." Marian merely smiled and Lord Richard continued talking upon such trivial subjects and finally asked her whether she had heard from her elder sister?

"She has only been gone from town a week, my lord," Marian said. "However, my cousin William said that he left her well and very happy to see her children again."

"How pleasant it must be to have a family of one's own!" Lord Richard said with a warmth which surprised Marian. "I'm afraid I have been rather dissolute and carefree in my youth, Miss Amberly. Caught up in the pleasures of the world, I have been blind to the pleasures of a more lasting nature. The current felicity of my cousin has made me think more seriously on these matters. I know I have been wont to make light of George's engagement, but I believe it has been only to shield my own envy rather than a lack of feeling. Envy, you see, is a feeling quite new to me." Marian turned to see if Rachel and Lady Emily were near enough to hear, but alas, they were not even in sight.

"We seem to have lost the others," she said. "Had not we better turn back?"

"No. I daresay Emma saw something she fancied and took your sister with her. Besides, Emily has a good sense of direction. I feel certain they will make it back to the others. They may perhaps arrive before us."

"Then perhaps that is all the more reason to return ourselves," Marian said. "What conjectures will there be if they hear we are walking alone in the woods?"

"They may think what they choose. We are doing nothing wrong."

"There are two or three in the party who will be happy to put it in the worst light," Marian protested. "I insist we return to the others, for the sake of my own honor."

"Stay but five minutes," Lord Richard said, taking her hand. "Surely that is not long enough to arouse suspicion." Marian stopped. "And I may venture to hope that by the time we leave this place, we will soon have the right to as much privacy as we choose."

"What do you mean?" Marian blushed and trembled as Lord Richard kissed her hand.

"I mean, dearest Miss Amberly—Marian—to tell you that I have never been so enchanted by any woman as I am by you. You have bewitched me and I am no longer master of myself." Marian pulled her hand away.

"You mock me, Sir," she said. "Do not think me such a simpleton! I know what you are about, well enough."

"Mock you! How can you say so? I love you! You are the only woman who could ever make me happy. You are intelligent and lively, and I need not speak of your beauty, I think. When you look at me, your eyes seem to read my innermost thoughts. Indeed I do not know how it came about, for never did I expect to fall in love. But say you consent to marry me and make the happiest of mortals!" Marian leaned against a tree for support, for she could hardly believe her ears. Never had she expected him to be seriously attached to her. He very delicately refrained from naming her supposed fortune among her attractions, but Marian made no doubt it was uppermost in his mind and he did not know of the transfer of her uncle's favor.

"I hardly know what to say, my lord. I cannot help but suppose you think my uncle's estate shall be at my disposal and such a supposition must add greatly to your affections. However, I feel it incumbent on me to inform you that I am no longer his heiress, due to a disinclination to submit to his conditions. My whole portion will be what my parents intend to settle on me and any small amount my uncle may choose to give me. My fortune will not be grand enough for a son of the peerage." Lord Richard's brow clouded during this speech.

"I suppose the condition was that you were to marry that impudent fop, Mr. Henderson. I suspected as much. It is no matter. Surely you did not suppose my affections were based on such material considerations? I am not wanting for money, I assure you. Your uncle's fortune may be what induces my family to permit, even encourage my attentions to you, but to me it is nothing. When we are married, you shall be mistress of my fortune, as well as my heart." He was now standing very close to her and leant in toward her. She felt as if in a dream and could not help returning the kiss he gave her, but felt, almost as soon as it happened, she ought not to have done it.

"Lord Richard, I believe we really must go back to the others."

"Will you give me no answer? I must hear you say it." They began to walk back up the path and Marian held on to his arm, for the mental turmoil had quite fatigued her.

"No—that is—I don't know. I need some time to think about it. I hardly know what I feel."

"You don't absolutely refuse me, then," Lord Richard said. "You allow me to hope, at least. I must thank you for that. But pray don't mention your uncle's transfer of his fortune to anyone. It will get out soon enough. There are those in my family who will base your worth on your fortune, rather than your merit, as they ought."

"You fear that your grandmother will revoke her invitation to me to attend her to Bath?"

"She is not so indecorous. But she may make your visit less comfortable. I shall, of course, do all in my power to make you not regret accepting her invitation."

"With such foreboding I almost regret it now," Marian said. "I do not think I could bear the brunt of her displeasure for a month."

"How I wish I had said nothing!" Lord Richard said. "For I am sure you would not let your private business become public if you could help it."

"Certainly not." Soon they were back with the rest of the party and Rachel and Lady Emily had not yet returned. Mr. Carlyle eyed Marian and Lord Richard suspiciously, Sir John noticed nothing out the ordinary and Lady Beauregard leant languid against a tree while her maid read to her, which also wholly engrossed Miss Henderson, who was determined to ingratiate herself with Lady Beauregard. Miss Seldon and her betrothed had walked off together, Mr. Wesley, Reggie and Laura had wandered off to find Rachel, Marian and Lady Emily and Miss Sheffield was commanding William's attention by their mutual knowledge of Ramsgate.

Lord Richard readily joined in their conversation and tried to include Marian in it also. He behaved so gaily it was almost as if Marian had in fact accepted his proposal. This did not escape the ever-discerning Miss Sheffield who suspected at least that proposals had been made, and from the state of Lord Richard's spirits, must have been accepted. Marian could not meet Miss Sheffield's eyes without a blush, which vexed Marian the more, for it seemed only to confirm Miss Sheffield's conjectures.

At length the different groups returned from their excursions and the whole party prepared to return to town. Marian returned home with her emotions in more confusion than when she had left and at their return, Lady Amberly was astonished at the new level of good spirits, even for Lord Richard, and a happy suspicion was soon aroused in her from some comments of her husband which he himself did not seem to fully comprehend the import of.

When alone with them in her dressing room, Marian told Rachel and Laura what had passed and asked their advice.

"Oh but you shall be a countess!" Laura said. "Will that not be charming?"

"You forget she has not accepted him, Laura," Rachel said. "But I had thought you rather preferred Mr. Sheffield."

"And that is just the point I cannot decide on," Marian said. "They are so different. Mr. Sheffield is always so very civil, and sometimes it really almost *seems* as though he were partial to me. But Lord Richard is so solicitous of my company, and now I must suppose his compliments were sincere, though I did not always believe them to be so."

"But what shall his parents think about the match?" Rachel asked. "When they know that Uncle Carlyle is to change his will, might they not want him to marry someone with a grander fortune?"

"Well he is past his majority," Marian said. "I suppose he may marry who he chooses. They might lament the loss of so grand a fortune, but I am hardly penniless."

"Do you love him?" Laura asked. "If I loved a man, I'm sure I should not care what anyone else thought, if he loved me enough to marry me."

"I hardly know if I love him," Marian replied. "I find him pleasant enough. I always have a strong emotion in his presence—I don't quite know what it is. However, I have a very strong regard for Mr. Sheffield. Mr. Sheffield is more sedate, but I believe he is by no means lacking in feeling. He has more care for the feelings of others. But Mr. Sheffield, you know, has not proposed or paid me any marked attentions. In short, I don't know what I feel."

"I believe you should see Mr. Sheffield again before giving Lord Richard a definite answer," Rachel said. "If then you feel certain you will not harbor feelings of regret, then you should marry Lord Richard. But Marian, you always counsel me not to marry a man to whom I cannot give my whole heart. Ought you not to follow your own advice?"

"Yes, you are right," Marian replied. "I shall wait to give my answer till I can better ascertain my feelings for Mr. Sheffield."

CHAPTER SEVEN

Though Marian's engagement with Lord Richard had not been confirmed, even between themselves, Lord Richard was not deterred from being just as attentive as he had been previously. Marian determined to carefully avoid being alone with him, lest he should press her for a more certain answer, which she was not prepared to give.

On Tuesday afternoon, he called with his sister and both the Mr. Wesleys to ask whether the ladies would not like a walk in Green Park? William and Laura, who happened to be there, were also invited, and Lady Amberly was eager to observe Lord Richard and her daughter in a less formal setting than her drawing-room, for she had not failed to observe that Lord Richard frequently called Marian by her Christian name, which he had hitherto not done.

After being assiduously attended by Lord Richard for some time, though not suffering her sister to leave her side, she found herself walking with George Wesley while Lord Richard and William were having an animated conversation on one of the very few things they had in common—horses. Marian could not but be amused by this and it rather endeared him a little in her feelings.

"Why did you not bring Miss Seldon?" Marian asked presently. "I do not think I have seen you out of one another's company for some time now."

"She was not at home," George replied. "But I imagine we shall soon have leisure enough for being in one another's company."

"Indeed! But how can you be so complaisant? If I were in love, I should be miserable whenever I was not in his company."

"Would you indeed?" George asked with a smile. Marian blushed at an allusion she was not certain he intended to make. "I understand indeed the sensation of wishing to be together as much as possible, but I shall not let it make me miserable when we are not. As long as one can be certain of possessing their beloved's heart, there can be no cause for distress." Marian did not reply and George moved on to another subject. "My brother seems to be enjoying your cousin's company."

"Does he? Well, and why may a gentleman not enjoy the company of a young lady? I daresay it is natural enough."

"To be sure, it is. But my brother seldom seeks the company of any particular young lady. He is civil to them all, certainly, but never takes any pains about them. Perhaps he has found a lady to match his moral capacity."

"Laura is the dearest creature in the world! But I must own she is very lively, and your brother seems rather serious. I cannot imagine what they have to talk about. But she has a very strong moral fiber, though she is just eighteen."

"I believe it is her very liveliness together with virtue that render her so agreeable to him. She is yet unspoiled by the dissipation of London and yet inflexible in her principles."

"Does he speak of her, then?"

"Not enough for me to ascertain his views. That he admires her is evident. He thinks highly of her character. But he never was very open with regard to his personal feelings."

"What of Lord Richard? Is he open with his feelings?" George smiled at this question.

"I think he is more open with me than with others. However, he has a very clever knack of concealing his feelings to the public when he chooses. He is a man of the world, Miss Amberly. I do advise you to take note of that. However, he is by no means deficient in feeling and if he clearly proclaims his feelings to you, you ought to believe him. He might deceive with actions, but not with words." Marian felt a little uneasy at this caution and was obliged conceal her discomfort from Lord Richard who returned to them momentarily.

"Thank you for entertaining my fair charge," Lord Richard said affably. "I should not have entrusted her to any man not already betrothed."

"Are you so distrustful, my lord?" Marian asked.

"Whenever there is a beautiful woman in question," Lord Richard replied, "It is always wisest to be suspicious."

"Of the lady or of other men?"

"That depends on the lady," Lord Richard said with a laugh. "Your heart I need not be worried about, once I have obtained it." Marian blushed at this assertion, but did not reply. Lord Richard kissed her hand, which did not escape Lady Amberly, who felt they must certainly be engaged, though she could not imagine why Sir John had not been applied to, nor the family informed. She endeavored to ask Rachel about it, but Rachel's evasive answers seemed only to confirm the engagement, secret though it was. Rachel would certainly been open if there had been no declaration or Marian had given a negative. That Marian could have given no answer did not cross her mind.

A fact which seemed to confirm even further the increasing intimacy between Marian and the family of Lord Richard, was Lady Emily's solicitation for Marian to attend them to Almack's. Lady Amberly would like to have subscribed, but Sir John would not allow it. However, for Marian to attend in such company was nearly as pleasing, though her younger daughters were not able to partake of it. But Marian was her favorite child, being the most like her, and Rachel was handsome and lively enough that she would certainly be well married off.

The next evening Marian went to Almack's with Lord Richard and his mother, grandmother and sister. Mr. Wesley and George Wesley also came with Miss Seldon and Miss Sheffield and Lord and Lady Wesley. Lord Richard automatically claimed Marian for the first two dances, and Mr. Wesley, at his grandmother's insistence, led Lady Emily to the dance.

"Have you thought anymore about my proposal?" Lord Richard asked Marian while they were dancing. "You put me in agony with this suspense!"

"I have made no decision," Marian said with a blush. "I shall give you an answer at the end of next week."

"Oh cruel tyrant!" Lord Richard exclaimed. "Do you conquer my heart only to leave me in despair?"

"What language is this? Surely you exaggerate. And I must beg you not to go on in such a manner in a public place. We must not feed gossip." Lord Richard dared not directly disobey her, but continued to pay her such compliments as gentlemen usually do when dancing.

When Lord Richard returned Marian to her seat, Miss Sheffield approached her.

"Well, Miss Amberly," she said. "Shall I tell you some news about my brother?" Marian blushed. "What do you suppose has taken him to Bristol?"

"You may tell me whatever you think appropriate to tell," she replied, though in fact burning with curiosity.

"Well my brother is *Mr.* Sheffield no longer! He is now *Sir Edward* Sheffield. What do you say to that?"

"How do you mean?"

"She means, my dear Marian," Lord Richard interrupted, "That Sheffield has ascended to the baronetcy held by his uncle, Sir Thomas. I take it the man has died then?"

"Yes—he was thrown off his horse and broke his neck about two weeks ago. He has left a wife but no legitimate children. However, I understand he has a mistress and a brood of natural children."

"How shocking!" Marian exclaimed. "But what has all this to do with Mr. Sheffield's going into Bristol?"

"Well Lionel—my youngest brother—is a rather impetuous youth," Miss Sheffield said, "And easily drawn in by what the other officers are doing. Therefore he has run up numerous debts and has written to Edward for assistance."

"Is that all?"

"All? Is that such a small thing?" Miss Sheffield asked. "Well, but you have not heard the most shocking thing of all. He was engaged in a duel and it is still uncertain whether the man will live, and he must wait trial. Edward has gone to see what he can do, but not much can be done except wait to see what the man's fate will be."

"Do you know what the duel was about?"

"Well, in the same letter he announced his engagement to a young lady by the name of Miss Darnell. As it happens, Miss Darnell is Sir Thomas' natural daughter. This lady is supposed to be excessively pretty, but she is said to have been carrying on with a young gentleman, though Edward has not yet discovered his identity. However, the duel was fought over this lady's honor."

"This is hardly a subject for a young lady to talk about," Lord Richard said, looking very disconcerted. "Pray talk of something else."

"Well if you don't wish to hear it, you may go sit over there, if you please," Miss Sheffield said boldly. "I'm sorry if I've said something to offend you, but this conversation really was not meant for your ears."

"It is I who should apologize," Lord Richard replied. "After all, it is never permissible to interrupt a lady." He bowed and retreated, but stayed near enough to hear their conversation.

"So Mr. Sheffield objects to the marriage because the lady's character is questionable?" Marian asked. "Is he to prevent it?"

"He means only to put his prospects into perspective," Miss Sheffield said. "Sir Thomas left his mistress seven thousand pounds and a thousand to each of the seven children besides the cottage he bought to maintain them in, just outside of Bristol. The four sons were entered into the navy and the girls were sent to a modest boarding school, that they might be enabled to earn their livings as governesses. However, they were not without hopes that the eldest Miss Darnell might marry well, on account of her beauty."

"Well, and did Sir Thomas intend to bring all these children into the world, that he might leave them with nothing?"

"Sir Thomas had not much to speak of himself. He was so dissipated and extravagant as a young man that his father left his estate to the younger brother—my father—and gave him only forty thousand pounds. He married a lady with sixty thousand pounds and bought himself a small estate outside Fulham."

"What was the name of the estate?"

"I believe it was Caverfield," Miss Sheffield said.

"Why, that is the estate my uncle is to purchase!" Marian exclaimed. "Why was it not left to his widow?"

"It has been mortgaged these two or three years," Miss Sheffield said. "After all remaining debts were paid upon Sir Thomas' death, all that is left for his widow is her jointure—which, however, is about a thousand pounds a year."

"Poor woman! Imagine what a shock it must have been to find her husband had so many children while she herself had none!"

"Well I daresay she knew about it for years. But what could she do about it? He only married her for the money and none of their children survived childhood."

"And so Mr. Sheffield has inherited his title. I wonder I did not hear of it before, if it has been two weeks."

"We did not know until Edward received the news in Bristol. Sir Thomas was not on good terms with our family, for reasons that may well be guessed."

"And do you know when Mr. Sheffield is to return?" Marian asked.

"He has to await the result of the trial," Miss Sheffield said. "Then perhaps he will bring Lionel to town with him."

"Well, I hope it all turns out well," Marian replied.

"I'm sure Edward will have it all sorted out," Miss Sheffield said. "But my dear Miss Amberly, why ever did you not tell me your cousin Mr. Forrester was to inherit an estate? You led me to believe he would have nothing but what a profession would earn him."

"Indeed, it is by no means certain he will inherit any estate. It legally belongs to his cousin Frederick, who though he is not in the best of health, may yet live to marry and produce an heir."

"Oh I like Mr. Forrester very well, with or without the estate."

"You must forgive my saying so, Miss Sheffield, but William is not to be attached as any other man may be. He is not a man of the world, but he is very discerning."

"You mean, I suppose, to discourage me. He cannot love me. I am too strong-willed. Besides, I have not had the advantage of being in front of his face his whole life. Oh, I know who he *is* in love with, well enough. Anyone with eyes may see *that*. However, *she* fancies herself in love with someone else."

"I don't know what you mean," Marian said coldly.

"Why, I can see, well enough, that Mr. Forrester is in love with your sister and she does not know her own power, for she secretly pines after—shall I tell you?"

"Miss Sheffield, I must beg you not to go on in this manner. It is not appropriate. Besides, if my sister were in love, she would certainly acquaint me with the matter." Miss Sheffield leaned closer so she would not be heard by anyone else.

"Not if the man were courting her sister."

"Surely you must be joking," Marian said scornfully. "I never heard anything so very absurd. I assure you, you have quite deluded yourself." Miss Sheffield smiled.

"You may think what you please," she replied. "But I assure you, I am very astute when it comes to these matters." Marian was relieved when their tete a tete was interrupted by George Wesley's requesting her hand for the next two dances.

When they sat down to a supper of bread and butter, lemonade and cake, Lord Richard asked Marian what she thought of the assembly.

"It is a little dull, I think," Marian replied. "The dances are rather insipid and the company is scarcely less so. Miss Sheffield, perhaps, is an exception, but I must confess, she can be a bit *too* overbearing. However, I don't wonder that my father deems it not worth his effort to subscribe here."

"Dull it may be," Lord Richard replied with a smile. "But to be admitted is considered a very great honor. Only the most exclusive society is allowed to subscribe here."

"Lord Richard, it is my belief that whenever a person conducts his or her self in a manner that is honorable and respectable, they will never want for good society. I have seen some people with little rank or fortune whose society would suit me better than those who have both in abundance, yet who live a life of dissipation and frivolity."

"Well said, Miss Amberly. And I may venture to add that this den of exclusivity is not always necessary to make a good match, for you had my heart before you ever set foot here, and I trust I am no mean conquest." Shocked by such a declaration, Marian besought him not to say such things.

"I will risk anything, rather than your displeasure, Marian," he replied. "And in token of my concern for your credit and well-being, my dear, allow me to advise you not to form an acquaintance with this Miss Darnell person if Sheffield should bring her to town. She does not strike me as a woman whose company would do you credit."

"Why should you suppose I will have any reason to form an acquaintance with this lady, except when she comes out with the Sheffields?"

"She sounds like just the sort of person I would expect you to form an intimacy with," Lord Richard replied. "Your good nature does you much credit if her situation excites your compassion. However, if she be so very handsome as Miss Sheffield describes, her beauty, mingled with your pity, might tempt you to an intimacy with her. But she is the natural daughter of a baronet and has probably had a very limited education and vulgar relations. Besides, we have reason to believe she is not of unexceptional character. I cannot allow it."

"Well, if the lady is to be related to Mr. Sheffield, I cannot see that there is any great impropriety in forming an acquaintance with her. And to be sure, she may have a very good explanation for any actions that might have seemed to censure her character. I hope I am not one of those persons who judge others by appearances. There are far too many of those in this town. That is how scandals are started."

"But consider who her mother is. What principles can we expect to be taught to one whose mother is a kept mistress by profession? What a charming connection that will be! A baronet and his illegitimate family. And the baronet could ill afford the extra expense. If he had been allowed to keep his estate, it would have been different. He might have been able to bring out the eldest, at least, in some style." Marian did not trust herself to reply to such a speech.

"You must excuse me, your lordship," she said, rising. "I see the company is returning to the dance and Mr. Wesley has engaged me for the next two dances." She walked away from Lord Richard, leaving him quite perplexed.

The rest of the evening passed as dull as it had been before supper and Marian resolved within herself never to attend an Almack's assembly again, for she could not remember when she had spent a more uncomfortable evening. She had much more pleasure in describing the assembly to Rachel and Laura the next day than she had actually taken in attending it. Descriptions of modish styles of dress took up more time than she had taken to look at them. She related all the particulars of her conversation with Miss Sheffield, excepting Miss Sheffield's hint about Rachel's being in love with Lord Richard. In the end, Marian left her sister and cousin quite envious at the high society she had been invited into, and Rachel failed not to hint that Laura would herself one day grace the doors of Almack's as the future baroness of—

Lady Amberly sent for Marian to the parlor and when Marian arrived, she saw Lord Richard's valet there with a package.

"Mr. Hobbs here has a package for you," Lady Amberly said, giving her daughter a significant look. "It is to be delivered into no hand but yours." Marian took the package which she instantly conceived to be a book.

"Is it from Lady Emily?" Marian asked.

"No ma'am," Mr. Hobbs said. "It is from my master. He said it does not require an answer, but I was to leave it to no one but you." Marian, much confused, thanked him for his trouble.

"And now, Mr. Hobbs," Lady Amberly said. "You may tell your master your commission has been carried out and tell him that I would be very glad if he would dine with us this evening." Mr. Hobbs bowed and left the room.

Much to the surprise of Marian, Lady Amberly did not say any more about the package, and immediately began question her about Almack's. However, she warmly remonstrated against Marian's declaration that she did not wish to go to Almack's again.

"How can you be so foolish, child? Do not you know that the most exclusive society assembles there? I know many ladies of my acquaintance who would give half their fortune for the privilege of attending there."

"Well they are welcome to it, with all my heart," Marian replied. "I never saw such a collection of dull people in my life! They are all so afraid of doing something that will put them out of favor with the patronesses, that there is not a bit of amusement to be had among them."

"And was Lord Richard duller than usual?" Lady Amberly asked. "I cannot imagine that he ever behaves in such a way as to make his company tiresome."

"Indeed, Lord Richard is all gallantry and scandalous talk, as ever. But allowances might be made for handsome young men of rank and fortune that might not be made for anyone else. Besides, I see Lord Richard often enough outside of Almack's."

"Yes, I've noticed that he is even more frequent in his calls, whether accompanied by his sister or not. I've also noticed that he calls you 'Marian' and it seems that he has sent you a present. Really my dear, I wish you thought your own mother worthy of your confidence. You know your father and I can have no objection to the match. Therefore I see no reason to keep it secret."

"There is no secret, mama," Marian said. "We are not engaged."

"Are you not? Well, such particular attentions as he pays you, it will be quite scandalous if he does not make an offer soon. After behaving so openly as a lover, his honor, if not his inclination, declare he ought to marry you."

"I certainly will not require him to do anything he does not desire," Marian said. "Nor shall I require it of myself. He is under no obligation to me, nor I to him."

"Pray, what has his lordship sent you? A little silver box with some trinket in it, I suppose." Marian blushed as she opened it to find a collection of Shakespeare's sonnets. Inside the front cover was written: My Dearest Marian, I could not forebear offering you some token of my affection, that you might not forget me when I am out of your sight. Allow me to recommend to your notice in particular numbers eighteen, one hundred six and one hundred sixteen. Richard.

"A book of love poems," Lady Amberly said, looking at the cover. "How thoughtful. Well, I make no doubt we shall see you a countess yet. I think far too highly of his lordship to suppose he would try to make a fool out of you. Very well. You may go now and read your little book, so you and he might sit in some corner after dinner tonight and discuss it." Much relieved that she escaped her mother's inquiries so easily, and with many blushes, Marian returned to her chamber.

Nearly a week passed without anything of consequence going by, except Marian remonstrating with Lord Richard about openly sending her presents when not engaged to her. He protested that he did not expect anyone else to be present when she received it. Lady Amberly continued to narrowly observe Lord Richard's behavior to her daughter, though she did not approach Marian on the subject again.

Sir John and his wife and all his children currently in town were invited to a dinner at the house of Mr. Parker, the brother of Mrs. Forrester, and in whose house Mrs. Forrester and her daughters resided while in town.

Marian was rather vexed to find that among those present were Mr. Henderson and his sister, who had come with Mr. Carlyle. There were few outside of her own party that Lady Amberly would have thought truly genteel, many of them being merely a degree or two above tradespeople, and would deigned not to have come, except that Sir John had put his foot down that it was common civility to the family of his particular friend.

Miss Forrester gave her fondest and most insincere welcomes to Laura and Rachel and cold civility to Marian. Marian, however, was above being offended at such behavior, though William was not above being offended for her, and gently remonstrated with Miss Forrester.

"La, William, I fancy you must be in love with Miss Amberly," Miss Forrester said, not troubling to take care the conversation was heard by no one else. "You are always so warm in her defense and so very indignant if you fancy she is slighted."

"Indeed, Miss Forrester, Marian and all my uncle's daughters, are as dear to me as my own sister," William replied. "And that is saying a great deal. However, it is not for the reasons you would attribute, but my regard for their elevated characters. They all of them have qualities I admire. Marian, for all her sharp tongue and wit, shows great delicacy in matters of importance. Her mind is so liberal she bears no ill-will toward anyone, even when openly slighted." Miss Forrester felt the last to be leveled at her, but rather than being penitent, she was rather resentful, but took more pains to hide it, that she might ingratiate herself in the eyes of her cousin.

There were three military officers there, two of which were young men and who did not seem to have been long in their majority and who seemed quite contented to have the attention of half the young females present. The third officer appeared to be in his thirties and was a married man, and therefore not worth the attention of the ladies. His wife was a very fashionable lady and was attended by another young lady whose beauty and air struck Marian as very elegant, though the young lady was alternately patronized and neglected by her companion.

It was not very long before Marian learned their identities, and what was her surprise when she learned that one of the young officers was Lionel Sheffield and that the elegant young lady was Miss Darnell. The other young officer was Mr. Harper and the senior officer was Colonel Pierson. Mrs. Pierson and Miss Darnell were introduced to Marian, and Mrs. Pierson, when she learned that Marian was the daughter of a baronet, gave her all her attention.

"And so it's Miss Amberly, is it? Pray, do you have a relation who used to be in the military?"

"I have a brother who was, and to my knowledge still is, a colonel," Marian replied.

"La! I did not suppose it to be a secret he kept from his own family that he has sold out," Mrs. Pierson exclaimed, evidently pleased to know something of Marian's relations which Marian herself did not know. "How extraordinary!"

"Sold out, ma'am? Indeed, you must be mistaken, for my brother must not sell out, for it cannot be supposed that he can live on only five hundred pounds a year. If he has sold out, he cannot expect that our father will let him live a life of leisure at home. But I cannot believe he would take such a rash action, for Albert has always been the most hard-working of my brothers."

"Indeed, I suppose I know what I'm about. I am no idle gossip, I assure you. Albert Amberly, colonel of the –th regiment sold out to my husband not three months ago. As to having five hundred pounds a year—well, I imagine it to be more like five *thousand* a year, with Miss Van Curen's fortune. A hundred thousand at least, to be sure."

"And who is Miss Van Curen?" Marian asked, growing alarmed.

"Who is Miss Van Curen?" Mrs. Pierson repeated, laughing. "Mercy me! I begin to think I have been very naughty in revealing everything! It seems he means to keep his family in the dark, and here I've gone and told it all!"

"Indeed you have not told me all, for you've not yet told me who Miss Van Curen is."

"Well you ought to know, for now she is your sister," Mrs. Pierson said. "She's the daughter of a Dutch merchant whom your brother met while stationed in the West Indies. They were married in January. She's a rather plain girl, but she has a very handsome fortune."

"I cannot imagine Albert would marry for mercenary motives," Marian said.

"Well I believe he thought her quite pretty—and she looked well enough, for all that finery could do for her. Only she is not what one would consider a beauty. Certainly nothing to Miss Darnell here. *She* was quite the belle of the ball in Bristol, I can tell you. Never once did she have to sit out a dance, if she did not like it. And men of rank and fortune, too. But I do not know that she was over-burdened with offers of marriage either, however. Though she is a beauty of the first water, she has not the fortune of Miss Van Curen, nor even one tenth of her fortune. However, there was a rumor some time ago that she was to make a match with a young lord. I don't remember his name. But nothing came of it after all. I suppose his family objected to the match. Mr. Lionel Sheffield will do well enough for her, however. Perhaps she will help him mend his wild ways. I understand his father required in his will that Mr. Lionel stay in the army till he is five and twenty, on account of his wildness, or he would not get his full inheritance. Fathers have very odd ways of controlling their sons, even after their deaths, don't you think?"

"Yes, very odd," was all the reply Marian would venture.

"He has fifteen thousand at his disposal now, which will be well enough to marry on, but what man would not want to get the rest if he could, with but a little exertion? For he will get twenty thousand more. And Miss Darnell will do very well for him, for she was raised in a very modest way, for all she's a baronet's daughter."

"That is fortunate for Mr. Lionel. Is he to have the same fortune as his sister?"

"I believe so, my dear. But Sir Edward Sheffield—for so Mr. Lionel's brother is called, now his uncle's died—would be a much better conquest. Do not you think she would be charming as *Lady* Sheffield? But I suppose Sir Edward would not think of her on account of her lack of fortune, though she is his own cousin."

"I have met Mr. Sheffield—that is, Sir Edward—several times, Mrs. Pierson, and I am by no means convinced he would base his choice of wife on anything mercenary. Nor can I suppose that he would enter an engagement with a lady who was at any time betrothed to his brother."

"Well, well, everyone is entitled to his own opinion," Mrs. Pierson said. "But I must hold to my own, that if Miss Darnell only had a little fortune, she would suit the halls of Sheffield Park better than an officer's quarters. Sheffield Park is a very grand estate, I understand, but Sir Edward is rather cold and reserved." Marian only replied that she thought he was very genteel.

"Oh to be sure!" Mrs. Pierson exclaimed. "Far be it from me to say otherwise. Only I think perhaps he is a little *too* nice about some matters. Poor Miss Darnell ought not to be held accountable for her unfortunate birth. 'Tis no fault of hers that her father was such a scoundrel. And furthermore, it is on the very account of his uncle's naughtiness that Sir Edward was raised as well as he was, for his father was the baronet's younger brother, who inherited Sheffield Park because his brother was so wicked. However, it was very kind of Sir Edward to come to Bristol and sort out that business about the duel for his brother. Far be it from me to deny praise where it is due. How shocked we all were about the whole affair! 'Twould have been a pity if such a gallant young man as Mr. Lionel had been hanged for coming to the defense of a young lady. Happily it all came to nothing, for the young rascal who caused the mischief survived."

"That is indeed fortunate," Marian replied. "And how came you to be acquainted with Mr. or Mrs. Parker?"

"Oh well Mr. Harper there is an old school friend of young Mr. Parker and it was on his account the invitation extended to young Mr. Lionel and my husband and, of course, us ladies." Mrs. Pierson lowered her voice. "I wouldn't have you think I keep this sort of company all the time, Miss Amberly, for I understand for all Mr. Parker has so very fine a fortune, he is but the first generation out of trade, and his father kept a greengrocer's shop." She ceased to speak in a low voice, but continued talking. "I must confess, I thought we were doing quite a kindness by Sir Edward, taking the young people out for a little amusement. But he seemed rather cold, to me, and said it was all the same to him. I'm sure he has a great deal to do, it being his first day back in town, but he might have been more civil. However, I shan't think bad of him for it, for that is not my way." Marian was beginning to grow quite weary of this conversation and it was to her infinite relief that dinner was announced.

The dinner itself was genteel enough, though the quality of the company left something to be desired. From the familiar way everybody spoke to one another, Marian might have fancied that they were in a family party. Young Parker and Mr. Harper carried on a conversation about horse-racing, despite the fact that they were by no means seated together, and Miss Parker was loudly enumerating her partners at a ball the previous night to Marian, Rachel and Laura. Mrs. Pierson was constantly pressing

Miss Darnell to take some more fish, another baked apple, or something of the sort and Mr. Parker and Mr. Carlyle were engaged in a dispute about business.

When the company retired to the drawing room, Mrs. Pierson attacked Lady Amberly with compliments on her daughters, etc. Sir John and Mr. Parker took up a game of Backgammon and Marian sat herself by Miss Darnell, who was at leisure and in whom she instinctively felt a keen interest. A few minutes' conversation sufficed to show Marian that she was a good-natured, modest young woman, not vulgar, as one might have expected from her background.

Miss Darnell had been received with great condescension by Miss Sheffield and kindness by Miss Seldon. Marian also found that the man with whom Mr. Lionel had dueled, was a rejected suitor, who found a vent for his spleen at a local ale house, where Lionel had been present.

"And you must know how open to scrutiny a young woman's name is, Miss Amberly," Miss Darnell said. "Imagine how much more an unsullied reputation means to a young woman with very little fortune and few connections."

"It would have been very shocking to have one's name so publicized," Marian agreed. "The man must have been a rascal. It was very chivalrous of Mr. Lionel to defend you against such a villain."

"I cannot help but be grateful to him for his good opinion," Miss Darnell replied. "Many other young men might have behaved quite differently."

"And were you—forgive me for asking—well received by Mr.—Sir Edward?" Marian asked. "I must confess Mrs. Pierson has made me quite curious, for she seems to think him unkind toward you."

"Oh no!" Miss Darnell said. "Nothing could be kinder. Indeed Sir Edward has been very attentive. Sir Edward's scruples concerning the match were for Lionel's reckless behavior in the past. He besought me not to marry his brother out of gratitude for his doing what any decent man ought to have done."

"I am very glad to hear it. That confirms the good opinion I already have of his judgment and his generous nature." They were called from their tete a tete by Mrs. Pierson's calling out to Miss Darnell to entertain them with a song, for, Mrs. Pierson declared, Miss Darnell had the most exquisite voice she had ever heard.

"Come, my dear," Mrs. Pierson said. "I shall play, and you sing. Miss Darnell, you know—" addressing the company, "is a great deal more practiced on the harp than the pianoforte, though she sings just as well at either." It was clear that Miss Darnell did not wish to perform before so many strangers, but she also did not dare disobey her professed protectress. Slowly, therefore, she accompanied Mrs. Pierson to the instrument.

Mrs. Pierson did not deceive them. Miss Darnell did indeed have a lovely singing voice. Miss Forrester could not bear for anyone to be on display if she herself was not, and therefore went herself to the pianoforte, though her voice seemed rather weak to that of Miss Darnell. Next, Marian was entreated to perform. She would have declined, but her mother insisted upon it. What was her confusion when Mr. Henderson came to turn her pages for her? He whispered all sorts of awkward compliments while she was choosing a song and assured her that he had by no means forgotten her.

Young Parker then declared that he should like nothing better than to dance, which several of the young people agreed to, and Mr. Henderson attempted to engage Marian. Marian, however, declared she had no intention of dancing.

"Ay," said John Amberly, "And Mary must play, for her beau is not here to dance with her." Much to Marian's consternation, the word "beau" raised a general enquiry, by which John was far too entertained to keep silent about. "I think we can all see that Marian and Lord Richard Beauregard are soon to be on the point of marriage." It was difficult to say whose face was redder—Marian's, Miss Henderson's, or, much to the surprise of anyone that happened to notice, Miss Darnell's.

"John, how can you say so?" Marian demanded, once she recovered her voice. "I've not told such a thing to anyone. And I'm sure Lord Richard has not, even in jest." John continued his raillery and Marian then retreated into a corner.

"John, you ought not to say things to distress your sister," William said. "Such teasing may be entertaining among unscrupulous young men, but it is truly injurious to the delicacy of a female mind."

"Nay, I know nothing of the matter," John said. "Except they have more than once begun a ball together and spend many evenings in a corner, in close conversation. I would not have the company believe I know anything for certain." Once such a hint had been given, however, not all that John or Marian could say would quiet the suspicions of curious minds.

Not more calculated to put Marian's mind at ease was the Misses Forrester and Misses Parker in close conversation across the room, occasioned by immoderate laughter. Laura alone looked as if she were not enjoying the conversation. Laura stood up and walked over to where Marian was sitting.

"Are you very angry with John?" Laura asked.

"I am quite distressed," Marian admitted. "I did not think John could be so thoughtless. Such gossip is just the sort of thing that uncultured persons, such as some present in this room, love to make sport with."

"I'm very fond of Julia," Laura said, "But I cannot say she is always kind to you, for she has just been telling us all that the reason Lord Richard pays you any attention is that you are very often of his own party, and she does not doubt that he thinks you the most pleasing to talk to, being young and handsome and not his sister. Furthermore, she says she has it on good authority that he pays very particular attentions to Miss Henderson when he is at home, for Miss Henderson is the very frequent companion of Lady Beauregard. Julia says it all so very convincingly, that if I did not know better from what you've told me, I really think I should believe her! It was all I could do to hold my tongue when I knew better."

"I'm very glad you did hold your tongue," Marian replied, "For Miss Forrester certainly ought not to be trusted with such information. I am sure Miss Henderson does all in her power to attach Lord Richard, and very likely deceives herself into thinking she is successful." Miss Forrester soon joined them.

"My dear Miss Amberly," she said, "My sister and I were just discussing how very forlorn you and Miss Rachel must feel when we take William and Laura away from you next week. I wish it were in my power to invite you both to join us in Bath."

"Is it so soon?" Laura asked. "But my time in London has passed so quickly! But we are to stay for the dance at Ranelagh on Wednesday, are we not? For Mr. Wesley asked me to save him a dance."

"We are to leave on Monday," Miss Forrester said. "However if a dance takes precedence over your own cousins, you are not obliged to attend us."

"Of course I did not mean that," Laura said, rather confused. "Of course my engagement to you must take precedence. Only I fear Mr. Wesley might be very vexed."

"Pish!" Miss Forrester said. "It is not for a man to be vexed with a lady. Really, Laura, I despair of ever bringing you to a proper way of thinking. Make yourself a man's servant before marriage and you certainly will be afterwards. Demand the adoration you deserve from the beginning and he will not question it later."

"And so that is how you think to attach William, is it?" Marian asked. "I must say I don't wonder at your failure, for it is well known that he will not marry a lady who does not show him proper respect." Laura was shocked at this speech and Miss Forrester was rendered speechless with fury.

"Oh Marian!" Laura said. "How can you say such a thing to Julia? I must say it is very indelicate of you, for you must know she has no designs on my brother."

"Really, Miss Amberly," Miss Forrester said, having somewhat regained her composure, "I must say I don't think your reception of me is very kind, when I came over on purpose to be cordial."

"Well, if that be the case," Marian replied, "Then I humbly ask your pardon." She curtsied and walked away.

"Well, Laura," Miss Forrester said, "And it is her side you always take."

"She apologized for what she said," Laura replied. "I'm sure she only walked away because she was embarrassed."

"Oh what a simpleton you are!" Miss Forrester exclaimed. "Do you deliberately take leave of your senses so that you may see Miss Amberly as a kind person with no mean tendencies?"

"Now it is you who are being unkind," Laura said, rather offended. "I hope one is not required to be stupid in order to be fond of their relations. And I believe you say more unkind things about her than she says about you."

"My dear cousin," Miss Forrester said, "I tell you I am certain she says *more* unkind things than I do, only you don't know it, for she is not always open with you as I am." Laura looked at her cousin incredulously, for she was certain that Marian was always open with her.

They were presently joined by Rachel, who had just left the pianoforte, and consequently, it was necessary that their conversation about Marian cease. So Miss Forrester turned the conversation to the newest and most interesting piece of gossip— Miss Darnell and her situation. Their minds were thus occupied until they were all called away to make up Mrs. Parker's card tables.

CHAPTER EIGHT

Much of Thursday was spent in anticipation and preparation for Sir Edward's ball. One incident that did occur in the course of the day was the appearance of John and William sometime after breakfast. Almost as soon as they entered, Marian suspected that something was not quite right, for John's gaiety appeared to be forced and William's looks were more serious than usual, almost to the point of vexation.

"John, is something the matter?" Marian asked. "You do not seem yourself."

"Do I not? I'm sure I don't know why you would say so. I've done nothing out of the ordinary today." When John said this, William gave him a look of consternation that was not lost upon Marian.

"I did not say you did," Marian replied, more suspicious than ever. "I only said you did not seem yourself. Are you unwell?"

"I'm very well," John said stiffly.

"May I offer you some refreshment, John?" Lady Amberly asked.

"I shall take a glass of port, if you don't mind, ma'am," he replied.

"Why, surely, John, you don't mean to have wine in the morning?"

"Why on earth not?" John demanded. "It is no uncommon custom with me. But if you prefer I take it in my own lodgings, it is just as well, for I cannot sit here long." Lady Amberly ordered some port to be brought in.

"Why John, I never heard you speak so rudely to Mother," Rachel said. "I agree with Mary. You are not yourself."

"Confound it!" John exclaimed, out of humor. "I certainly did not come here to be interrogated." He rose to depart and Marian came over and touched his arm. Almost in an instant, John let out a cry of pain and Marian felt a chill, for John's coat was wet. She looked at her hand and saw blood on her fingers. She nearly fainted at the sight and was assisted to a sofa by William, and Rachel revived her with smelling salts while Laura wiped her hand with a handkerchief.

"John, what is this?" Lady Amberly demanded, quite horrified.

"Well John, I should not have told, but your own foolishness has discovered you," William said. "I told you we should have returned to your lodgings."

"None of your preaching, cousin!" John cried. "For that is more irritating to my ears than this bullet to my arm!"

"Bullet!" Marian cried. "Why John, you don't mean you were in a duel?"

"And what if I was?" John replied angrily. "You see I'm still alive."

"And—and the other man? What is his condition?"

"Missed," William answered for him. "Little did I know that a morning walk would turn into a duel."

"Was it not by appointment then?"

"Between the duelists no doubt it *was* by appointment," William said. "However *I* was not informed in advance, else I should not have been his second."

"You always were too squeamish for your own good," John told him. "Now, help me back to my lodgings and fetch me a surgeon."

"John, you had better stay here," Lady Amberly said. "You should not move about anymore."

"'Tis only a bullet in my arm," John said peevishly. "I daresay the surgeon will remove it and I shall attend Sir Edward's ball tonight." John then took his leave of the ladies, despite their several protests and returned to his lodgings with William.

After Lady Amberly's servant returned with word that the wound was not serious, the day continued to pass as usual until time to prepare for Sir Edward's ball. Marian took more care than usual when dressing for the ball and made liberal application of lavender water. The girls took turns adorning one another's hair until it was quite to their satisfaction.

When they arrived at the ball, Marian looked about anxiously for her brother, fearing that he might make a scene. Fortunately, he was nowhere in sight and Sir Edward greeted her very warmly. Lord Beauregard and his family arrived not very long after, and Lord Richard lost no time in reminding Marian that she had promised him the first two dances. Marian assented, but was vexed to find that Miss Henderson was of his party, and so Lord Richard had a cold reception from his lady without knowing why.

When Lord Richard had left Marian's side for a few minutes, Sir Edward came and asked Marian to open the dance with him. Never was Marian so dejected than when she had to turn him down because she was already engaged to dance with Lord Richard.

"I see I shall have to be a little quicker next time," Sir Edward said, smiling to cover his embarrassment. "Then perhaps the next set of dances?"

"I should be delighted," Marian replied. Sir Edward then left her feeling more vexed than ever with Lord Richard, and her vexation had not much subsided by the time the dancing started. She became more irritated still when she saw that Sir Edward stood up with Miss Perdue, and Lord Richard was left to reap the consequences of Marian's ill humor. Marian was silent as Lord Richard led her to the dance and gave him very short and cold replies to all of his attempts at conversation.

"What is the matter, my love?" he asked at last. "Have I done something to offend you?"

"My lord, I beg you not to address me so," Marian replied. "It is highly improper." At this reply, Lord Richard looked positively alarmed.

"I would not wish to give you any displeasure," he replied. "But I cannot help but notice you are not yourself this evening. Has anyone—said anything to you?"

"Like what?"

"I don't know. This change in your behavior seems rather sudden. I can't help but think that something rather extraordinary must have happened."

"I don't know what you mean," Marian said. "I'm the same as I've always been." Lord Richard ceased to ask her questions and felt more uneasy than he had felt in a very long time. When the first two dances were over, he escorted Marian back to her party and left her, resolved to discover what time supper was to be, so that he might escort her thither after her good humor had returned.

Marian's good humor did return while she was dancing with Sir Edward, and she began to wonder how she could have, even for a moment, considered marrying Lord Richard. Surely Sir Edward was not indifferent to her, for he had seemed truly disappointed that she could not open the dance with him. And yet, he was still very reserved. All politeness, but whether he expressed any true signs of love remained doubtful. Perhaps he cared nothing for her after all and Lord Richard was her best chance of happiness.

Lord Richard took Marian into supper when the time came. John also showed up during supper and made his way to Marian.

"Mary, my dear, how are you enjoying your ball so far?"

"John, have you been drinking?" Marian demanded. "I think you had better go home, John."

"Pish!" John said. "And is this the affectionate welcome I'm to expect from my favorite sister, when I've come on purpose to see her?"

"Why should you come to see me at a ball, John?" she asked. "You can see me just as well at home. And better, for we are not in so much company."

"I see how it is!" John said. "Your young lord here is enough company for you at present. Aye, and a very handsome lad he is, too!"

"You ought to be at home resting," Marian said. "I advise you to go at once."

"A woman's advice!" he exclaimed. "A fine thing, that! If men always took the advice of women, we should be always at home and have no fun. Well, I shall leave you to your charming beau." He did not leave, however, but went into the ballroom.

Marian and Lord Richard returned to the ballroom and John came and started talking to Lord Richard, congratulating him on the conquest of his sister, and saying he hoped they would be very happy together.

"Thank you," Lord Richard said. "But how did you know? Marian did not wish to inform the family until the engagement was final."

"How now?" John asked, as Marian went pale. "Am I to understand that you truly have made proposals to my sister? And I thought I was in jest!" Now it was Lord Richard who went pale.

"John, you must swear not to say a word!" Lord Richard said anxiously as Marian angrily walked away. "I would not have dreamt of saying it if I did not suppose she had spoken first."

"Posh and nonsense!" John exclaimed. "She's got no reason to refuse. And to be sure her mother has been going on about it for weeks."

"Just the same, I beg you to keep it secret," Lord Richard said. "She shall be very vexed with us both if it gets abroad."

"She's always vexed with me," John replied. "That's the fun of it."

"Well it is not fun for me," Lord Richard said. "I certainly do not wish to have your sister angry with me."

After supper, when the couples went back to dancing, Lord Richard walked with his cousin George to the refreshment table and then back to Miss Seldon and Miss Darnell. Miss Darnell got pale when she saw Lord Richard approaching. George asked Miss Seldon if she were ready for another dance.

"Only if Lord Richard will dance with Miss Darnell," she replied. "For I cannot bear to leave her all alone here."

"I'm sure Richard will be happy to oblige," George said. "Will you not?" Lord Richard looked uncertain for a moment, then bowed.

"Far be it from me to deny any request of a lady," he replied. He led Miss Darnell out to the dance. They danced at first in silence, then Miss Darnell spoke.

"At last, I have a chance to speak to you. Why did you not come when I sent for you?"

"Were you so good as to send for me?" Lord Richard asked.

"Come, Lord Richard," Miss Darnell said. "Let us not play this game. Why are you trying to avoid me? Such cold replies you sent to my letters. You never intended to marry me, did you?"

"I must beg to defer this conversation until another time, Madam," Lord Richard replied. "We are in company at present."

"And this is the most privacy we shall be afforded without arousing suspicion," Miss Darnell replied. "All of my attempts to discuss it in a more private setting, you have rejected."

"I have nothing further to say on the subject," Lord Richard replied. "If I have raised expectations I did not intend, I am most exceedingly sorry. My affections have been engaged elsewhere for some time, and you are on the point of marriage. Therefore I see no reason to continue on the subject. I must beg you to let the matter rest."

"I only—I shall," Miss Darnell said, breathing heavily.

"Miss Darnell? Are you unwell?" Lord Richard asked.

"I think I shall faint." Lord Richard caught Miss Darnell by the arm and Laura, whom Lord Richard only now noticed was next to them, immediately offered her assistance. Anxious and mortified at the thought that he and Miss Darnell had been overheard, Lord Richard followed behind the two ladies. As soon as Miss Darnell was seated, he went to get her refreshments. Miss Sheffield came to see what the matter was and Laura and her partner returned to the dance.

"Why Jane, my dear child!" Miss Sheffield exclaimed. "Are you unwell?"

"I fear that the excitement of the dance has been too much for me," Miss Darnell replied. "I hope you will not be angry if I retire early."

"Of course not," Miss Sheffield replied. "I shall go with you, if you like."

"You're very kind," Miss Darnell said. "But I prefer to go alone. I need some time to repose myself, then perhaps I might return."

Lord Richard, seeing Miss Darnell walk out of the room, followed her and would have addressed her had there been less of a chance of being seen. The simple fact that he followed Miss Darnell at all did not escape the shrewd eyes of Miss Sheffield, nor did a note delivered to Lord Richard about half an hour later by one of Sir Edward's footmen. Upon being questioned by Miss Sheffield, the footmen admitted that the note had come from Miss Darnell. Miss Sheffield of course, lost no time in relating this interesting discovery to Marian as soon as Lord Richard was not by.

"I think you had better keep a closer watch on your young lord," she told Marian. "I shall advise my brother to do the same with his lady."

"What do you mean?" Marian asked.

"I believe my sister elect and Lord Richard have met before," Miss Sheffield said. "My brother's footman just delivered a note to Lord Richard from Miss Darnell. I do not know what it could be about, but I don't want my brother's heart to be broken."

"I don't know what I'm to do about the business," Marian replied peevishly. "Lord Richard is certainly nothing to me at present."

"Is he not?" Miss Sheffield asked. "Well, I understand your disappointment, then. But I must say, from my observation, you do not always give him so much encouragement as you could. I have always thought it very important for young ladies to give encouragement as often as they can, for they are only allowed so many opportunities before losing him to another woman."

"You quite mistake me, Miss Sheffield," Marian replied. "I have no wish to encourage Lord Richard. I am not so desperate for a husband."

"Why then, you do not know what you are about," Miss Sheffield said. "Lord Richard is one of the most eligible bachelors in town. He's handsome and titled and, to be sure, he adores you. Those are qualities one does not often find in a husband."

"I am not so mercenary to wish to marry a man with a title with no regard to his character," Marian replied indignantly. "It is not Lord Richard's good looks I am uncertain of. It is his sincerity. And if what you are implying about he and Miss Darnell is true, he ought not to attempt to marry me."

"La! What an inexperienced child you are!" Miss Sheffield exclaimed, as if she were much older than Marian. "Don't you know men will be men? They always do just as they please. And if my sister elect were not the girl in question, I should not care one jot about it. But as it happens, I do not want my brother to break his heart."

"As I said before, Miss Sheffield, the matter really has nothing to do with me. You might speak with Miss Darnell about it yourself. Or you may complain to Lady Emily. Her brother holds her in high confidence, I believe. I, however, cannot help you." Marian curtsied and walked away to find Rachel or Laura. When she found the latter, she related what had passed between her and Miss Sheffield.

"And so she would convince me," Marian concluded, "that Lord Richard was carrying on some sort of flirtation with Miss Darnell, whom he never saw in his life before tonight, I suppose."

"Perhaps there might be something to Miss Sheffield's assertions," Laura replied. "I do not know the particulars, but it does seem that there is some sort of history." She then related what she had heard pass between Lord Richard and Miss Darnell. "I'm sure it cannot be as bad as Miss Sheffield would suggest, however. Certainly Miss Darnell would not marry Mr. Lionel if she did not care very much for him, now would she?" Marian smiled at her cousin's artless simplicity, but nevertheless felt very perplexed.

Marian was not left very long to wonder, for the next morning, when she was in her room writing a letter, a servant came in and said that Miss Darnell wished to speak with her privately. Though surprised, Marian readily assented and Miss Darnell was allowed to enter. Marian noted that she looked rather agitated.

"I beg your pardon for calling on you in such a familiar way," Miss Darnell said. "I know I have not been acquainted with you long, but—" She stopped.

"Be assured, I am not offended," Marian said. "I beg you not to make yourself uneasy. Won't you sit down? You look quite unwell."

"Thank you. I—I don't quite know what to say. I understand—that is, I suspect—that there is a sort of—of an understanding between you and—a certain Lord Richard Beauregard." Marian stiffened at the mention of Lord Richard and began to anticipate some sort of information.

"Miss Darnell, I fear that your sister elect is a bit of a gossip and at present one of her favorite subjects is my supposed engagement with Lord Richard. I am sorry she has employed an innocent person for the satisfaction of her curiosity, but neither Lord Richard nor myself have ever made any such information public."

"Nay, Miss Sheffield does not even know of my calling upon you," Miss Darnell replied. "I swear if it is a secret to be kept, you may depend upon my silence. I have no intention or reason to tell Miss Sheffield or anybody of your situation. But I would know if you are positively engaged to Lord Richard." Marian hesitated for a few moments as she looked at Miss Darnell.

"We are not engaged at present," Marian said at last.

"Ah! Then it is as I feared!" Miss Darnell said, much to Marian's surprise. "Miss Amberly, you seem to me a very deserving young woman, and I would not have you throw away your affections on such a man as Lord Richard, for I believe they will receive but a poor return." She paused, but Marian was rendered speechless with astonishment and Miss Darnell resumed. "I believe Sir Edward to be a much more deserving young man and it is evident that he likes you very much. And you cannot conceive how generous he is, Miss Amberly. He has given me five hundred pounds for wedding clothes and he has been very kind to me. As to Lord Richard—well, I daresay you have a stronger heart than I, but even the strongest hearts, you know, may be deceived by professions of love and a handsome face."

"You quite amaze me, Miss Darnell," Marian replied. "Is it possible you are acquainted with Lord Richard yourself?"

"Alas that I ever was!" Miss Darnell exclaimed. "I have known him since he was in Brighton nearly a year ago. He has broken my heart in a most barbarous manner! I presume, Miss Amberly, you have heard something of my history?"

"I know a little," Marian replied reluctantly. "I understand that you are—a cousin to the Sheffields."

"Yes, I suppose you know that I am the natural daughter of the late Sir Thomas. Ever since I have understood the nature of the relationship between my parents, I have strived to make a name for myself separate from that of my mother and father. I have always been most careful of my conduct, until that fateful day when I put my trust in the wrong person!"

"And that person Lord Richard," Marian said, in a breath.

"My sisters and I were sent to a cheap, but respectable boarding school," Miss Darnell resumed. "My father could ill afford his extravagant lifestyle, you see. I endeavored to make respectable connections. About this time last year I received an invitation from one of my school-fellows to spend some weeks with her family in Brighton. Eager for a taste of public society, I readily accepted. I first met Lord Richard at an assembly. I thought him extremely handsome and one of the most agreeable young men I had ever met. I continued to meet him in public places and I found myself falling in love with him, and he assured me he was in love with me too. At last, when the time for my departure was drawing near, he told me he adored me more than anyone he had ever met and that to be separated from me would make him the most wretched man in the world! In short, he asked me to elope with him to Gretna Green. I told him that surely we ought to ask my father, for there could be no objection to our marriage. But he convinced me it must be, for *his* family might object while it could still be forbidden. He said we must be married first, and then reconcile his family to the match. I believed it, for I had no fortune and his family is very proud. I allowed myself to be convinced."

"So how came it that you are not married?" Marian asked, afraid of the answer.

"Well I went out of the house after all the family was in bed and Lord Richard had a carriage waiting for me outside," Miss Darnell said. "We stopped in the middle of the night at an inn and took rooms, so that we might sleep a few hours before continuing. What was my shock when—but no, I will spare you the details, Miss Amberly. Let it suffice to say I then began to realize that perhaps his design was not marriage after all." At this, Miss Darnell burst into tears.

"Surely you do not mean—" Marian stopped, unsure of what to say next.

"Lord Richard is a scoundrel and a rake, Miss Amberly," Miss Darnell said. "But though he may have tainted my reputation, he has not robbed me of my honor. I begged him to allow me to retire for the night and not see me again until the morning. He obliged me, and I resolved within myself to forgive him if he truly did intend to marry me after all. In the morning, however, instead of him, I was met by the inn-keeper with a note from Lord Richard informing me that he was obliged to go to town on urgent business, but he had paid the innkeeper for a week and would send his valet to attend me either to my friends in Brighton or my home in Bristol. Even so, he left me with some hope, for he said he would send me word when his business was concluded. Thus I was abandoned, though provided for. I could not bear to return to my friends in Brighton so disgraced. Lord Richard's valet arrived as promised and spoke very little all the way. I went home to my mother and confessed to her what had happened. She was vexed that I had damaged my chances of a good match by my foolish actions. I sent a letter to Lord Richard by his valet, but never received an answer.

"I wrote him three letters altogether, and at last I received an answer. Oh cruel letter it was! In short, my hopes were dashed forever, though I long ceased to hope in earnest. It was inevitable, I suppose, that word of my elopement somehow reached Bristol. The details were not known—it was only said that there was some imprudent behavior between me and a young man. Some few suspected it was a nobleman, but no one, I believe, knew the whole truth. I was still accepted in polite society, though I was shunned by some over-scrupulous ladies. Mrs. Pierson took pity on me, I think, and I was grateful for her attention, for it kept it from being said I only kept company with men. Miss Van Curen, who I believe is now your sister, was also kind to me, and that was a great help to my good name, for she is very well respected in Bristol. It was at these assemblies that I first met my cousin Mr. Lionel Sheffield. He told me that as my cousin, he felt it was his duty to play the part of my protector during the absence of my brothers. I fully felt his kindness, I assure you. A young woman, in such a situation as I am in cannot fail to raise impertinent remarks—particularly from men. I suppose you remember that at the Parkers' dinner party you were told I had rejected a suitor, which was the cause of his duel with Lionel?"

"I do," Marian replied.

"The proposals he made were of a less innocent nature than marriage," Miss Darnell said. "He attempted to make me—his kept mistress."

"How abominable!" Marian exclaimed.

"I suppose the whole town expected me to become what my mother was only because I was her daughter. It was just after this that I privately confessed to Mr. Lionel what had passed between Lord Richard and me, though I did not give him Lord Richard's name. I am assured of his confidence however. When he made proposals to me, I did not see how I could refuse. My heart has been so trampled upon, that I know not whether I can love again—but if I could, it would certainly be Lionel. I hope you won't think me very wicked, Miss Amberly, if I marry a man that I do not yet love as I ought. He is indeed as dear to me as any of my brothers, and I believe I shall be happy with him. And I shall grow to love him—I know I shall."

"I'm sure you shall," Marian said. "If you believe you shall be happy with him, then I wish you all the best."

"The worst part is that after seeing Lord Richard at the ball last night, I believe I love him still!" With this statement, Miss Darnell burst into tears again. "And yet—he has done me as much wrong as any man can do! All I ever did was love him, and he broke my heart! Oh, I ought—I wish I could hate him! But I'm afraid I cannot! But let me warn you, Miss Amberly, do not let your heart become ensnared as I have! Extricate yourself while you can. Find some worthier object for your affections, for he will break your heart! If he does not break your heart before marriage, he will surely do it after." Miss Darnell continued sobbing and Marian tried to comfort her. In return for her confidence, Marian told Miss Darnell that Lord Richard had proposed and was still waiting for an answer.

"But after such a tale as you have told me, I will surely refuse him," Marian said. "He must be the wickedest of men if he can behave so cruelly and unjustly! I thank you for your confidence. But let me advise you, Miss Darnell, to take more care of your actions concerning him, for Miss Sheffield is very clever and she has already noticed there is something amiss."

"I believe, Miss Amberly, that all communication between Lord Richard and myself is over, unless he seeks me out. I have done with him, and I must endeavor to forget him. But here are the letters he wrote me." Miss Darnell had taken two papers from her pocket-book and presented them to Marian. She read the first, which had been written before Lord Richard had left the inn.

My dear Miss Darnell,

I have been called away on urgent business in town. I regret that I am unable to have the honor of escorting you to your destination, but I have resolved to send my valet, Mr. Hobbs, to attend you. You shall want for nothing under his care. If I have caused you any embarrassment, I most humbly beg your pardon, and I assure you I shall do all in my power to refrain from doing so in the future. If you wish to return to your friends in Brighton, it shall be done. If you think it better, however, that you should return home to your mother, Hobbs will be happy to escort you. I shall write to you after my business has been concluded. Until then, I remain your humble servant,

R. Beauregard

"Was I not a simpleton to believe such a letter?" Miss Darnell asked when Marian had finished reading. "Notice how careful he was not to make any reference to his professed intentions. And in the other letter—but no, you shall read it for yourself, and tell me where such another man is to be found!" Marian read the second letter, which had been written some months after Lord Richard's desertion.

Dear Madam,

I hardly know how I have been so unfortunate as to incur your displeasure, but I assure you it was done most unintentionally and I am grieved to be the cause of your sorrow. I must regretfully inform you, however, that those sentiments which you have assigned to me are not in my power to return. I beg you to forgive my candor, but I cannot suppose it right to ignore my duty to my family in order to oblige the wishes of a young lady, however amiable she may be. I am truly sensible of your merit and I would have you transfer your affections to a worthier object than I. Be assured I believe you to be a most deserving and modest young lady, and if I have ever appeared to suppose otherwise I shall bitterly reproach myself. For the sake of your character and reputation, I have destroyed those letters you have addressed to me hitherto and I advise you to do the same with this I write you now. Not that there is anything censurable in our correspondence, but scandalous tongues will be only too eager to surmise their own reasons for our having it at all. For this reason I beseech you to let this be the end of our correspondence. Please be assured that I am most solicitous for your welfare and happiness and allow me to extend the warmest wishes for your future prosperity.

R. Beauregard

"Can this possibly be the Lord Richard I am acquainted with?" Marian exclaimed, throwing the letter aside. "Oh he is very careful in how he writes his letters. In this way he saves himself from paying damages. Oh how shocking it is! It is no wonder you were so ill at the sight of him."

"Indeed I had some suspicion he would be there," Miss Darnell replied. "And I even had my suspicions about the nature of your relationship to him, after what your brother said at Mrs. Parker's dinner party."

"Oh my foolish brother!" Marian exclaimed. "John can be so very troublesome sometimes. He fancies himself very witty, though he sometimes carries it too far. I should not mind it so much if he would restrict his comments to family parties—but he does not, as you have witnessed. His jesting does not always have any foundation. But why did you dance with Lord Richard last night if he made you so uncomfortable?"

"I wanted to speak to him and he would not see me privately," she replied. "He spoke to me as if everything that had happened had been my own imagination. In short, he will not admit to having been engaged to me at all. I must suppose then, we were never engaged at all—only I thought we were!" Miss Darnell's tears began afresh. "I only wanted him to face me once again. I wanted to hear him reject me with his own lips. Now it is over. I shall move on. I know that I am better off with Lionel. And to be sure, one Lionel is worth fifty of Lord Richard. However, I have done. I shall be much obliged if only you will allow me a few moments to compose myself. I don't want anyone to be suspicious. I thank you for seeing me, Miss Amberly."

"Not at all," Marian said. "I only wish I could do more. I can hardly believe that Lord Richard could behave in such an inhumane way. I shall avoid him as long as I can. Indeed, I cannot avoid him forever, for I am to accompany his grandmother to Bath next week. Oh, how sorry I am now to be going! I must go, however, for my family cannot afford a break with the dowager. Have you spoken to Lady Emily? She would be very sympathetic to you, I am sure."

"To what purpose, Miss Amberly?" Miss Darnell asked. "She cannot undo anything. And it would be simply to make my situation more public. I am eager to keep it concealed—not only for myself, but for the sake of Lionel's family. I only told you as a warning against Lord Richard's character."

"You may be assured your secret is safe with me," Marian said. After having sufficiently gained her composure, Miss Darnell took her leave and Marian was left with her thoughts and the internal anguish that they brought with them.

CHAPTER NINE

Marian remained alone for some time before Rachel came to her. She had not decided how much she ought to tell Rachel and Laura, as the secret was not her own.

"What did that girl want?" Rachel asked her. "Did you find out anything about this mystery between her and Lord Richard?"

"I am not at liberty to disclose certain parts of our conversation," Marian said. "Let it suffice to say that I have been shown the plainest evidence that Lord Richard is a scoundrel and I am now quite certain I ought not to marry him."

"Oh Mary," Rachel said. "How can you make such a declaration and not tell me why? Surely I must be an exception to the rule of secrecy."

"I would spare you the details, Rachel. Indeed, I almost wish I had been spared myself. Please tell Mother that I am not feeling well and shall stay in my room until dinner. I have reason to expect Lord Richard might be here and I do not wish to speak to him at this time."

"But are you really unwell, Mary?"

"I do have a headache. At any rate, I am certainly in no mood for company tonight. But pray only tell Mother that I am unwell—do not mention Lord Richard."

"I hope I know better than that," Rachel said. "But she is so certain of your engagement to his lordship that you really ought to break the news to her."

"She shall know it soon enough," Marian replied. "That I assure you."

Marian came down exactly when everyone was going down to dinner and quickly took the arm of William and made Laura stay close to her, so that she might sit on her other side.

"I was sorry to hear you were unwell," William said, as they sat down.

"Perhaps more disturbed in mind than in body," Marian replied. "I have been anxious most of the day. I wish to avoid a certain person present."

"I think I can guess who," William said, "Though I'm sure I don't know why. You have seemed rather inclined toward him lately. It is no business of mine, however. But I think you will be pleased to hear that Arthur has returned to town. He has only just arrived, and I rather expect him to drop in."

"Yes. I shall be very happy to see him. But I believe I shall return to my room after dinner—before the gentlemen go into the drawing room."

"You are very determined, I see. I must say, Lord Richard looks very hurt by your negligence." Marian determined not to meet Lord Richard's eye.

"It is no worse than he deserves," she said. "He is only hurt because he has just realized he has no power over me."

"Had he ever any power over you?"

"That I cannot say. But if ever he had, he has certainly lost it." William wisely pressed the subject no further and talked of something else.

After dinner, when the ladies retired to the drawing room, Marian returned to her own room against the protestations of her mother. She was not very surprised when Rachel came to her room later that night, bearing a note from Lord Richard. She read the note aloud to her sister.

My Dearest Marian,

I am at a loss to know what can be the matter with you, my love. Your mother informs me that you are ill, but I fear there is something more. I have many questions within myself. Why did you not walk down to dinner with me? Why would you not even look at me? You cannot know what an agony I have been in all the evening, surmising any reason you could possibly have to be angry with me. I am acutely aware that I do not deserve you, but I am also aware that I cannot bear the pain of living without you. I had hoped to finalize our engagement tonight, but I had no opportunity of speaking to you. I beg you to send me a reply—a line, a word, anything to relieve me from my sufferings. I know you love me, though perhaps not as I love you—therefore I see no reason to delay making our intentions known to our families. Your devoted lover,

R. Beauregard

"Arrogant presumption!" Marian exclaimed. "Is he still here?"

"Yes—he told me he will not leave until he receives some sort of reply, even if it be only a promise of a letter or a time that he may call upon you tomorrow."

"I shall give him a reply," Marian said, taking the book of sonnets he had given her out of her desk. She sat down and wrote on a piece of paper:

Lord Richard,

As you ask for an answer, I most readily give it to you. My answer is that I cannot consent to be your wife, if indeed you did propose in earnest, which I now have reason to doubt. From this point I beg you to consider us as no more than common acquaintances. I am returning your book of sonnets and your letters so that you may not question my resolve on this subject.

Marian Amberly

Rachel carried the letter and the book down to Lord Richard who read it eagerly, and Rachel reported to her sister that she had never seen any man look so grief-stricken and that she felt quite sorry for him. Marian, however, could feel no such sympathy.

Monday morning brought the departure of Laura and William to Bath. Marian was consoled in the thought that she herself would be in Bath in a week, though Rachel had no such journey to look forward to.

After their departure, Marian received a letter from her governess, Miss Smith:

Dear Miss Amberly,

It has been very dull since the departure of you and your sister. Your brother, Mr. Arthur, has been here conducting some business for your father's estate. The first day or two he was here, the children would not attend to their lessons, but after the novelty was gone, they settled down again. I cannot break Miss Jane of her boyish habits, and I despair of ever doing so, as long as Master Henry is here with her. Fortunately, Henry goes to school in the fall, and perhaps then we can turn your sister into a lady.

Miss Anna continues in her Latin lessons. I believe your father only allowed her to take them because he thought Anna would lose interest before long, but she persists in her lessons and I understand from Mr. Carter she is an excellent pupil. I must confess I rather fancy that her dedication might be due more to Mr. Carter's handsome face than her own interest, for he is very well to look at. Therefore I always insist they take their lessons in the school room where I might keep an eye on them. However, they have taken up a new pastime, which they know I cannot participate in, and that is riding. As you know, I am no horsewoman. Whether or not this is a calculated attempt to escape my supervision, I cannot be certain. I always make sure Miss Jane and Master Henry join them, but I can never be certain that the two latter do not run away from the others. But I would not wish you to suppose I distrust Mr. Carter, for he is very amiable and I have no doubt of his morals, for he is a clergyman, even if only a curate.

I sometimes go to visit your aunt, Mrs. Forrester, at the parsonage, but her company is not the same as having you and your sister here. Mrs. Forrester is quite desolate without her children here, but I believe Anna is some comfort to her. Anna has developed a great zeal for visiting the poor, but I cannot think what has brought it about. Anna, as you know, has always been rather flighty. Perhaps she fancies it is the only way for her to get out and see the world.

This young lord of yours sounds like quite a scoundrel. You must tell me how it all ends with him. I should like to see him, for Miss Rachel informs me that he is extraordinarily handsome, though she does not tell me much else about him. She also informed me in her last that the young man who was so gallant—Mr. Sheffield—is now a baronet. I do wish you would write me, my dear, for I've not heard from you in a few weeks. I must go attend to the children. Mr. Arthur leaves us tomorrow and we have promised them a picnic.

F. Smith

In the afternoon, Marian began to feel that she had been indoors too long and decided to pay a visit to Miss Seldon and Miss Darnell, both of whom seem pleased to see her. Marian privately told Miss Darnell of her difficulty avoiding Lord Richard at home, and Miss Darnell immediately went to Sir Edward to request permission to ask Marian to stay a few days. The request was readily granted and the next order of business was to send for Marian's clothes, including the dress she was to wear to Ranelagh on Wednesday.

On Tuesday Miss Sheffield went shopping with Miss Darnell and Miss Seldon in order to give those ladies the benefit of her advice on wedding clothes. Marian, wishing to have some time by herself after the incessant prattling of Miss Sheffield, stayed in her room. The gentlemen had left early in the morning and were not expected to return until dinner. The ladies had not been gone ten minutes, when a servant informed her that a gentleman wished to see her in the drawing room.

At a loss to decide who it might be, Marian obeyed the summons and found Lord Richard waiting for her. She would have turned immediately away and walked out of the room, except Lord Richard stopped her by taking hold of her hand.

"Hold, Marian," he said. "I must speak to you. I have been watching since I learned you were here, for an opportunity of seeing you alone. I could not come while Miss Darnell was here."

"I supposed I had made myself quite clear, your lordship," Marian replied, pulling away her hand, "That we were not to meet except as common acquaintances. Understand I have nothing to say to you, nor do I wish to hear anything you might have to say."

"My love, I have far too high an opinion of your justice to suppose you would refuse to hear both sides of a story before passing judgment on the accused. Hear me but for a few moments, I beg you." Marian sat down.

"Very well. But I must beg you to refrain from those terms of endearment which you are by no means authorized to use."

"I have been a rather wicked man, I must admit, though not so heartless as you appear to think. I did my best under the circumstances I had placed myself in. The fault was mine, from a lack of forethought and I have bitterly regretted my foolishness since that time.

"When I first met Miss Darnell in Brighton, I was enchanted with her beauty. I met her on several occasions and because she was beautiful and amiable, I began to think I might be in love. She appeared to grow very attached to me and it soon became clear that she expected me to marry her. I did not know what to do, but at last we decided to elope. I wrote to my cousin Charles to ask his advice. I advised him at which inn we would be on what day, should he choose to write me.

"When we were at the inn, Miss Darnell and I had a late supper in her room. We had some conversation and she was very coquettish. My passions began to get the better of me, but Miss Darnell called me to my senses. I apologized for my behavior and returned to my own room. I then began seriously to think about what I was doing.

"Miss Darnell was very beautiful, but rather dull, you see. She lacked passion and wit and I knew I would soon grow weary of her company. I should be faithless in my attempts to drown my regret and she would be unhappy. As I was reflecting on these melancholy thoughts, my cousin surprised me by appearing himself at the inn.

"He further reasoned with me against continuing to Gretna Green. Miss Darnell was virtually penniless and an illegitimate child. Not to mention that my family would be violently opposed to the match. Charles also opened my eyes to the fact that Miss Darnell would be made miserable because she would surely be looked down upon by those of the aristocratic circle because of her humble birth and there would be implications that she had married for mercenary reasons. Furthermore, her indifferent education had but ill prepared her for the intrigue of the aristocracy and she must always feel like an outsider.

"To all these reasons, Charles added yet another, in that my mother was at that time taken seriously ill and to receive such a shock as that I had married beneath me, and without my family's approval, might be fatal to her nerves. So reasoned, my decision was made. I ought not to marry Miss Darnell, both for the sake of her happiness and my own.

"I slept very ill that night. Charles and I arose early in the morning and I wrote a letter to Miss Darnell informing her that I had business in town—that was to see my mother—and I would send her my valet to see her home. I determined she should not want for anything between then and her return home, and I hoped that she might someday find a more suitable man for her than myself.

"So you see, Miss Amberly, my intentions were not always bad, as Miss Darnell might have led you to believe. But I swear I have never loved any woman as I love you, and I beg you to reconsider my offer."

"You made the offer to another first," Marian replied. "You ought to have upheld your promise to her."

"I was to marry her out of obligation," Lord Richard said. "You I should marry from my own desire. Would you have Miss Darnell made miserable because she felt like an outsider? Do you not agree she is much better off as she is? I beg you to tell me you do not think so ill of me as you did before."

"I hardly know what to think, my lord. When you say you should become faithless to Miss Darnell when you grew weary of her, what assurance do I have that the same should not happen with me? Shall you not grow weary of me?"

"I should not. You are clever, passionate and lively. I could not grow weary of you. I should only love you more every day."

"And what about your family? If money is a primary object to them, what makes you think they will approve our marriage once they find out I am not to inherit my uncle's fortune?"

"Hang the family!" Lord Richard exclaimed. "I shall brave all their wrath for the sake of your love. Besides, can you really suppose that the legitimate daughter of a baronet with 20,000 pounds and who is, moreover, connected to our own family, is not preferable to them to a natural daughter with hardly enough to purchase a trousseau? Come, my love, I know you cannot be serious in thinking of such a thing."

"Perhaps you are not so *very* heartless as I supposed," Marian said. "However you do have a great many vices, it seems. I'm sorry my lord, I still feel I cannot marry you. Even if you are not heartless, you are certainly thoughtless. You do not seem to have a moment's concern about that poor girl's pain."

"If you only knew how often I look back at that time with regret, you would not wish to torture *me* so."

"Torture *you*!" Marian exclaimed. "Oh yes, you are a most unfortunate creature! Well, I daresay you shall get over your disappointment, as others have done before you. You shall move on and find another victim. Only next time take care to fancy yourself in love with a woman of fortune and there shall be no obstacles for you."

"Your words cut me to the heart. My sweet Marian, can this be your true opinion of me? No, I cannot suppose you think so ill of me. Only tell me what I must do to regain your trust. I swear that nothing shall be left undone which will serve to reconcile you. Please, my love, I beg you not to say I've lost you forever." Lord Richard softly placed his hands on either side of Marian's face and Marian felt her resolve begin to waver. "You must leave me with some hope—with something to live for." This would not do. Marian pulled herself out of Lord Richard's grasp and turned away from him.

"I think we have quite done here, your lordship," she said. "I have heard your side of the story which was all I promised to do. I do not think it prudent for you to remain here any longer. I must beg you not to call here again." Lord Richard looked as if he would protest and Marian said, "If you have any consideration for my ease and happiness, you will go at once. I ought not to see you before tomorrow night at Ranelagh, and even then only as common acquaintances." Lord Richard bowed.

"I shall do as you wish, much as it pains me," he replied. "But I cannot help but cling to my hope that you might someday relent, for that hope is all that sustains me at present." They were both startled by the opening of the drawing-room door and the entrance of Sir Edward. After a moment of surprise, Sir Edward apologized and would have left the room, but was stopped by Marian.

"Pray don't go, Sir Edward," she said. "We have quite done here. Lord Richard, please give my regards to your sister."

"Thank you," Lord Richard said, rather awkwardly, glancing from Marian to Sir Edward. Then he went away.

"I apologize if I interrupted anything important," Sir Edward said.

"Not at all," Marian replied. "Lord Richard only came to give me some information on something I had been wondering about."

"I see." Sir Edward was silent a few moments before speaking again. He took a few steps toward her. "Miss Amberly, I hope you know—how much I—how well I think of you." Marian's heart began to beat faster. "I would not wish to see you injured."

"Injured, Sir Edward?"

"I would only have you consider—" Here Sir Edward paused again as if searching for the right words. "I would have you be cautious in giving your heart."

"Indeed?" Marian felt the color rising in her cheeks. "And why should such a matter be your concern?"

"Because I feel—that is, I cannot answer you without—" Sir Edward made a motion as if to reach for her hand, but thought better of it. "I am not so eloquent as Lord Richard is. I beg your pardon, Miss Amberly. I did not wish to offend you. Forgive me for my boldness." He bowed awkwardly and quickly left the room, leaving Marian as confused as ever.

On Wednesday came the night of a ball at Ranelagh, hosted by Boodle's. Marian had a dress specially made for the occasion, for all ladies attending were to be dressed in white and silver. She felt elated to be a part of Sir Edward's party, though her happiness was somewhat tempered by the presence of Mrs. Pierson. This amiable lady came for the purpose of playing the part of chaperon, and it may be said that she thought herself very well-suited for the purpose.

Much as Marian did not relish the idea of spending an evening with Mrs. Pierson, even less calculated for her pleasure was being in the company of Miss Perdue, who came along as Miss Sheffield's particular friend. However, she was fortunately spared from having to enter into much conversation with either of them, for those two ladies were of dispositions exactly suited to entertain one another. Mrs. Pierson always took extreme pains to ingratiate herself into the favor of wealthy ladies who might give her consequence, and Miss Perdue dearly loved to be admired. Marian, who had a less splendid gown and fortune than Miss Perdue and was less inclined than Mrs. Pierson to pay her homage, was therefore of no particular interest to either of them.

When they arrived at Ranelagh, Marian thought she had never seen anything so magnificent as the Rotunda, and when they went inside, it was more amazing still, for it was a very large round ballroom with a fireplace in the center and a place for the orchestra. The crowd was a flurry of ladies in white dresses and gentlemen in dress-coats. A booth was set up where there was a raffle for ladies' trinkets, or if a lady chose it, a gentleman might draw for her.

Marian saw her father's party and stole away to greet her family. She took Miss Darnell with her, in case Lord Richard should happen to be with them. Sir Edward, who might have otherwise asked Marian to dance, was prompted by his sister to ask Miss Perdue in Marian's absence.

"Oh Mary!" Rachel said. "Why have you left us? It was very cruel of you to leave us the same day as Laura. It has been very dull without you. Even Reggie is not there, for he is staying with our Uncle Carlyle. John has only been to dinner once this week and Lord Richard has made two very short calls. Arthur has come and gone sometimes, but it really is very dull without you."

"But I shall be back for dinner on Friday, you know," Marian said.

"Yes, but then you are going away again on Saturday," Rachel replied. "And then I shall have no chance of seeing you! Oh I wish we were all going to Bath, but Mama will not allow it. She says that now she's got you almost married off, we must set about finding a husband for me. And it is better done in London than in Bath."

"What nonsense," Marian said. "Mama knows very well I am not engaged. She does not even know that Lord Richard has proposed."

"But Lord Richard is so very obvious in his attentions, that I believe it is almost impossible to doubt it. Indeed, I myself believe he is sincere, for he was quite pitiable after I gave him your letter on Friday."

"Lord Richard is a man of the world, Rachel. Do not imagine him so vulnerable in his emotions as he might appear. He has disappointed many young ladies. Surely he can stand a bit of disappointment himself."

Despite the minor inconveniences of the evening, Marian enjoyed herself. She refused to dance with Lord Richard more than once, convinced she was right in doing so. She did dance, however, with Sir Edward and George Wesley. In the middle of the ball, soon after supper, she was presented with a very pretty locket by a servant who would not tell her who had sent it. She recognized it as one of the raffle prizes. A hint Sir Edward had dropped earlier in the evening, however, convinced her that it might be from him and that it might be a prelude of something more substantial in the near future. His manner the previous morning had seemed as if he really cared for her. If it were so, she determined to accept him, for she felt an inclination in his favor at least equal to any she felt for Lord Richard.

No proposal was made the next day, however, but Marian wore the necklace down to dinner. Sir Edward looked thoughtfully at it a few moments before speaking.

"Do you know who sent you that locket, Miss Amberly?" he asked.

"I have my suspicions," Marian replied with a slight smile. "However he may be assured his secret is safe with me." Marian thought she saw the color rise to his cheeks as he looked away. Sir Edward looked thoughtful for the rest of the evening until he retired for the night. If Marian was disappointed in her expectations, she still hoped that Friday would bring better luck.

However, Friday morning came and went and still Marian was disappointed in her hopes. If anything, Sir Edward seemed more distant than before. Marian returned to her family Friday afternoon, only to leave them again Saturday morning.

Bath, however, opened a whole new realm of possibilities and in her excitement of the journey, Marian endeavored to forget about Sir Edward Sheffield. The Dowager Lady Beauregard had a good house in the best part of Laura Place, and after the ladies were settled, Marian was allowed to refresh herself in her room before dinner and she took the time to write a short letter to her sister.

At dinner she was placed next to Lord Richard, but she tried to keep her comments very general and promptly changed the subject when Lord Richard attempted to allude to more personal matters. After dinner, she kept close to Miss Seldon and retired to her room as soon as she could politely do so.

On Sunday afternoon, the dowager and her party paid a visit to the Pump room and put their names in the book. The dowager and Lady Beauregard found one or two of their acquaintance there, until the young people began to be quite impatient to go out into the Crescent Fields. Lord Richard came to Marian's side and said "Come, Marian, and let us leave this dull company to themselves. You and I shall walk about the fields together. We need not wait for them."

"I hear you, you naughty young man!" Lady Emily said playfully, before Marian could reply. "Do not fear, Miss Amberly. I shall protect you from my wicked brother." She took Marian's arm in hers. "There now! He shall not have one of us without the other!"

"Then I shall gladly take you both," Lord Richard replied. "I can hardly be the worse off for being in the company of *two* very pretty young ladies, rather than one. Let us walk out into the field."

"But we cannot leave Mama and Grandmother," Lady Emily protested. "They should never forgive us if we leave them alone."

"We shall leave them in the care of Charles," Lord Richard replied. "He will take care of them."

"Richard, I tell you we shall not," Lady Emily insisted. "Miss Amberly, I am sure, will not wish to vex them any more than I do."

"Indeed I do not," Marian said. "It would ill repay their hospitality, I am sure."

"You shall ill repay their hospitality by anything besides your marriage to me," Lord Richard said. "For you must know that is the main reason my grandmother wanted you to come."

"Richard!" Lady Emily exclaimed, as Marian grew quite red from either embarrassment or anger. "How could you say such a shocking thing? And in a public place, too! You have quite crossed the line there. Come, Miss Amberly. He shan't bother you about it anymore. You mustn't take him very seriously. Richard likes to say sensational things and seldom knows when he has gone too far, unless he is checked. But I shall speak to him for you." Marian thanked Lady Emily as best she could manage, but was otherwise left quite speechless until she saw William and Laura and their cousins enter the room. She went eagerly to meet them and Laura had so much to say about Bath, having never been there before, that she would scarcely take time to draw breath between sentences. They had been to the ball, to the bath, to the concert and they had met so many interesting people and handsome young men. In short, it was just as delightful as any young woman of eighteen *should* find it.

In addition to the Forresters who had been in London, there were two new members of the party—young Mr. Frederick Forrester and his tutor, Mr. Harding. Frederick, at sixteen, ought to have been at the flower of his youth, but instead was plagued with a poor constitution that made him seem aged beyond his years. Had he been a picture of health, he might have been said to resemble his cousin William.

Mr. Harding was a serious, not unhandsome man of about thirty. Mrs. Forrester clung to the arm of this young man with a fervor not unlike that with which her eldest daughter clung to the arm of William.

All the warmest regards were expressed and the necessary introductions and re-introductions were made, and it was agreed upon that they should all dine together at some time on some evening in the not-too-distant future. When Lady Beauregard and the dowager joined Marian, Lady Emily and Lord Richard, the dowager gave a slight nod after having the Forrester family introduced to her and declared the room was becoming too hot and she wished to be out-of-doors. Laura promised to call on Marian as soon as she could manage it.

First thing on Monday morning, Lady Beauregard and the ladies in her company went down to the bath. Marian found the water very hot and the bathing clothes extremely ugly, though the ladies adorned themselves as best they could with what could be worn above the shoulders. Marian had her own tray of nosegays and rosewater, should the smell of the water be too much.

"I spoke to my brother last night," Lady Emily told her, when they were a little separated from the others. "I gave him a terrible scolding, and I assure you, he won't say such a thing again anytime soon. He is made very uneasy by your displeasure, and I almost think it punishment enough."

"Come, Lady Emily," Marian replied. "You and I both know your brother is too gallant to be sincere. He is just the sort of man who knows exactly what to say so that no one is vexed with him."

"Indeed, Miss Amberly, you wrong him if you suppose he does not feel very deeply. I shall be the first to admit he has studied—or perhaps inherited—a very pleasing address and is well-practiced in the art of flattery and gallantry. But I also know that when his heart is truly touched, he feels it very deeply—perhaps more so than others. I beg you not to dismiss so lightly what you possess—what is so coveted, yet so difficult to obtain."

"And what is it I possess, Lady Emily?"

"His heart. Nay, do not look at me so skeptically. He has confided in me the whole story. You may be assured I will not speak of it to anyone else. But let me entreat you on his behalf, to reconsider your refusal. Richard has his faults, I know—but I don't believe you could find a better or more devoted husband."

"I thank you for your concern in my happiness," Marian said, a little peevishly. "But I have quite made up my mind for the present. And it will take a good deal more than a few pretty speeches to change it." Lady Emily was silenced and spoke no more on the subject and her behavior toward Marian the remainder of the day was rather cool.

Lady Emily appeared to forget her resentment, however, when they went to a ball at the Upper Rooms. The party did not arrive until tea, when all the classes might mingle about in any order they chose. Marian felt very warm, for it was very crowded, though there was plenty to divert the eye.

Immediately after tea, when the assembly was returning to dancing, Lord Richard walked away from the party, at which Marian could not decide whether she felt relieved or offended. Mr. Wesley requested Lady Emily's hand and George naturally went with Miss Seldon, leaving Marian alone with Lady Beauregard and the dowager. The dowager was in the process of declaring she did not know what Richard was about when Marian was rescued from her embarrassment by William's appearing and asking her to dance.

"Will not Miss Forrester be offended?" Marian asked, as they walked to the dance. "She fancies that she ought to always be your first partner."

"And so she was tonight," William replied with a smile. "I was obliged to ask her, you know, as the eldest daughter of my hostess—besides being family."

"And you never were one to shirk your duty," Marian said. "I trust Mrs. Forrester and her children are well?"

"The ladies are very well. Frederick is as well as can be expected. He is dancing with Laura as we speak."

"He is dancing? Well, he must be doing very well to exert himself so."

"I fancy he has other inducements as well. I predict this will be the only dance he dances this evening. And I may very well be summoned away sooner than I like, on account of his exhausting himself."

"I thought you weren't very fond of large assemblies." Marian looked thoughtfully at her cousin. "Or perhaps the large assemblies, tedious as they are, are preferable to the alternative?"

"It would be very ungrateful of me to *say* so," William replied, with a meaningful smile. "But I give you leave to surmise what you wish."

"Oh, I can sympathize with you very well," Marian said. "You see, I am quite in the same position, only I do not have Laura to comfort me."

"True," William admitted. "It would have been very well if Rachel had accompanied you."

"Yes, I have no doubt she would be a true comfort." Marian smiled. "But Miss Seldon is very kind. Though she is a betrothed woman and quite preoccupied with other matters." After the dance was over, William sat with Marian a few minutes before returning to his party. Lord Richard also returned to Lady Beauregard at this time, accompanied by Miss Henderson.

"Look here, Mother," Lord Richard said. "I have found your friend. She and her brother have just recently come to Bath." Lady Beauregard acknowledged the young woman who immediately began her civilities. How Marian wished she could escape such a scene!

Mr. Wesley and Lady Emily returned from the dance and Mr. Wesley, upon seeing William, inquired after Laura. William told him she was well and Mr. Wesley replied that he was very glad.

Soon William felt obliged to return to his Forrester cousins, though it was evident he did so with much reluctance. After he was gone, however, Marian hazarded a glance at Lord Richard, whom she caught with his eye upon her. She blushed and looked away, but Lord Richard spoke.

"Forgive me, Miss Amberly, I have been remiss in my duty. I have not asked you how you are enjoying your first assembly in Bath."

"I cannot say it has been disagreeable," Marian replied in some confusion. "Though perhaps it is too early to say anything about it at all. I have, after all, only danced one set of dances."

"Yes, Richard," the dowager interjected. "I must say it was very ungentlemanly of you to walk away after tea instead of asking Miss Amberly to dance, as you ought. It was by sheer coincidence that Mr. William Forrester happened along to ask her."

"Was it indeed?" Lord Richard said with an amused smile. "How very fortunate."

"Never mind that," the dowager went on, "You may dance with her now, I'm sure." Marian was indignant and not a little alarmed at this statement of the dowager's.

"Oh, but your ladyship, I was just about to ask Miss Henderson for the next two dances," Lord Richard said. "Surely you would not wish me to forsake my honor."

"Well there is no difficulty if you have not yet asked Miss Henderson. I am sure she will not take it amiss if you should put off your request for the present." The look on Miss Henderson's face, however, plainly stated that she *would* take it amiss.

"But we have been engaged to dance some time now," replied Lord Richard. "Besides, I have a feeling Miss Amberly does not wish to dance with me at this time."

"I certainly would not wish anyone to beak an engagement on *my* account," Marian said coldly. "I would not be responsible for any breach of decorum."

"Miss Amberly is a model of all that is right and proper," Lord Richard said with a bow. "Shall we, Miss Henderson?" Marian watched them walk away with unaccountable pique and was angry at herself for feeling it.

She was not left to her self-reproach for long, however, for the master of ceremonies came to her, accompanied by a young captain and begged leave to introduce him to her. Marian turned pale, then red as she accepted, for he was the same Captain Jennings who had jilted her for Miss Perdue a year previously.

The re-introduction being made, Captain Jennings asked her to dance. Marian looked uncertainly at the dowager who told her to go on, and perhaps it would "teach Richard a lesson."

"How very happy I am to see you in Bath again," Captain Jennings said, as they joined the dance. "You cannot imagine how I've wished to see you again."

"Indeed I cannot imagine it," Marian said. "The last time we spoke, you asked me to dance and stood up with another lady." Now was Captain Jennings' turn to color.

"Miss Amberly, you cannot imagine how I've regretted—it was a very delicate business, you see. My brother was most eager to close a matter of business with the young lady's father and begged my assistance in taking her out of the way. I was obliged to do my brother's bidding—for, you see, I am almost entirely dependent on him for any advancement I may make in my profession. But I assure you, Miss Amberly, that it was most certainly you I wished to dance with. I have been in agony ever since, wondering what you must think of me." Marian was not sure whether or not she ought to believe a word of his story, but she desired nothing more than to provoke Lord Richard in return for his flirtation with Miss Henderson, and the surest way of doing so was to permit the attentions of a smart young captain, for it is well known among gentlemen that, in general, the female half of the population holds a soft spot in its heart for a man in a red coat.

"Well since you have indulged me with an explanation," Marian said, "I suppose it is my duty to forgive you."

"You are too generous, Miss Amberly." He was silent for a few moments before speaking again. "Have you been long in Bath?"

"No—only since Saturday."

"I thought not. Otherwise I would have seen you before, I daresay. I presume you are not here with your family? I did not see them."

"I was invited to Bath by the dowager Lady Beauregard, who is a relation of mine."

"Indeed? I ought to have realized you were descended from nobility. She is your grandmother, perhaps?"

"She is not." Marian began to feel these were very impertinent questions and wondered what Captain Jennings could mean by asking them. Had she really been so foolish as to ever have fancied herself in love with this man? He looked well enough in his red coat, to be sure, but after the gallantries of Lord Richard and sincere addresses of Sir Edward, Captain Jennings made for a very awkward comparison.

CHAPTER TEN

The next morning Laura and William came to call and found Marian sitting with Miss Seldon, Lady Emily, Mr. Wesley and George Wesley.

"How sorry I was not to see you at the ball!" Marian said to Laura, after everyone made their bows and curtsies. "You must have left very soon after our arrival."

"Yes—I had hardly finished my two dances with Mr. Wesley when poor Frederick took ill," Laura replied. "We fancy the exertion of the dance was too much for him. Had I known the ill consequences—Oh I should not have! Surely it would have been proper for me not to dance with him, had I known his health was at stake?"

"Laura, dearest, you cannot blame yourself," Marian said. "You could not possibly have predicted such an occurrence."

"But I know his constitution in general—I should have been more careful."

"Marian is right," William interjected. "It certainly is not your fault that Frederick's constitution is not the strongest. He is old enough to think for himself. If he exerted himself too much, the responsibility must be, at least partly, on his shoulders."

"Miss Seldon and I were just thinking of going for a walk in the Crescent," George announced. "The weather seems to be fine, and we would be very glad to have the pleasure of your company. We would make quite a merry little party, I think."

"What do you say, Laura?" Marian asked. "Would you like to go for a walk?" Laura readily agreed to it, and soon the young people were setting out. Miss Seldon quite naturally walked with George Wesley, Marian walked with Laura and William, Lady Emily and Mr. Wesley followed behind.

"Oh Laura, Lord Richard behaves in a most provoking manner," Marian said, as soon as they were away from the others. "He must either pay me as little attention as possible or be excessively gallant. Why can he not be properly civil?"

"Which was he last night?"

"The former. He found Miss Henderson at the ball, and brought her to our party only to lead her out to the dance. I am certain he did it only to provoke me. He knows how much I dislike Miss Henderson."

"Why should you dislike her?"

"Because she is an insinuating little social climber," Marian said after some hesitation. "She is artful and insincere and a coquette."

"And you are certain he does not simply enjoy her conversation?"

"One can never be certain of what Lord Richard is thinking," Marian said peevishly. "He has so many whims and fancies that he is forever changing them." They were joined by Lady Emily and so had to put a stop to that conversation. Mr. Wesley and William also caught up with them, and soon Lady Emily had managed it so that she was between Marian and William and Laura was walking with Mr. Wesley.

When they came near the Forresters' house, Laura owned herself rather tired and William took his sister home. It was not until this time that Marian realized they had quite lost George Wesley and Miss Seldon. Marian and her two remaining companions turned back in search of them, but with no success. Even more unfortunate was that it started to rain, as it is wont to do in Bath. They quickened their pace, but were soon obliged to seek shelter in a nearby pastry shop. After treating his fair companions to ices, Mr. Wesley felt he must go for the carriage, that the ladies might not get anymore wet than they were. After he had gone, Lady Emily spoke.

"Mr. Wesley seems to like your cousin very well. And *she* is more responsive to his attentions than *you* are to my brother's."

"Your brother is either very liberal with his attentions, or else very stingy."

"Oh! If you're talking about last night, he was only so cold because I told him of our conversation earlier in the day."

"You ought not to have discussed that with him," Marian said, rather annoyed.

"Well, he was very disappointed, to say the least. However, he assures me he shall attempt to overcome his affection for you, and he said I might tell you so. So you see I am quite as open with you as with him."

"A little reserve is not a bad thing," Marian replied. Lady Emily did not reply and, looking around, Marian noticed that Captain Jennings had just walked in. He saw them almost immediately and came to pay his respects.

"Miss Amberly!" he said. "Whatever are you doing out in this weather? Are you quite stranded here?"

"Your ladyship, allow me to introduce to you Captain Jennings. I think perhaps you saw him at the ball."

"A pleasure, Captain Jennings," Lady Emily replied. "We are indeed waiting for the rain to stop, or for my cousin to return with the carriage."

"My chaise is entirely at your service," Captain Jennings said. "I can take you anywhere you wish to go."

"That is very kind," Marian replied, "But someone is going for a carriage as we speak."

"Well I see no reason to wait about here forever if there is no need," Lady Emily said, quite unexpectedly. "We accept your offer, sir."

"I'm not quite sure it would be proper," Marian told Lady Emily in a low voice as Captain Jennings was opening his umbrella to escort them out of the shop.

"Nonsense," Lady Emily replied. "There is nothing improper about accepting the escort of a friend when one is stranded."

"But as it is, Mr. Wesley will be back any moment." But Lady Emily would hear none of it and boldly got into Captain Jennings' carriage as if it had been her brother's. Marian could not refuse to follow, as the alternative was for her to remain in the shop alone and suffer Lady Emily to leave in a carriage with a man she had just met.

Captain Jennings went through such a strange labyrinth through the streets of Bath that Marian began to suspect that he was either lost, or intentionally confusing them. However, as they eventually approached the King's Bath, Marian supposed it must not be the latter. The rain, though it was heavy for a time, did not last long and Lady Emily asked Captain Jennings if they might not step into the Pump room for "just a few minutes." Captain Jennings was always willing to be agreeable, and certainly had no objection to being seen in a public place with two attractive young ladies, and so he willingly assented.

More to Marian's irritation than pleasure, the only people she knew there were Mrs. Forrester and her son and daughters. Marian would rather she had not seen any of her acquaintance at all. However, as the parties were too close to one another before they saw one another, neither party could escape before they were discovered by the other. Marian had good cause to be annoyed, because she soon noted that Mr. Henderson was of Mrs. Forrester's party and his was a look of thinly veiled jealousy of Captain Jennings.

"How charming to meet you here!" Miss Forrester said. "Though I would have expected you to be accompanied by a rather larger party. Our cousins deserted us for your sake, you know."

"Yes, we were all out walking together," Marian replied. "But they have since returned home, and I rather expect that is where they are now."

"I saw Lord Richard here not very long ago," Miss Forrester continued. "However he did not stay long and left just before you arrived. I suppose he was only searching the room for some acquaintance."

"Oh your ladyship," Marian said, turning to Lady Emily. "Do not you see your brother must be searching for us? Mr. Wesley has had more than enough time to return to the shop and discover we are gone. Are you not at all concerned what they must all think? What will your grandmother say?" Lady Emily did seem truly apprehensive of what the dowager might think of their little detour.

"Perhaps you are right," Lady Emily conceded. "We shall go home at once." The two parties took their leave of one another and Marian and Lady Emily hurried to return to Captain Jennings' carriage.

When Captain Jennings had escorted them home, Lady Emily suggested they attempt to get to their room to change before presenting themselves before the dowager. While they were walking up to the first floor, they were met at the landing by Lord Richard.

"Marian! Emily!" he exclaimed. "Where have you been? We have all been quite beside ourselves with worry!"

"We just came from the Pump room," was Lady Emily's feeble excuse.

"I was just there," Lord Richard replied. "I did not see you."

"I understand you left just before our arrival," Lady Emily said.

"Why did you not wait for Wesley?"

"We were bored," Lady Emily replied. "You can't think how extraordinarily tiresome it is to be sitting in one place with all manner of people coming in and out. When Miss Amberly's handsome young captain offered to escort us, I could not refuse."

"Miss Amberly's handsome young captain?" Lord Richard repeated, looking both confused and disturbed.

"Oh yes—you remember the young man she stood up with last night, after you publicly refused to dance with her?" Lord Richard colored.

"I did not refuse," he said, not looking at either of the ladies. "I supposed I was respecting her wishes—as I think you well know, Emily." He turned to Marian. "If I have offended you, I am very sorry."

"Not at all," Marian lied, though not convincingly. "But if you will excuse me, your lordship, I must get some dry clothes. I'm quite wet through."

"Of course," he replied. "Emily, you had better change as well. It would be a pity to spend your first week in Bath being ill."

Half an hour later, Miss Seldon came to Marian's chamber and, seeing Marian still arranging her hair, apologized for interrupting her toilette.

"Not at all," Marian replied. "I am sorry I have not had many chances to speak to you since we came to Bath. It seems we are always going here and there. And of course you are staying with your father now."

"Yes. I think he missed me while I was away in London. He likes George very well. He says he seems to be a respectable young man. Father says that although George is a younger son, he can tell he is no fortune hunter and cares for me very much."

"I believe he does," Marian said with a smile. "I am glad your father approves, however. Fathers cannot always be depended on to give their blessing in such cases."

"Oh! Father is no miser. Besides, George is of good family and is by no means lacking in connections. And he will have an inheritance—only no estate."

"That is true. And family and connections are always recommendations, even when there is no estate. When shall the wedding be?"

"I believe we will have it in July. I have scarce begun to shop for wedding clothes. But I daresay Bath has quite as much to offer as London. I would prefer to have the wedding here rather than London, anyway. Edward and Catharine must come here and I suppose Catharine will be my bridesmaid, for I have already promised her. Then of course we shall take our wedding tour to the North, and perhaps even to Scotland."

"I understand the country is very beautiful in the north," Marian said. "I have never been. My mother prefers the diversions of the city. We cannot marry lakes and mountains, you see."

"Ah, but you are fortunate to have your mother still with you. I must rely on my own judgment to make a good match. However, I daresay I have not done so very bad for myself." Miss Seldon smiled. "Oh, I almost forgot. Lord Richard sent me to say you may come down at your leisure, for he has abated the annoyance of her ladyship. He assured her he was convinced your disappearance was the doing of Lady Emily, not yours, by Lady Emily's manner of explanation."

"It was," Marian agreed. "I tried to convince her to stay and wait for Mr. Wesley, but she would go with Captain Jennings. I have not the faintest notion why."

"Perhaps she likes a redcoat. I understand, however, that he fancies you."

"And so he will, until a young lady with a better fortune comes along. You are fortunate to be engaged. You perhaps are safe from him. Though I should not be surprised if he has changed his affections to Lady Emily already. Men like Captain Jennings have very transferable affections, you know." Miss Seldon did not reply to this comment, but simply smiled. So ended the conversation and they walked down together to join the rest of the company.

Marian was not to suffer a very long absence from Captain Jennings. Although for such a place as Bath, it might have been considered a long separation indeed, for a whole two days passed before she saw him again at the next assembly.

Another week passed in the same manner, and Captain Jennings was sure to dominate the attention of both Marian and Lady Emily anytime they met in a public place, and it was not long before the captain made free to call at Lady Beauregard's residence. Lord Richard, to conceal his irritation and resentment at never finding a chance of speaking to Marian alone, settled for starting a mild flirtation with his mother's young friend, Miss Henderson. So a week passed, and they all met again at a breakfast in Sydney Gardens.

Still, Marian could not quite make up her mind about Captain Jennings. As Marian and Lady Emily were together during the morning, and Captain Jennings was equally attendant upon both of them, Marian could not decide for which of them the captain held more deference.

After breakfast was over, the company were free to roam about the gardens at their pleasure. Marian, for one, had a great desire to go into the labyrinth, and Lady Emily and Captain Jennings both expressed their willingness to go. Miss Henderson, however, who had latched herself onto Lord Richard, expressed a wish to go down one of the other walks. Lord Richard was obliged to go with her and left the happy Captain Jennings with the other two young ladies.

Once the three of them had lost themselves in the labyrinth, Marian extricated herself from the group, and she quite enjoyed wandering about the hedges, except for some rather impertinent remarks from some young men in the Merlin Swing.

At last she came across her cousin William and Miss Forrester.

"Marian!" William said, evidently pleased to see her. "Are you alone?"

"It seems I have lost my companions," Marian replied. "I was with Lady Emily and Captain Jennings."

"And where is your young lord these days?" Miss Forrester jeered. "In London it seemed as though you were never away from him, and in Bath I have yet to see you *with* him. I do hope you have not let him slip through your fingers."

"You need not concern yourself over that matter, Miss Forrester," Marian replied. "But if I ever did need advice on maintaining my hold on a young man, you should certainly be the first person I would ask." Miss Forrester looked daggers at this remark and William cleared his throat.

"I do believe I see an opening," William said. "Now we may tell all our acquaintance we have successfully navigated the labyrinth." Lady Emily and Captain Jennings were strolling about outside the labyrinth when Marian and her new companions joined them. Captain Jennings gave William a very skeptical look which disappeared after William was introduced to him. Furthermore, the way that Miss Forrester clung to his arm assured the captain that William was no competition.

When they met Lord Richard and Miss Henderson again, they had been joined by Mr. Henderson. Lady Emily left the group to join her brother, and Marian half expected Captain Jennings to follow. When he did not, however, she supposed she really ought to give him credit for his story concerning Miss Perdue. However, she resolved to write to her sister about it, for Rachel would surely know the particulars, and if she did not, she could soon discover them. Meanwhile, Marian saw no harm in taking the captain's offered arm and making herself a very pleasant companion.

Mr. Henderson, realizing he could be no competition for a red coat escorted his sister away for a pressing social engagement and Lady Emily addressed her brother.

"I need not ask where your thoughts are, Richard, but no amount of malicious staring from you will make him go away."

"What are you talking about?"

"You know very well what I'm talking about. I'm talking about that brash young captain who fancies every young lady is ready to fall in love with him because he wears a red coat. He is out to catch an heiress, I daresay."

"And Miss Amberly is his next victim?" Lord Richard started. "I cannot allow that. Surely Miss Amberly would see through such a scheme."

"I don't think he is any real cause for worry. His technique for playing the charmer is quite sloppy. He certainly has nothing to you. The only things he really has in his favor are his red coat and good looks."

"Those are no mean assets, I assure you," Lord Richard said distastefully. "She certainly seems very pleased with him. And I should not be surprised if he should discover she has qualities beyond her fortune."

"Miss Amberly left us when we were in the labyrinth, no doubt by design. I asked the captain if he would follow her and he said he was quite content to remain with me, if I found his company acceptable. I made it quite clear it did not matter to me one way or another, and I further gave him to understand that he needn't attempt to court me, for I was not interested, and if he wanted any chance with Miss Amberly, he must not allow her to suspect he had ambitions elsewhere."

"And so you encouraged him in his pursuit of Miss Amberly! Oh Emily, how cruelly you have complicated matters!"

"Nonsense," Lady Emily said. "I only meant to have a bit of fun with him, for I am certain he has no chance with Miss Amberly. He cannot compete with you, despite his uniform. He has a red coat, you have a title, an estate and infinitely more charm."

"Look how she holds to his arm! What I would give to be in his situation now, despite his lack of fortune! You have never been enamored with officers, so you cannot understand other young ladies who are. They are a formidable rival, I assure you."

"Shall you give up, then?"

"I shall go away to town tomorrow. I cannot say how long I will remain there. But I am resolved that I shall go before breakfast."

"Oh, you think your absence will make Miss Amberly realize she cannot live without you? A good plan, to be sure. But what do you think grandmamma will say when she sees you are gone? You must know the main reason she invited Miss Amberly is so that you would be thrown together."

"I have done all she can require me to do," Lord Richard replied. "I made my proposals to Marian. They were not accepted. There is now nothing for me to do except endure my misery as best I can. I cannot stand back and watch her court the attentions of that young officer. By separating myself from her, I hope I shall cease to be tormented. To forget her seems to me unthinkable, to replace her impossible—but I shall try."

It was not until dinner the next day that Marian realized Lord Richard was no longer in Bath. Lady Emily had said nothing concerning the matter and it was not until George came to dinner in the evening that anyone else discovered it.

"I wonder that Richard has not shown himself today," Lady Beauregard said. "Usually he has come by now. Pray, George, do you know where he has hid himself?"

"He left before breakfast this morning," George replied. "He charged me to say he was called away to town on urgent business and does not know when he may return."

"Nonsense!" the dowager interjected. "What business can he possibly have in town? He means only to indulge himself in revelry away from the watchful eye of his mother and grandmother. I will write to him at once and let him know I shan't allow it."

"Pray grandmamma, what can you do?" Lady Emily asked. "He is five and twenty and his own master. He does not wish to displease you, I am sure. I'm certain something very particular has taken him to London."

Meanwhile, Marian did not dare look at Lady Emily, lest she should betray some of her own internal confusion. Lord Richard had gone away. Why? Had she been too cold to him? He was a wicked and thoughtless young man, to be sure, but he was almost Marian's sole source of entertainment in Bath. Without him, their parties would be very dull indeed. And yet, Lord Richard had hardly spoken to her all week and had quite devoted his attention to Miss Henderson. Why, then, did she have such a sinking feeling within her? This was something Marian had still not settled with herself when they left the dining room and she retired to dress for the evening ball. She really had quite a headache by now and truly did not wish to go, but she would not give anyone the satisfaction of seeing her affected by his lordship's absence. Truly, it ought not to affect her at all and certainly it was not worth her thoughts.

Marian completed her toilette with a fresh determination and when she joined the others downstairs, it was in vain that Lady Emily, or even George Wesley searched her countenance for a trace of discontent. She smiled as gaily as if she were the happiest creature on earth.

When they arrived at the Lower Rooms, they were immediately joined by Captain Jennings and a handsome young naval officer.

"Miss Amberly," Captain Jennings bowed. "My companion here has expressed a wish of becoming acquainted with you. Allow me to introduce Midshipman Darnell." Marian, though surprised, graciously inclined her head and instantly concluded that this must be a brother of Miss Darnell, so striking was the resemblance, though his hair was darker than his sister's. Though why he would wish to be introduced to her, she could not imagine.

Captain Jennings did not allow for further explanations, for he asked Marian to dance and it was too early for her to claim fatigue. As they joined the other dancers, Captain Jennings kept up much of the conversation himself while Marian answered with "yes" and "no." Finally she asked how he was acquainted with Mr. Darnell, for it seemed Mr. Darnell was some years younger. The captain colored and hesitated before answering.

"Yes, he is younger. He is soon to take the lieutenant's exams and I am not quite certain he has reached his majority. As to how we are acquainted—well my brother used to fancy himself in love with the eldest Miss Darnell and I was commissioned to discover the particulars of the family. I was much struck by the good nature and common sense of young Darnell. Unfortunately, the family is deficient in both fortune and connections. Their father was a baronet, it is true, but surely none of his acquaintance would deign to acknowledge his *natural* children. And his circumstances were too bad to leave them in any decent condition."

"What came of your brother's affection?"

"Oh! Well you see we are dependent on our uncle and he has made it clear it will be highly in our disfavor to dispose of ourselves poorly. And so he had to give the young lady up. Besides, there was some hushed up matter about an indiscretion. I understand she is engaged now."

"Yes, to her cousin," Marian replied. "One of those very acquaintances you supposed would have nothing to do with the family."

"You are acquainted with the family then?"

"I have met Sir Edward and his sister in town on several occasions. They are a very generous family, each in their own way. They were very welcoming to Miss Darnell. She is staying with them until the wedding."

"Yes, I understand you are already acquainted with Miss Darnell. It is through her that her brother recognized your name. However, I am glad to hear she is well provided for. I sincerely wish her well, for she is a sweet girl."

After her dances with the captain were over, Marian allowed herself to be led out by Mr. Darnell. They danced the first few minutes in silence, then Mr. Darnell spoke.

"You must be wondering about my wish of becoming acquainted with you." Marian inclined her head and waited for him to go on. "I hope you will not think me too bold, only I wished to meet the young lady who was spoken of so highly by my sister. She wrote about you in her last letter and spoke of your kindness and condescension. And when my friend Jennings said that you had walked in, I told him I would be happy to make your acquaintance."

"Miss Darnell strikes me as a very sweet girl," Marian said. "I'm sure I'm happy to be acquainted with anyone related to her. Have you met Mr. Lionel Sheffield?"

"Oh, yes. He called very frequently while he was in Bristol. I have yet to meet my other cousins, however. Miss Sheffield, I believe, is very close to my own age. And my sister writes that Sir Edward has been very kind to her. I daresay it is no less than Jane deserves, though perhaps beyond our expectations."

"And you are the eldest?"

"I am the eldest but one. My eldest brother is in service in the West Indies. He has done very well for himself, considering his obscure connections. I hope I shall be as fortunate as him. I'm concerned about my younger brothers, however. John, who is fourteen, was sent to sea the first time not long before my father's death. Now none of us will have our father's influence to assist us in the profession. And I don't know what shall be done for the youngest, for he is still too young to go to sea."

"And what about your younger sisters?"

"They shall have to be governesses," Mr. Darnell replied. "Unless they can marry, like Jane."

"How long shall you be in Bath?"

"I shall return to Bristol tomorrow. I can be there and back in a day, you know. It is but twelve miles. Perhaps I shall come back next week, when Jane is here. She is to be married Monday, you know, and then she and her new husband are to come to Bath."

"So soon? I did not realize—and they are coming to Bath? Why choose such a place for their wedding trip? I had thought they might go to the sea or the mountains."

"I suppose Lionel must return to his commission soon. And Bath is near enough to Bristol that we might visit one another. Mother is very anxious to see them before they go away. Susan, I am sure, would like to visit Bath. Have you ever been to Bristol, Miss Amberly?"

"No. I have been only to Bath and Ramsgate, besides London. Bristol is much like Bath, is it not?"

"Bristol is not so grand as Bath, but it is well enough to suit our purposes. And it has always been home to me." They talked on about Bath, daily routines and the various places Mr. Darnell had seen on his travels, which very much interested Marian. They continued their conversation after they returned from the dance and poor Captain Jennings began to think he had made a foolish mistake in introducing them.

When it was time for tea, his young usurper had not quitted Marian and escorted her into the tea-room. Captain Jennings himself was required to offer his arm to Lady Beauregard, in order to keep himself included in the party. He could, easily enough, have attempted to monopolize the conversation with Marian, but he did not dare be so obviously inattentive to Lady Beauregard. He had to satisfy himself, therefore, with listening in on their conversation from time to time and wonder how a mere boy, with no fortune or connections could so completely engage the attention of such a lady as Miss Amberly.

After tea, Captain Jennings pulled Mr. Darnell aside and requested that he see about the party of officers they had arrived with, but alas, while he was so ingeniously paving the way for his own tête-à-tête with Miss Amberly, she was asked to dance by Mr. George Wesley.

"You seem quite popular with the officers this evening," George said. "Neither of those young sparks have left your side since we walked in the door."

"I did not suppose I could send them away if I wished to," Marian replied. "Besides, Mr. Darnell is very agreeable and we have been having a great deal of conversation."

"So I have noticed," George said dryly. "And what of the other gentleman?"

"Captain Jennings? Oh, he is well enough I suppose. I'm really not sure what to make of him. I had fancied myself in love with him once, but I think better of it now."

"Indeed! I would never have thought that. And dare I mention another gentleman, who is not present this evening?"

"I don't know what you mean," Marian replied, coloring.

"Do you not? I daresay my poor cousin has not been on your thoughts this evening. Indeed, how could he stand a chance against such competition as he faces tonight?"

"I'm sure I don't know why he should be on my thoughts at all," Marian replied peevishly. "I daresay I am not on his." George smiled.

"You and I have not had much time for conversation this week," he said. "I have been much engaged with Miss Seldon and her father, and you have had pursuits of your own, I believe. And my grandmother thinks you are quite at her disposal."

"I suppose I am," Marian said. "I am her guest and I am expected to be available for any social engagements she wishes me to attend with her. I believe I shall dine with my cousins sometime, but I don't know when."

"Miss Seldon and I were thinking of forming a walking party to Beechen Cliff tomorrow," George said. "Providing, of course, that the weather is fine."

"Yes, the weather is rather unpredictable in Bath. And last time you induced us into a walking party, it rained after you had deserted us."

"Never could I have suspected such a turn of events!" George protested. "But upon my honor, we shall all remain together this time. And so I suppose it was your gallant captain that had the privilege of driving you about while the rest of us fretted about your disappearance?"

"Lady Emily was tired of waiting, and certainly I could not allow her to go with the man alone, as she was not acquainted with him. It would have had a very odd appearance."

"Indeed it would. And I am well acquainted with the obstinacy of Lady Emily. I can easily believe her thoughtlessness about the matter."

"I do not wish to put her ladyship in a poor light."

"No one suspects you of it, Miss Amberly. She is a very good-natured girl, but

a little too used to getting her own way, as most young ladies in her situation are. She is much like her brother in that respect."

"I would never have thought that Lord Richard was used to getting his own way," Marian said saucily. "He has such a humble air about him." George laughed.

"I see you have not given up your former opinion of him. Or if you have, you hide it very well. I had hoped by now you would have formed a better opinion of him."

"My opinion of Lord Richard is constantly changing. He is no less enigmatic to me than Captain Jennings, or any other man. However, your plan to walk to Beechen Cliff is a good one, and I should like very much to see it."

By the time the walking party commenced, it included Lady Emily, Miss Henderson and Mr. Wesley, besides Marian, Miss Seldon and George Wesley. And before they arrived at their destination, yet two more were added to the party, for they were joined by Captain Jennings and Mr. Darnell whom they met, quite by accident, on the way.

"But had you better not begin on your way?" Captain Jennings asked Mr. Darnell. "You've got a long ride ahead of you."

"I can spare a few hours," Mr. Darnell replied. "We've got an early start. As long I leave by two, I daresay I shall be in good time for dinner." As Captain Jennings could think of no reply to this, he was forced bear yet again his defeat by a lesser man.

Miss Henderson claimed Mr. Wesley for herself in the absence of Lord Richard and as Marian voluntarily began a conversation with Mr. Darnell, Captain Jennings was obliged to walk with Lady Emily, which may be imagined was very awkward for them both. But the Captain bore it well and did not allow himself to sulk in his own defeat.

"Do you read?" Marian asked Mr. Darnell.

"I haven't much spare time for reading," Mr. Darnell replied. "I have been studying for my lieutenant's exam and hope to receive my commission soon. I hope now I shall have more time for such leisure activities. What do you recommend?"

"Well that all depends on your tastes," Marian replied. "A young man and a young lady often have very different tastes. I prefer novels, but novels are commonly considered fit only for idle young ladies."

"And I suppose that, being a young man, I am to prefer a commentary on the war or politics?" Mr. Darnell replied, with a smile. "I assure you, Miss Amberly, I get quite enough of that in my life without reading about it. Therefore, as soon as we are back to town, I shall get the most sentimental, romantic novel I can get my hands on. And now that we've settled on my reading material, we must go about setting my social tastes. Now tell me—should I prefer the theater or the opera?" Marian laughed and they continued the conversation until they reached the cliffs, and then it was time for them to join the others in exclaiming upon the magnificence of the view. And after they had all walked about, rested and admired, it was time to return again.

After they returned home and the gentlemen had left them, the rest of the day was spent loitering about the Pump Room, shopping, or whatever the ladies could find to occupy them. It rained all day Sunday and Monday and on Monday evening they went to Mr. Seldon's house for dinner.

Mr. Seldon was a middle-aged, gouty gentleman who was good-natured, but set in his ways. Besides the party she came with, what was Marian's surprise when she saw that Captain Jennings was there, as well as an older gentleman who turned out to be Captain Jennings' uncle, Mr. Cox, who was a very great friend of Mr. Seldon. Miss

Seldon had seen Mr. Cox often enough, but was not aware until this evening of his connection with Captain Jennings.

When they went down to dinner, the happy captain had the privilege to escort Marian and take a place beside her.

"My dear Miss Amberly," he began, "How can you have been so cruel as to run away from me this afternoon, when I expressly wanted to talk to you?"

"What did you wish to talk about?" Marian asked. "I am very ready to listen."

"I did not mean I had anything *particular* to speak to you about. Only that I wished for your company."

"Well you could have very easily joined our conversation, if you wished," Marian replied. "But I supposed you were in company more to your liking."

"Her ladyship is very amiable, I am sure," Captain Jennings said, "But you see, even the most amiable company is dull when one wishes himself *elsewhere*."

"Am I to understand that you prefer *my* company to that of Lady Emily? I cannot believe it."

"Are you so ignorant of your own charms to suppose otherwise?"

"Accuse me of ignorance, by all means," Marian said with a good-humored smile. "But do not wonder that I should believe that as elegant and sophisticated a lady as her ladyship cannot take second place to a country nobody like me."

"You would turn my compliment into an insult."

"By no means! I am extremely gratified that you would spend your powers of gallantry on me rather than the daughter of an earl. It is very kind of you, for you must know I am much more wanting for admirers than her ladyship can be." The captain looked as if he did not know quite how to respond to this, and so he simply asked if she had found herself in pleasant company with the young midshipman.

"Oh yes. He is much more agreeable than I might have expected. He has an artlessness of manner that I find very appealing. His conversation is pleasant, he has a good countenance and he does not appear to be wanting in common sense."

"Yes, it is a pity that he has no better prospects," Captain Jennings replied. "He has few connections now that will advance him and while our ships are at bay and he remains on shore, he has little chance of improving his fortune." Marian felt certain this was calculated to lessen her esteem for the poor young man and so replied,

"Well, perhaps he may make a good marriage. There are many young ladies of fortune, I'm sure, that like a man in uniform. He seems a modest young man. I daresay he would do well enough with four or five hundred a year. Therefore, if he could find a young lady with ten thousand pounds and catch her fancy, it would be very well." This reply had the desired effect of silencing the captain and allowing her to finish her dinner in peace.

After dinner, the young ladies were requested to sing at the pianoforte, each in their turn. When Marian's turn came, Captain Jennings followed her and hovered about her until her song was finished.

"Come, captain," Mr. Seldon said. "You must give the young lady room to breathe. I imagine she knows what she is about without your assistance."

"I would not presume to offer assistance where it was not wanted," Captain Jennings replied, "But I cannot help but offer admiration."

"Ah, Mr. Cox," Mr. Seldon said. "These soldiers and all their gallantry—'tis no wonder they have the ladies pining after them. Why, my own nephew, Lionel Sheffield, had nothing particular to recommend him, except his red coat, and was married just this morning. And they say his bride is the handsomest young lady ever seen, though worth next to nothing."

"Papa!" Miss Seldon exclaimed, shocked.

"Not that I see anything wrong with young people marrying, provided there's enough between them to live on," Mr. Seldon continued. "For me it doesn't much signify whether it comes from the gentleman's side or the lady's."

"But surely there are other things to be taken into consideration," the dowager interjected. "A pure blood-line might be acceptable, even without a large fortune. And I suppose with a large fortune obscure blood might be overlooked. I see far too many noble families obliged to connect themselves with this vulgar new class of merchants and such because their family fortunes have been squandered away. Thank heavens such is not the case in *our* family!"

"Exceptional connections are also a strong recommendation," Mr. Cox added. "But I understand this young miss hadn't *any* of these recommendations. Young Mr. Sheffield could have done much better for himself, I am sure."

"What is your opinion, Miss Amberly?" Captain Jennings asked. "You look as if you don't agree."

"My opinion is that we ought not to discuss so freely that which is no concern of ours," Marian answered. "It is not the young lady's fault that she was not born a duchess or with thirty thousand pounds. Therefore it is not right we should judge her."

"My dear, we don't require the lady to be a duchess," Mr. Cox told her. "If she be only a gentleman's *legitimate* daughter with ten thousand or so, it would be enough."

"I am quite of Miss Amberly's opinion," Miss Seldon said. "Miss Darnell is a dear girl who always conducts herself with grace, despite the expectations of vulgarity that others have about her. No one can be more ashamed of her situation than she is herself, but what can she do about it? It is most ungenerous to gossip in this manner, and I must beg that we choose another subject for our conversation." No objection being made to this proposal, the subject was dropped and the party moved on to other, more seemly matters.

CHAPTER ELEVEN

On Tuesday evening Marian attended the Dowager Countess Beauregard to the theater, where it seemed to Marian that nobody could possibly be at the Lower Rooms, for all of Bath was at the play. Lady Beauregard did not feel well and so did not attend them, though it could not be said that anyone languished for the want of her company.

While Marian was searching the room for William and Laura, Miss Seldon exclaimed, "Why there's Lionel Sheffield! And Miss Darnell—that is, Mrs. Sheffield." Marian looked to where Miss Seldon indicated, and what was her surprise when she saw not only the newly-wed couple, but her own brother, Albert, and a well-dressed lady she did not know. It must be his new wife, she supposed, for she recollected that Mrs. Sheffield had had some acquaintance with Albert's supposed bride.

"The play is that way," said a voice. Marian looked up and saw Captain Jennings smiling at his own wit.

"Indeed, *one* of the plays is that way," Marian replied. "But the play happening in the boxes is of more interest to me, for I have already seen the play on the stage."

"You provoke my curiosity," replied the captain, "For I would know what causes so much interest in the boxes. I see no players and no one is making speeches."

"Life, Captain Jennings, is what I speak of. What secrets, what intrigues are behind the colorful masks that those of the polite world put on everyday? Perhaps you recall the lines of the great playwright—'All the world is a stage, and the men and women in it merely players.' There is much truth in those words, as much today as two hundred years ago. Would you not agree?"

"Indeed, there is much comedy, as well as tragedy that may happen in a man's life," Captain Jennings said. "Such things cannot be predicted."

"True. And that is precisely what makes watching life much more fascinating than watching a play, where everything is predictable."

"You put it so eloquently, Miss Amberly, that I find myself compelled to agree with you."

"I don't know which is more abundant," Miss Seldon said in a low voice after Captain Jennings had gone. "Your wit or his gallantry."

"He is rather excessive, as men tend to be, when they have motives for it. *His* I cannot pretend to know."

"Perhaps he admires you," Miss Seldon said. "He would certainly not be the first, I'm sure. I believe my own cousin, Sir Edward, holds you in very high esteem and admires you greatly."

"I had thought so," Marian replied. "But I am by no means certain. Sir Edward is at different times so distant, and so cordial. I cannot know what he thinks of me."

"But why should you care what he or any other man thinks?" Miss Seldon asked. "I daresay you have a number of admirers, each for their different reasons. But the sooner you make your engagement public, the sooner you will be rid of unwanted suitors."

"Engagement!" Marian exclaimed. She lowered her voice again. "What can you possibly be talking about?" It was Miss Seldon's turn to look surprised.

"Why, are you not engaged to Lord Richard?" She asked. "We have been expecting it to be announced any day now."

"Engaged to Lord Richard!" Marian repeated. "No! However did you come to such a conclusion?"

"Why, I had thought—so had we all. Lord Richard has been too pointed in his attentions to be ignored. You seemed to accept them without question. What else are we to suppose but that there was some sort of understanding? George said Lord Richard intended to make proposals, though we never knew the result. Even Edward believes you must be engaged, though he cannot imagine why it is kept a secret."

"I am not engaged!" Marian said. "You shall, perhaps, despise me when I tell you, but Lord Richard did make proposals and I refused them! You must know the reputation he has—I could not be certain of my future happiness. I hope you do not blame me."

"I admit there was never a doubt of his being accepted," Miss Seldon replied. "But I cannot blame you for acting as you felt right. I shall be the last person to tell you to marry for mercenary reasons. And I suppose that explains his attentions to Miss Henderson last week. He was angry over your refusal."

"Doubtless his lordship is used to getting everything he desires. But I have been endeavoring not to think about him. And I beg you not to mention what I have told you to anyone else. I dare not openly reject him until I must, for I fear it would only result in a breach between our families. My mother would never forgive me for it."

"I shall not speak of it to anyone," Miss Seldon assured her. "But are you sure you will not reconsider?"

"I cannot deny that there is much to admire in him. He has a good person and address, moves in the first circles and is in line for a title. And to many young ladies, I've no doubt that these would be attraction enough. But I have many reasons to believe he is not to be trusted. I fear that he should be faithless and I could not be happy in such a marriage, though some more ambitious ladies may find it acceptable."

"But many young men like to carry on a flirtation with one or two young ladies," Miss Seldon said. "Particularly charming young men. But they usually settle down once they are married."

"I have a feeling Lord Richard is not one of them. But why do you wish me to marry him?"

"I don't wish anything about it," Miss Seldon replied. "Only I had thought—you seemed to like him very much. I only think that if he is the man you like best in the world, you should consider carefully before giving your final answer."

"But I am not at all certain he is the man I like best," Marian said. "There is another I like at least as well, and one who I am certain would not trifle with a young lady's affections as Lord Richard has. But he has made me no offers."

"Pray who is this man that so merits your admiration?" Miss Seldon asked.

Marian colored and looked away. "Forgive me, Miss Amberly. I have no right to know your private concerns. You have confided so much already. It would be impertinent in me to desire more. You may depend on my silence." Marian thanked her, and they were soon obliged to give their attention to the rest of the company.

The next morning, Marian met her cousins at the Pump Room and when she told them of Albert's being in town, William proposed they look him up in the books and pay a visit to him. Before they left the Pump Room, however, they met Lionel Sheffield and his wife. Mrs. Sheffield was, of course, pleased to see Marian again and pleased again to hear she had met her brother.

"And what do you think of him, Miss Amberly?" she asked. "Is he not very handsome?"

"He is very agreeable in person and in manner," Marian replied, smiling.

"I knew you would think so," Mrs. Sheffield said. "And we are to go to Bristol tomorrow, and spend the day there. Mama will be so happy to see us. Should you like to come with us, Miss Amberly?"

"Come with you?" Marian repeated.

"Oh yes!" Mrs. Sheffield said. "I daresay it shall be a great deal of fun. Have you ever been to Bristol, Miss Amberly?"

"I have not."

"Well I don't pretend it is so grand as Bath, but there is certainly enough to give us a fair bit of amusement. And you might meet my mother and sisters." Marian had no great wish to be acquainted with Sir Thomas' former mistress, but she did not wish to offend her friend and therefore said she would be pleased to accompany them, provided the Dowager Lady Beauregard allowed her to go.

When Marian requested permission to go, the dowager declared a great desire to see Bristol herself, and proposed they make a party of it. No one made any objection and soon the party grew to include Mr. and Miss Henderson and Captain Jennings.

The next morning, Marian at last had the opportunity of meeting her brother, who expressed great surprise at seeing her in Bath and warmly saluted her. He then introduced her to his wife, who curtsied and walked over to Mrs. Sheffield.

"I suppose, Albert, if you were a little more open in your correspondence, we might have been spared the shock of discovering at once that you are married and had left your commission," Marian said, rather reproachfully. "I should have been very happy to come to the wedding."

"Oh! Well, as to that—we were married in the West Indies, you see."

"The West Indies! What an interesting affair it must have been!"

"Indeed it was," Albert agreed. "And that is where we met, you know. Greta's father has investments in a plantation there. And the cost of living—and entertaining—is much lower there."

"Well, now you shall have the honor of introducing your wife to the dowager," Marian told him. "She doesn't know of your marriage. Only days ago she was boasting of how none of *her* family had to dilute their blood with the families of *tradespeople* for the sake of money."

"Marian! What a dreadful thing to say!" Albert exclaimed. "I might have expected it from her ladyship, but not from you."

"I was only telling what *she* said," Marian said. "My own opinion has nothing to do with it. I never supposed you would marry for money."

"And so I did not," Albert replied. "Greta is a dear girl and her fortune had nothing to do with my admiration for her. Her father even tested me to see if I was a fortune hunter by informing me that he had lost nine of his ten ships and was ruined. I replied that if his daughter could consent to living on five-hundred a year plus a colonel's wages I should do all in my power to make her happy. And so it turned out he was very well off after all and we have 120,000 between us."

"And so you've sold your commission," Marian replied. "What a touching story. I imagine our father would have liked to have been informed, at least."

"You know his opinion of foreigners," Albert said. "Even though she brought a fortune, what would Father have said to my marrying the daughter of a Dutch merchant? No, I thought it best to break it to him after the fact, for then he has no choice but to reconcile himself to it."

"Well you might have told some of your less prejudiced brothers and sisters about it," Marian said. "As it was, I heard about it from your successor's wife."

"I wrote to John about it," Albert said. "I did think he would tell you, at least."

"He did not," Marian said. "John only communicates whatever will give him the most entertainment. His favorite subject, of late, has been the supposed engagement of myself to Lord Richard. And he speaks about it in public, which is what distresses me."

"Oh yes, Sarah told me there was some sort of flirtation going on between you," Albert replied. "Especially on his part."

"When did you speak to Sarah?"

"Oh! Didn't you know? Greta and I just came from Fort de Mar. We paid a visit for a few weeks and came straight on to Bath."

"If you had deferred your visit for a few weeks, you might have met us all there," Marian said. "For Mama and Father and Rachel are to go to Ramsgate on Monday, and I am to join them a week later."

"Yes, I am aware of that," Albert replied. "I am no hurry to meet my father yet. However, we shall be at Rosewood in the fall, so you needn't concern yourself that I am attempting to avoid him forever."

At last the Dowager Lady Beauregard complained that if she had known she was to be kept waiting in the heat for an indefinite amount of time, she might have stayed home. And so the seating arrangements were hastily made, with the minor difficulty of Mrs. Amberly not wishing to be separated from her husband, though he was to drive one of the carriages. Albert at last prevailed on her to ride in the carriage with Marian, Mrs. Sheffield and Miss Seldon while he and George rode up top. Another carriage carried the other four ladies and Mr. Wesley and Lionel Sheffield. Captain Jennings and Mr. Henderson rode on horseback, supposing that they appeared to better advantage that way.

Marian found that any attempts at conversation with her new sister were in vain, for she could receive nothing but short replies, and no attempt to meet her efforts. However, she did seem to be fond of Mrs. Sheffield and was much more talkative with her.

When they arrived at Bristol, the first order of business was to find a tea-room to refresh themselves after their journey. Mrs. Sheffield quickly wrote a note to her brother to inform him of their location, in case he should want to join them. Marian was obliged to sit at a table with the Dowager Lady Beauregard and her daughter-in-law. Mr. Henderson would have taken the fourth seat, but Captain Jennings was too quick for him and secured the place for himself. No sooner was everyone seated, than the dowager began commenting on Albert's marriage.

"Oh! That I should live to see the day my own grandson was married to the daughter of a sugar merchant!" she exclaimed. "I don't believe I have ever been so shocked! What do you suppose made him do it?"

"Money, without a doubt," Captain Jennings answered. "For I hear she has a very large fortune."

"That may very well be," the dowager replied. "But his family is in no financial difficulty, and therefore I see no reason to taint the blood unnecessarily."

"But Albert is not to inherit my father's estate and surely we could not expect him to wish to remain dependant when he could have a house of his own," Marian said, rather irritated. "Besides, your ladyship, our family has already been tainted, as you call it, for my grandmother was the daughter of a merchant. And if I am not mistaken, she was your sister." The dowager was quite dumb-founded for a few moments and then she recovered herself.

"Our father was a very respectable man," she said. "And besides, he was no foreigner like this girl's father. I don't know what could have put such foolishness into Albert's head. To go to the West Indies and find a wife! I daresay he could have done better for himself in his own country."

"His fortune alone would hardly be enough to support a wife of any fashion," Marian replied. "And English heiresses of genteel birth are difficult to come by. Would you rather he married an *English* lady with a very small fortune?"

"Certainly no promising young man should marry a young lady with little fortune if he may do better for himself," the dowager said. "No matter how pretty she may be." Marian felt certain this was a remark upon the late marriage of Mr. Lionel Sheffield, for she glanced in Mrs. Sheffield's direction as she said it.

"And it seems Albert has done better for himself," Marian said. "For he has managed to find a wife who will provide him with a very comfortable income."

"And what of young ladies, your ladyship?" Captain Jennings asked. "Are they to be held to the same strict standard?"

"I believe it to be the duty of young ladies to raise themselves in rank if they have the opportunity," the dowager replied. "If a young lady be of genteel birth and good fortune, she may, perhaps, aspire to be the wife of a baronet or lesser nobility. With an exceptional fortune, she might hope even to ally herself to one of the greater houses. Even girls who are very well-born, like my granddaughter, Lady Emily, must be careful with whom they make alliances, lest they tarnish their family names with low connections. And furthermore," she added before anyone could reply, "Young ladies must take special care of whom they choose as their female companions, for, as the Good Book says 'evil communications corrupt good manners'."

"And how must we judge the suitability of our companions, your ladyship?" Marian asked. "By their birth or their conduct? I have known young ladies of what some would call 'inferior birth' who conduct themselves in a very respectable manner and I have likewise known ladies of superior rank who can be as mean-spirited and ill-mannered as anyone in the working-class."

"But surely, Miss Amberly, you must be aware that nothing good may come of associating unnecessarily with persons of obscure birth and dubious connections." *Surely this conversation is directed at my friendship with Mrs. Sheffield*, Marian thought. *But what concern should Lady Beauregard have about it? Unless she supposes I shall marry her grandson—in which case she supposes I must sever any associations of a dubious nature. Well she shall not have the satisfaction.*

"Indeed, your ladyship," she replied. "I assure you there is no need to warn *me*, for I have no friends that are wholly without good connections. However, allow me to thank you for your very kind advice." And what could her ladyship say to such a reply? Nothing, to be sure. For surely she could offer no more hints about Mrs. Sheffield's connections without being very obvious in her meaning, and even the Dowager Lady Beauregard could not deny that an alliance with the influential Sheffield family was a very good one.

Marian was not released from her ladyship until Mr. Darnell arrived, and even then, she was never out of her sight. Mr. Darnell brought with him a pretty young lady, about fifteen or sixteen, whom Marian soon discovered to be his second sister, Miss Susan Darnell. Mr. Darnell also announced, on behalf of his mother, that they were all very welcome to attend a garden breakfast she was giving that morning.

"But it's nearly eleven thirty!" Marian exclaimed. "We could not possibly come on such short notice."

"But the breakfast shall not be until one," Mr. Darnell replied. "My mother is very fashionable, you see, and keeps London hours. Her house is barely a mile out of Bristol." The dowager at first declared she had no desire to attend such an engagement, but when all the young people of the party showed a great inclination to go, she changed her mind and declared she would not have them all attend such a place with nobody but a freshly married couple for chaperones.

Lady Beauregard having been consulted as to her ability to walk a mile, the party began their walk toward the house where Mrs. Sheffield's mother resided. It was not until this time that Marian and Mrs. Sheffield had any chance of speaking together out of the hearing of any others.

"I want to apologize for bringing such a large party," Marian said at the first opportunity. "I asked for the dowager's leave to accompany you to Bristol and it seems that she thought it right to invite herself and everyone else. It was certainly not my intention."

"Don't trouble yourself about it, Miss Amberly," Mrs. Sheffield replied. "I can see well enough how it happened. I shall always consider myself fortunate that I escaped being her granddaughter. If Mrs. Amberly, with her large fortune, cannot escape her censure, how could I, with almost nothing, ever hope to be acceptable to her? No, I see now everything that happened was for the best."

"And only think," Marian added, "Lord Richard is her favorite grandson, and the future earl of—. Albert is only the second son of my father."

"What would Colonel Amberly say if he heard her speaking of his wife in such a manner?" Mrs. Sheffield asked.

"He would be quite angry, I believe," Marian replied. "For he was piqued when I simply told what her ladyship's opinion *would* be. But, like everyone else, he is far too afraid of her to make any complaint to her face. She can be very intimidating."

"So I've noticed," Mrs. Sheffield said. "But you don't suppose she would insult poor Mrs. Amberly to her face, do you?"

"One can never tell with such a person. Their prejudices can cause them to behave in a manner quite unbecoming. My father, for instance, is prejudiced in a different way. He is violently opposed to foreigners of any kind. Therefore it is likely he will disapprove of my new sister not because she is a merchant's daughter, but because she is not English."

"I would have thought her fortune would be enough to overcome any prejudices."

"In some families, perhaps it might. In some families, money is very welcome in whatever form it comes. In others, blood is a higher priority. The dowager and my father are the latter. I don't envy my new sister."

"I have a new appreciation for my good fortune in marrying into a family that is kind enough to overlook my lack of both good blood and fortune," Mrs. Sheffield said. "I did not realize how difficult it was to be accepted on one's own merit."

"Such littleness of mind is more common than it ought to be," Marian replied. "But pride is a very common sentiment that is felt a little too strongly by some families. The higher a family's rank, the more likely they will have such views. But Sir Edward's mind is superior to such vain concerns and looks for the good in everyone, I believe."

"You could not praise Sir Edward too highly for me," Mrs. Sheffield said. "I've told you already how kind he has been. But are there enough well-born ladies of fortune in the country to make such views practical?"

"It depends on what you call a fortune," Marian replied, with a smile. "If a fortune is ten or fifteen thousand pounds, I suppose it is common enough. The dowager Lady Beauregard would probably consider anything less than fifty thousand too insignificant to marry her favorite grandson. She fancies my fortune to be much larger than it is, and so she allows, perhaps even encourages, Lord Richard's attentions to me."

"Perhaps you should simply give her to understand that is not the case," Mrs. Sheffield suggested. "Then your refusal of Lord Richard would not irritate her."

"I daresay she shall find it out soon enough," Marian said. "I leave Bath at the end of next week. If she discovered my fortune was only twenty thousand, instead of the hundred and twenty thousand she supposes, it would considerably lessen me in her esteem. I hope you understand why I have no wish to hurry the discovery. Besides, Lord Richard is away—so what purpose would it serve?"

"You are quite right," Mrs. Sheffield said. "I can believe well enough that she might become rather cold."

"I'm surprised she has not found it out already. Lady Emily knows, I believe, but she is an advocate for the match because she believes Lord Richard is sincere."

"Do you believe he truly loves you?"

"He has certainly fooled a great many people into thinking so, if he does not," Marian said. "And I must admit he has almost convinced me. But do not alarm yourself—I am by no means prepared to accept his hand. Nor do I believe I shall be."

"Do not imagine you will *offend* me by a marriage to him," Mrs. Sheffield said. "I have no right to be angry with anyone for marrying him. But I would wish for you a man who better deserves you. But, Miss Amberly, I know you are very capable of judging for yourself."

Soon they arrived at a pretty little cottage with a large, neat garden in which Mrs. Sheffield's mother and her other guests were already assembled. She was very attractive and looked to be no more than thirty, though Marian knew she could not possibly be less than forty. She was dressed at the height of fashion and rather more gaily than Marian had expected.

"I had thought she would be rather more solemnly attired," Marian said as Mrs. Sheffield walked ahead to greet her mother. "One would suppose she is not in mourning at all." She was speaking to no one in particular, but it was the Dowager Lady Beauregard who replied.

"How very fortunate for her that Sir Thomas was not her *husband*," she said. "Therefore she is not obliged to wear mourning." The color rose to Marian's cheeks as she was forced to acknowledge the justification of the dowager's remark. Introductions were made and naturally their hostess was pleased to make all their acquaintance.

Much to the surprise of both Marian and Captain Jennings, Mr. Cox was present. Before Mrs. Sheffield's mother had had a chance to introduce her other guests, whom Marian could not fail to notice were all men, Marian noticed a small reaction to a young man of about thirty. Instantly upon seeing him, Lionel Sheffield had grabbed hold of his sword, as if involuntarily, and let go after his wife gently placed her hand upon his arm.

"My dear Mrs.—Sheffield, is it?" the young man said with a smirk. "Please allow me to extend my warmest congratulations on your recent nuptials. I hope you will be very happy."

"Thank you, Sir Walter," Mrs. Sheffield said coldly. "I'm sure we shall be."

"I find myself very taxed for congratulations this morning," Sir Walter said. "Pray, how many more marriages am I to bless today?"

"Hush!" their hostess said, playfully tapping the young baronet on the arm with her fan. "You shall give away my secret!"

"A thousand pardons, madam," Sir Walter said. "I did not realize it was so great a secret."

"What would you say if I told you all you were at a wedding breakfast?" This time she addressed not Sir Walter, but the assembly in general. There was a slight murmur.

"Oh Mother," Mrs. Sheffield said. "Don't tease us so. Why, who is getting married?"

"My dear," her mother replied. "I was married this morning. To Mr. Cox." The astonishment of nearly everyone present was extreme. Mrs. Cox had evidently not shared her intentions with even her children and only days before, Mr. Cox had spoken against marriage with anyone without connections or fortune.

Mrs. Sheffield and Mr. Darnell immediately retired to the copse, whither they were followed by their sister.

"What can our mother mean by marriage at this time?" Mrs. Sheffield asked her brother. "So soon after our father's death?"

"I know nothing of the matter," Mr. Darnell said. "I noticed that Mr. Cox has been to visit sometimes—but then so have other gentlemen. She loved our father, I believe, to have stayed with him so long. But now he has gone and she has an opportunity to gain some respectability. It is no more than you or I have tried to do."

"But she chose to live a life where she would be despised in certain circles," Mrs. Sheffield replied. "We did not."

"My dear sister, what wrong is there in her marriage to a perfectly respectable man? I daresay she knows her life has not been one of innocence. But shall we blame her for wishing to redeem her character to some degree?"

"Her character or her fortune?" Mrs. Sheffield asked, rather acrimoniously. "For I understand that Mr. Cox is very well off."

"You almost sound bitter, Jane," Mr. Darnell said. "Surely you don't envy our mother when you've made such a fine match yourself?"

"Perhaps I am a little bitter," Mrs. Sheffield admitted. "Only not because of envy. I'm bitter because of the disrespect and the gross insults her manner of living has caused me to suffer. No matter how I tried, I never could escape the shameful manner in which I was brought into this world. It seemed everyone supposed I would become what my mother was."

"But all is well now," her brother replied. "For now you have got a respectable husband and no one can doubt your honor. And you are not without well-connected female friends. Mrs. Pierson, for example—is she not the wife of your husband's colonel? Mrs. Albert Amberly and Miss Seldon are bound to have some influence in the fashionable world. And even Miss Amberly, I have no doubt, will make her mark upon the world. She seems to me a lady who cannot fail of making an impression on everyone she meets."

"And what of you, Robert?" Mrs. Sheffield asked. "Has she made an impression on your heart already? I must say nothing would please me better."

"Hush, Jane. I cannot think of such a thing. I find her very amiable. And I must say I could very easily find myself—"

"What?" Mrs. Sheffield pressed. "Find yourself what?"

"This subject will not do," Mr. Darnell said. "Such a thing is out of the question. You might as well put it out of your head and stop trying to put it in mine."

"But I believe it has put itself into your head, whether you willed it or no. And why is it so very unlikely? She has a small fortune of her own. I daresay you could live very well on twelve hundred a year, and her family is very likely to have some influence in the navy."

"I believe you have a little wickedness in you, Jane," Mr. Darnell said. "You are trying to inspire ideas in me that will never come to pass. Were I a captain, or even a commander, with a little money of my own, I might perhaps dare make the attempt. But as a mere midshipman on half-pay—no, I could not even think of asking her to make such a sacrifice when she might do so much better for herself."

"Would you call marriage to Captain Jennings doing better for herself? For I see well enough that *he* has designs on her. And his reasons are no more noble than yours would be."

"Captain Jennings is my good friend, Jane. I hope you are not trying to make me think ill of him. I have no doubt of his honor."

"I do not doubt his honor," Mrs. Sheffield said. "Merely his motives. There is nothing *dishonorable* about marrying simply to improve your fortune. But it is highly mercenary. Just as our mother's marriage is not dishonorable. I must postpone my judgment on whether or not it is mercenary. But her marriage has already taken place. Miss Amberly's has not. I hope you have not forgotten Captain Jennings' manner of tossing *me* aside because of my lack of fortune."

"My dear Jane—"

"No, Robert, there is no need to defend him. It does not matter now. But do you really wish Miss Amberly to fall into the hands of such a man?"

"You speak as though it is a settled thing that Miss Amberly shall marry Captain Jennings. I must say I don't believe she has any more regard for him than for any other man. When we went to Beechen Cliff last week, she had any number of chances of walking with the captain, yet she remained in my company almost the whole time."

"There you have it!" she exclaimed. "You see, she likes you very well."

"Just because she finds me a pleasant walking companion, it does not follow that she must like me for a husband. I, for one, should not make such a presumption. I have known her only a week. Who would not suspect me of having mercenary motives after so short an acquaintance? No, let Jennings make proposals if he will. I should not do it under such conditions no matter how well I might like her."

When Mrs. Sheffield and Mr. Darnell returned, the rest of the party was assembled for the breakfast. Once they were all seated, however, the dowager refused to eat anything, so that she might not seem to support any of the doings of her hostess.

After the comparably short repast during which no one was very talkative, except

Mrs. Cox's gentlemen guests, Mr. Cox and his nephew went into the house where at first they sat in silence in a poorly furnished library.

"Is this some sort of joke, Uncle?" Captain Jennings asked at last.

"I beg your pardon?" Mr. Cox returned, rather indignantly. "Have you ever known me to play jokes?"

"I have always supposed you to be a man of openness and integrity," Captain Jennings replied. "I can scarce believe you have secretly married yourself to another man's kept mistress, with seven children of her own, no less."

"I get lonely sometimes, you know, in that big house," Mr. Cox replied. "I fancied I might like to have a pretty wife. Mrs. Cox is still handsome, though old enough to not be over-particular in a husband. I did not wish for a young lass, young enough to be my granddaughter, or an elderly widow, though she be wealthy. Besides, she has shown great loyalty to remain so long with the baronet, though she was not bound to him."

"I cannot believe you are in your right mind. And so I was to be denied the daughter while you courted the mother? All the lectures you gave me about doing my duty and finding a wife of good family and fortune, forcing me to give up Miss Darnell—was that nothing more than hypocritical talk?"

"You will hold your tongue!"

"You would not let me take the daughter," Captain Jennings pressed on, "Innocent though she was, because she was virtually penniless. Yet you take to yourself her mother, who has spent more than half her life so far in social and moral disgrace! You have taken exactly the kind of wife who will bring shame to your door. Do you suppose she will not make a cuckold out of you in the end?"

"Do not concern yourself on that account! I have taken care of that in the marriage settlements. Believe me, she will think twice before crossing me."

"And if she remains faithful? Are you to leave her your entire fortune?"

"So that is it, is it?" Mr. Cox said. "You are concerned about how your inheritance will be affected. And I had flattered myself you were concerned with my well-being. But on the contrary, you are concerned about what happens after I'm dead."

"I beg you not to say such things, Sir," Captain Jennings protested. "My concern is how our family's respectability will be affected. I trust to your honor concerning me, for I know you are aware I am almost entirely dependant on you."

"My dear boy, I will not leave you completely unprovided for, though I cannot deny it is now out of my power to leave you my whole fortune. You will have enough to live fairly comfortably, provided your habits are not extravagant. But what about that pretty young heiress you were bent on catching? Miss Amberly, is it? If she is, in fact, to have 120,000 pounds, why then, with what I shall give you, you shall be able to live almost as well as a lord."

"I rather suspect I have a lord for competition, Uncle. Though he has gone from Bath for now, he may return at any time. And during his absence, your own new wife's son, though only a midshipman, seems to have caught Miss Amberly's fancy.

And I have no doubt he will press his advantage, once he discovers it."

"Then you had better find an opportunity," Mr. Cox told him. "You have known the young lady longer than young Darnell, have you not?"

"They met only last week. Yet already she seems to like him very well."

"Well you have a longer acquaintance to your advantage. You should take it."

"And may I ask how much young Darnell will profit from this marriage of yours?"

"Not so much as you will, provided you don't let the heiress slip out of your grasp and into his."

While Mr. Cox and his nephew were having this amiable discussion, the object of it was taking a turn in the shrubbery with Miss Henderson.

"What an interesting day this has proved to be," Miss Henderson remarked. "We come to Bristol to see the sights and spend half the day at the wedding breakfast of people whom we have never met before."

"True," Marian replied. "Though I have met Mr. Cox once before. I am not well acquainted with him, of course, but I must say this marriage is very surprising indeed." They came to a bench and Marian proposed they sit for a few minutes.

"I shall never understand how people with shameful lifestyles manage to come to a respectable end. First Miss Darnell, and now her mother."

"I grant you that the lifestyle of the mother has been dissolute," Marian said. "But the children cannot be blamed for what could not be helped."

"Oh if you suppose that Miss Darnell—Mrs. Sheffield, rather—was not as practiced in the art of coquetry as her mother was, I daresay you are sadly mistaken. She was raised by her mother, wasn't she?"

"My understanding was that she spent a great portion of her youth in school. Perhaps she received a very good moral education there."

"Hush, I hear someone," Miss Henderson said. They ceased talking and heard both a male and a female voice approaching on the other side of a tall hedge.

"And are you quite certain no one can see us here?" The man asked his companion.

"Perfectly certain, Sir Walter," his companion replied. "I've lived here ever so long. I think I know all the best hiding places."

"I'm sure you do, my dear," Sir Walter replied. "But I suppose your brother and sister must know about them too."

"Jane was always much too dull to play in the garden," the girl replied. "And Robert was scarcely any better." So the girl must be Susan Darnell.

"Pray, why did your sister marry that young man? He very nearly killed me, you know. He challenged me to a duel with very little provocation."

"I don't know why she married him. He's not dashing at all. And he's certainly not nearly as handsome as you."

"You flatter me, my love," Sir Walter said. "And who was that tall, thin girl with the rather sharp nose?"

"Oh! I believe she is Miss Henderson. One of the young ladies told me she scampers about after the great ladies, supposing she must gain some consequence by being in their company." Marian could scarcely keep her countenance at this description of Miss Henderson, though Miss Henderson was furious.

"And the girl with the brown eyes?"

"She is Jane's friend and I think my brother is in love with her. He might make her an offer if he were a higher ranking officer and had a better situation. As it is he won't say a word, for he does not want to seem like he would marry her for her fortune."

"She is a lady of fortune then?"

"I don't know," Susan replied. "Captain Jennings says she is to have 120,000 pounds, but I heard Jane say that if she married Robert they would have twelve hundred a year. But, my dear Sir Walter, did you bring me here merely to talk about other ladies?"

"No indeed," Sir Walter said. "I have a much more amusing use to make of my time with a lovely creature like yourself." Susan responded with a girlish titter.

Marian led Miss Henderson away, and as soon as she had an opportunity, she told Mrs. Sheffield of her suspicions about the baronet and Mrs. Sheffield's sister.

"Oh how I loathe that man!" Mrs. Sheffield exclaimed. "He is the man I told you about, Miss Amberly. He is the one Lionel fought a duel with. Sir Walter Lovell is a first-class rake, and everyone in town knows it. He also has scarcely enough income to support his extravagant life-style and therefore he must marry a lady of fortune."

"And what about your sister?"

"Susan is very foolish," Mrs. Sheffield answered. "I suppose she expects him to make her a lady, but he shall not. If I attempted to warn her, however, she would only be angry and accuse me of jealousy. No, I had better invite her to go with us, while we're in Bath. Mother shall take her away soon, for Mr. Cox plans to sell the cottage and they shall move to London. Then Susan will return to school. Sir Walter must find another object of prey."

"What will you tell Mr. Sheffield?"

"I must tell him that Susan wishes to see Bath. And I daresay it is true. I'm afraid if I tell him the real reason for removing her, however, he might challenge Sir Walter again, and that is something I would rather avoid."

When they at last took their leave of Mrs. Cox, they ventured back into town. Mr. Darnell suggested they all walk to the port and see the merchant ships, Miss Seldon and Lady Emily were for looking at the shops and Lady Beauregard and Mrs. Amberly declared they were very much fatigued. So it was decided that Lady Beauregard, Miss Henderson and Mrs. Amberly would take a private room at an inn for a few hours, George Wesley and the dowager would accompany Lady Emily and Miss Seldon to the shops, and everyone else would go to the harbor.

If Miss Susan had expected that she would have the baronet's undivided attention while they were in public, then she was sorely disappointed, for Sir Walter had gathered from the dowager that Marian was the niece of a wealthy banker and was to inherit nearly his whole fortune. Sir Walter's situation being what it was, he could hardly pass up an opportunity of trying his charm on a pretty young heiress so conveniently in his way. So, he immediately attached himself to Marian and asked if it were her first time in Bristol.

"Yes, Sir," she answered rather curtly.

"And how do you like it?"

"I have not seen very much of the city, Sir Walter," Marian replied. "But I must confess it is not as grand as Bath."

"Very true," Sir Walter said. "I am very fond of Bath myself, and I generally go there at least once a week when I am in this part of the country."

"Do you not live in Bristol?"

"Oh no! I do come to Bristol every year, but my estate is in Hertfordshire."

"I see." Marian did not wish to encourage the man, so she offered no other remark to this information.

"Have you been long in Bath, ma'am?"

"This is my third week."

"And how much longer shall you remain?"

"Only a week, Sir."

"Only a week!" Sir Walter exclaimed. "Well then, I shall try to go to Bath every day in hopes of meeting with you."

"I beg you not to trouble yourself," Marian said contemptuously. "Surely there can be no reason to go back and forth so many times and waste your time and tire your horses."

"You are quite right, Miss Amberly. Perhaps I shall simply take lodgings there for the week."

"You may do as you please, Sir Walter, with no reference whatever to me. Perhaps you might lodge with Mr. Darnell. I'm sure he would be happy to oblige anyone who has paid such particular attention to his sisters." Marian gave Sir Walter a meaningful look which disconcerted him for a few moments, though he quickly recovered.

"Of course Mr. Darnell must know I hold all of his family in the highest esteem," he said. "He is an honorable young man, I daresay, and his sisters are sweet girls. Though as to *particular attentions,* I'm sure I don't know what you mean."

"Do you not?" Marian returned. "Well, I suppose it depends on what you mean by 'particular attentions.' You see, *I* would call it very *particular* for a young man to have a secret meeting behind the bushes with a young girl, but for *you*, it may well be a common occurrence. I really could not say. But, as I said, everyone must judge for himself." This time Sir Walter was more thoroughly rendered speechless, and Marian took her opportunity to excuse herself to go to Mrs. Sheffield, from whose side she did not remove herself until the dispersed Bristol party was reunited.

CHAPTER TWELVE

On Monday Albert planned an excursion to a castle in which he included his sister and all his cousins. A quite natural extension to this party was Mrs. Sheffield, as his wife's particular friend, and of course her husband, sister and brother, for Miss Susan had indeed come to spend a week or so in Bath. Mr. Wesley invited Miss Henderson and her brother, though Mr. Henderson declined going, for he had business to attend to. Mr. Darnell requested that Captain Jennings also be invited, for artless as he was, he still held his friend in high regard. The dowager declared that Lady Emily should not go, though her grandsons and Miss Amberly might decide for themselves, the former being grown men, beyond the jurisdiction of their grandmother, and the latter to be under the protection of her own brother.

Other than the fact that she had to ride in a carriage with Miss Henderson, Marian found the ride rather enjoyable, for they also shared a carriage with William and Laura. Naturally, they could not speak of anything interesting in the presence of Miss Henderson, but they were a very lively party all the same. There were times when Laura was not participating in the conversation and Marian thought she looked rather preoccupied. When they finally arrived at their destination and everyone divided into pairs or threesomes, Marian was finally able to inquire into the cause.

"Indeed, Mary, I will own I am rather distressed," Laura said. "And I shall tell you why. First let me ask you—did it ever appear to you that my cousin Frederick was very fond of me?"

"Naturally," Marian said gaily. "But then I should think it very unusual for anyone *not* to be fond of you."

"Don't tease me," Laura said. "I am quite serious. But the other day I came upon him in the drawing room and he was quite alone. He asked me to come sit and talk to him, for he was feeling out of spirits. Well, he and I have talked often enough before, after dinner and at other times—but there was always someone else present. Well, at length he took my hand and—in short, he told me he loved me, and that he always has!"

"I must own I am not surprised," Marian replied. "I've always suspected a partiality. Indeed, how could it be otherwise? He has had very little social intercourse beyond our families. And you always take the time to speak to him and his sisters hardly take any notice of him when there are other young men in the room."

"But then," Laura continued, "He went on to say that he would not ask me to marry him, though he had no reason to suppose his mother would object. But that he knows he shall not live long and he would not make me a widow before I reach my majority. He told me if he knew I loved him just a little, it would be enough and he would be happy. I was more distressed at this than anything else! How could he talk so! I began weeping, and then *he* was distressed. Oh what a scene!"

"My poor cousin!" Marian said, embracing her. "And what did you say?"

"I told him that of course I was very fond of him and I had no idea he was so partial to me. I begged him not to distress himself and told him that I very much doubted I would be getting married anytime soon."

"What about Mr. Wesley?"

"What about him? I must say I like Mr. Wesley very much, but he has given me no reason to believe he has any particular regard for me. And even if he did, I'm sure I do not meet his family's expectations of his prospective bride. I am only a clergyman's daughter with five thousand pounds. He is the eldest son of a baron. Besides, did you not see him walk away with Miss Henderson?"

"With Miss Henderson!" Marian exclaimed. "No, I must own I did not. I was too concerned about you to notice Miss Henderson. And you must not be so hard upon yourself. I promise you that you are a better connection for him than Miss Henderson. His grandmother has proved she can be harder on those who have no real genteel blood than on those who have a small fortune."

"I would not wish to be the lesser of two evils," Laura said.

"My dear cousin," Marian said, "You are far from even remotely resembling evil. I'm not so sure I can say the same of Miss Henderson."

"Marian! What a thing to say!"

"You are more concerned about her than she would be about you," Marian told her. "I have no doubt she's using her arts to lure Mr. Wesley away from you. I only hope he sees through it in time."

After about an hour of exploring the castle and grounds and joining and separating from the others, Marian and Laura discovered a narrow staircase in one of the towers. When they arrived at the top, they could see the entire garden and beyond. Laura thought it was a wonderful sight and in a quieter way, Marian agreed with her. Looking down, Marian saw Miss Seldon approaching with Miss Henderson.

Marian and Laura were just preparing to descend when they heard Miss Seldon's voice echoing through the tower.

"But Miss Henderson," she said, "Why are you determined to engage all of Mr. Wesley's attention? I, for one, was quite certain he was fond of Miss Forrester. You might have taken away her best chance of a good match."

"Oh! Is that all?" was Miss Henderson's cool reply. "She may have him, if she pleases. I mean to get Lord Richard, if I can, but Mr. Wesley is a fine beau in his absence. When his lordship returns, however, Miss Forrester may have him back."

"I don't see how you can be so very heartless," Miss Seldon said. "That poor girl would be the last person in the world to give offence."

"Well, it is her fault for being so slow about getting him. If she had any sense, they would be engaged by now, and I could not have any effect on him. But if she gives him so little encouragement, is it any wonder he should look elsewhere?"

"You are being quite as thoughtless of Mr. Wesley as of Miss Forrester, I daresay," Miss Seldon said. "And I'm afraid you will not gain your end. It is surely no secret that Lord Richard is in love with Miss Amberly."

"Oh, I shall soon cure him of that," Miss Henderson said. "Besides, Miss Amberly treats him with a coolness that would quench the warmest passion, if kept up long enough. And if she is not clever enough to take advantage of her good fortune, you may depend upon it that I will be there when his lordship most wants comfort."

"You have it all planned out, I see." Marian thought she heard a little disgust in Miss Seldon's voice. Marian however, had heard enough, and began to speak to Laura rather loudly, so that the other ladies might know of their proximity. When they all met each other near the top of the stairs, they greeted each other cordially enough, though Miss Henderson's cheeks were flushed, lest she had been overheard. Marian and Laura soon continued down the stairs and when they were out of the staircase and in the garden, Marian asked Laura what she thought of Miss Henderson now?

"Do not ask me that," Laura said. "I would not wish to speak ill of anyone, no matter how they choose to speak of me. I am hurt, certainly, but truly, I pity Miss Henderson. She must be very miserable to have such wicked thoughts about people."

"You are too angelic," Marian said, embracing her. "I am more angry for you than you are for yourself, I think."

"I would not have you be angry, Mary," Laura said. "It is not worth your concern. Really, it is not."

"I believe you! I shall try to hold my tongue for your sake, but I must say she is the most designing, artful hypocrite I have ever met. I always thought it was a bad trait in a man, but you see it is far worse in a woman!"

"True hypocrites are their own worst enemies," Laura said. "They are always found out eventually. They need no help from us."

"True enough," Marian replied. They were presently joined by Captain Jennings and Mr. Darnell.

"There you are!" Captain Jennings said. "We have been searching the whole grounds for you."

"We were in the tower," Marian told him. "There is a very good view of the garden there."

"Oh, we have all the view we could desire right before us," Captain Jennings said gallantly. "Do we not, Darnell?" Mr. Darnell looked rather confused at this question so Captain Jennings spoke again. "Well, why don't you take Miss Forrester to see the chapel? I wish to speak to Miss Amberly alone." Mr. Darnell did as he was told, though he looked quite miserable to be leaving the two of them together.

"I hardly think all this ceremony necessary," Marian said. "People will talk."

"Let them talk if they will," Captain Jennings replied. "But surely you can guess why I wished to speak to you alone?"

"If you force me to guess," Marian said evasively, "I should surely draw the wrong conclusion." They sat down on a nearby bench.

"Very well, you little tormentor," Captain Jennings said. "I shall be plain. I have come to throw myself at your feet." Here, the captain got down on his knees. "Miss Amberly, I beg you to relieve my current distress and consent to marry me."

"Captain Jennings," Marian said, "I will not have you make proposals under false notions of my fortune. I might as well tell you at once that I am not to inherit my uncle's fortune, as is commonly supposed. He placed conditions on my inheriting the fortune that I did not choose to follow. Therefore my fortune will only be twenty thousand, besides whatever small amount my uncle chooses to give me. And now I give you leave to take back your proposals, as they were surely made with consideration of my fortune." Captain Jennings was completely dumfounded by this reply and could not speak or move for some minutes. He certainly did not know what to say. Fortunately for him, he was spared the necessity of a reply by an interruption. And who should it be that walked right into the middle of this scene but Lord Richard!

"Lord Richard!" Marian's astonishment was extreme. Captain Jennings quickly stood up and Lord Richard looked at the captain with an indefinable expression.

"Captain Jennings," Lord Richard said. "Will you excuse us? I have something of great importance I must speak to Miss Amberly about."

"Of course, my lord," Captain Jennings said, perhaps too awed to dare to refuse a direct request from Lord Richard, but more likely he was happy to be spared being obliged to reply to Miss Amberly's information concerning her fortune.

"What is the matter, my lord?" Marian asked. "What is so urgent you must send Captain Jennings away?"

"Can it be that you are so very sorry to see him go?" Lord Richard asked, looking at her anxiously.

"If I were," Marian replied, "Why should you be concerned about it? But pray tell me what your urgent business is with me."

"Exactly the person who we were just discussing," Lord Richard said. "Tell me, are you engaged to the man?"

"He has only just now made his proposals," Marian answered. "I have not yet given him an answer. You happened upon us during a very particular time."

"I am glad of it. But surely you do not intend to accept the man? I feel myself obliged to you both by honor and the particular regard I have for you, to tell you that this dashing young captain is a mere fortune hunter and it is your supposed inheritance he is after, with no particular regard for you."

"Is it?" Marian smiled slightly. "My, what a valuable commodity I seem to have become! It seems I have any number of admirers. However, I am glad to be informed that they are all after my money, so I shall be on my guard."

"My dear Marian," Lord Richard protested, "This is no laughing matter. I had returned to London, determined to escape you, for you seemed to like that young officer very much and I could not bear to watch you slip further and further away from me.

"But I discovered that this young man has numerous debts, which he has somehow managed to keep secret from his uncle, who is his benefactor and only chance at fortune, for he has some little property, I believe. He has made several failed attempts at marrying a fortune, including your own sister's friend, Miss Perdue.

"These discoveries made me very uneasy, and I resolved to return to Bath, where I arrived this morning, only to find you had gone. I had some conversation with my sister and was informed that Jennings' uncle is now married—to Miss Darnell's mother, no less! But at any rate, I knew that his uncle's sudden acquisition of a large number of dependents would likely make him desperate. And it is not unlikely that Mr. Cox may eventually have an heir of his own.

"However, I came directly here to warn you against accepting him. And here I am. Uncertain as I was of your feelings toward Captain Jennings, I could not bear to stand aside and watch you ruin your life, knowing his situation as I do."

"I am much obliged to your interference, I'm sure," Marian replied coolly. "And to take so much trouble to meet me here, when you might have just waited for me to return to Bath—how very kind of you!"

"How could I?" Lord Richard asked. "I could not sit idly about while that scoundrel lured you right into his trap."

"I'm sorry you doubted my good sense, your lordship. Did you suppose I would not be as thorough in considering him as I have been with others in the past? I am not such a simpleton as you may think, let me assure you."

"By 'others' I suppose you mean me. He and I are nothing alike. I love you, not your money. And I don't believe you are as indifferent to me as you would have me believe. I see you are still wearing the locket I gave you." Marian looked at her locket which she had been wearing nearly every day.

"The locket *you* gave me!" she exclaimed. "But it was from Sir E—" She stopped herself and Lord Richard frowned.

"I see!" he said. "So it is Sir Edward you pine after, and not the captain. I might have known. Solemn and passionless as he is, he is the fortunate recipient of your regard. And yet I doubt he will do you the honor of returning your sentiments, for I am afraid I must tell you he is engaged to Miss Perdue."

"I cannot believe it!" she said, after a moment of stunned silence. "I daresay you have your own reasons for telling me such a story."

"I have no reason to tell you anything but the truth," Lord Richard protested. "I have always laid my heart open to you. Why cannot you open yours to me?" He took Marian's hand and pressed it to his lips. "Surely you could never doubt *my* heart, though you may doubt others."

"I do doubt it. Why shouldn't I, given your behavior with Miss Henderson?"

"Miss Henderson! Oh, my dear Marian, please be serious! Surely you do not suppose I could think seriously of Miss Henderson while you are constantly on my mind? I should never have paid her so much attention had I not thought you wished to avoid me. But think how cold *you* have been, my dear. Whenever I speak to you, you seem to be wishing me away. Besides, it seems that Miss Henderson has made herself quite indispensable to my mother. I have my suspicions about her motives—but still, I cannot be insensible to anyone who has taken pains to entertain my mother when many others would not take the trouble." Marian could not deny the truth in this and felt a slight pang of guilt.

"Would your mother be pleased if you chose to marry Miss Henderson?"

"I cannot say for sure. My grandmother I know would have objections. But what does that matter? I do not choose to marry Miss Henderson. How could you suppose it possible, while I still cling to the hope that you will consent to be my wife?"

"Why do you persist, my lord? Have I not made myself perfectly clear? I cannot marry you."

"My heart refuses to accept such an answer. I have tried to give up hope, but I cannot. Though you may prefer Sir Edward, I know you cannot be as indifferent toward me as you would have me believe. If I am mistaken, look me in the eye and tell me so."

"It is not a matter of feeling, Lord Richard, but of trust. How can I trust you after you've shown so little concern about the feelings of Mrs. Sheffield and Miss Henderson?"

"Must a man's mistakes condemn him forever?" Lord Richard cried, exasperated. "Have I not already explained the situation concerning Mrs. Sheffield? And as for Miss Henderson, it is not me she is infatuated with—it is my title and estate. You need not pity her." He came closer and touched Marian's cheek. "Come, my love. As it appears Sir Edward is out of the question, perhaps you might reconsider me. I believe I could make you happy, if only you would give me the chance."

"I still cannot believe Sir Edward could possibly marry Miss Perdue," Marian said. "She is vulgar and insincere."

"Money is a very great attraction in society," Lord Richard told her. "And one that Miss Perdue is fairly well supplied with."

"I cannot believe that Sir Edward is mercenary," Marian insisted. "He has no reason to be, nor is it in his character."

"When you know more of the world, you may discover that those who appear to be most righteous are often the greatest hypocrites, and those who seem to have many vices are the most honest. But wait. I have something for you." He produced a letter from his pocket. "It is from your sister. She entrusted it to me when I told her I was returning to Bath. Perhaps you may believe her where you did not believe me."

"Thank you," she said, taking the letter. "I've been waiting to hear from her."

"Then I shall leave you alone to read your letter. I will be just through the hedge, guarding you from impertinent curiosity." Marian was grateful to him in spite of herself, and sat back down on the bench to read her letter."

Dear Marian,

How pleased I was to hear from you! I cannot say it has been altogether dull since you left, for Mother has taken me to a great many balls and dinners and parties. Last Monday we went to a very late breakfast at Ranelagh and at five o' clock, a Mr. Garnerin ascended into the air in a balloon. It really was quite a sight. I thought I would have liked to go in one. What a sight it must be to see London from the sky! However, I believe these amusements are not the same without you to share them with. Mother has not yet fixed upon any particular man for me to marry and I own I am not very distressed by the delay. It does get rather lonely during the day, however. Reggie is staying with our Uncle Carlyle now and John seldom comes anymore. Our uncle has made Reggie his heir now, on the agreement that Reggie will marry Miss Henderson. Reggie made no objection, but I don't know whether Miss Henderson will like it. I daresay she hopes to make a grander marriage. Arthur sometimes joins us for our evening engagements, but he has other things to do during the day. I have only been riding once since you went away. John accompanied me to Hyde Park one day, but I suppose he can hardly be expected to do it all the time. I have been spending many mornings with Miss Perdue, but you know she is not fond of riding.

Speaking of Miss Perdue, I asked her about Captain Jennings. She laughed when I asked her if he had a brother and told me he had not. It seems he is the only nephew of an old bachelor from whom he is to inherit some little property. She also said he made proposals to her last spring, but her father would not allow her to accept him. She did not break her heart about him and says that Sir Edward is much better worth her hand and fortune. She also advises you to be on your guard concerning Captain Jennings and says that you should secure Lord Richard as soon as possible. I went with her the other day to shop for wedding clothes, for you know she is to marry Sir Edward. I know you liked him very much, Marian, but I really think you ought to reconsider Lord Richard under the circumstances. I know you are fond of him, in spite of yourself, and I really do believe he could make you happy, when once you got over Sir Edward. And I really believe he loves you, for he spoke of you whenever he came to call. Mama has invited him to Rosewood for a few weeks after we return there from Ramsgate and of course he has accepted.

We shall be making preparations to go to Ramsgate soon. How I look forward to seeing you there! I would be very happy if William and Laura were to accompany you, but I suppose they are very happy with their other cousins. You must tell me if Laura is in good looks. I got the impression from her last letter that her spirits are not high. Is her romance with Mr. Wesley going badly? But of course she would say there is no romance at all. However, as I said, I cannot wait to see you in Ramsgate. Part of me will be sorry to leave London, as I am sure you will miss Bath. But what fun it will be to go sea bathing! I hear it is a very refreshing experience, once you get into the water. Give my love to Laura and William and the Misses Forrester. We shall see one another soon. Your affectionate sister,

R. Amberly

Marian could scarcely believe what she had read. Sir Edward was in fact engaged to Miss Perdue. How could that be? What could possibly have caused him to make such a decision? Surely he could never be truly happy with her. Perhaps Rachel was mistaken? No, she had her information from Miss Perdue herself. And so there it was. Marian felt a sense of despair come over her and she was forsaken by the hope that she had not even known she was clinging to. Rachel's letter fell from her loosened grip and a single tear rolled down her cheek.

After she had remained in this state for some time, Lord Richard returned. He was naturally alarmed by Marian's pale complexion, drooping shoulders and blank stare. He instantly rushed to her side and begged to know what the matter was. He received no answer, and, seeing the letter on the grass concluded that some news therein had caused this sudden loss of animation in Marian.

"Marian!" he exclaimed. "I cannot bear to see you like this. Tell me truthfully—has your sister confirmed Sir Edward's engagement? Is that the reason for this melancholy?"

"You have the letter in your hand," Marian replied. "Cannot you answer your own question?"

"You do not suppose I would read your letter without permission do you?" he asked. "I am not so dishonorable as you like to think. However, if I have your leave, and you think my reading the letter will make me understand, then I will." Marian suddenly became conscious of what Rachel had written concerning Lord Richard and took the letter from him.

"I think not, my lord," she replied. "But I cannot deny that Rachel did inform me of Sir Edward's engagement to Miss Perdue."

"And do you still pine after Sir Edward?"

"Indeed I ought not—cannot, if he is to be another lady's husband. I dare not hope that it will be broken off. Sir Edward is too honorable to jilt a lady, and Miss Perdue surely will not leave him, for she has been pursuing him ever since they met." Lord Richard was wise enough to discern that he was gaining an increasing advantage and pursued it. He took her hand and she did not resist.

"My dear Marian," he said. "Perhaps I presume too much, but I believe—that is, I flatter myself, that of all *unattached* young men, I am the one you prefer above the rest. And you know you have my entire devotion."

"My lord!" Marian exclaimed, pulling her hand away and turning from him. "Have you no modesty? Or care for mine?"

"I believe that your modesty is what so far has barred me from happiness," Lord Richard replied, seizing her hand again. "I would not distress you, but I must speak the truth. You will get over Sir Edward, and I could give you anything you desired, if you would let me. You shall be a countess, mistress of three grand estates, a leader in society—you shall have a carriage of your own, jewels, anything you could desire."

"You do not know me very well, my lord, if you suppose I am to be tempted by such offers as these. They would be enough to entice Miss Henderson, no doubt, but I am above such material considerations." Lord Richard took Marian's face in his hands.

"You shall have a husband that adores you," he said softly. "What of that? I know I could make you happy—and you could make me a better man. Indeed, I believe you have already made me a better man." He put his forehead against hers. "Oh Marian, see what a fool you've made of me? Proud as I am, you have made me grovel. Used to everything I have ever desired, you have made me desperate for what seems to elude me. Such trials may seem insignificant to you, but for me, they have been most difficult to endure, I assure you. After such sufferings, how can you deny me?"

"Indeed my lord, I do not know that I can deny you," she replied. Lord Richard kissed her.

"Oh my dear Marian!" he cried. "How I have longed to hear you say those words! Tell me again that I may know it is true."

"I have made no promises, your lordship," Marian said pulling away again. "I only mean that I do not absolutely refuse you at this time."

"When will you cease to torture me, my love?" he asked her. "Last time you refused me an answer and ended up rejecting me at last. How can I bear it again?"

"You must not force me," Marian said. "I cannot give you an answer until I have made up my own mind. I do not wish to be hasty."

"Hasty! That, I assure you, you are not! How long will you tax my forbearance? I have been more patient than I ever thought I could." Marian did not reply. He took her hand again.

"Forgive me," he said. "I know that anything worth having is worth waiting for." Just then William came upon them.

"I beg your pardon," he said, coloring and turning away from them.

"William!" Marian said, "Pray, do not go. We shall be very glad of your company, shall we not, my lord?" Lord Richard merely bowed and did not reply, for it so happened that he would *not* be very glad of another man's company at that time, no matter what the relation. What Lord Richard wished, however, was of very little consequence to William, if it conflicted with the wishes of his cousin, so he stayed.

"Everyone has been wondering where you are," William told them. "In fact, your lordship, there are several who doubt your presence here. Miss Henderson was quite certain she had seen you, though Miss Seldon did not believe her. I happened upon Captain Jennings who informed me you were both to be found at this spot. I had no idea I was interrupting a tete a tete."

"Nonsense!" Marian said, taking her cousin's arm. "No interruption could be more welcome! But perhaps we had better return to the others, before we become the objects of very scrupulous observation." They walked toward the more populated area of the park and Lord Richard had no choice but to follow.

When the time came for them all to return to Bath, Miss Henderson broadly hinted that the carriage she had come in was decidedly crowded. Lord Richard offered to remedy this by requesting that Marian ride back with him. No doubt this was not what Miss Henderson had in mind. Marian protested that she would go only if he did not plague her with undesirable subjects of conversation and on his promise that she should choose all topics they should discuss, she agreed to go with him.

The rest of Marian's week in Bath passed without much further incident. She did not see much of Captain Jennings, for he had suddenly felt a great inclination to visit his uncle and his new wife in London. Marian and Lord Richard had very few chances to be alone and Marian's brother, Arthur, came two days before Marian's departure, in order to escort her to Ramsgate. Arthur eyed Lord Richard suspiciously any time Lord Richard attempted to enter into private conversation with Marian and frequently kept Marian's attention to himself.

Marian was not sorry to be prevented from having much private discussion with Lord Richard, for there was something in her heart that kept her from wishing to give his lordship a definite answer to his proposal. The day of departure came at last and just outside the carriage, Lord Richard managed a few private words to Marian while Arthur was taking leave of the others.

"I shall come to Ramsgate as soon as I can get away," he told her. "And then I shall speak to your father."

"Oh, my lord—" Marian began to protest.

"Pray, don't use such a formal address to me anymore," Lord Richard said. "If we are to be married, you must learn to call me 'Richard,' or 'my love,' if you will, but no longer 'my lord,' or 'your lordship.' And it is madness to put the marriage off for so long. Now that buffoon Jennings knows that you are no longer your uncle's heiress, it is only a matter of time before word gets 'round to the Dowager and she will make objections. If we are safely married before she knows, she cannot attempt to stop it."

"I would not wish to marry you against your family's wishes."

"All will be well, my love," he said, taking her hand. "The dowager will get over it and my mother and sister will have no objection. My father is too involved with his own concerns to care. I shall be at Ramsgate within a fortnight. In the meantime—" He kissed her hand. "I shall write to you and dare to hope you may write to me."

Arthur returned and Lord Richard handed Marian into the carriage. As soon as they were on their way, Arthur began questioning his sister about Lord Richard's attentions.

"Mary, what was Lord Richard saying to you just now?"

"He was only taking leave of me," Marian replied, trying to sound unaffected. "It is possible he may soon come to Ramsgate."

"Oh Marian, I thought we were rid of his company for some time," Arthur said. "And you—I thought you were above taking such attentions as his seriously. What can you be thinking?"

"Perhaps he is not as undeserving as I thought at first," Marian said. "He has many good qualities—and the match would make my mother happy."

"But would it make *you* happy?" Arthur asked her. "Furthermore, I know what kind of character he is. He is not the marrying type. Oh he may marry by the time he is our father's age, only to produce an heir, once he is past his youth. But he is too successful in his amorous conquests to think of settling with only one woman. I have often heard him boast about how he made this lady or that lady in love with him."

"Perhaps he has changed," Marian replied. "Many people make mistakes in their youth."

"Oh Mary, I have dreaded this!" Arthur exclaimed. "I never would have thought *you* could be so blind to your own danger! And do you flatter yourself he will marry you? Has he made you any proposals?" Marian did not reply. "He is a rake, Marian. He will no doubt marry some heiress who is of noble blood."

"I do not wish to continue this conversation, if you please," Marian said

angrily. "I hope you did not volunteer to fetch me just so you could lecture me."

"Very well," Arthur said. "But don't be surprised if all turns out badly."

"Thank you, Arthur. I shall consider myself warned." The remainder of the trip was a somewhat silent one as Arthur did not bring up the subject of Lord Richard again, though it pressed heavily on his mind. He was very anxious for the emotional well-being of his sister, as he was very fond of her. He did not like to think that her spirit would be broken because of Lord Richard's carelessness.

Marian and Arthur were both relieved when their journey came to an end and Rachel and Marian were very happy to be reunited after a month's separation—the longest separation they had endured for two years.

"Oh Marian," Rachel said, "I am afraid that Ramsgate is a dreadfully dull place after London and, I daresay, Bath. It is considerably more quiet, I think. There are fewer balls and parties and there is not as much variety in the shops. There is to be an assembly on Wednesday and Sarah says she shall give a ball when the count is returned in a few weeks or a month. I suspect Sarah will invite you and me to stay with her for a week or two, though Father says he prefers to stay in our lodgings in the town."

"How came Reggie to be here instead of in London with Uncle Carlyle?" Marian asked.

"Our uncle fancied the London air was disagreeable to Reggie and sent him to the sea hoping it would do him good. They are to return to London together after Uncle Carlyle's visit to Rosewood."

"I suppose our uncle is not yet acquainted with Reggie's taciturn disposition."

"What of Lord Richard?" Rachel asked. "Are you engaged to him yet?"

"Somehow I cannot bring myself to give him a definite answer," Marian said. "Yet I do not know how much longer I can avoid it. I cannot deny he has very patient. He says he will come to Ramsgate and wishes to speak to Father. What am I to do?"

"I cannot make your decision for you," Rachel said. "But if Mama hears of it, she will surely oblige you to accept him."

"Mama cannot force me to accept him. She can only advise me. Anyway, I suppose I shall accept him, since Sir Edward is to marry Miss Perdue."

"If we cannot have our first choice," Rachel said, "I suppose it is best to accept our second."

On Tuesday, Lady Amberly took her daughters sea-bathing and then they went shopping before returning to their lodgings to prepare for dinner. They were to dine with Sarah at Fort de Mar, a few miles out of town. Reggie was aloof, as usual, and Arthur was in a fairly amiable mood. Arthur and Sarah had always been close and Arthur naturally looked forward to seeing Sarah. He would find some time for a private conversation with Sarah concerning the state of their younger sister's heart and whether it was truly affected by a rascal such as Lord Richard.

Marian also looked forward to a conversation with her elder sister about the same subject—the state of her heart. She wished very much to consult with her older, more experienced sister on what she ought to do concerning Lord Richard.

When they arrived at Fort de Mar, Sarah was not alone, as expected. The Hendersons were present, and it was soon discovered that they were there on a visit for a few weeks, at least until the count was returned. Besides this, Mr. Henderson hinted that Mr. Carlyle had told Miss Henderson about his plan for her to marry Reginald and inherit the bulk of his fortune, and so Mr. Henderson had brought his sister to Ramsgate so that she might become better acquainted with her intended. But he added to Marian, when he thought no one was listening, that he could not deny he had another reason for coming to Ramsgate—that he wanted to see her out of the company of her several suitors. He did not completely despair, he said, of gaining her favor.

"But you have nothing to gain by such a pursuit," Marian said haughtily. "My uncle already plans to leave his estate to Reggie."

"I believe we may make him change his mind back," Mr. Henderson replied with a wave of his hand. "After all, it was his dearest wish, once."

"In any case I cannot marry you," Marian said, thoroughly disgusted. "You and I are completely incompatible. Besides, I—am already engaged." She spoke the words before she realized what she was saying, for she still did not quite consider herself as engaged. It was *almost* true, however, and that was quite good enough for putting Mr. Henderson off. Mr. Henderson's expression went from lazy assurance to extreme consternation at her declaration.

"Engaged!" He exclaimed. "To whom?"

"I am by no means obliged to relate my affairs to you," Marian said. "Nor do I choose to make it public at this time."

"It's not that milksop of a midshipman is it?" Mr. Henderson demanded.

"If it were," Marian said, bristling, "It is nothing to you. And I would ask you not to speak so slightingly of my friends. Mr. Darnell is a very good, kind young man. He has grown up very well, considering his circumstances."

"His circumstances, as I understand them, are that he is a poor, fatherless sea officer of the lowest kind, who lacks the connections to become even a lieutenant."

"If that were the case, it ought to excite your compassion, not your contempt."

"I see it has excited your compassion," Mr. Henderson said. "Well enough for you to bestow your hand on such a vagabond. For now I see plainly enough he is the one you spoke of." Marian stood up, curtseyed and walked away.

After dinner, Sarah made up a card-table with herself, Sir John, Lady Amberly and Arthur. Mr. Henderson and Rachel played Backgammon and Reggie and Miss Henderson were sitting near one another, attempting conversation, but not getting on well. Marian was playing with her niece and nephews, whom the nurse had brought in for a short visit, on Sarah's request.

Sir John smiled fondly at them, as they were his only grandchildren so far. He did not wish to interrupt Sarah's card-table, however, and so did not leave his seat. After the nurse had taken them away again, Sarah said, "I really ought to invite William and Laura for a few weeks after their visit to the Forresters is over. What do you think?"

"I think it is a very good idea," Marian replied.

"I think so much time away from home will spoil the poor child," Lady Amberly said. "We all know that, with her fortune, she is very likely destined to be a country parson's wife. A little amusement is all very well, but if she becomes too accustomed to it, she may become dissatisfied with her lot in life. She has been in London and Bath and was she not here already this year?"

"One might think you begrudge Laura her season of enjoyment, Mama," Marian said. "Have I not been in London and Bath already this year? And am I not in Ramsgate now? Yet that is perfectly acceptable to you."

"That is different," Lady Amberly replied. "I have no doubt you will be a great lady and will spend a great deal of time in London and Bath."

"Mama!"

"Nay, I shan't say his name since it distresses you, but I believe most of us in the room know to whom I am referring." There was an uncomfortable silence and Marian was distressed and Miss Henderson and Arthur both wore darkened expressions.

"I think Laura enjoyed her time here very much," Marian said finally. "And I for one will be very glad to see both her and William and their addition surely could not make our family parties *less* agreeable, though they may very well make them *more* so."

"Yes, I agree," Sarah said. "Laura is far too sensible to be truly harmed by an extended season of entertainment. Besides, if it is as you say, ma'am," turning to Lady Amberly, "it is best to let her enjoy her youth before she must settle down into a less eventful life."

"You may do as you please," Lady Amberly replied. "I shan't tell you whom you may and may not invite to your own house."

"I know your advice was most kindly meant, ma'am," Sarah said diplomatically. "But think of it—if she went back to the country, she would be very lonely. Most of her cousins are away. She would have no one to keep her company."

"They shall not be always living at home," Lady Amberly said. "But I have no wish to argue about it."

When the evening was drawing to a close and Sarah and Marian were a little separate from the others, Sarah asked Marian if Lady Amberly had been referring to Lord Richard earlier.

"I'm certain she was," Marian said with a blush. "And that is just what I wished to speak to you about. What shall I do? I cannot deny I have some measure of feeling for his lordship, but shall I make myself miserable in marrying him? For he has made marriage proposals, despite what Arthur may think about it."

"Arthur fears that Lord Richard has been insincere," Sarah said, "and that your happiness would be doubtful even if his lordship were sincere."

"I very nearly accepted him," Marian said. "And he seems to think I have. For he vows he will come to Ramsgate and speak to Father. But something in my heart tells me to withhold my hand and heart a little longer. Yet how can I go on like this?"

"If his lordship is indeed sincere," Sarah replied, "And if he has been very patient, then you surely must give him an answer by the end of the week. If you remain in doubt of your heart, you had better deny him."

"You are right, of course," Marian said, unwilling to admit even to herself that the cause of her hesitation was a lingering hope that Sir Edward might not marry Miss Perdue after all. "Shall you be at the assembly tomorrow?"

"I believe I shall." Sarah smiled. "I must chaperone my young guests, I suppose."

"I shall think about it again tonight." But how could Marian become any more certain of what she ought to do? Could she throw away her last chance of happiness because she had lost another? It was a very difficult decision indeed.

CHAPTER THIRTEEN

When they arrived at the assembly rooms on Wednesday night, it was considerably more crowded than Marian had expected. For this reason, she was all the more surprised to see someone outside of her own party with whom she was acquainted, and certainly not someone she expected to meet in Ramsgate. It was Sir Walter Lovell, and he was coming towards them.

"Oh good heavens!" Marian exclaimed before Sir Walter was in earshot. "What on earth is he doing here?"

"Do you know him?" Rachel asked. Before Marian had a chance to answer, Sir Walter was before them. He immediately expressed his satisfaction at meeting Marian there and inquired after her health.

"Mama, Rachel," Marian said, "May I present Sir Walter Lovell?"

"Sir Walter is it?" Lady Amberly replied. "And may I ask how you are acquainted with my daughter, sir?"

"I had the pleasure of meeting Miss Amberly in Bristol, ma'am," Sir Walter replied. "And I look forward to becoming acquainted with her family."

"And are you here with friends or family?" Lady Amberly asked.

"I have one or two friends in Ramsgate," Sir Walter replied, "But here at the assembly, I am quite alone."

"And are you here for society or your health?"

"Both, I may say," Sir Walter replied, with a slight smile. "There are many kinds of health to be taken into consideration."

"I see," Lady Amberly replied. "And look—here comes my daughter-in-law, the Countess de Roche." Sarah had just come in with Mr. and Miss Henderson and was coming towards them. More introductions took place and while Sir Walter was busy charming the other ladies, Mr. Henderson lost no time in requesting Marian to dance with him. Marian accepted, for even the gallant stupidity of Mr. Henderson was to be preferred to the rakish attentions of Sir Walter.

Sir Walter, meanwhile, danced with Rachel and when both girls were returned to their mother, Sir Walter attempted to engage Marian for the next two dances. Marian declined dancing those two dances, hoping that Sir Walter would be discouraged enough to go away.

Sir Walter was not discouraged, however, and contented himself with exercising his powers of pleasing on the ladies present and was invited by Lady Amberly to attend them to the tea-room. Sir John joined them from the card-room but made no comment on Sir Walter's presence. Sarah also said nothing, and only observed this young man's calculated attentions to Marian. Sir Walter, scoundrel though he was, certainly knew how to make himself agreeable. Lady Amberly was quite charmed and would only wait until she knew more of his situation before urging him in the direction of Rachel, for Marian she considered as already spoken for by Lord Richard.

After tea, Sir Walter again importuned Marian to dance, and she really felt she must accept him, or she would be forced to sit out the whole evening. Besides, one of the dances was to be the Boulanger and they would be constantly changing partners.

"At last I have an opportunity of speaking to you alone," Sir Walter said.

"And why would you need such an opportunity, Sir Walter?" Marian asked. "We have been acquainted so short a time that you can hardly have anything to say to me that anyone else may not hear."

"If you think so, you do not know the impression you have made on my heart."

"If you think to impress me with these exaggerated gallantries of yours, then I must warn you, you are wasting your time."

"Charming, even as she plunges a dagger into my heart!" Sir Walter exclaimed. They were separated by a movement in the dance during which she could only wonder what his intentions truly were. She immediately discounted all of his claims of admiration, but it was possible he still thought her fortune much larger than it really was. She knew he sought to marry a lady of fortune.

"Well," Marian said, when she returned to Sir Walter, "I trust you will get over it soon enough. I have never been one for idle flirtation. If such empty professions are what you wish, I might direct you in a more profitable direction."

"Idle flirtation! Miss Amberly, you misunderstand me."

"Oh? Then pray, tell me your meaning."

"My meaning?" Sir Walter seemed a little confused. "I only sought to improve my acquaintance with you. Is that so very unbelievable?" They separated again before Marian had a chance to answer and she found herself face to face with Sir Edward Sheffield!

"Sir Edward!" she exclaimed in a voice hardly above a whisper. "What are you doing here?"

"Miss Amberly!" Sir Edward said. "Might we discuss my motives for being here at a more private time?"

"I—I—yes, of course," Marian faltered. "Forgive me. I did not expect—" She grew pale and gripped Sir Edward's hand tighter, for she felt as though she might faint.

"Miss Amberly, are you feeling well?"

"I don't quite know," Marian said, rather distracted. "I'm not sure what I feel." The dance separated them again and she returned to her partner.

"Sir Walter," she said. "I feel rather faint. I think I must sit down." They left the dance and Sir Walter went to fetch Marian something to drink.

"What is the matter, Dearest?" Lady Amberly asked. "Are you ill?"

"Only a little shocked," Marian answered. "I saw Sir Edward Sheffield."

"Why should that be so very shocking?" Marian didn't answer.

"Mama, she is already distressed," Rachel said. "Would it not be best to refrain from questions which will distress her more?"

"My dear," Lady Amberly said, ignoring Rachel. "Why should you be concerned with Sir Edward when you already have a much greater conquest?"

"Sir Walter is hardly a great conquest," Marian mumbled.

"I'm not talking about Sir Walter, you silly girl," Lady Amberly said. "I'm talking of Lord Richard, of course." Sir Walter returned with some refreshments and engaged the others in conversation while Marian tried to sort out her emotions.

Very soon after the set of dances was over, Sir Edward himself came over to their party. He expressed real concern for Marian's well-being, which made the sense of what she had lost much more acute. Sir Walter regarded him with jealous suspicion, but Sir Edward took no notice of this. After Marian assured him she was quite well and only needed a rest, Sir Edward seemed a little more at ease. Marian inquired after Miss Sheffield and Miss Perdue, both of whom were very well. They were still in Bath, but were to join him at the end of the week.

"Are you here alone?" Marian asked him.

"I came to the assembly with Mr. Perdue and his youngest daughter," Sir Edward replied. "It was Miss Fanny whom I was dancing with just now. She is Miss Perdue's sister."

"What is she like?"

"Very shy," Sir Edward replied. "She has not been out long. She is just sixteen, I believe. She is very different from her sister."

"Oh, Sir Edward," Marian said finally. "May I offer you my congratulations?"

"Congratulations?" Sir Edward repeated. "What for?"

"Your engagement, of course," Marian replied. "To Miss Perdue." Sir Edward looked so puzzled that Marian was extremely vexed with Sir Walter for interrupting the conversation by attempting to re-engage her to dance. He said that it was only fair, for they had left during the dance. She wanted very much to decline, but could not bear that Sir Edward should think she had very bad manners.

"You seem displeased," Sir Walter said as he led Marian back to the dance.

"I am," Marian said frankly. She did not care how rude she seemed to Sir Walter. "Your interruption was a most untimely one."

"I beg your pardon, Miss Amberly," Sir Walter replied. "I had no idea I was contributing to your displeasure. I will make every endeavor not to repeat the offense." Marian did not answer. "Pray, who is Miss Perdue?"

"She is a young lady of larger fortune than mine," Marian answered, seizing the opportunity of ridding Sir Walter of his sudden and mercenary infatuation with her. "For she is to have seventy-five thousand pounds and I am only to have twenty. I suppose she is to be here at the end of the week." Marian could hardly hope that Miss Perdue would exchange Sir Edward for Sir Walter, but Sir Walter could very well drop Marian in hopeless pursuit of Miss Perdue.

"Perhaps a greater monetary fortune," Sir Walter replied. "But there are other things to be taken into consideration." Marian was surprised at this reply and reflected that Sir Walter might be a rake, but he was certainly clever enough not to discard one prospect before he was sure of a better one. If only he applied such prudence to his spending habits, he might not need to marry for money at all.

Just because Sir Walter envisioned a better prospect for himself, there was no reason he could not make himself agreeable to the young lady who was present. Besides, he was not yet acquainted with this Miss Perdue and he would need a medium through which to be introduced to her.

When they returned from the dance, Sir Edward had gone back to his party and Marian was distressed to hear from Rachel that Lady Amberly had thrown out several broad hints about Marian and Lord Richard. She was somewhat appeased by Rachel's informing her he might possibly call tomorrow, but even that did not relieve Marian of her vexation with her mother.

The next morning, Sir Edward called on Marian and proposed a walk a short time into the visit. Arthur walked with Rachel and Marian walked with Sir Edward
"Pray, Miss Amberly," Sir Edward said when they were alone. "What sort of man is this Sir Walter?"

"I know little of him myself." Marian hesitated. "I understand he is an extravagant spender and quite a rake. He is no particular acquaintance of mine, though he pretends to be."

"I only ask because he was introduced to Miss Fanny last night and she danced with him," Sir Edward said. "She is a very impressionable girl and she seemed charmed by him. I only wondered whether I ought to caution her father against him."

"It would be advisable," Marian replied. "He is just the sort of man young girls ought to be protected from."

"Thank you for your information," Sir Edward said. Neither one of them spoke for a few moments, though Marian tried to think of something to say. At last Sir Edward spoke again. "I understand Lord Richard is to be joining you this week."

"He—I believe he said he might come to Ramsgate soon." Marian blushed and Sir Edward gazed at her thoughtfully. He stopped and Marian studied the ground.

"What kind of man would you say Lord Richard is?" Sir Edward asked. "Is he the sort young ladies ought to be protected from?"

"He is certainly not like Sir Walter, if that's what you mean," Marian said, a little defensively. She looked up. "I believe even Lord Richard has principles which Sir Walter does not. And he is certainly no fortune hunter."

"If I have upset you, I apologize," Sir Edward said. Marian did not reply, but returned her gaze to the ground. She could hardly bear to look into the penetrating eyes of Sir Edward. She was surprised when he suddenly seized her hand. "Miss Amberly, forgive me if I seem too forward, but what exactly is the nature of the relationship between you and Lord Richard? I must know—are you engaged to him?"

"I—I hardly know," she said. "I'm not engaged to him. That is, he has made proposals, but I have not answered him, because—" She could not tell him why. "I know he expects an answer, but—no, we are not engaged."

"What chance do I stand against Lord Richard?" Sir Edward asked at last. Marian noticed he was still holding her hand. "Do I dare to hope that I am the cause of your hesitation in accepting him? I hardly know how to believe that is the case, but my heart refuses to give up hope, though my reason may declare otherwise." He stepped closer and put his hand on her cheek. "Is it possible you could care for me at all? Is it possible you should care enough to agree to marry me?" Marian could scarcely believe what she was hearing and dared not believe it.

"I can hardly believe you are in earnest, Sir Edward," Marian replied, scarcely able to breathe.

"Indeed I am," Sir Edward said. "I have spent many weeks uncertain of your feelings toward me. Uncertain of where Lord Richard stands in your heart. I know I'm no lord, but I cannot let this opportunity escape me while I have it. I must know for certain if it is indeed in vain that I ask you to marry me."

"But are you not engaged to Miss Perdue? I don't understand how Miss Perdue could believe herself engaged to you, as she clearly does, if it were not so."

"I have never proposed to Miss Perdue, or any other young lady, before today," Sir Edward answered. "My sister has always attempted to make me believe I ought to marry Miss Perdue, but I have always resisted. I respect Miss Perdue very much, and I wish her well, but I do not love her. I have always tried to be considerate of her, and as she is a constant companion of my sister's, I can understand why an outsider might suppose more than there is. But I have always thought of her as just that—my sister's friend."

"Did you ever pay her very marked attentions?"

"Not intentionally. Nothing beyond what I felt was expected of me. If she misconstrued my meaning, it must be due to my sister's encouraging expectations which I cannot fulfill."

"Perhaps that was why Miss Sheffield was always encouraging my marriage to Lord Richard," Marian said. "She was always telling me I ought to marry him."

"My sister was always one for prying into the affairs of others," Sir Edward replied. "Especially to meet her own ends. It was she who helped convince me that you were engaged to Lord Richard. I saw that Lord Richard certainly paid you a great deal of attention, but I could not be sure it was more than an idle flirtation. My sister insisted it was more, as if you had confided in her. There were some times when I thought you were encouraging me, but I thought you were already engaged and—I'm ashamed to say—I thought you were playing the coquette and I grew very irritated. I realize now it was only jealousy that I could not believe it was more than that."

"And what made you change your mind about my coquetry?"

"When I arrived at Bath on Saturday Miss Seldon told me you were not engaged to Lord Richard," Sir Edward told her. "Had I already known that, I might have come to Bath sooner, in hopes of meeting you. As it was, I wished to avoid you and any unnecessary pain. As soon as Miss Seldon and George Wesley were married, I resolved to follow you here and see what my hopes of success were. I had the additional excuse of coming ahead to procure lodgings before my sister comes with Miss Perdue on

Saturday. But last night at the ball I was thrown into confusion again, for your mother seemed to think of your engagement to Lord Richard as quite a certain thing."

"Oh yes. My mother is quite determined on the match. But I shan't base my life decisions on her wishes. My father, I assure you, will be more reasonable."

"Now that explanations have been given, do you accept my proposal?"

"Yes," Marian replied, scarcely able to conceal her happiness. "I do accept."

The rest of their party had wandered a good ways before they noticed that Marian and Sir Edward had disappeared. When they finally found them again, there was a very suspicious glow in the faces of the unannounced lovers. Rachel looked questioningly at Marian, for she could not imagine what would make Marian so happy when Sir Edward was engaged to Miss Perdue.

When they arrived at their lodgings, Sir Edward went to speak to Marian's father and the footman presented a letter to Marian. First, however, Marian recounted the conversation to Rachel, which she did as soon as Sir Edward was out of the room. Rachel, of course, was all astonishment and felt very concerned for Miss Perdue.

"She bought her wedding clothes and everything!" Rachel said. "I'm very happy you got what you wanted, of course, but it's very hard not to feel that Miss Perdue has been very ill used. What a shocking disappointment for her!"

"Perhaps she was ill used," Marian conceded. "But if so, it was not by Sir Edward, but his sister. She has very likely been convincing her friend that Sir Edward's attentions meant more than they really did."

"Well I have no doubt that Lord Richard will think himself ill used," Rachel said. "For if it is as you say, and he has gone to fetch his lawyer, he has been making wedding preparations as certainly as Miss Perdue. What shall you do when he arrives?"

"I don't know," Marian admitted. "But Rachel, do try not to be very angry with me for agreeing to marry Sir Edward."

"I'm not angry," Rachel protested. "I only worry about what others will think. And I can't deny I'm a little sad for Miss Perdue and Lord Richard. But I am really happy for you. Truly I am." She embraced Marian and Marian had to believe her.

"Now," Marian said, "All that is left is to break it to Mama."

Lady Amberly took the news much as was to be expected. But as she was not aware that Lord Richard had ever made any actual proposals and Sir Edward had a large estate and Marian would still be called "my lady," she was tolerably consoled. After this great feat was accomplished, Sir Edward went to call on Mr. Perdue and inform him of his engagement before his eldest daughter came to Ramsgate and stirred up false and mistaken impressions. Sir Edward was to return for dinner, and meanwhile Marian went to console herself with her letter, which was really no consolation at all, for it was from Lord Richard.

My Dearest Marian,

How I have missed you these few days! But I find comfort in the thought that we shall soon be permanently united. I am in London now but I shall make my way to Ramsgate soon. I shall be there perhaps late Thursday night. I shall call on you Friday morning and hope that I may speak to your father. I have been consulting with my lawyer, who shall accompany me to Ramsgate. I do not think Sir John will find anything in the settlement not to his liking.

I have been extremely busy this week. George was married yesterday morning, and I rode straight to London from there. You will probably not receive this letter much sooner than I shall arrive myself, but I was strongly inclined to write to you. I hope you don't think it too impetuous of me. That is all I have to say for the present. I have to settle several business affairs while I'm in town. I have no social engagements. I only long to return to you. Until Friday, then, think of me at least half as often as I think of you. Eternally Yours,

R. Beauregard

Sir Edward called on Friday morning and proposed a walk. Lady Amberly declared herself not unwilling and Marian was eager to be out of the house in case Lord Richard should call. Rachel, Arthur and Reggie also came as a matter of course. The party had hardly stepped out of the front door when they saw Lord Richard coming toward the house. He stopped when he saw them, gave a look of alarm to Marian, who was holding the arm of Sir Edward and asked whither they were all going.

"Lord Richard!" Lady Amberly exclaimed, looking somewhat confused. "I did not know you were coming to Ramsgate."

"Did Mar—Miss Amberly not tell you?" he asked. "I thought she might have mentioned it. Or perhaps she has had more important matters to think about." He gave Marian such a look of cold displeasure that she would have never have expected from him. She looked away.

"Now that I think of it," Lady Amberly replied, "I do believe she mentioned that you might *possibly* be coming sometime. But we were just starting out for a walk. Will you not join us?"

"Thank you, ma'am," Lord Richard replied gallantly. "I think I shall." He was very silent during the walk, however, and hardly anyone else ventured into conversation except Lady Amberly, who could very gaily make small talk in any situation.

Lord Richard attempted to separate Marian from the others, but she would not allow herself to be separated from Sir Edward.

"Did you leave everybody well in Bath?" Marian asked him at last.

"Yes, everyone was very well," Lord Richard replied.

"Mr. and Miss Henderson are on a visit to Sarah," Marian said. "And we shall soon be receiving other friends here. Sarah has also invited William and Laura to stay with her. And Miss Sheffield and Miss Perdue will be here tomorrow."

"And did you not see fit to escort them here, Sir Edward?" Lord Richard asked. "I'm sure if two women so dear to me were to be travelling, I would not let them go alone."

"My brother Lionel is to escort them here and return to Bath on Monday," Sir Edward answered, taking no notice of Lord Richard's tone of contempt. "And surely, your lordship, yours is not one of those weak minds that sees an attachment where there is none? You of all people ought to know that common courtesies and good manners are not always acts of love." Lord Richard paled at the implication.

"When a man shows such pointed marks of attention so that all of society expects an engagement," Lord Richard retorted, "It is not honorable for that man to shirk his duty by refusing to marry the young lady in question, as his attentions may have kept other suitors away."

"No doubt those sort of scruples are what you are counting on," Sir Edward replied. "But I assure you I paid no attention to Miss Perdue that was not due to a guest in my house. There will always be those with malicious tongues, but I assure you I do not care for such idle gossips and I shall not allow them to run my life."

"What about the expectations of the young lady?" Lord Richard asked. "I suppose her feelings are not to be taken into account?"

"If she has formed a mistaken impression, I am sorry for it," Sir Edward replied. "But as it was done without any encouragement from me, I cannot hold myself accountable."

"I wish I could relieve myself so easily from my responsibilities!" Lord Richard exclaimed.

"Perhaps we had better turn back to the house," Marian said, not wishing the young men to provoke one another any further.

"Yes," Lord Richard agreed. "I have something to speak to Sir John about." Marian was alarmed by this but as she could not do anything about it, she said nothing.

When they had returned to the house, Lord Richard went into Sir John's study and Marian expressed her apprehensions to Sir Edward.

"Lord Richard will think himself very ill used," Marian said. "I never absolutely said I would marry him, but he clearly chose to take it so. I'm sure my father will be very perplexed at receiving two requests for my hand in the same week."

"Lord Richard must learn not to assume everybody is at his disposal," Sir Edward said. "He is far too used to getting his own way."

"But do you suppose others will think so ill of us?" Marian asked. "If it is indeed so generally expected for me to marry Lord Richard and you to marry Miss Perdue, will they not think we have shamelessly jilted them?"

"Well they can hardly accuse us of jilting them for material gain," Sir Edward assured her. "Lord Richard has a higher rank and more estates than I and Miss Perdue's fortune is larger than yours. Those with honest minds will have no choice but to conclude that there was never any sort of understanding between Miss Perdue and myself or you and Lord Richard. As for the rest of the world—well I don't really care about them, and neither should you, my dear. Idle tongues will soon find another subject for their derision." Lord Richard returned to the drawing-room came over to Marian, looked as if he would say something, but did not. At last he took leave of them and left.

A footman came in and informed Marian that her father wished to see her.

"Well, my dear," Sir John said when Marian entered his study. "I was under the impression that once I had granted one young man permission to marry you, I would not be petitioned by another. But now, you see, Lord Richard has come asking for your hand and, moreover, informing me that he has a prior claim, for he says you have already accepted him." Marian colored. "My dear, you know I only wish to see you well-settled and happy. Only tell me at once which of these young men you prefer and we will get the matter settled. But it will never do for you to be engaged to two young men at once. It is not modest, you know."

"I was never actually engaged to Lord Richard," Marian replied at last. "He did ask me to marry him, but I told him I would think about it. He chose to believe I accepted him simply because I had not given him an absolute refusal. However, I have accepted Sir Edward and it is him I wish to marry."

"Very well," Sir John said. "Sir Edward seems a very good, moral young man. I don't know how much I would have liked you to be among the very high society. There is a great deal that goes on there that ought not to. But you shall have to inform his lordship of your decision."

"Did you not tell him then?"

"I was so surprised by Lord Richard's application for your hand that I did not know what to say. I supposed he had had sufficient encouragement to justify it so I told him I would speak to you about it. He seemed very out of spirits. Usually he is so eager to please everybody. I hope you have not permanently damaged his cheerful manners."

Marian went to her room to write the following note to Lord Richard:

Dear Sir,

I am obliged to inform you that after this note it will not be appropriate for us to exchange correspondence. I was engaged to Sir Edward yesterday morning. He is not engaged to Miss Perdue as you informed me. I am certain that, as a man of honor, you will not press the matter. I do not blame you, for Miss Perdue herself was misled by persons other than Sir Edward. I wish you well and I hope you will learn to reconcile yourself to your disappointment.

Marian Amberly

Marian entrusted the note to Arthur, who was to pay a visit to Lord Richard. Arthur was naturally suspicious, but when Marian assured him that the note would ensure that Lord Richard would cease his particular attentions to her, Arthur agreed to take it.

When Arthur returned later, he seemed deep in thought and Marian asked him privately how Lord Richard had received her letter.

"In truth, Marian, I do believe that perhaps he truly loved you," Arthur said. "I had always doubted the seriousness of his attentions, for he always was a rake, but I do believe he had some feeling."

"What did he say?" Marian asked.

"It was a more a matter of what he *did*," Arthur replied. "He crumpled up the paper and put his hand on his head. He was completely silent for a few minutes and then, without warning, he went into a passion and began throwing things about the room, shouting incoherent things all the while. He overturned a table, threw a chair at the wall and set about abusing the dresser. Then he leaned his back on the wall, slumped down to the floor and buried his face in his hands."

"Good heavens!" Marian exclaimed. "Do you know what was in the letter?"

"Yes, I saw it."

"You saw it!"

"Why yes," Arthur said. "For he sat there for rather a long time before I finally asked him what had made him so angry and he told me to read the letter. So I did, for I own I was very curious. I was a great deal puzzled by it and I asked if he had made you proposals and he replied that he had offered you his hand and fortune and anything you could possibly wish for and in return you ripped out his heart and threw it in his face."

"He must be very angry to make such remarks," Marian said. "But, Arthur, knowing as you do now that his attentions were serious, do you think I ought to have accepted him?"

"No, I think you were right to refuse him," Arthur said. "Perhaps his attentions to you were honorable, but they have not been so toward every woman. Lord Richard is accustomed to getting everything he wants. His fit of passion earlier was probably due to his inexperience in being denied anything. I think you are much better suited to Sir Edward."

"I always liked Edward, you know. Even before he became a baronet. But he was always so polite to me and everyone that I could never tell his feelings. Then last week Lord Richard told me Edward was engaged to Miss Perdue and I came very close to agreeing to marry Lord Richard. But still I hesitated."

"Well, it has been for the better. And I'm sure you will be very happy."

On Saturday, Miss Sheffield came to dinner with her brother. Lady Amberly had invited Miss Perdue and Lord Richard but they had declined. Miss Perdue sent the excuse that she had not seen her father and sister for some time and could not possibly leave them on her first night with them. Lord Richard sent no excuse at all. Sarah came with Mr. and Miss Henderson. Sarah warmly offered her congratulations and Miss Henderson was scarcely less elated, for Marian's engagement to Sir Edward meant that she was no longer Miss Henderson's rival for Lord Richard's hand and perhaps now Lord Richard was in need of a pleasant young lady to be conveniently in his way. Mr. Henderson received the news with a very sullen expression and could hardly be induced into conversation the rest of the evening.

"Miss Amberly," Miss Sheffield said, taking Marian's arm. "Or I suppose I may call you Marian, since we are to be sisters. And you must call me Catherine, or Cathy, if you choose. What a wonderful thing that you should be engaged to my brother! I never would have expected it. I thought you were engaged to Lord Richard."

"I'm afraid you were mistaken," Marian said. "It seems there have been a great many misunderstandings in this whole business."

"Well I'm sure I was not mistaken about Lord Richard's attentions," Miss Sheffield replied. "I feel quite certain he would have made you an offer soon, for he certainly shows all the symptoms of love. And to be sure, *I* shan't blame you if you should marry him after all, for I certainly would if I were in your situation."

"What kind feelings you have toward your brother!" Marian exclaimed, trying to make light of Catherine's unfeeling speeches. "Would you have me jilt Sir Edward and break his heart?"

"Oh, as to that, he will get over it soon enough," Miss Sheffield said. "He would be rather piqued, to be sure, but I don't believe he would break his heart about it. He is too serious to have very deep feelings."

"I'm sure you're wrong. I cannot believe his feelings are not strong."

"Do you suppose you know my brother better than I?" Catherine asked. "But you may believe what you choose." It was impossible that Marian should not be made uncomfortable by such a conversation, but she endeavored to forget it and to remind herself that her sister elect wanted Sir Edward to marry her friend.

Sarah invited the whole family to stay with her at Fort de Mar, for it made no sense, she said, to pay rent for a house when she could quite comfortably fit them all. Sir John protested that he must be near the bathing machines in case he should wish to go, but the children might go to Fort de Mar if they chose. Lady Amberly, however, agreed with Sarah's argument and it did not take long to convince Sir John that Fort de Mar was so close to town that they might walk, and if they came by carriage it would take no time at all. Besides, Sir John preferred the country to town and was he not tired of being confined to the limited space of a house in town? Lady Amberly knew well enough how to work on her husband to get what she wanted. Sir John agreed at last that it would be pleasant to be in the country. So it was arranged that they would all go to Fort de Mar the following Monday.

Sir Edward and Miss Sheffield were also invited. Sir Edward would have declined, not wishing to impose, had he not been informed that Sarah had already invited Lord Richard when she found he was in town. Miss Sheffield declined, saying she would stay with Miss Perdue. Marian was not altogether sorry for this, for Miss Sheffield's company was well enough in small doses, but she was so free in her speech that one must have a great deal of patience to listen to her.

If Miss Perdue received Catharine a little coolly on account of Sir Edward's engagement to another woman, it was not long before Catherine consoled her friend by declaring that she thought Edward had used her very ill and it was a most shocking business. Furthermore, by dropping a few well-placed hints and lamenting that it would be very trying to stay in the same house with her brother and his intended bride who were responsible for so much heartache, she was able to procure an invitation to stay with her friend.

After all of Sarah's new guests were installed in her house, she began devising entertainments for them. She had written to William and was pleased to say that he and Laura would join the party at the end of the week. Marian rather suspected that their residence with Mrs. Forrester and her children was becoming rather strained because of Miss Forrester's aspirations to a marriage with William and Laura's uneasiness concerning Frederick Forrester. Besides, the Forresters were to return home soon.

Sarah had also written to her aunt, Mrs. Charles Forrester, and that lady had replied that naturally she longed to see her children again, but as there was little to entertain them there with so many of their cousins gone, of course they must be allowed to lengthen their time of enjoyment when they had so many kind invitations. Besides,

Laura had so enjoyed the very short time she had spent by the sea that she would be very happy to return for a longer visit. So it was arranged that William and Laura would return to the parsonage when Sir John and his family returned to Rosewood Manor.

Much to Marian's surprise, Lord Richard neither sought nor avoided her company when they were in the same room, nor did he seek to find her alone. He was very grave but no less polite and to Marian it was a very painful thing to see Lord Richard, who was usually charming and lively, so out of spirits. Sarah was very sorry for him, but like Arthur, felt that Marian was better suited to Sir Edward. Miss Henderson was frustrated to find that her efforts to attach Lord Richard were fruitless and he was less disposed than ever to be particularly attentive to her. Instead of making him more susceptible to her charms, as she had expected, his final rejection by Marian rather increased his indifference toward Miss Henderson.

A little more successful in cheering Lord Richard up was Rachel, for they shared an interest in music and horses. It was they who went riding with Sir John and Arthur. Sir Edward was in Lord Richard's company as seldom as possible, for he was constantly provoked by the young lord.

On Tuesday Marian and Sir Edward were walking about the garden and Marian was thinking about her conversation with his sister, for some of what Catherine had said weighed heavily on her mind. But how could she approach such a subject? When Sir Edward commented on her silence, she no longer hesitated.

"Edward, do you truly wish to marry me?" she asked at last. "Are you certain?" Sir Edward looked at her in surprise.

"Why, my dear Marian, what a question to ask! Why should you have any doubt?"

"But, Edward," she persisted, "You have not answered my question."

"Well of course I want to marry you," he replied. "I should not have asked you if I did not. But in return for my answer, you must answer my question. That is, what could cause you to ask me such a question? Surely you do not doubt my affection?" Marian hesitated for a moment, but decided at last that nothing would do except to be very open with the man who was to be her husband.

"Well Miss Sheffield seemed to think that you would not be *very* deeply hurt if I were to marry Lord Richard after all," she said. "She said you would not like it, to be sure, but that you would get over it soon enough." Edward looked at her in astonishment.

"And is it possible you should give credit to such assertions?" he asked her. "Surely you did not believe it?"

"I did not know what to think," Marian replied. "At first I did not even consider it, but when I told her so, she said she knew you better than I and that you were too serious to feel very deeply. What, indeed, could I say to such a claim? I cannot deny that she does know you better, for she has known you her whole life and I have not known you a year." Edward was silent and thoughtful for a few minutes before he spoke again. When he did speak it was in a softer tone.

"You must not credit everything Catherine says—particularly concerning my feelings. I love my sister, but she loves nothing better than to talk and gossip. She often makes assumptions and then treats them and speaks of them as fact. You and I might have been spared many weeks of pain were it not for her meddling. And do try to keep in mind that she wanted me to marry Miss Perdue and no doubt thinks it still possible, if only she could get you to break your engagement to me." He paused and took her hand. "I have not, perhaps, the gift of speaking so eloquently of my passions as Lord Richard has, for he is considerably more practiced in the art. But, indeed, I do love you—more than I can say. I admired you almost from the first time I saw you. I cannot say exactly when my admiration became love, but I have spent many weeks trying to suppress a feeling which I knew I ought not to have, because I supposed you an engaged woman. My sense of propriety has quite tortured me, you see, for it kept me from even daring to approach you on the subject. But tell me—if I had asked for your hand before you came to Bath, would you have accepted me?"

"Of course I would," Marian said candidly. "In fact, I was half expecting, hoping that you might. That time when I was staying at your house with Miss Darnell—that is, Mrs. Sheffield—I *thought* you seemed to care for me. I must admit I was slightly disappointed when nothing came of it. I thought that locket was from you, you know."

"Did you?" Edward asked in surprise. "And I thought you knew it was from Lord Richard and your acceptance of such a gift confirmed your engagement."

"Your sister led me to believe you were drawing on behalf of a certain young lady who did not mean to draw herself," Marian said. "I suppose she meant Miss Perdue."

"She assumed Miss Perdue," Edward said. "But I did not have the winning ticket. I knew Lady Emily had won it and no doubt gave it to her brother. But how could you not know who it was from?"

"A servant brought it to me and did not give the name of the gentleman it had come from," Marian said. "I did not know who had won, only what your sister had told me. It was very foolish of me, I know, to make such an assumption."

"I had considered proposing before you left," Edward said. "If it had not been for *that* misunderstanding, I might have. But how could I, under the circumstances?"

"Well, it does not do to dwell on the past so much," Marian said at last. "All is well now, is it not?"

"Yes, for now it is time to look to the future," Edward said. "But are you sure you wish to marry me? Catherine thinks I make a very dull companion."

"Surely you are not doubting *my* affection now, are you?" Marian asked with a slight smile. "I'm sure you are not dull, and I do wish to marry you. I am sure I shall be very happy." Edward squeezed her hand and kissed her. Then they walked on, talking of the future and not noticing how far they had walked until they had been missed for nearly two hours.

CHAPTER FOURTEEN

On Wednesday was the regular assembly in Ramsgate and it was the first time Miss Perdue had been seen by anyone from the Fort de Mar party since the announcement of Sir Edward's engagement to Marian, for though Sir Edward had called on Mr. Perdue and his daughters on Monday, Miss Perdue had pleaded a headache and would not come down.

Miss Perdue did not look as dejected as generally becomes a young lady who has had her heart broken. It was necessary, of course, that the friendship between Rachel and Miss Perdue must suffer a little, for what young lady could reasonably be expected to be intimate with the sister of the young lady whom she viewed as responsible for the destruction of her hopes?

Nevertheless, Rachel was disconcerted by the slightly cool reception she received from her friend when she went to greet her. Miss Perdue regained some degree of her cordiality toward Rachel over the course of the evening, but there was an inevitable barrier that was not there formerly. But what surprised both Marian and Rachel was that Miss Perdue went to Marian and offered her congratulations in a manner so enthusiastic that an engagement between Marian and Sir Edward might have been what Miss Perdue most wished for in the world. This was particularly unexpected by Marian, because Miss Perdue had seldom taken so much notice of her before.

Marian danced first with Sir Edward and Miss Henderson broadly hinted at her wish for a partner to Lord Richard, but Lord Richard apologized and said that he had already engaged Miss Rachel Amberly for the first two dances. It is impossible to say exactly what Miss Henderson's feelings were at this time, but it can be supposed that she was extremely indignant that just as one sister was out of her way, the place should be taken by the second. She had quite forgotten that she herself was supposed to have been intended for Reginald, for who could think of Reggie Amberly with only five or six thousand a year when Lord Richard with thirty or thirty-five thousand a year was near? But since Lord Richard had not asked her, she rather ungraciously accepted Reggie's hand for the first two dances.

Miss Perdue danced with Sir Walter Lovell, for though Mr. Perdue had been warned about the baronet, Miss Perdue had already met him and was extremely pleased with him. Sir Walter had noted Mr. Perdue's change of attitude toward him and was clever enough to direct his attentions to the elder daughter who had reached her majority, though the younger was considerably more handsome and had the same fortune. He did not like the younger daughter so much better that he was willing to go through the hassle of arranging an elopement when he might have the elder, who did not require the consent of her father, much more conveniently.

After the first two dances, Marian danced with Lord Richard. She supposed it might be safe since he had hitherto not pursued her. They danced in silence for a few minutes until Marian commented on his lack of anything to say.

"What shall I say?" he asked her. "What may I be allowed to say to an engaged woman? You have made your choice and I must endeavor to accept it."

"Can we not speak of music, or books, or Bath, or London?" she asked.

"Surely there can be no danger in those subjects."

"And what shall we say about Bath?" Lord Richard asked. "Shall we speak about how it was in Bath I supposed I was to be made very happy? Never did I expect what a blow I was to have."

"I suppose you think I was very wrong to accept Sir Edward," Marian said coolly. "No doubt you feel that I used you very ill."

"What shall I say to such a speech?" Lord Richard asked. "I cannot deny that I have been deeply wounded. But to accuse you of doing anything wrong—I cannot bear it. I know you made it all too clear that we were *not* engaged. I see now I only fooled myself into believing it because I wished it so."

"I suppose you must hate me now."

"I could not hate you," Lord Richard said. "Oh that I could! I wish that I could even trick myself into supposing that you were guilty of a disloyal heart. But your heart was never disloyal, was it? Only its loyalty was not to me. Its loyalty has only ever belonged to Sir Edward!" Marian had felt prepared for pleas to desert Edward for Lord Richard, but she had not been prepared for Lord Richard's dejected acceptance of defeat, and it almost brought tears to her eyes in spite of her best efforts to remain indifferent.

"Oh my lord," Marian said. "What can I say?"

"Nothing you say can be any consolation to me," Lord Richard replied. "There is only one thing you might say that would give me any comfort, and I am not fool enough to hope for it." Marian did not ask what that one thing was, for she rather suspected she already knew.

"I regret being obliged to cause you pain," Marian said. "I would much rather avoid giving anyone pain, if I could. But in such cases as these, it is inevitable that someone must suffer. I myself am a sufferer for knowing myself to be the cause of unhappiness."

"I would not have you trouble yourself about it," Lord Richard said. "It does no good, unless you mean to change it."

"You know I cannot, my lord."

"Indeed I know all too well that you cannot, or will not. Whatever the case may be, I had rather try to forget all unpleasant matters. I had thought to leave Ramsgate when I heard of your engagement, but I have tried before to drive you out of my mind without success. Why should this time be any different? No, if I must be miserable, I might as well give myself the consolation of seeing your face. It will be but a bitter-sweet comfort, it is true, but it is better than what I shall endure out of your presence."

"Perhaps it would be better for you to go away, if my company will cause you to have thoughts you ought not to have," Marian said. "Perhaps my presence will only make matters worse."

"Surely you cannot be so cruel as to send me away," Lord Richard replied. "Not when you have denied me everything else?"

"You are your own master, Lord Richard. I cannot command you to do anything or go anywhere you do not wish. I would only spare you additional discomfort."

"Oh but you can command me anything you wish, and you know I will not hesitate to do it."

"You ought not to say such things, my lord. You will make me reproach myself most severely if you continue in this way. You have already made me quite miserable."

"That was not my wish, I assure you," Lord Richard replied. "I consider you entirely innocent and irreproachable." Marian did not reply and Lord Richard's words made her no less uncomfortable. The dance soon ended and Lord Richard and Marian returned to the rest of the party. Sir Edward was alarmed at the agitated expression on Marian's face and asked if Lord Richard had been troubling her with unseemly petitions and comments. She replied that, on the contrary, it was his tone of helpless defeat that troubled her so.

Lord Richard walked away and engaged Miss Sheffield for two dances and Marian danced with Mr. Henderson. Sir Edward, out of politeness, asked Miss Perdue to dance, but she declined and he danced with Miss Fanny Perdue instead. After those two dances were over, Sir Edward brought his partner to be introduced to his family elect, for Miss Fanny had expressed a particular wish to be introduced to Marian.

Miss Fanny Perdue was different from her sister in every possible way, for she had a slight figure and a fair countenance and was very shy and quiet. Marian thought she was a sweet girl and was pleased to make her acquaintance and if Miss Fanny had been slightly prejudiced against Marian by her sister's way of talking about her, it was very soon dispelled.

Sarah also was pleased with the young girl and invited her to come to Fort de Mar whenever Miss Sheffield should be pleased to come and Miss Fanny went back to her party quite overwhelmed with the kindness of Miss Amberly's family and wondered how her sister came to be so deceived as to think that Miss Amberly herself was anything but charming.

In observing Lord Richard's unanimated expression, Marian lost much of her enjoyment in the evening for knowing herself to be the cause. It really was a most unfortunate thing that Lord Richard should have taken it into his head to fall in love with her. Marian could not be completely indifferent to him, for she really had a great liking for him and it could not be denied that she had once had a strong inclination in his favor. But she loved Sir Edward, and besides that, her relationship with Sir Edward had the foundation for a more lasting affection in mutual trust and respect between them. No, certainly she could not regret the decision she had made.

The next few days continued in much the same way they had been, with the welcome addition of William and Laura to their party and an occasional visit from Catherine Sheffield. Sarah was constantly planning diversions of some kind for her guests, for she was most anxious that they should always have something to entertain them. She invited Catharine to a picnic on Tuesday and told her she might bring Mr. Perdue and his daughters with her. Catharine then asked if they might bring Sir Walter Lovell with them, for Miss Perdue seldom went anywhere without him. Sarah raised no objections, though secretly she might have wished to avoid such company.

Marian at last discovered there was a motive in Sarah's keeping herself surrounded by company and busy with entertaining and reproached herself with being so wrapped up in her own concerns as to prevent her from discovering it sooner. Sarah, indeed, was always a hospitable person, but at this time she was exerting herself even more than usual to keep her mind occupied. Marian at last happened upon her in one of her rare idle hours, for Sarah was sitting in her dressing room staring at the fire, deep in thought. She had been attempting to read, for she held a book in her hand, but it now rested in her lap, open but unread. She did not hear Marian's knock, nor did she notice her approach until Marian was directly in front of her.

"Sarah, what is the matter?" Marian asked her.

"Oh! There is nothing the matter," Sarah replied placidly. "I only had a few moments with nothing to do, so I thought I might read a little."

"And yet you are not reading."

"Oh, well one does get distracted when one spends so much time in such a quiet occupation," Sarah replied. "I am quite ready to give it up. Shall we go play with the children?"

"No, Sarah," Marian said. "We shall talk about what is occupying your thoughts so. I really think you might tell me."

"Oh, but Mary, you are quite—" Sarah stopped. "Yes, yes, you are quite right. I have got something on my mind. And I might as well tell you, as it shall not be a secret much longer. But here—" She went to her desk and took out a letter. "This might explain matters better than I can." She handed her the letter, which was from the count.

My Dearest Sarah,

I know not how to open this subject before you, but it really ought not to be put off any longer. I could not bear to tell you these things when we were last together, so I am taking the first opportunity, before my arrival in Antigua, of sending this letter to you to explain somthings which might not be altogether pleasant for you to hear. I will likely be there only two or three days before the voyage back and I ought to be back in England by the end of July.

I know you are not altogether aware of the business that takes me to the West Indies, except that it has to do with the recent death of my uncle. In fact, this business of mine may have a very great effect upon our lives and I must prepare you for it. As you are aware already, my father was killed by the revolutionaries in France when I was hardly more than a boy and my mother survived him only four years.

What I have never told you is that when I was not even of age, I was married to my cousin. My mother was very ill and it was her dearest wish to see me married to her brother's daughter. My uncle also wished for the match, and I did not like to deny the request of my dying mother. I had a high regard for my cousin, but not the passion which one ought to have for a wife. Anabelle died giving birth to our daughter who was named for her. I was overwhelmed by grief and guilt, feeling that I had not loved her as I ought to have done. Anabelle was her father's only child and his grief was severe. He proposed raising the child himself, a plan that suited us both, for he needed the child to soften the loss of his own daughter and I was a young man, barely in my majority and did not relish the thought of being tied down by a child.

I resumed my life as a bachelor and my uncle took the child to his estate in Antigua. My uncle, however, has now died, and I must take the girl back into my care, so I go now to Antigua to fetch her. I am ashamed to say I have not seen my daughter since she left England ten years ago, nor have I had much correspondence with her. Therefore the situation will be awkward for us all. I ought, perhaps, to have told you of this long ago, but I never could bring myself to do it. We may, perhaps, be obliged to obtain a governess rather sooner than we otherwise intended. I know that once you have gotten over the initial shock, you will be able to accept her into your care and, I daresay, affections, for such is your nature.

I have no more to say on the subject at present. I might, perhaps, add a word of apology for my behavior at Vauxhall before I left the country. I was under a great deal of mental anguish and the thought of telling you what business took me to the West Indies was almost too much for me. However it is done now, and I only hope you might find it in your heart to forgive me for keeping you in the dark for so long.

Philippe de Roche

"Good heavens!" Marian exclaimed. "Do you mean he has had a child all these years and he never told you of it? I can hardly believe it."

"It was indeed a shock to me," Sarah said. "I hardly know what to think about it. I shall do my best to welcome the poor child, of course—but I fear that she will feel my partiality for my own children, though I don't mean to show it. She is but a child and will not understand. And surely she deserves my utmost compassion, for she shall be a stranger in a country unfamiliar to her."

"You show your good nature in your very eagerness to welcome her," Marian replied. "I admire you for it. I wish I could think I would be so selfless in your situation. But I rather fear my energy would be exerted on my irritation with my husband. What a shock it would be for me to find that Sir Edward had already been married!"

"Surely my situation is not a very common one," Sarah said. "I have seldom heard of such an occurrence as a man being previously married without his wife's knowledge. And that it should happen to me—it is very strange."

"Very strange," Marian agreed. "I only hope that this new daughter of yours will not be dreadfully spoilt and teach bad habits to your children."

"I shall try to be a good mother to her," Sarah said. "I daresay I will be as much a mother to her as Philippe is her father. Poor Philippe! He shall not know how to act himself. I feel quite as sorry for him as anybody. He did not like to distress me and so suffered alone. What a burden it must have been on his mind!"

"Still, he ought to have told you of this before you were married," Marian said. "Then you would not have this shock seven years later. One consolation you may have, however, is that the child is not a boy. Otherwise Jacques might have been robbed of his inheritance."

"That is true," Sarah said thoughtfully. "I had not thought of that. It would indeed have been very hard for Jacques to lose his place as the next count. Though the title is very likely no longer acknowledged in France, for I hear they have quite done away with the aristocracy there. Philippe's father lost the family estate, you know, in the Revolution. But still, whether there is anything to it or not, the title is a very good thing to have."

"Besides the title, the eldest son must have the right to Fort de Mar," Marian pointed out. "So it is indeed fortunate that the child is a girl."

"I do hope you will be kind to her when she comes," Sarah said. "I would not like her to be made uncomfortable. Do think—she has just lost her grandfather, who was no doubt very dear to her and she never had a mother. And she has never set eyes on her father, dear man that he is, and must be a complete stranger to her. My difficulty is—how shall I explain it to the children? But I must prepare them."

"Moreover, you must tell everyone else," Marian said. "For will not the count return with the child before we are all gone?"

"Yes, you are quite right," Sarah said. "And I must make inquiries for a governess. I shall make no decision without Philippe, of course, but I must make a beginning. A good governess is sometimes very difficult to come by."

"It is a pity we have two younger sisters not yet out," Marian replied. "Otherwise Miss Smith might come to you."

The rest of the family was naturally shocked when Sarah told them of the coming addition to her family, but eventually it was accepted as a matter of course. Lady Amberly echoed her daughter's sentiments in thinking that it was fortunate the child was a girl.

"But I suppose her grandfather shall leave her his fortune?" she asked. "Has he any other dependents?"

"I know only that her mother was an only child," Sarah replied. "Otherwise I do not know the details of the will."

"Certainly he will leave our mother something," Mr. Henderson said. "After all she is his sister and by her account he was very fond of her."

"Not that *we* have ever met him," Miss Henderson added with some asperity. "Nor has he ever bothered to invite us to visit him."

"Eleanor, you know very well Mother would not be able to make the voyage," Mr. Henderson reminded her. "And it would not do for you to go without her."

"Well he might have invited you, at least," was Miss Henderson's reply.

"And so he did," Mr. Henderson said. "But you know that even I could not be spared away from England. What if something should happen to our mother and I was a month's sea journey away?" Miss Henderson did not reply.

"Miss Henderson," Lord Richard said suddenly. "Would you play that charming little ballad you played Tuesday night? It has been constantly in my head, only I'm afraid I do not remember it correctly. I should be very much obliged."

"Certainly, my lord," Miss Henderson said, making her way to the pianoforte. Lord Richard took this opportunity to glance at Marian who admired his discretion and prudence to avert what threatened to become a family quarrel embarrassing to all present. Marian tried to express her gratitude with an approving look and Lord Richard managed a ghost of a smile before he looked away again.

CHAPTER FIFTEEN

On Tuesday, Sarah hosted an outdoor party and invited one or two of the principal families in the neighborhood. Count de Roche owned a small pleasure boat and everyone who wished took turns in groups of ten going out on the water for an hour or so while everyone else took refreshments and walked about the lawn.

Catharine came with Miss Perdue and her sister, attended by Sir Walter. Sir Walter and Miss Perdue immediately walked off by themselves and Catherine took Miss Fanny's arm and came over to her brother who was sitting with Marian and Laura.

"What a pity I did not bring my easel and water colors!" Catharine exclaimed. "This would have made such a charming picture."

"I shall go and fetch you some from the house if you wish, Miss Sheffield," Laura said. "I know Sarah has got some in the school room she has set up for Count de Roche's new daughter. She will not mind."

"Count de Roche's new daughter!" Catharine said. "And what shocking new development is this?" Marian gave Laura a warning look.

"It is a long story," Marian said. "It really is not worth going into."

"Oh but I think it is," Catharine persisted.

"Cathy," Sir Edward said. "You know impertinent curiosity is a vulgar trait."

"Pho pho, Edward," Catharine said. "You are far too nice. Do try to bring your thinking into this century. Nobody else makes so much fuss about such trifles."

"Shall I fetch the watercolors for you?" Laura asked again.

"No, thank you," Catherine said. "I can never draw out of doors. Do you want to go out on the boat, Fanny?"

"Oh yes," Miss Fanny replied. "I would like it very much. I went out on a boat before, you know, and I did not get sick at all."

"That's very nice dear," Catharine said absently. "Say, Miss Forrester, is your brother about?"

"I believe he is on the boat with Miss Henderson and my cousin Arthur," Laura replied. "They ought to be back soon."

"Is your sister well?" Marian asked Miss Fanny.

"Yes, she is here, somewhere," Miss Fanny replied. "I believe she is walking about with Sir Walter."

"And what do you think of Sir Walter?" Marian asked her.

"I think—he *seems* to be an agreeable man," Miss Fanny replied, blushing. "I do not know him well and Papa seems to doubt him, but I'm sure I don't know why."

"I'm sure your Papa wants what is best for you," Marian said. "He is very wise to be careful of your acquaintances."

"Oh you know fathers are sometimes a little *too* particular," Catharine said.

"They can be suffocating, really. And sometimes elder brothers are not much better." She glanced at Sir Edward as she said this. "I think Sir Walter is charming enough in his own way. But I daresay Georgiana might do far better."

"Surely she is not to marry that shameless scoundrel?" Sir Edward said.

"Well, he has made no proposals yet," Catharine replied. "And I daresay you are not so against the match as to take preventive measures."

"You ought to be ashamed of yourself, Cathy, for making such implications," Sir Edward said. "You know I wish Miss Perdue as well as anyone could, but you know that—" He stopped, for it would not do to continue his thought in the presence of Miss Perdue's own sister. Catharine knew this and gave him a most provoking smirk.

"Surely Miss Perdue is much too clever to bind herself to such a rake," Marian said, wishing to direct Catharine's thoughts away from provoking her brother.

"Well, not everyone can expect *your* good fortune, Marian," Catharine said. "Some people must choose what is more important—a title, a fortune, a handsome face or a dull, moralistic character. If I must do without any, I think I would do best without the last, and I daresay Miss Perdue is not so over-particular."

"If by dull, moralistic character you mean someone who has morals," Marian replied, "Or who is not so free with their tongue, then I confess I believe that to be a rather important trait. My cousin William would very likely fall into such a category."

"But he has, at least, a handsome face to recommend him," Catharine replied. "To me, that is as important as anything."

"But if that is your only consideration," Marian said, "One day you may find yourself married to an unattractive old rake without anything to recommend him."

"In any case, it is only important for the first year or so of marriage," Catharine said. "Everyone gets tired of their husband or wife by then and they find other ways of entertaining themselves."

"I wish you would not put such poisonous ideas into the head of my intended bride," Sir Edward told her. "I hope you will not encourage her to believe such things."

"Well, she seems very set in her opinions," Catharine said. "I doubt *I* will be able to influence her mind in any way." Marian took Laura and Miss Fanny away so that Sir Edward and Catharine could continue their argument unheard.

Though Sir Walter had not made proposals by the day of the picnic, it was not very long before he did and was accepted. Their engagement was announced a mere two weeks after Miss Perdue's arrival in Ramsgate. Marian was disgusted, though she did not share her opinions with anyone. She could not decide what disgusted her more—that Miss Perdue should marry Sir Walter for his title, or that Sir Walter should marry Miss Perdue for her fortune.

Mr. Perdue, though against the match, did not make very many difficulties, for he would rather have some say in the marriage settlement so that all of his daughter's fortune would not go directly into the hands of Sir Walter in consequence of a hasty and rebellious marriage. It was arranged so that Sir Walter would receive a generous annual sum for Georgiana's maintenance and she would have a good jointure.

Sir Walter protested that he was insulted by the implication that he would ever desert his wife, but he agreed to the terms of the settlement Mr. Perdue had drawn up. This being done, there was not much to wait for, because Miss Perdue had already bought her wedding clothes when she had thought she was on the point of marriage with Sir Edward. So Sir Walter succeeded at last in catching an heiress and they were married within a week of their engagement.

Though Sir Walter and the new Lady Lovell were to stay another few weeks in Ramsgate, Miss Sheffield saw fit to avail herself of Lady de Roche's renewed invitation a few days prior to the wedding. The small town house, she feared, would become rather too crowded when Sir Walter removed himself there.

Two days after Sir Walter's wedding, Count de Roche arrived with his daughter. Annabelle de Roche was rather taller than expected, and though she was but ten years old, appeared to be twelve or thirteen. She had light colored hair and her features were not particularly remarkable, save that her eyes were filled with a look of great apprehension. She was attended by a rather plain woman of middle age. The count looked anxiously at his wife for her reaction and Sarah immediately went to the child and took her and her maid upstairs to their rooms.

After they had left the room, the count stood awkwardly in his own drawing-room with a substantial number of house guests he did not know he had. It had only been a family dinner and everyone was sitting in their various occupations, but still, there were still thirteen people where he had not expected to find any. There was nothing for it, however, but to greet everyone, accept their words of welcome and allow himself to be introduced to those he had not already met—that is Sir Edward and Catharine Sheffield.

Sarah soon returned and told her husband that she had sent some dinner up to Annabelle and her maid. The count did not say much in reply and soon retired himself.
    "I have some interesting news for you, Marian," Sir Edward said as he and Marian sat by themselves in one part of the room. "I believe you have met my cousin, Mr. Darnell, have you not? I understand you've taken a keen interest in him."
    "He seemed to me a very good young man," Marian replied. "I do think very well of him. I think one must be very calloused not to think well of him."
    "Well, as one interested in Mr. Darnell's welfare," Sir Edward said, "I thought it might interest you to know that he may soon be offered a commission."
    "Oh, I am glad of it," Marian said. "It does seem a pity that he should be forced to remain a midshipman. And I confess it did seem rather unlikely that he would get a commission, since we are at peace and he has no great connections in the navy."
    "Well there, you see, I have done what I could for him," Sir Edward said. He took a letter out of his coat. "My uncle on my mother's side is a commodore in the navy, who, though he is but six-and-thirty, has a considerable influence. He is the only son of my grandfather, who was an admiral until he died. When I first met my cousin Robert a few months ago, I was struck by the same thought as you—that it seemed a terrible pity that such a deserving young man should not have the promotion that was his due simply because others had better connections. So I wrote to my uncle about the merits of this young man and requested that he should do what he could for him, if he should find him as deserving as I did."

"And has he written you back?" Marian asked.

"Well he had already replied that he should be happy to meet the young man who had such a recommendation from me, for he knew I certainly would not give it if it were not deserved. He told me next time that Mr. Darnell was in London I should direct him to pay a visit to the commodore. So when I was last in Bath, just before I came here, I told Mr. Darnell what my uncle said and provided him with a letter of introduction, whenever he should go to London. He went by the end of the week."

"This letter here is what I have just received from the commodore. He says he has met the young man and is very satisfied both of his merit and of his naval knowledge. He will see what can be done for him. Though commissions are not as readily available as they are in a less peaceful time, several officers are retiring at this time, and lesser officers are being promoted. He will do what is in his power to secure a place as fourth lieutenant for young Darnell. Here is the letter." Marian briefly read through the letter, which merely confirmed what Sir Edward told her.

"Well I am glad of it," Marian said. "Mr. Darnell and Mrs. Sheffield, at least, deserve to have some good fortune in their difficult lives. I cannot speak for the rest of the family."

"I have not met the eldest brother," Sir Edward said. "He is already first lieutenant I believe. I'm afraid he has fallen in with bad influences, however, from what his brother tells me."

"I fear Miss Susan will be led astray," Marian added. "She seems easy prey for a rake who knows what he is about. I feel certain she would have fallen into Sir Walter's clutches if her mother had not taken her away and he had not followed me here."

"He followed you here?"

"It certainly felt that way. He seemed to have no particular acquaintance here and he thought my fortune much larger than it is. You see how quickly he dropped me for Miss Perdue, however."

"Perhaps Miss Susan needs guidance more than anything," Sir Edward replied. "Do you think we ought to invite her to stay with us sometime after we are married?"

"I see no objection," Marian said with a blush. It was still difficult to think of herself as soon to be married. "But I think I would rather invite Miss Fanny Perdue."

"Perhaps we might invite them both," Sir Edward replied. "I think both of them might benefit from your example. Though Catherine's influence won't do them much good." Marian merely smiled.

On Monday, William was walking in the park with Marian and Catharine when a servant brought him a letter. As he read it, his countenance grew very serious.

"What is the matter, William?" Marian asked. "Is it bad news from home?"

"My father has written to tell me that my cousin Frederick died yesterday," William said. "It was one of his fits. It proved fatal at last."

"Well now you shall inherit his estate," said the thoughtless Catherine. "Does not that, at least, please you?" William looked at her in disbelief.

"No, Miss Sheffield," he replied. "It does not please me in the least that my cousin has died, even if it does mean I inherit the estate. I would rather have been a clergyman my whole life than acquire a fortune in such a way."

"Well I'm sure that you are very singular," Catharine said defensively. "I know of many young men in your situation who would be very happy to get a fortune and estate any way they could."

"Doubtless there are people in this world who are callous enough to be as satisfied acquiring fortune by the death of another as any other way. But I shall not be counted among them. And I should be sorry to think that *you* would, Miss Sheffield."

"Are you to leave us then?" Marian asked.

"I'm afraid I must," William said. "It is only proper. I shall leave today. Laura may stay here, as she cannot attend the funeral anyway."

"Sarah will be disappointed you must miss her ball," Marian said. "She's worked very hard on it."

"Unfortunately these things cannot be planned," William said. "I'm sure she will understand."

William left within three hours of first receiving the news of his cousin's death and when Sir John heard the news, he began to talk of leaving as well. Lady Amberly protested, but Sir John was determined to leave on Wednesday and he only agreed to stay till then because of Sarah's ball on Tuesday night, since it meant so much to her.

Sir Edward and his sister were, of course, invited to accompany them, but Sir Edward said he needed to return to his estate, for he had not been there some time. He would, however, go to Rosewood Manor as soon as he could. He said he would very likely leave his sister at home, but Catharine declared he would not. He might leave her alone in London or Bath, if he pleased, but surely he did not expect her stay out in the country with no company at all? And what's more, if her brother insisted on leaving her there, the moment he was gone, she would hire a coach and go wherever she pleased. Sir Edward did not doubt his sister's capability of carrying out such a scheme, so there was nothing for it but to keep her with him.

Lord Richard was invited to come to Rosewood when he could. He did not like to deprive Sarah of all her company at once, but he would come as soon as was proper.

"And is Miss Amberly so complaisant to be out of my presence?" Lord Richard asked Marian when he found her alone. "I wish I had your fortitude!"

"You ought not to say such things," Marian replied. "I am engaged."

"How can I forget it?" Lord Richard replied, leaning toward her. "Am I not reminded of it every day? One conquest was not enough—you must make another!"

"My lord, that is unjust," Marian protested. "You know how it all was. I have done you no wrong, yet you make me feel as if I have!" She turned and walked away.

"Marian!" he called. He seized her hand.

"No, my lord," Marian said, pulling her hand away. "I shan't let you work upon me like this!" She turned away again and this time Lord Richard did not try to stop her, though he looked miserable.

At the ball, Lord Richard seemed inclined to stay near Marian. Not willing that his attention should provoke Sir Edward, Marian attempted to direct Lord Richard's attentions another direction.

"May I make a suggestion, your lordship?" Marian asked him.

"You know your wish is my command," Lord Richard replied.

"Why do you not ask Miss Henderson for the first two dances?" Marian asked.

"I'm afraid that is not in my power," Lord Richard replied. "You see, I am already engaged to your sister for those two dances."

"My sister?" Marian repeated. "Why, do you mean Rachel or Sarah?"

"Well, I am to open the ball with Lady de Roche," Lord Richard answered. "Then I have engaged Miss Rachel for the two after that. And I was very much hoping that you would honor me with your hand for the third set."

"I shan't dance with you until you dance with Miss Henderson," Marian said.

"Why such an advocate for Miss Henderson all of a sudden?" Lord Richard asked, rather taken aback. "I was of the impression you were not the greatest of friends."

"I only think it is time you exercised your romantic inclinations toward someone who might better appreciate them," Marian said. "I am not at liberty to accept your attentions, and I only mean to direct you where they might be best received."

"I see how it is. You mean for me to fall in love with Miss Henderson so that I shall forget you. But it is not that easy. You are too deeply branded on my heart. Nay, before you reproach me for my language, let me assure you that if any woman were to drive you from my mind, it would not be Miss Henderson. And I know too much of your delicacy to suppose you would wish me to give her encouragement where there are no intentions."

"Well such encouragement as you've given her in the past must merit her expecting an offer, by your own calculations."

"My own calculations?" Lord Richard exclaimed. "Surely *I* never thought of such a thing."

"But you have shown Miss Henderson as many attentions as Sir Edward ever showed Miss Perdue," Marian said. "If not more. Yet you would have it that Sir Edward used Miss Perdue shamelessly and you are innocent." Lord Richard could not immediately think of anything to say to this all but too just remark of Marian's.

"Would you really have me marry Miss Henderson when you know very well that you are the woman I love?" Lord Richard asked her at last.

"That is not my decision," Marian replied. "I only know that you cannot marry me, so you will have to fall in love with someone else." They were interrupted by the commencement of the dancing and Sir Edward came to claim Marian's hand and Lord Richard went to claim Sarah's.

In spite of his reservations, Lord Richard did ask Miss Henderson for the third set of dances and was rewarded by Marian's agreeing to dance with him for the fourth. Laura did not feel inclined to dance all evening, for her head was full of melancholy thoughts about Frederick. Besides, she ought not to dance, for she was supposed to be in mourning, though she did not have anything black to wear until she returned home.

Most of Sir John's party retired relatively early, since they were to leave the next morning to return to Rosewood. Miss Sheffield was now included in the party, since Sir Edward was to only go home for a week, and Miss Sheffield was to come to Rosewood anyway. Reggie had been planning to stay at Fort de Mar and go to Rosewood when Sarah and her husband went, but Miss Henderson's obvious indifference toward him determined him to take no pains. He should marry her if his uncle still insisted upon it, but otherwise he should prefer not to. She was ill-tempered and five years his senior, neither of which qualities were particular recommendations.

It was not very long after Sir John and his family returned to Rosewood Manor that the family was faced with another domestic confusion.

Not a week after Sir John's arrival, Miss Smith, the governess, went home for a short holiday. Thus, there was no one to keep a particularly close eye on the children still under Miss Smith's care. Miss Anna Amberly, a younger sister of Marian and Rachel, was a pretty girl of fifteen. This young lady was very eager to go out into society, despite her mother's declaration that her girls should not attend even public country balls until they were sixteen.

Anna felt herself quite ready to be out, as she was as accomplished in music, dancing and drawing as any young lady of the same age. In addition to this, she had undertaken to learn Latin and Mr. Carter had been engaged to be her tutor.

Mr. Benjamin Carter was the eldest son of the local attorney, who had determined to educate him in the style of the gentleman. Much of the family's income had gone to educating the eldest. The only other son was to continue his father's business. They had three sisters who had three thousand pounds apiece.

Though he was clever and good-looking, Mr. Carter had been unable to procure a living, as those with better connections were to be preferred to him. Mr. Charles Forrester had therefore engaged him as his curate, more out of a desire to be of use to the young man than out of a real need for a curate. What he received from Mr. Charles Forrester, though generous for a curate's salary, would hardly be enough for him to marry on, should he ever take it into his head to do so, so he also took on the task of tutoring for the children of two or three of the principal families in the neighborhood. When he was told the daughter of Sir John Amberly wished to take lessons in Latin he could not refuse, though it was a singular subject of interest for a young lady, for the wages were considered to be very decent.

As Miss Smith was away, Lady Amberly told her two eldest daughters to sit in the schoolroom while Mr. Carter and Anna had their lesson. So Marian and Rachel worked on a rolled paper box while Mr. Carter and Anna sat in the far corner of the room. Marian watched them carefully and tried to listen, but she could not understand what they were saying. She could not help but think, however, that they seemed a little too pleased with one another to be taking part in something as serious as a Latin lesson.

After the lesson was over, Anna took her Latin book and walked out of the room with Mr. Carter. She stood in the hall until Mr. Carter was gone, then she turned to hurry back to her room. But she ran directly into Catharine Sheffield and a piece of paper came out of the book and onto the floor. Of course the ever astute Catharine saw this and grabbed the piece of paper at once.

"What's this?" she asked, obviously pleased. "I own I had wondered what a pretty young miss like you would want with Latin, but now that I see your tutor, I quite understand you."

"Pray, Miss Sheffield," Anna said. "Please give me my letter."

"Oh a letter is it?" Catharine said. "Does your father know you are having private correspondence with your tutor? I think perhaps not."

"I beg you, Miss Sheffield, please return my property at once."

"No, I think it is my duty to advise Sir John of such improper goings-on in his house," Catharine replied, really quite elated at the prospect of a scandal, for she was longing for something to entertain her. "Your father must approve your correspondents, you know. And if by a mistake I confiscated the letter from a *female* correspondent, then my folly shall be exposed and you shall no longer be molested." She turned and walked away as Anna tearfully pleaded with her not to go to her father. Catharine, however, was unaffected, and continued to Sir John's study.

Sir John was evidently surprised at Catharine Sheffield coming to see him, but did not deny her admittance. Anna came in after her, still tearful and now quite red.

"Papa!" she exclaimed. "Miss Sheffield has been quite cruel. She has something that belongs to me and she took it by dishonest means."

"I think you might decide whether or not I took the right course in confiscating this thing, Sir John," Catharine said, giving him the letter. "I must tell you I rather *suspect* that it is from that young man that Miss Anna has been taking Latin lessons from. Sir John began to open the letter and Anna protested.

"Papa!" she exclaimed. "Is it gentlemanly to read a lady's correspondence?"

"My dear," Sir John replied, "I shall look directly at the signature, and if it be from Miss Forrester, or your cousin Laura or some other female correspondent, I shall not read the contents." Anna looked quite miserable, for she had no argument against this. So Sir John read the letter and looked and his expression was very serious. He called a servant to have Mr. Carter summoned at once and then he expostulated with Anna about the impropriety of having a private correspondence with a young man she was not engaged to. Catharine retreated, lest she should be asked to leave, but went to a corner of the room rather than out of it.

Mr. Carter was soon ushered into Sir John's study and had a look of great puzzlement on his face. He then glanced at Anna, who was looking downcast and miserable and his jaw stiffened.

"Do you know why I have called you here, Mr. Carter?" Sir John asked him.

"I would be very obliged if you would tell me," Mr. Carter replied. Sir John held the letter out to him and Mr. Carter took it reluctantly.

"Now I ask you, sir," Sir John said, "Is that your handwriting?"

"It is, sir," Mr. Carter answered after a few moments.

"Is this the first letter that has passed between you?"

"It is not."

"And do you care to explain yourself, sir, as to why you would keep a private correspondence with a girl of such tender years?"

"She does not seem to me to be merely a girl," Mr. Carter replied. "She has charms and accomplishments equal to any grown lady."

"And so you thought it would be acceptable to write her private love-letters?" Sir John asked. "I beg your pardon, sir, but whether the girl be fifteen or twenty, a correspondence without the knowledge or consent of her parents is nothing short of a deceit that shows the greatest degree of disrespect for the family of the young woman. Did you commence this correspondence?"

"I was the first to speak of marriage, when I should have better prospects," Mr. Carter said evasively.

"Oh Papa!" Anna exclaimed. "I can't keep silent anymore while you question Mr. Carter so cruelly. I was the one who wrote to him first. He did not think we ought to be so secret about it, but I was sure you would object on account of his having no fortune. But he loves me, and I love him."

"And what have you to say for yourself, Mr. Carter?" Sir John asked.

"It is as Miss Amberly says," Mr. Carter replied. "We are exceedingly attached to one another and were I in a position to marry, I should not have hesitated to formally ask for her hand."

"And I suppose her fortune is of no consequence to you?" Sir John asked. "No doubt it adds substantially to her other girlish attractions."

"Sir, I am insulted by such an assertion," Mr. Carter said. "Were her fortune nothing at all, it would change nothing. Except perhaps to make it even more necessary to wait until my situation were improved. But I must wait until I obtain a living."

"Papa," Anna said, "If we did not respect your opinion, we might have run away to Gretna Green any time these three months. Indeed, I suggested it once, but Mr. Carter would not hear of it. So I must wait patiently until he feels worthy to ask for my hand."

"But Anna," Sir John said, "Even if he had a living, do you think you should be happy being the wife of a clergyman?"

"I daresay I should like it very well," Anna replied.

"Well then," Sir John said. "Under the circumstances, I suppose you ought to get married, as soon as Mr. Carter has a living. And it shall be in my power to give him one, if Charles Forrester means to give his up, as I believe he does. I ask only that you wait half a year."

"Oh Papa!" Anna exclaimed, throwing her arms about his neck. "How very happy I am! Mr. Carter, are not you happy?"

"Of course," Mr. Carter said. "I am indeed grateful for your father's kindness and condescension."

"This one lapse of judgment aside," Sir John said, "I've always thought very well of you, Mr. Carter. I daresay you will be a fine clergyman."

"Thank you, sir," Mr. Carter said.

Catharine, who had been listening the whole time, took this opportunity to slip out of the room and spread her new piece of news among the ladies of the household. It was not long before the news reached the parsonage and by extension, Mrs. Forrester and her daughters. And in return for this interesting piece of news, they shared a very similar one, for Mr. Harding and Miss Diana Forrester had long been attached to one another, unbeknownst to Mrs. Forrester. Since, by the loss of Frederick, Mr. Harding's presence was not required in the capacity of tutor, he openly avowed his attachment to Miss Diana to Mrs. Forrester. Mrs. Forrester was shocked and it took her some time before she could bring herself to realize it, or even look at her daughter without agitation, for she had had some hopes of Mr. Harding herself. These details were, of course, left out when she related the story to her sister-in-law in which she only added in a tone of slight derision that the young couple had thoughts of starting a small school in a local village.

Sir Edward finally came to Rosewood and told Marian he hoped that Sheffield Park would be fit to receive its new mistress by the time they were married, which by this time was rapidly approaching. During the day, Sir Edward went hunting with Sir John and his sons and in the evening, read aloud to the ladies, played a duet with Marian or helped make up Lady Amberly's card table.

With Anna's engagement, Lady Amberly was obliged to give up the notion that her daughters could not appear at public gatherings before the age of sixteen. She therefore resolved not only to take her daughter to the public assemblies, but to throw a ball for both of her engaged daughters at once. Lord Richard soon came and he had recovered but little of his spirits since they last saw him, and allowed Sir Edward to continue as the principal entertainer.

"Now that both I and our sister will soon be married," Marian said to Rachel one day, "Our mother will be very eager to get you married off."

"I have thought of that," Rachel said. "But fortunately there are not many young men in the neighborhood who our mother would count as worthy of an alliance with our family. I believe I need not fear at least until we next go to town."

"Oh, but I believe I know of someone in our own circle who thinks very highly of you," Marian said. "If you could but return his affection, perhaps Mother's ball might be for all three of us." Rachel blushed.

"I don't pretend not to know who and what you mean," Rachel said. "But surely I have no reason to think he has so *very* particular a regard for me."

"Oh, but I am quite certain he does," Marian told her. "He smiles when you come into the room and always seeks out your company. I am very certain he is a great admirer of yours. It would be a very good match for you. He is kind and handsome, to be sure, and now he is heir to a very substantial fortune."

"But, Mary, surely you would object to me having an alliance with him, even if he should offer."

"Certainly not!" Marian exclaimed, "Nothing could please me more, I assure you."

"I scarce know what to think," Rachel said. "I always liked him very well, you know. Only I was afraid to tell you, for fear you might be angry. And do you really think he's so very partial to me? Do you not think it is too soon?"

"Too soon?" Marian asked. "Whatever do you mean? I suppose you must wait two or three months until the mourning period is over, but otherwise I see no objection."

"Mourning?" Rachel repeated. "Is he in mourning, then? No, you must mean his attachment to you. I know he felt it very strongly."

"Attachment to me? He is not attached to me at all, in the way of a lover. I know he has a great brotherly affection for me, but his devotion has ever been to you."

"Brotherly affection?" Rachel said. "Surely you must be joking. Mary, you know very well that Lord Richard had much more than a brotherly affection for you."

"Lord Richard!" Marian exclaimed. "Did you think I meant Lord Richard?"

"But of course," Rachel said. "Who else might we be talking of? Surely you not mean—you were not talking of our cousin William?"

"To be sure!" Marian said. "You mean you did not know? You did not think I would encourage you to marry Lord Richard?"

"I ought to have known it was too much to wish for," Rachel said, sitting down. "You only meant to push me toward *William*, of all people. You don't want Lord Richard yourself, but it is too much to endure seeing *me* with him."

"Rachel, that is not fair!" Marian exclaimed. "If I were certain of his lordship's character, I would have no objection at all. But he is very inconstant. You would never have to doubt anything with William. And now, you know, William shall be very well able to provide for a wife."

"Well it shan't be me," Rachel said stubbornly. "How could you think it? I'm very fond of William, but I've only ever thought of him as my brother. We grew up seeing one another every day, had the same governess and masters—why should I think of anything more?"

"William thinks of more, I do believe," Marian said.

"Well I do not," Rachel said. "I am sorry if what you say is true, for it grieves me to think of giving him pain because I will not have him. And why does he not speak for himself, if he cares for me so very much? Why commission you to speak for him?"

"He did not commission me," Marian said. "He does not even know I am speaking to you on the subject. I believe he would be very mortified if he did."

"Well you are not thinking much about other people today at all, are you?" Rachel asked.

"Oh yes," Marian said sarcastically, "I am very selfish indeed to be thinking of the happiness and well-being of my sister and cousin. Well, I *do* apologize!" She left the room abruptly, leaving Rachel to reflect on what Marian had said and what she had said in return.

After Rachel had had some time to think, she went to find Marian to apologize for being so ungrateful for her good intentions. She inquired for her sister about the house and was finally told she had gone for a walk with Sir Edward. So, Rachel went outdoors to look for them. When she did, however, she found the very person who it was most awkward for her to see—her cousin, William.

"Rachel!" William exclaimed. "Are you out walking alone?"

"I am going to look for Marian," Rachel said. "We had some words earlier and I need to speak to her about it. It is nothing you need be concerned about."

"Ah, but I am concerned about any affairs of my two favorite cousins," William said with a smile. "Especially if it puts them at odds with one another." *Ah* Rachel thought, *so we are equally his favorite cousins. Perhaps Marian was mistaken after all.*

"But you wouldn't want to pry into the confidential conversations of young ladies, would you?" Rachel asked him.

"Certainly I would not wish to do that," William said. "But if there is anything *I* can do, please do let me know." *He is too good*, Rachel thought.

"Thank you William, but I think I can manage."

"I'm sure you can," William said. "And you know you can always tell me if anything is troubling you."

"We were discussing the possibility of my marrying, if you must know," Rachel told him. "I did not suppose I had any particular admirers, but Marian assures me I have at least one." She looked at William for his reaction and he did indeed color slightly. *Perhaps he suspects that Marian has given away his secret.* "Now, what should you think if Lord Richard were my admirer?"

"I should think that it would be good if he could divert his mind from Marian," William said, after some surprise. "But at the same time it would show how very changeable his emotions were. He cannot love very deeply if his affections are so quickly changed from one young lady to another in the course of a month. I'm sure *I* shall not—would not—so soon forget the woman I loved. Particularly if I've loved her a long time. I feel for Lord Richard. To love, with no hope of a return, is the most dreadful thing imaginable."

"Are you in love, William?" Rachel asked him. "Have you been in love with Miss Forrester after all? I'm sure she would be very happy to have you."

"How could *you*, of all people, think of such a thing?" William asked her. "Do you not know me, Rachel? Do you not even suspect what I—" He stopped.

"Perhaps you ought to marry Miss Forrester," Rachel said, not willing for William to resume his speech, for fear of what he might say. "After all, you are to inherit her home. Would it not be kind in you to give her the means to stay in it?"

"My father has told Mrs. Forrester and both her daughters that they may stay as long as they like," William said. "They have eagerly accepted his offer and I have reason to believe they mean to stay some time. I suspect the only thing that will make them move out is my marriage to someone besides Miss Forrester. And *that,* I fear, will not soon come to pass."

"Why ever not? You are perfectly eligible. Why should you not marry?"

William took her hand.

"If I could hope that *you* would accept me," he said, "I would offer you my hand at once. For my heart, you know, has always been yours, and always will be. And now that I have more to offer than the life of a clergyman, perhaps—"

"Oh William," Rachel said, distressed. "You are not serious."

"I am perfectly serious, I assure you. I have no wish to distress you, believe me. But I cannot help telling you what I feel when presented with the opportunity."

"I have the highest regard for you," Rachel replied. "You know that. But I think of you quite as my brother. And I did think that was all you ever thought of me."

"So it was, until I went away to the university," William replied. "I saw you so seldom then, and you had grown into such a young woman meanwhile, that it was quite easy to forget we had even been in the same schoolroom."

"I wish I could give you the answer you wish," Rachel said. "But I cannot! I can think of you in no other way."

"I did not really expect it," William said with a sigh. "I could only hope. But Rachel, do let me advise you not to throw your heart away on Lord Richard. I know he is rich, charming and amiable, but he has not the strongest morals. I would hate to see you make yourself miserable with such a man."

"I suppose I can manage my own affairs," Rachel said defensively. "Besides, I have no reason to think that Lord Richard has any particular regard for me."

Meanwhile, Marian and Sir Edward were walking about the grounds and Sir Edward was describing his estate when they saw a carriage coming up the lane. It slowed as it approached them and Marian soon found that it was her brother Albert and his wife. Marian greeted them warmly and said she was very happy they had come.

"I'd get out and walk with you if I could," Albert said. "But Greta would never forgive me if I left her to ride to the house by herself, when she does not know anyone."

"Indeed I would not," Mrs. Amberly agreed. "I don't know why you would rather walk anyway, if you could avoid it."

"I'm an active man, my dear," Albert said. "I always prefer to walk."

"Well you had better go then," Marian said. "We will go to the house directly."

As was to be expected, Sir John was shocked in a most unpleasant way to learn that his second eldest son had married a foreigner, for Marian had told only Rachel of the affair and Laura had quite forgotten about it during all the confusion of Frederick's death and then of Mr. Carter's engagement. William, of course, did not feel it was his business to tell.

Lady Amberly received Albert's wife much more cordially than Sir John did, though she had been just as surprised. She told her husband in private that it was very well for Albert that he had married such a wealthy lady and Sir John replied that he would rather his son had married a woman of small fortune who was of English blood.

Marian introduced her brother to Sir Edward, and Albert professed himself quite delighted with his new brother elect, and had already been predisposed in his favor by

Sarah's account of him. Marian tried to warm to Mrs. Amberly, but she was always repulsed by her short, curt replies, and so she soon gave up the effort. Catharine Sheffield, however, considered it a challenge and persistently followed Mrs. Amberly about until Mrs. Amberly had grown quite used to her company, and even found Catharine rather amusing.

John finally returned to Rosewood, now that nobody was in town anymore, and he found it considerably dull. John and Lord Richard spent much of their time in company together, riding into the local village, playing backgammon, and discussing world affairs in the library. Arthur went away on business for a few weeks, and not very long after he left, Sarah, her husband and her children also arrived at Rosewood.

Jane, Marian's youngest sister, was thirteen years old and displayed no interest in becoming a proper young lady. She was excessively fond of her brother Henry, who was twelve, and frequently joined him in the boyish activities of climbing trees, playing at swords, and catching frogs and insects by the lake. Jane and Henry took Sarah's children in hand, but Annabelle did not particularly relish playing in the dirt. Annabelle, therefore, was left to her own devices.

She made the schoolroom her own retreat, and nobody bothered her there, for Jane and Henry were on holiday until Miss Smith came back and would not go near it meanwhile. Anna and Mr. Carter no longer had their Latin lessons there, for they no longer needed such a cover for their courtship. Anna's enthusiasm for the subject had indeed been inspired by her regard for Mr. Carter.

Little did the young people know that their holiday was to be longer than they expected, for Sir John received a letter from his son Arthur, informing him that he had just been married to Miss Smith and that he was removing himself to a small aspiring seaside resort to practice medicine there. He and Miss Smith, or Felicia, as he might now call her, had in fact been secretly engaged for several months and were only waiting until Sir John and Lady Amberly returned to Rosewood so she might take her holiday to see her parents and Arthur might soon follow so that they could be married.

"I don't see why my children see such a need to keep secrets from me," Sir John said to his wife, after he had shown her the letter. "I feel as if I don't know them. Shall I have any son who will not prove a disappointment?"

"What about Reginald, my dear?" Lady Amberly asked. "He seems to be doing well for himself, and always does as he's told."

"I wanted him to go into the church, you know," Sir John replied. "But it is true he has redeemed himself more than his elder brothers."

"But consider, John," Lady Amberly said. "Did you not say you would rather your son married an English lady of little fortune than a foreign heiress? So you see, that is exactly what has happened. Do you not like it so much as you supposed you would?"

"It is not his choice of wife that bothers me so much as his way of going about it," Sir John said. "Why so secret about it?"

"Well I should think *that* was obvious, my dear," Lady Amberly said. "Had he asked your consent, would you really have given it? You might *say* you would now, for it is no longer required, but if your son had asked you if he might marry the governess of his younger brothers and sisters, would you really have said yes? Do be honest."

"I only hope he will not come to regret this rash action," Sir John said. "Oh, how have I failed my sons that they make such foolish choices? First Albert marries a foreigner, and what must Arthur do but marry a governess? Not to mention John, who can do nothing useful with his time."

"They are grown men," Lady Amberly said. "You cannot blame yourself. Of course, you did send John to the university where he first got into such dreadful habits. And you did send Albert into the army, by which means he met his wife. And you did hire Miss Smith as governess. But still, young people will make their own decisions, regardless of what their mother or father may say about it. I must own, however, that I am better pleased with Albert's marriage than with Arthur's. And even John may redeem himself after he has sown his wild oats."

A few days after the revelation of Arthur's marriage, Marian showed Catherine around the house. Catharine expressed a particular desire to see the gallery, and so they went. They were not there long, however, before they were joined by Lord Richard.

"Your lordship!" Catharine exclaimed. "Fancy meeting you here! Marian was just showing me her great grand-mother and I told her they look very alike. What do you think?" Lord Richard looked at the painting, then gazed at Marian.

"An extraordinary likeness indeed," Lord Richard replied. "The same dark eyes, brown curls—the expression of the mouth." Catharine laughed outright at this.

"My lord!" she said. "Do not you see you are making Miss Amberly blush? I daresay you quite shock her modesty with your remarks."

"Indeed he does," Marian said coldly. "Pray, Catharine, shall we move on?"

"Oh well I quite forgot, I was engaged to walk with Mrs. Amberly in the garden," Catharine said. "She must be waiting for me now." Catharine ran away, leaving Marian paralyzed with astonishment and Marian began to suspect, rather angrily, that it had all been planned from the beginning.

"Good morning, my lord," Marian said, curtseying. She turned, but Lord Richard seized her hand. "Lord Richard! Pray, let me go at once!"

"Do you think I can let such an opportunity escape me?" Lord Richard asked. "I beg you to appeal to your better feelings of compassion and the small regard you have for me, though you do not like to admit it. Marry me! It is not too late to change your mind. Let me save you from a life of dullness and misery."

"I thought we had quite finished with this sort of talk," Marian said. "It would be very wrong to break my engagement with Sir Edward. Particularly for such a reason. How should I tell him such a thing? And surely my parents would not hear of it."

"We can elope," Lord Richard said. "Let us go tonight."

"I will not listen to you," Marian said, turning away in disgust. Lord Richard still clung to her hand.

"You shall kill me if you refuse me!"

"You are too dramatic," Marian said. "You shall not die. You shall only feel sorry for yourself." The gallery door opened and Sir Edward came in. He stopped when he saw them and looked from one to the other. "Sir Edward!" Marian exclaimed, pulling her hand away from Lord Richard, who let her go. She walked over to Sir Edward.

"Is there something you wish to tell me, Marian?" Sir Edward asked gravely.

"It is nothing," Marian said, not wishing to make Sir Edward angry at Lord Richard, who had just at this time joined them.

"You are very fortunate, Sir Edward," Lord Richard told him. "Nothing can move her." He then left the room.

"What am I to think of this, Marian?" Sir Edward asked. "My sister told me I might find you in the gallery. Little did I expect you would be having a private meeting with Lord Richard, of all men!"

"It was certainly not by appointment!" Marian said, a little angry that Sir Edward seemed to be accusing her. "I did not even know he would be here. I came with your sister, and she went away as soon as Lord Richard appeared."

"If Lord Richard does not cease his impertinence, I shall be forced to challenge him," Sir Edward said. "Which is certainly something I would rather not do. But I can't have him constantly causing distress. And if my sister tries such a trick again, I advise you to follow her and not allow yourself to be left alone with Lord Richard. I can see nothing good will come out of it."

After Sir Edward left her, Marian received a letter from her former governess and took it somewhere she could be alone. Marian's favorite retreat was some ruins of a castle which had been the house of the previous owners of her father's property, some centuries before. They had never been completely removed and there were a few wide arches and a substantial section of stone floor that had once composed the main hall of the castle. There were some steps that led from this stone floor up to what was now grass. These arches, steps and floor were overgrown with grass and ivy and on the whole, Marian thought it made a very pleasant retreat. She often went to this place when she wanted to be alone and no one bothered her there. Miss Smith's letter read as follows:

My Dear Marian,

I'm sure you will be greatly surprised to be receiving a letter from me at this time. I know that Arthur has written to your father by now, and so I take this opportunity to write to you, not as your governess, but as your sister. I'm certain you have heard that Arthur and I were married a few weeks ago, and if your father has not yet seen fit to share this news with your family, I ask you not to mention it yourself. However, I take this first opportunity of writing to you, so that you may be assured of the very great regard I have for you and your family and to beg you not to despise me, as I know you now must. I have always liked your brother very well and you yourself are aware of the effect he has always had on young ladies, for we have discussed it many times, if you will recall.

I hope you do not blame me for marrying your brother, though I fear you must. But Marian, do consider, though I am very fond of you and your sisters, when you are all grown and married, there shall be no more need for me there, and I should have to find another family, who might not be as kind and generous as yours. Fortunately Arthur, though he is a younger son, has a small fortune and I have managed to save a little money, so we shall do well enough, I think.

Arthur told me about Mr. Carter and Anna. Is that not very odd? I must own I rather suspected a partiality on the part of Anna, but I did think that Mr. Carter would be more sensible. But he is a young man himself. He is newly ordained and not yet five-and-twenty. And your father is to give him a living. I only hope that Miss Anna will be a suitable wife for a clergyman.

Now let me tell you of our new home. We are happily situated in the small seaside resort of B—. We have a small, pleasant cottage. It is nothing to Rosewood Manor, of course, but it is our own. It has six bedrooms, two parlors and a dining-room. We have a nice yard with a kitchen garden and a flower garden with an arbor. Arthur has his horse, in case he should need to travel quickly, and we have two maids and a cook. We have several pleasant neighbors who have been to call on us since our arrival. We are only a short walk from the sea and there are many other pleasant walks besides. We have only a few shops here, but they are quite sufficient for our needs. We should both be very happy if you would come to visit us. Perhaps in the summer you might come with your new husband. I'm very sorry I did not see Sir Edward myself. Do try to reconcile your parents to our marriage. If anyone can, it is you. And please do yourself try to forgive,

F. Amberly

Marian remained pensive for some time after reading her letter, not only about Arthur's marriage, but her own troubles with Lord Richard and Sir Edward. She was finally wakened from her reverie when she felt a drop of water hit her face, then another, then another. She sat up and realized it was getting dark and starting to rain. She hurried to one of the arches for shelter and tried to determine what to do. Should she run home in the rain, or wait until it was less heavy or someone should find her?

While she was thus contemplating, Lord Richard came with an umbrella.

"Your brother told me I might find you here," Lord Richard said. "We missed you at dinner and I came out to find you."

"And why have *you* come, instead of Sir Edward?" Marian demanded. "Surely he did not sit at dinner while you came out in the rain?"

"Sir Edward did not choose to come down for dinner," Lord Richard said. "He dined in his room and sent word that he was suffering from a dreadful headache." Marian did not reply.

"You know you cannot stay angry at me for long," Lord Richard replied. "You know that all the foolish things I do are because I love you."

"Stop it!" Marian said. "I beg you to stop plaguing me with such assertions! You don't love me. If you did, you would not torture me so. Why cannot you leave me to live my life in peace?"

"I have tried," Lord Richard said. "But I cannot bring myself to give you up."

"I will not stay with you a moment longer in this way," Marian said. "I'm walking home, rain or no." Lord Richard called after her as she ran across the stones.

All of a sudden she slipped on the wet stones and hit her head on a stair. Lord Richard immediately ran to her in a panic. He felt her head and lifted her up, lifeless.

Lord Richard carried Marian back under the arch where they were sheltered from the rain and laid her down there.

"Marian!" he cried, kneeling down next to her and stroking her hair and face. "No, you *must* speak to me." Marian remained unconscious and a small trickle of blood ran down from where she had hit her head. Lord Richard took off his coat and laid it over her, lifted her up and carried her back to the house through the rain.

Meanwhile, Sir Edward had just been informed of Marian's absence and had just begun walking in their direction when he saw Lord Richard carrying the unconscious Marian. His first thought was panic and he ran over toward them.

"What happened?" Sir Edward asked.

"She fell and hit her head," Lord Richard told him.

"I shall take her now," Sir Edward said, taking Marian into his own arms before Lord Richard could protest. He was met at the door by one of the servants and someone was instantly dispatched for a surgeon.

"Yes, take her!" Lord Richard cried, when no one could hear him. "You always do! Dull and pragmatic as you are, yet she prefers you!" He sank down to his knees. "You shall all be the death of me! She shall drive me mad!" He stayed there some time in the rain before he finally came to himself enough to realize he was extremely cold and wet and went into the house.

The surgeon came and examined Marian and said he could detect no fracture of the skull and that she would soon wake up without serious damage, but he recommended she stay in bed a few days. He would return the next day to see how his patient fared. Rachel stayed by her bed all night until she should wake up and promised Sir Edward, who sat in a chair outside Marian's room, that she would inform him when she woke.

Sir Edward was feeling the pangs of guilt, for he knew that he had been ever so slightly angry with Marian for her interlude with Lord Richard and that she had very likely felt it. Such was the real reason he had dined in his own room. The thought that he could have been part of the cause, however indirectly, was torture.

Marian slept through the night and woke to find Rachel asleep at her bedside, her hand clasping her own. Marian squeezed her hand and Rachel slowly lifted her head.

"Mary!" Rachel exclaimed when she opened her eyes. "Thank heavens you're alright! We've all been so worried!"

"What happened?" Marian asked.

"Lord Richard brought you home," Rachel answered. "He said you fell."

"Where is Edward?" Marian asked.

"I almost forgot," Rachel said. "He's outside the door. I promised him I would inform him the moment you woke up. He's been quite beside himself with worry." She got up to tell Sir Edward that Marian was now awake. Sir Edward had fallen asleep in his chair, but Rachel roused him and informed him that Marian was now conscious,

177

much to his relief. The surgeon returned later in the day and declared that Marian would be perfectly well within a week. He stopped in also to see Lord Richard, for Lord Richard's valet, Mr. Hobbs, said that his master was unwell. After visiting his second patient, the doctor's diagnosis was less optimistic. Lord Richard had developed a very dangerous fever and was presently in a state of delirium. The situation was grave, though not hopeless. Nevertheless, Sir John thought it best to inform Lord Richard's family of the matter.

Over the next few days, Marian was well enough to leave her room and participate in quiet occupations, though Lord Richard remained in bed and was not much improved. The doctor had come to the conclusion that Lord Richard's illness was caused by a combination of exposure to the cold and wet for an extended period of time, lack of sleep and proper nourishment and extreme emotional anxiety. When Marian heard this, she could not help but feel that she was at least partially to blame. Her spirits were only more depressed by a conversation with her eldest brother.

"Why Marian," John said, sitting next to her one evening after dinner. "What have you done to Lord Richard? You have made him positively ill."

"I have done nothing wrong," Marian said. "If anyone has transgressed the lines of what is proper, it is him."

"What womanly compassion is this?" John asked. "I think we all know what his 'emotional anxiety' is. *That* in turn led to the lack of sleep and appetite. As for the cold and wet, was that not from his rescuing you from the same fate he suffers now?"

"Pray stop, John," Marian said, almost in tears. "I cannot bear to hear you say such things. Surely I do not *wish* him to be ill. But what would you have me do?"

"I suppose there is nothing," John said with a sigh. "But I say, he was a lot more fun before you made him in love with you. He has not been himself these three weeks. The most blasted melancholy disposition you can conceive."

"And you urged me to encourage him," Marian replied.

"So you did, did you not?" John asked. "Dancing with him twice at a ball, having private conversations—did you not accept a gift from him once?"

"He sent one," Marian replied. "But I have a long time since returned it. And I do not care to discuss this subject further. I am engaged to Sir Edward, and it does not do to discuss the past."

"Speaking of Sir Edward," John said, "What should you think if I were to marry his sister, Miss Sheffield?"

"You? Marry Miss Sheffield?" Marian exclaimed in astonishment. "Why surely you are not serious?"

"Why not? She comes from a good family, has a good fortune and high spirits, which is just what I like in a woman. None of your dull, 'accomplished' misses for me!"

"I must say I never thought of you marrying Miss Sheffield. She gossips a little too much and laughs about serious matters, but I suppose that would suit you."

"Yes indeed," John said. "I shall start paying her small attentions and see how she receives them. Her behavior shall be my guide."

It was not long before the Dowager Lady Beauregard and Lady Emily arrived with Mr. Wesley, for the dowager, hearing of the danger her grandson was in, immediately determined to set out to see him. Lady Beauregard was not well enough to travel and Lord Beauregard had business to detain him.

"Well, Miss Amberly," Lady Emily said, after she had been to visit her brother, "I must say Richard looks very ill. I'm not sure he is not half mad. He's very fretful—not like himself at all. I fancy I know what might help his recovery. But it is not something I can give him. Nor can you, in the present circumstances."

"I don't know what you mean," Marian said, coloring. "I'm sure *I* have nothing to do with it."

"I hear I must congratulate you on your forthcoming marriage," Lady Emily said. "I heard all about it from Miss Sheffield. I *hope* that you will be happy." Marian could not help but think there was a little bit of spite in Lady Emily's congratulations.

"Thank you," Marian said. "I'm sure we shall."

"I only wish my brother could recover from his disappointment as easily as Miss Perdue seems to have recovered from hers," Lady Emily went on. "I hear she is Lady—something or other."

"Yes, she is Lady Lovell now," Marian replied. "She married an unprincipled fortune hunter who was a baronet. Do you remember meeting Sir Walter in Bristol?"

"Oh yes, I think so. Not that I thought that much about him. I should not think of throwing myself away on an impoverished baronet. I suppose he may be good enough for *her* however. Everybody has their level of what they expect in a match."

John began his project of courting Miss Sheffield, but though he admired her for being spirited, he soon discovered she had little pleasure in horses, interrupted him without scruple when she did not like the subject and laughed immoderately at the least appropriate times. Furthermore, he rather suspected that she made light of his love-making to Marian and Lady Emily, and as it turned out to be true, it was almost too much to bear. The knowing looks of Lady Emily were very provoking.

Lady Emily borrowed Rachel's horse to go for a ride about the grounds and she and John went to the stable at the same time.

"How does your brother fare?" John asked, merely to make conversation.

"I believe he is a little better, thank you," Lady Emily replied. "He cannot yet leave his room, but I believe he is improving."

"I'm glad to hear it," John said. "I do hope he is more himself when he comes out of it. He has been uncommonly dull of late."

"Indeed," Lady Emily said coldly. She mounted her horse and galloped away. John mounted his own and went after her.

"Have I said something to offend you?"

"I would rather not speak of my brother's dullness, if you don't mind."

"You handle your horse very well," John told her. "For a woman, of course." Lady Emily's expression darkened and she stopped her horse on the bank of the lake.

"Pray do not speak to me so insolently," Lady Emily said. "Miss Sheffield may laugh at you, but I shall do worse if you cross me."

"Are you threatening me, your ladyship?" John asked her with a smirk. "What, pray, shall *you* do to me? Kill me with your coquetry? Plague me with details about your gowns and parasols?"

"I shall—I shall horsewhip you!" Lady Emily said, raising her whip at him, anger flashing in her eyes. John grabbed her wrist.

"Have a care, my lady," he said in a low voice. "I do not take kindly to threats. Particularly from silly young women." He released her.

"Come, John," Lady Emily said. "Let us not quarrel anymore." She held out her hand and he took it, then with a violent strength he would not have expected in her, with both hands she pulled him off of his horse and down John went, into the mud.

When he recovered from the initial shock, John reached up and caught hold of Lady Emily's foot, pulling her down into the mud with him.

"How dare you!" Lady Emily shrieked as John laughed. John continued laughing until his coat was splattered with mud by Lady Emily, who haughtily stood up. John then stood up and stroked Lady Emily's cheek, wiping mud on it.

"Perhaps that will teach you a lesson," John said with a malicious smile.

"You vile—serpent!" Lady Emily cried. "I hate you! I *despise* you! You are the most ill-mannered pig I have ever met and I hope I never see you again!" As she said these words, she gave John several hits on the coat with the horsewhip.

"I despise *you*," John said, grabbing both of her hands so that she might not strike at him anymore. "You are just a spoiled, selfish brat." They stood for a few moments, staring fiercely at each other until suddenly, and a little violently, John pulled her close and kissed her.

"How dare you!" Lady Emily exclaimed, looking at him in anger and astonishment. "You are nothing but an ill-mannered, vulgar beast!"

"Perhaps," John said. "But I'm used to getting my own way, as well as you. Besides, I think you enjoyed that, though you don't like to admit it."

"I *what*?" Lady Emily exclaimed. "You are quite mistaken, sir, if you think I enjoy being attacked by ill-bred young men." John came forward and kissed her again, and this time she did not resist. John embraced her, and they were thus positioned when Marian came next to them with her horse.

"John!" she exclaimed. "What are you doing?"

"We were just—Mr. Amberly was just helping me back to my horse," Lady Emily said, rather confused. "I fell in the mud you see, and—"

"And I was just assuring myself that there were no injuries," John added. "Her ladyship appears to be perfectly sound." Marian did not ask any more questions and when she was not looking, John and Lady Emily looked at one another and smiled.

Marian was, perhaps, the only person who was not particularly surprised at the engagement of John and Lady Emily. There was no real objection to the match, though the dowager had hoped Lady Emily would marry Charles, who would someday be Lord Wesley. John would only be a baronet. Lady Emily might have done much worse, however. Sir John could be pleased that one of his sons at least had made an honorable marriage. Miss Sheffield was a little piqued, for she really meant to have accepted John, if he should have asked her.

Lord Richard was reported to be well enough to leave his bed, though he would not yet venture downstairs. He sent word to Lady Amberly begging that she would not postpone her ball any longer on his account. So Lady Amberly began rewriting the invitations she had not yet sent out.

Two more weeks passed by and Lord Richard was able to come downstairs and eventually gained a degree of his health back, though not his spirits. Henry, meanwhile, had been sent away to school, to the disappointment of his sister, Jane. Mr. Wesley had resumed his attentions to Laura, much to the alarm of the dowager, who immediately found some errand for him to return to town to complete. The title of baroness, in the dowager's opinion, would be quite thrown away on the daughter of a country squire just recently in possession of an estate. Charles might do much better for himself in town. So, Mr. Wesley was sent away to safety.

One afternoon, Lord Richard ventured to go riding with his sister, despite his grandmother's objections that he was not strong enough. He, of course, laughed at her protests, declared he had never felt better and led Lady Emily out by the hand.

"I do hope you are not overexerting yourself, Richard," Lady Emily said. "I could not bear it if you took a turn for the worse."

"Nonsense," Lord Richard replied. "Riding comes as natural to me as walking. It does me much better than staying indoors all day would do."

"Yes, perhaps it is better for you to get away from certain indoor scenes. It cannot be agreeable for you to always see Miss Amberly and Sir Edward together."

"Agreeable? No," Lord Richard said. "But if it will afford me a glance, a chance to gaze at her, see her smiles, hear her laugh—it is the most I can hope for."

"You do realize you must give her up, Richard, do you not?" Lady Emily asked him earnestly. "I know you fancied yourself in love with her, but it will not do for such an infatuation to continue, now the possibility of fulfilling it is past."

"I *fancied* myself in love?" Lord Richard repeated, rather indignantly. "Do you suppose, then, that my feelings are not very sincere?"

"I believe you think them so. However, you have been in love before and you always got over it tolerably well."

"It has never been like this, Emily. I don't know how to explain it. Certainly I will agree that the girls of my past were mere fancies, but this, I assure you, is not."

"We shall see. Did you not believe it so with the others as well?"

"Not like I do now. Marian has penetrated my soul, and try as I will, I cannot get her out again. I cannot force myself away."

"But Richard, this is the first time your love has failed to be reciprocated. If she had given in as easily as the others, she would have been the same."

"I cannot agree with that."

"Do you mean to stay for Lady Amberly's ball?" Lady Emily asked.

"Yes, but I shall leave very soon after," Lord Richard replied. "I could not think of staying for the wedding. It would be too much."

"I believe that is wise," Lady Emily said. "But do you know, I fancy that Miss Rachel is rather like her sister and I believe she likes you very well."

"Miss Rachel is a good girl," Lord Richard said. "But to suggest that she could compare to Marian—well, one would have to have a great imagination."

"I think she would do very well for you. She is a great rider, as you are, and you both have a passion for music. Besides, her looks and coloring are very like her sister. If you cannot have the one, why not settle for the other?"

"I do not think she would have me if I should ask her," Lord Richard said. "She knows I'm in love with her sister. She is too clever to think I could have changed my opinion overnight. Besides, I don't know if I wish to marry anyone besides Marian."

"You must not say so," Lady Emily said. "You *must* marry. You are the only one who can carry on the family name. It is your *duty* to marry and produce an heir."

"Would you have me unite myself to one lady as I am hopelessly in love with another?"

"You must endeavor to forget Miss Amberly. You shall be miserable the rest of your life if you do not. I should have liked it well enough if she had accepted you, but as she has not, I daresay you could do much better."

"Do not say so," Lord Richard said, a little angrily. "I will not have you suggest that there is anyone better. I shall take it as an insult."

"To be sure," Lady Emily said, "I cannot conceive her obstinacy in refusing you with all you might offer her. But I understand she once fancied that impudent young officer in Bath, which does not speak very well for her taste, I'm sorry to say."

"A young person's first fancy is seldom their greatest accomplishment. I am not proud of all the women *I* have fancied myself in love with in the past. There are very few now that I tolerate with anything like patience."

"What of Mother's friend, Miss Henderson?" Lady Emily asked. "You know she is quite in love with you, and you might have her for the asking. I hear that on the death of her uncle she inherited an additional fifteen thousand pounds, so now her fortune is twenty five thousand, which is no less than what Miss Amberly will get."

"Do you suppose I take fortune into the least consideration when choosing a wife?"

"Only if you have no better reason for which to marry," Lady Emily replied. "If you cannot marry for love, you might as well marry for money as not. Besides, Mother likes her very well and they might keep one another company. Of course, I do not know that Miss Henderson's attentions will not cease as soon as you are married, for I'm sure her chief reason for attending our mother is because she wants your good opinion."

"I'm sure you're right, Emily. And if I do as you suggest, and marry for money, I'm sure I could do better than that. Besides, I cannot abide Miss Henderson. I used to find her charming enough, but now I find her quite provoking."

"Well I don't suppose it would do for you to despise your wife," Lady Emily said. "You must at least be able to *pretend* some affection for her. I suppose Miss Rachel might not be the best choice for you either, congenial though you may be. For she and her sister are very close, and no doubt you would be in Miss Amberly's company very often, and that cannot be good for you."

"You know, I think you have hit upon it," Lord Richard said. "If I married Miss Rachel Amberly I would be in Marian's company often. Then at least I would have some opportunity of seeing her."

"I hope you don't fancy seducing her into some intrigue. It won't work."

"How could you suggest I have any but the most honorable of intentions?"

"Because, my dear brother, I know you far too well."

"I have changed, my dear Emily. I am quite a different man now."

"That would be an amazing feat indeed," Lady Emily replied. "If Miss Amberly has accomplished *that*, I shall have to give her a good deal more credit."

The day of the ball finally came and Anna was in high spirits, for this was to be her first real ball. The only thing that gave her any chagrin was that Marian was to open the ball by reason of having been the first engaged, being the eldest and having a higher ranking fiancé. Anna felt that this was to be both her coming out and her engagement ball and she ought to have precedence. But it was not to be, for Lady Amberly had declared that Marian and Sir Edward were to open the ball.

Lord Richard decided to devote his attention to Rachel, for he knew that attentions to Marian would be unwelcome and pointless. Besides, if he wanted to make himself a credible suitor to Rachel, he must pretend that he was becoming indifferent to Marian.

Anna was enjoying herself immensely, for she had never been in the company of so many young men before. While dancing with a handsome young gentleman from a neighboring town, she even began to wonder if she was throwing herself away on a country clergyman. Surely with her youth, fortune and accomplishments, she ought to be worthy of at least a gentleman with a decent estate.

"What a year this has been for our family!" Albert said to Marian when they were sitting together. "We have got half the family married off now. Arthur and I were both married this year, and you and John and Anna are all engaged. And is there not some sort of arrangement for Reggie to marry Miss Henderson?"

"Oh yes, though I don't know how *that* will turn out," Marian replied. "I daresay Miss Henderson thinks herself quite too high for Reggie now that her fortune has increased."

"What will your uncle Carlyle think of that?" Albert asked.

"I don't know," Marian answered. "Why do you not ask him?"

"Why, is he here?"

"Yes, he arrived yesterday. Did you not notice? I believe he means to stay for a month and take Reggie back to London."

"Does he approve of your engagement to Sir Edward?" Albert asked. "Surely he cannot deny it is a good match for you."

"I believe he thinks better of him than he thought of Lord Richard," Marian replied. "But I don't know that he has quite forgiven me for not marrying Mr. Henderson. But Mr. Henderson is such a vulgar, odious creature. I could not like him."

"Whatever happened with Lord Richard?" Albert asked. "I hear he was quite in love with you. Did he ever make you an offer?"

"Yes," Marian said. "And I came very near to accepting him. But somehow I could not bring myself to irrevocably bind myself to him."

"It is perhaps as well. I hear he has a reputation among the women of London."

"I never was sure if I could trust him," Marian said. "He claimed he would always love me, but as inconstant as he has proven in the past, I had no assurance he would not grow bored with me after we were married."

"What do you know of his inconstancy?"

"I have *heard* a great deal. And such things as I heard were not likely to give me any reassurance."

Meanwhile, John asked Miss Sheffield to dance, and as soon as he had led her out, she immediately began attacking him with her raillery.

"How very versatile you are," she said with a saucy smile at him. "You pay very pointed attentions to one young lady and within the week you are engaged to another. I wish *I* had such admirable flexibility."

"Why Miss Sheffield," John replied. "When a gentleman pays his addresses to a young lady and she does very little short of laughing in his face, what is he to do?"

"Since when are gentlemen offended by a little bit of laughing? Any man who is too stuffy to support a little gaiety is not worth *my* time, I assure you!"

"Well then it is fortunate for you that no man has wasted your time enough to make you any proposals," John said peevishly. "I wish you all the luck in finding a half-witted man who will not notice when you are making fun of him." Catharine laughed.

"I'm glad you think so well of my taste! I shall have to take care in the future not to incur the displeasure of young men who think too highly of themselves."

"No man of sense likes to be laughed at," John said.

"Yes, all men have such a fragile sense of pride," Catharine replied. "They all prefer wives who will hang about them and tell them they are more important than they really are. Every man, if he has the right kind of wife, thinks he is the most handsome, amiable, witty, charming man in the world, because his wife lets him think so."

"Men do not wish for any such thing, and certainly *I* don't. I only wished for someone with spirit, for only such a woman could support my ill-humors without shrinking into a meek little mouse, which I hate. I despise weak women. I would tire of my wife very quickly if she were that, no matter how beautiful and accomplished."

"Well *I* am no weak woman, I assure you," Catharine said. "I'm sure *I* may do better than to marry an heir to a baronetcy with scandalous manners." John flushed.

"Well Miss Sheffield," he said stiffly. "I hope you may." When they parted after the dance, needless to say it was with very ill-humors on both sides.

Mr. Carter looked on while Anna flirted with several handsome young men and Laura greatly pitied Mr. Carter and lamented her cousin's ill-judgment. Mr. Charles Forrester and his wife brought Miss Forrester and Miss Diana with them, and much to Laura's shock, Miss Forrester danced every dance she could. When Laura asked how she could be so callous as to dance so very much when she was only a month in mourning for her brother, Miss Forrester laughed at her and told her it was not the same as a *public* ball, where of course she ought not to dance so much, but it was quite harmless at a *private* one. Neither was Miss Forrester convinced that she ought not to perform during supper with the other young ladies and did not see why, after the very great misfortune of losing her brother, she must also suffer the loss of her enjoyments.

Now that Catharine had been disappointed where John was concerned, she refocused her attention on her former favorite, William. To William, of course, these attentions were less than welcome, but he knew not how to escape from them, for Catharine was much more clever and no less determined than Miss Forrester. William did not dance at the ball, pleading the excuse of his cousin's recent death.

William spent most of his time at Rosewood and was rewarded by seeing Rachel's looks of annoyance when she saw him talking quietly to Catharine. William was not so small-minded as to attempt to provoke jealousy in Rachel, but he could not help but be gratified that it seemed to affect her in a small way. Rachel was particularly affected by this after Lord Richard went away and she had no one else to pay her attentions.

Lord Richard, as he had said he would, left two days after the ball in company with his sister and grandmother. Instead of going directly back to their estate, they went to London to order wedding clothes for Lady Emily, for John and Lady Emily wished to marry as soon as possible. John would soon meet them, after they had left London.

Marian's wedding day was rapidly approaching. Rachel, of course, was to be her bridesmaid and Sir Edward's brother Lionel had come a few days before with his wife.

"How pleased I am that you are to marry Sir Edward!" Mrs. Sheffield said. "You see, I always thought you would suit very well. And now we shall be sisters!"

"I would like to have news of all your family," Marian said. "How is your mother? And your brothers and sisters?"

"My mother does very well, I suppose," Mrs. Sheffield said. "She is very much the same as she ever was. Only now she can afford to give parties on a larger scale than before. I daresay she thinks her new position suits her very well."

"And the others?"

"I think perhaps you already know, but Robert has finally received a commission. Sir Edward brought it all about."

"I knew that he had spoken to his uncle," Marian replied. "Sir Edward thought it *likely* Mr. Darnell would get a commission, but I had not heard any more than that."

"My sister has just been sent to school, but she heard of Sir Walter's marriage before she went away, and she was very distressed. She would eat hardly anything for a week, but then she got over it tolerably well."

"She is still very young," Marian said. "She will fall in love again. I hope next time it will be with someone more worthy."

"Oh yes," Mrs. Sheffield said. "I tried to explain to her that Sir Walter would not have married her because she had no money. That is a hard thing to have to explain to a young girl, but it could not be helped. I tried to soften the details about Sir Walter's habits and certainly said nothing about the vulgar proposal he made to me."

"Well I must say that Miss Perdue—or Lady Lovell, as I suppose I should call her now, was properly warned of his character before she was even engaged to him. But she would do it."

"Oh, did he marry Miss Perdue? I had heard only that he was married and did not care to make further inquiries. But was she not always after Sir Edward?"

"So I understand. But then Sir Edward and I got engaged and within a month she met, was engaged and married to Sir Walter. I suppose she was determined to marry a title and Sir Walter happened along at the right time."

"I confess I never really liked Miss Perdue," Mrs. Sheffield said. "I'm glad Sir Edward did not marry her."

"Yes, so am I," Marian said, laughing. "Otherwise I might have been forced to marry Lord Richard."

"I did not mean—I only meant—"

"I understand you perfectly," Marian said. "And I confess I never much cared for her myself. But I don't believe I would have wished Sir Walter on her."

"Perhaps she will reform him," was Mrs. Sheffield's comment, at which they both laughed.

"Yes," Marian said. "Perhaps she will."

Sir Edward and Marian were married among their family and they all returned to Rosewood where a larger crowd was present for the wedding breakfast. Marian could hardly believe she was married and she felt almost lightheaded. It was a very long while before she could be alone with her new husband, for there were people to be met, congratulations to be accepted and wedding toasts to be made.

The next morning, Sir Edward and Marian made the journey to Aberdeen, but they were to travel onto the continent after a very short stay at Sheffield Park. Catharine was invited by her brother, Lionel, and his wife to stay with them in Bath until the return of Marian and Sir Edward. It was about two weeks since the wedding before Rachel received a letter from her sister.

My Dear Rachel,

How strange it seems to be married! We are to leave for the continent tomorrow, but I had to write and tell you about Sheffield Park. As you know, the day after the wedding, Edward and I came here. How strange it was to have them all call me "Lady Sheffield." I don't know if I shall ever become accustomed to it. The servants were very polite, though I think they were very curious to see their new mistress. Mrs. Jameson is the housekeeper and she seems to be a steady character. She is short and plump and has a kind face. Besides Mrs. Jameson and the steward and butler, we have thirty maids, sixteen footmen, two cooks, and a scullery maid. There are also the outdoor servants, such as ten gardeners, a coachman and a stable-hand. The house itself is a little larger than our father's house and there is a summer house and a labyrinth, which I daresay will be a great deal of fun in the summer. There are some woods on the north part of the property and I'm told there is a stream there, but we did not have time explore all of the grounds, because we have to leave again tomorrow and have spent much of this time looking about the house and preparing for the journey.

I must go now. Mrs. Jameson wants me about something and there is still much to do. Do write to me and tell me how everyone at home is getting on.

Marian Sheffield

Dear Marian,

I hope you are enjoying yourself and can only wish that you had thought to take me with you. It is extremely dull hereabouts, now that everyone has gone away. You have heard, of course, that John and Lady Emily were married earlier this month. My one consolation in being left behind is that they have invited Anna and me to come and stay with them when they go to town after Christmas. I shall try to convince John to invite Laura too, for I'm sure it will do her good to see Mr. Wesley again. She has confessed to me that she likes him very much, but she is afraid he does not think of her and even if he did, certainly his family would not approve. I told her no rational person would object to their marriage and certainly the dowager should not be attended to. The Dowager Lady Beauregard, for all she gives herself so many airs, is no better than anyone else. And she was not born a lady, but she has clearly taught herself to think so. Father says that John and Lady Emily may use his townhouse this winter, if they please, for he does not intend to go this year. He has had quite enough, he says, of being away from his own house for the present. Mother is not at all pleased, but she is glad that Anna and I are to go. She thinks Anna ought to have at least one season in town before being tied up in the country. No doubt she hopes that *I* shall find a husband. That puts me in mind. Do you know, I have been thinking about William's declaration and I *begin* to think that *perhaps* I could think about him as something other than a brother. I have not necessarily decided to accept him, nor have I spoken to him about it. I only mean that I have been considering it. I think I need not ask what your advice would be. Reggie of course has already gone to town with our Uncle Carlyle. Jane has gone to Fort de Mar with Sarah. Did Mother tell you? Sarah offered to take Jane home with her so that Mother might be spared the trouble of finding another governess. Jane is really the only one of us who needs a governess and Sarah thought that Jane's manners might be improved if she was separated from Henry. Besides, she will be a good companion for Annabelle. I think Mother is almost pleased she is to be rid of all of her children at once, but she wishes to convince Father to at least go to Bath, if he will not go to London. I shan't write again until after Christmas, for then perhaps I may have something to tell. Until then, do not cease to think of,

R. Amberly

Dear Marian,

Perhaps you will be surprised to hear from me, but it is raining outdoors and I was looking for some occupation this morning and thought I would write to see how you and my brother fared. As you know, I am in Bath now staying with Lionel and Jane. Mr. Perdue and Fanny have also come to Bath, for it is now too cold to go sea-bathing, and Mr. Perdue thought he might try the Bath waters. Sir Walter and Lady Lovell have just come to Bristol and they come to Bath sometimes. I believe Sir Walter did not know what he was getting when he married Georgiana, but I believe she keeps him in line. How I laugh to see it! No more high living for Sir Walter! If he supposed he was to have her fortune to do what he pleased with, he has been, most unfortunately for him, undeceived. She handles all the accounts, gives him an allowance and she told him if he spent it unwisely, she should reduce it. She is quite dedicated to improving his estate which she says has much potential, if only the owners would take it into hand to improve it, rather than going about the country and living beyond their means. In short, she has quite whipped him into shape. I invited Fanny to stay here for a few weeks with me, and I must tell you what monstrous fun we had! Well, Jane's brother, who is a newly made lieutenant in the navy, has also been visiting here. He is a handsome enough young man, though rather green, and I thought I would start a pleasant flirtation with him. So, one day, when one of his officer friends was with him, I made all sorts of hints of how much I liked a man in uniform—particularly a sea officer, and I mentioned my fortune and all that and though Mr. Darnell took no heed of me, his *friend* did and began paying me a great many attentions. When we went to an assembly at the Upper Rooms, what do you suppose happened but that another fortune hunter began courting me? Well, I told both of these young men at different times that they ought to come to their point or stop wasting my time. Naturally, of course, both of these young men proposed marriage and I feigned that I had not yet reached my majority, and therefore the only option was to elope to Gretna Green. So I arranged for them both to come with a coach at the same time very late at night and I would meet them outside. Both of them believed me, and Fanny and I sat at the window at the appointed time, very low down, so they would not see us. How we laughed at their confusion! They very nearly came to blows and one of them drew his sword. Fanny pretended not to be as diverted as I was, but I know otherwise. The next day one of the young men called and demanded an explanation and I told him I begged his pardon, but my brother was up very late, and I could not possibly get out without his noticing and perhaps we ought to try again tomorrow night. He went away satisfied and I thought the other young man would have quite given up, but at last he too came, and I told him I thought we had arranged it for Thursday, not Tuesday. And what do you think, but the two fools came again! One declared he felt himself very ill-used, went away, and I have not seen him since. The other, however, did return and when he asked what had happened this time, I told him I had a previous engagement. He, too, was quite angry and went away. I hope that will teach those two men a lesson. I wish I could have gotten more young men to come— how much more fun it would have been! Do you know, I believe Fanny and Jane's brother rather fancy one another, but I am afraid nothing will come of it. Jane and I are going to the shops now. Whenever you have something to tell, please to not hesitate to write to,

Catharine Sheffield

Marian and Sir Edward returned from their trip to the continent in January. They stayed at Sheffield Park for a month before going to London. Just two days before their departure for London, Marian received a letter from Rachel informing her that she had just become engaged to Lord Richard. Marian, of course, could not believe what she read, but she would be in town in a few days and it would be better to wait until then to discuss it with Rachel.

Meanwhile, Sir Edward had gone to Bath to bring Catharine home. Catharine professed herself very happy to see Marian and quite ecstatic that they were to go to London together. Catharine asked if Marian had heard the latest concerning her sister. Lady Emily had written to her and informed her of Lord Richard's proposal to Rachel and its acceptance.

"Did I not tell you that your sister was in love with his lordship all the time?" Catharine asked her, most provokingly. "But you did not believe me."

"I had thought my sister had more sense," Marian said.

"Oh, well you can't hold the poor girl accountable," Catharine replied. "Lord Richard is what every normal young woman ought to want. She would have to be perversely obstinate to refuse such an offer."

"He is rich and handsome, I admit," Marian said, "But those are not the things to make one happy. We have discussed this point several times before, Catharine, and we do not agree, so I do not think it needs to be discussed any further."

"But if we agreed on everything, it would make for very dull conversation, would it not?"

"There is only so much we can discuss a certain point," Marian said. "I have grown quite weary of it."

Sir Edward traveled with his wife and sister to London the next day, and Marian's first order of business when she arrived there was to call on her sister. The ladies were out shopping, but John and William had lately arrived from White's and William was looking particularly pensive as he sat in his chair.

"Well Mary!" John exclaimed. "How was your journey to the continent? Did you bring back some French fashions for your sisters? They will never forgive you if you did not."

"Some of the French fashions were not suitable for my sisters to wear," Marian said. "Indeed, they ought not to be worn by any respectable lady."

"Well, but besides all that," John said. "Surely there are *some* acceptable fashions."

"I have brought presents for my sisters, John," Marian said. "You need not be concerned about that. How is Lady Emily?"

"Oh, she is well enough," John said. "We had a monstrous fight last night, but it is all over now. She can keep up her side of an argument pretty well."

"Well I'm very happy you are so suited to one another," Catherine said. "I would hate for you to have a *peaceful* marriage, since you don't seem to like it."

"Thank you, Miss Sheffield," John replied. "So would I."

"William, what is the matter?" Marian asked him. "You have said nothing since we got here."

"Oh don't mind him," John said. "He is only out of sorts because he is engaged in a duel."

"John!" William exclaimed. "Have you no more sense than to go about alarming the ladies?"

"It is not true, is it William?" Marian asked. "Who would challenge you to a duel? You've never done anything to offend anyone, I'm sure."

"Oh, but *he* is the challenger," John said. "Shall I tell them who the challenged is?"

"No," William answered.

"Yes," said Marian and Catherine.

"Well then, it is Lord Richard," John said triumphantly. "We were at White's this morning, see, and Lord Richard was at a nearby table with our cousin, Mr. Wesley. Somehow the subject came 'round to his lordship's engagement to Rachel and Lord Richard actually let slip that he made proposals to Rachel only because of the opportunities it would afford him of being in *your* company more frequently, and for the similarities between you. William declared that was a base insult to his cousin and challenged him on the spot."

"And you allowed him to do it, Mr. Amberly?" Catharine asked. "Mr. Forrester, it is nothing but idle talk, I am sure. Surely such a thing is not worth a challenge."

"To speak so about a lady in a public place is a bit beyond 'idle talk' Miss Sheffield," William said. "That he would even speak so tells how little he deserves her."

"Good heavens!" Catharine exclaimed. "You people are too nice about some matters. You make no allowance for anything." William did not trust himself to reply to such a remark, and so remained silent.

The ladies eventually returned to the house and Rachel, of course, was happy to see her sister and blissfully announced that she and Anna had been buying wedding clothes.

"Come to my room, Marian," Rachel said, "And see what I have got." Marian followed her sister up to her room and went on. "Look at this piece of muslin. It shall make a lovely morning dress, don't you think?"

"I daresay it will," Marian answered. "But Rachel, about this engagement—are you quite certain it is what you wish?"

"Of course it is," Rachel said. "And naturally Mama is very happy. Which reminds me—she wrote to say that she is coming to London and shall stay with Uncle Carlyle. She fancies that my taste is not adequate for buying wedding clothes suitable to the future Lady Beauregard. I daresay she is right, but I should like to choose my own clothes, just the same."

"Yes, but Rachel, how did all this come about?"

"The engagement, you mean? Well, very soon after I arrived in London, Lord Richard called on his sister here. When he saw me, he told me he was very happy to see me and that he had been thinking of me ever since he left Rosewood. After a couple more weeks passed, and we had spent quite some time in one another's company, he confessed to me that he had been in love with you, which of course I already knew, but that he had forced himself to get over it and before he had stopped loving you, he had begun to feel a stronger inclination for me. He feels now, he says, that I am much better suited to him than you, for we share many of the same tastes. In short, at last he proposed and I accepted."

"Rachel, I would advise against your marrying him," Marian said. "You cannot trust him."

"No, Marian," Rachel said. "Perhaps *you* cannot trust him. *I* can, and I do. You were always ready to suspect the worst of him, even before you really knew him."

"I have always made my judgments from my own observations. From the very first time I met him, I knew he was a terrible flirt, and since then I have heard worse."

"You are jealous," Rachel said angrily. "You did not want Lord Richard for yourself, but you don't want *me* to have him. You cannot bear to have your younger sister placed above you in society."

"Rachel, that is unjust."

"Is it not true? Then you must want to punish him for having ever loved you. It is not enough for you to reject him—you must have me reject him too! Well, I shall not. You had your opportunity and you chose to marry someone else. Now my turn has come and I shall not throw it away as you did! Don't try to make everyone else miserable!" Marian did not trust herself to reply to such a speech, so she excused herself, left the room and joined the company downstairs.

The next morning at breakfast, Rachel asked William if she might speak to him alone for a few moments. Naturally, he did not refuse her, and as soon as breakfast was over, everyone else went to the sitting room, leaving the two of them together.

"We are quite alone now, Rachel," William said. "What is it you wish to say to me?"

"It has come to my attention that you have challenged Lord Richard to a duel," Rachel said. "I want you to retract your challenge."

"I cannot do that."

"You must," Rachel said. "Or I shall never forgive you!"

"Do you not understand it is a matter of honor?" William asked. "Do you even know what the duel is about?"

"I understand that you might kill one another!" Rachel exclaimed, tears rolling down her cheeks. "What should I ever do if one of you were killed? I would be killed myself!"

"What do you know about why I challenged him?" William asked. "Who spoke to you about it? Was it Marian or John?"

"It was Lord Richard!" Rachel said. "He told me you challenged him for some trifling matter. He seemed to take it as quite a joke and assured me that he should try to fire amiss, for he really did not wish to harm you. But you might not have the same consideration and might hit him. That would not be fair."

"It was because I care about you, Rachel," William exclaimed. "You know I hate duels. But *I* cannot bear to see his *lordship* make a fool out of you, as he surely will, if he's allowed to go on."

"What do you mean?" Rachel demanded.

"He does not love you," William said. "He loves Marian still. He only wishes to marry you because you are her sister. He said as much himself. In a men's club, no less!" Rachel sat back down.

"I cannot believe it," Rachel said. Then her eyes flashed at him. "I cannot believe that you would be so base as to create such an accusation only to sink him in my esteem."

"Why would I create such a story?" William asked, growing angry at Rachel's stubbornness. "What motive could I possibly have?"

"I wish you would tell me," Rachel said. "But if you truly love me as you say you do, you would grant my request and retract the challenge." They looked at one another for a few moments before William finally spoke.

"Very well," he said. "I will retract it."

Later in the morning, Lady Emily, Rachel, Anna and Laura went to see Marian. Unlike formerly, when she was not the mistress of the house, Marian could not sit and talk in a corner with one of her friends, so Rachel asked if she might borrow a pen and paper. Marian directed her to the writing desk while she entertained her guests. When they left, she gave Marian the note she had written during the visit.

Dear Marian,

Please forgive my harsh words yesterday. I did not mean to be so hard. I know you fancy you are doing what is best, but please be assured I am very certain in my decision. I love Lord Richard and I have for some time now. I always thought you would marry him, so I held my tongue. Perhaps it is I who am a bit jealous, because of the regard he had for you in the past. But it is time for us both to look to our own futures. Pray, forgive me for what I said and do not hate me.

Rachel

It was several weeks before Marian spoke to Lord Richard, though she had seen him at several balls and parties. He prudently refrained from seeking her out, and pretended to be devoted to his fiancé. At last however, he could no longer keep himself away.

"Lady Sheffield," he said with a simper. "It is a pleasure to see you again."

"Thank you, my lord," Marian replied. "I understand I am to offer you my congratulations. I hope you will be happy together." Lord Richard looked around to see if anyone was listening and lowered his voice.

"If you wish me not to marry her, I shall not," he said. "I shall incur the world's censure only to please you."

"I only wish you not to marry her if you are not sincere," Marian replied. "If you do not love her, as you have told her, you ought not to continue allowing her to believe so. For she will believe no one else who disclaims your affection for her."

"I have the highest regard for her," Lord Richard replied. "Who would dare to suggest otherwise?"

"Apparently you would. I certainly would not like to believe such an accusation, but I have it on good authority."

"You know that I only love you," Lord Richard said. "But alas, you are denied me."

"Such a speech is very ill-calculated to raise you in my good opinion," Marian said. "When will you cease to say such things?"

"Never."

"Then I can never speak to you, for it is not proper for me to hear them."

"Well perhaps I may never *speak* them, if you wish, but may I not *think* them?"

"You ought not."

"But I can't help it."

"Then you should not marry my sister. Indeed, you should not marry anybody with that attitude."

"What would you have me do then?"

"Go on a tour around the world," Marian told him. "Forget about me. The pyramids of Egypt and the temples of Greece ought to drive me from your mind. After a few years, perhaps you will have gotten over me and may move on. Perhaps I may have smallpox, then you will not want me."

"To be sure I shall," Lord Richard protested. "It is not only your face I care about. You would still be the same."

"That is what all the young men say until their lady really does have it," Marian said.

"Will you dance the next two dances with me?"

"No," Marian said. "I shall not dance with you at all tonight. I do not believe it is quite safe."

"Yes, your husband would be sure to see me, and then I would be challenged to another duel."

"Well, perhaps it would do you good," Marian said.

"Well, I will not make the same promise by your *husband* as I did for your cousin."

"I will pretend I did not understand that," Marian said. "But I would ask you to leave me now. You have neglected your party too long to talk to a married woman."

"Very good, *Lady Sheffield*," Lord Richard said, pressing her hand to his lips. "Until we meet again."

Mr. and Mrs. George Wesley came to London at the beginning of March. Mrs. Wesley came to call on Marian and Catherine, both of whom expressed great pleasure at seeing her. They were only to stay in town about six weeks, as Mrs. Wesley was approaching her confinement.

"I am very sorry you are not staying until summer," Marian said. "But I'm sure the country is a better place for you to be at that time."

"And of course you and Sir Edward must come and visit us this summer," Mrs. Wesley replied. "I quite depend upon it, you see."

"Well then, how can I refuse?" Marian replied, smiling. "But only if you agree to visit us as well."

"I'm sure we shall be very happy to," Mrs. Wesley said. "But you know, George has become such a favorite in our little village, that I think it possible he may be soon elected to Parliament. I wonder what his father would think of that."

"Would Mr. Wesley be pleased to sit in Parliament?" Marian asked. "I thought it was not quite to his taste."

"Well, I know he will consider it his duty, whether he likes it or not," Mrs. Wesley said. "Of course I should not like him to be obliged to do anything he does not wish, but I also know his disposition, and if he is petitioned to run for office he will not refuse."

"Well, I wish him very well, then."

"Have you anything interesting to talk about?" Catharine asked at last, unable to bear any longer a conversation that held no entertainment for her. "You know I detest politics and the like."

"You are not obliged to take part in the conversation, if you do not wish to," Marian replied coolly. "But it is not polite to dictate to others what they may talk about."

"Oh, I am to have a lecture on manners now, am I? Well, I should like to know how my sister-in-law, who is a year younger than I, may educate me in anything."

"Have you noticed a change in your brother-in-law's behavior lately, Mrs. Wesley?" Marian asked, choosing not to reply to Catherine. "He has seemed a little cold and aloof this past month."

"I have seen him but once since we came to town," Mrs. Wesley replied. "He dined with us two nights ago. He seemed a little preoccupied, but I understand he has been visiting a good deal at your brother's house. I think he must have a very great inducement to be there so often. I shall be very surprised if he does not soon make a proposal to your cousin. But it would be better for us not to discuss it just now."

"Yes, perhaps the reason for his pensive attitude is that he is contemplating marriage with *somebody*," Catherine said. "I have my own opinion on the matter, but I shall not disclose it."

"I'm very glad you can show some degree of discretion," Marian replied, not taking the bait to plead for an explanation.

"Is it true that Mr. Carter is due to arrive tomorrow?" Catherine asked. "I'm sure he is quite longing to see Miss Anna again."

"I suppose it is true," Marian said. "At least, that is the news from Rachel."

"Well then, I propose that we pay a visit tomorrow," Catharine said. "I should like to see how her attitude toward him has been affected by her stay in London. It might have lessened her opinion of a retired life in the country. She fancied she was in love with Mr. Carter simply because he was the only man she was in company with."

"I do not like to hear you say such things," Marian said. "Really, Catherine, I think you want everybody to do what they ought not. Why do you take pleasure in such speculations?"

"It is much more interesting if people break the confines of society," Catherine replied. "We are quite prisoners in this world of manners."

"You are influenced too much by the Romantics," Marian said. "But one needs only to look at the lives they lead to see they are not to be imitated."

The next morning, Mr. Carter arrived at John's house when the family was still at breakfast. Anna had not yet come down and Lady Emily sent her maid, Elizabeth, to inform Anna that Mr. Carter had arrived and cordially invited him to join them while he waited. He sat down, but declined eating anything.

"I hope Miss Anna has not become too accustomed to life in town," Mr. Carter said. "She is used to such luxuries as I cannot afford."

"I'm sure Anna will be happy wherever she is," Laura said. "A happy home with the man you most love and respect is better than anything London can offer." Everyone looked at Laura and she blushed deeply and looked down at her plate.

"A noble sentiment, to be sure," John said. "But I doubt it is Anna's. She has been quite aching to get away from home since she was fourteen."

"Perhaps now she has had her taste she will be ready to settle down," Lady Emily said. "She ought to be content with the life she has chosen for herself."

"Certainly she *ought* to be," John said. "But it does not necessarily follow that she *will* be."

"Oh hush, John," Lady Emily said. "You will only distress poor Mr. Carter. How can you suggest she would be otherwise than happy when she returns home?" Elizabeth came back presently, wringing her hands and looking pale and nervous. She did not speak at first.

"Well, untie your tongue, Elizabeth," John said. "Is she coming down?"

"I'm afraid not," Elizabeth said at last. "Miss Anna—is gone."

CHAPTER EIGHTEEN

This revelation of Elizabeth's caused many exclamations of astonishment and consternation. She produced a letter addressed to Rachel.

"What do you mean 'she is gone'?" Lady Emily asked. "Where is she?"

"It appears her bed has not been slept in," Elizabeth said. "The curtains of the bed were all drawn, and when I opened them, the bed was still made and there was only a letter addressed to Miss Amberly."

"She has eloped," Rachel said, looking at the letter. "She does not say with whom. She says only that we may assure ourselves he is a man of character with whom her marriage should raise no objections, other than that she broke her previous engagement. She assures us all that he is a man of birth and fortune and charges no one to follow her, for they shall surely not be overtaken before they reach Gretna Green."

"Of course we must *try* and overtake them," John said, standing up. "Even though I know we cannot. For what shall I tell my father? That I allowed Anna to elope with nobody-knows-who while under my watch? And I did not attempt to prevent her?"

"We must hope for the best," Lady Emily said. "We can only hope that she was right in taking him to be a man of fortune."

"Well, I shall go after them and meet them on the road if I can," John said. "If he turns out to be a fortune hunter after all, I shall challenge him and kill him."

"Oh John, don't do that!" Rachel said. "It will do nobody any good for you to become a murderer."

"It's not murder if it's a fair challenge," John said.

"But you might be killed," Lady Emily cried. "Promise you won't attempt it."

"I must still go after them. I will send you word as soon as I have news. I hope I shall bring my sister back." Mr. Carter finally spoke after some moments of silence.

"If I had known she did not wish to marry me, I would have released her."

"Oh Mr. Carter!" Laura said. "How you must be suffering!"

"Do not think of me," Mr. Carter told her. "I must join with the rest of your family in hoping that Miss Anna has not thrown herself away."

Lady Emily noticed that her maid's paleness did not go away after the initial shock of Anna's disappearance was over. In fact, when she thought about it, she realized that Elizabeth had been looking progressively more ill for some time, but had said nothing. Lady Emily sent her to bed and had a physician sent for as soon as John had gone on his way to find Anna and her new husband.

By the time Marian and Catherine arrived at John's, the house was in confusion. The doctor was just coming down the stairs, shaking his head as they were being shown into the drawing room to wait for Rachel, for Lady Emily was busy just at that moment.

"What is the matter?" Marian asked, when Rachel came in. "Is someone ill?"

"Lady Emily's maid," Rachel replied. "She has been ill some time, I believe, but

Lady Emily never noticed until this morning. She sent for the doctor and he has examined her. I don't know what the diagnosis is, but Lady Emily has gone into her room."

"The doctor shook his head," Marian said. "It must be serious."

"I don't know," Rachel said. "But too many things have gone wrong today."

"What do you mean?"

"Where are Mr. Carter and Miss Anna?" Catherine asked. "I had rather expected to see them this morning."

"William and Mr. Carter have gone out," Rachel said. "Anna—has run away. She eloped last night, and we know not with whom." Rachel related what had happened that morning and when Lady Emily came down stairs, Rachel had just finished her narrative. Her face was red and she looked very much as if she had been weeping. Catherine went upstairs to see Laura.

"Oh, Miss Amberly—I mean Lady Sheffield," Lady Emily said, holding her handkerchief to her eyes. "Pray sit down." All the ladies sat down. "I don't know what I shall do. I am very fond of my maid. She has been with me since I was thirteen."

"Is she very ill?" Marian asked. "I hope she is in no serious danger."

"She is—she is—" Lady Emily paused and lowered her voice as if afraid the walls were listening. "She is *with child*."

"How shocking!" Marian exclaimed. "Why, surely she must have been seduced by some rogue. But what young men have had such an opportunity?"

"I know who it is. She confessed it to me herself. And that is what hurts me most. It was—my brother." Lady Emily buried her face in her handkerchief.

"Your brother!" Marian repeated. "I must say I never would have expected that, though I always knew he was a flirt."

"I don't know what possessed him to do it," Lady Emily said. "I know he has done such things in the past, but I never thought he would have seduced *my* maid."

"But anyone else's is acceptable, I suppose?" Marian asked.

"You needn't be so self-righteous," Lady Emily said coolly. "It would never have happened, had you married him."

"You cannot possibly think to blame *me* for your brother's actions!" Marian exclaimed. "He is his own master, is he not?" Marian looked at Rachel, who had a stony expression on her face. "What do you think of this, Rachel? Do you still wish to marry Lord Richard after this?"

"Do not ask me that right now," Rachel said. "I don't know what to think."

"How can there be any doubt? Do you wish to have such a man for a husband?"

"So you seek to poison your sister against Richard now," Lady Emily said. "Rachel, don't allow one lapse of judgment on Richard's part keep you from him. He was suffering a great disappointment at the time and had not the comfort of your affection."

"Do you condone his actions?" Marian asked Lady Emily. "Can there be anything that justifies seducing a young girl? You yourself claimed you were much injured by what he has done."

"It is only because I know that my maid shall be the chief sufferer, for she must know that Richard cannot and will not marry her. And I fear I must lose her." Catherine came downstairs with Laura, and Marian stood.

"Come, Catherine," she said. "I think we must go now. Rachel, I advise you to think about what you've heard today." Catherine protested, but she followed Marian out.

Two days later, John returned with Anna and her new husband who, everyone was not a little surprised to find, was Mr. Wesley. It seemed that they had met frequently and Anna had confided that she was engaged, but did not wish to marry her intended. Her only hope of escaping the match was to elope with someone else. Mr. Wesley had at one time been inclined toward Laura, but he was struck and charmed by the easy playfulness of Anna's manners, her youth and her beauty. He did not like to think of such a promising young woman confined in the country. The girl was of good birth and fortune, so there was no reason not to marry her, besides that she was publicly engaged to someone else. Mr. Carter returned to the country feeling rather dejected and Laura had to bear her disappointment as best she could.

One morning after Sir Edward had gone out, Marian was writing a letter to Sarah informing her of the recent events and of the happier news that Sir Edward might soon have an heir. While she was reflecting on these things, one of the maids announced a gentleman who desired to see her on a matter of urgent business. She ordered that he be directed into the drawing room and she stood up. Lord Richard came in and closed the door.

"Lord Richard," she said. "I have nothing to say to you." She went toward the door, but he would not suffer her to pass.

"I have let you escape me once too often," he said. "I've been waiting for Sir Edward and Miss Sheffield to leave, and so I know you are quite alone. Therefore you must hear me while I have the opportunity to speak to you. I offered you everything and you rejected me. For what? For a life of dullness and insipidity. What kind of life is this for someone of your wit and vivacity? I cannot allow you to live so. I have resolved, therefore, to rescue you from such a fate. I have come to propose that we run away together. I have already got passage on the first ship to Calais tomorrow morning."

"Are you mad?" Marian asked him, in extreme astonishment. "You cannot possibly expect that I will go anywhere with you. I must suppose you are in jest, even if it is very poor taste. But pray, be assured I am by no means unhappy with my life. It may be dull for *your* taste, but *I* am perfectly satisfied."

"I have never been more serious," Lord Richard said, holding her arms to hold her still. "I love you and cannot live without you." He kissed her and she slapped him.

"How dare you!" she exclaimed. "So this is your urgent business, is it? To attack and insult me in this barbarous manner? I command you to leave my house at once! I never wish to see you again!"

"Oh no, my dear," Lord Richard said, grabbing her hand lest she should attempt to strike him again. "I shall make the commands today. I have given you the option of refusal too many times. Now come." He pulled her over to the writing desk. He saw Marian's letter to Sarah which was but partially concealed, pulled it out and read it. "Now, sit down and you will write a letter which I will dictate." Marian had a brief glimpse of a pistol in Lord Richard's waistcoat and sat down as he had commanded her. Her heart started pounding and she began to think that perhaps Lord Richard really had gone mad. She took up the pen slowly, determined to take as long a time as possible, in hopes that Sir Edward would return home earlier than expected.

"Write 'My Dear Edward'—is that how you would begin a letter to your husband?"

"No, my lord!" Marian exclaimed, suddenly realizing what he was about. "I shan't do it! You may kill me if you wish, but I shan't do it!" He leaned toward her.

"Do you have the same apathy for the sake of your child?" Lord Richard asked her. "For your dear Edward's heir?" Marian began to weep. "Oh don't cry. You know I could never really harm you. If you refuse to do as I say, however, I might very well make you a widow." This assertion was not well calculated to cease Marian's tears, but she wrote the first line of the letter, though perhaps a little badly.

"'I hold you in the highest esteem,'" Lord Richard continued, "'But I find that I am unhappy in the life I have chosen, and that you and I are not suitable for one another. I have decided to save us both from a life of misery. I will be gone from London by the time you receive this letter. Please do not attempt to follow me. Be assured that this is the best course. I wish you every health and happiness in the future and urge you to forget one you once held so dear.' And then sign your name and seal it."

"Please don't make me do this," Marian said, even as she wrote the words. "What can you possibly have to gain? Edward will be heartbroken."

"He will get over it," Lord Richard said coolly. "He does not love you as I do. And I should think it would be quite obvious what I have to gain."

"This is not love," Marian said. "This is cruelty. This is cold selfishness and contempt for the feelings and wishes of others."

"However you choose to see it," Lord Richard replied, leaning close to her again. "You must and will be mine. I always told you that you would drive me mad, and now you see the result. You may congratulate yourself on your success. Now come." He held her by the wrist and pulled her with him.

"No, my lord, no!" Marian protested.

"What's going on?" asked a young maid who came to the bottom of the stairs.

"Margaret," Marian said. "When Sir Edward comes home, tell him I was taken by force by Lord Richard."

"I advise you to do no such thing," Lord Richard told her. "I say give this letter to your master when he comes home and say your mistress went out and did not tell you where. Here is a guinea, and if you hold your tongue properly, you shall have a hundred pounds." Margaret looked confounded at such an offer of money and accepted the letter.

"Nay, but if you do as *I* ask," Marian told her, "You shall be my lady's maid and have a hundred pounds every year."

"*I* shall give you enough money so that you never have to work as a servant again," Lord Richard countered. "You may open a shop or get married or do whatever you please. But do keep in mind that though I can be very generous to those who oblige me, I can exact very thorough revenge on those who cross me." He continued pulling Marian out the door and into his carriage which was in the street.

"You won't get away with this," Marian told him. "You will be found out."

"But I think I really will get away with it," Lord Richard said. "Sir Edward will know nothing until it is too late, and you and I will be on the continent. Then, of course, when it is plainly known that you and I have run away together, Sir Edward will not be able to take you back, even if he wishes to. He will have too much pride and it would be quite the scandal."

"You are taking me quite against my will," Marian said. "I think even society will understand that. Do you not care about your own reputation?"

"I care about nothing but being with you," Lord Richard said.

"Your family might take it very ill if you do not marry and produce an heir," Marian told him. "Where will your title go then?"

"If Sir Edward divorces you, you will be free to marry me."

"I would not marry you," Marian said. "And I am very glad now I did not agree to marry you before. You have used me very ill. My only consolation is that now Rachel will not marry you."

"Do you think I really cared to marry your sister anyway?" Lord Richard asked. "Only because I could not have you. But now I think it is possible to have you, and then my happiness will be complete."

"You have destroyed any measure of pity I had for you before," Marian said. "Now I can only hate you and hold you the most contemptible of men."

"I think you will change your views," Lord Richard said. "I don't expect it today, but I think you will, in time."

"Nothing you can do or say would ever make me think well of you again."

"When once you have gotten over this unfortunate, but necessary measure of mine, you will be happy enough. You shall still have every luxury you could wish, and we will not come back to England for a long time. We can see the whole world."

They arrived at Lord Richard's house and Marian went in with relatively little fuss upon Lord Richard's renewing his former threats. She was taken to a room at the top of the house that was well furnished.

"Never mind your screaming," he said. "No one can hear you up here." He turned and left the room, locking the door behind him. Marian looked around for any means by which she might escape. She could bear being ill-used, but she could not bear that Sir Edward would really think she had deserted him.

"Well, she shall be very difficult to manage, Hobbs," Lord Richard told his valet when he came back downstairs. "She was very desirous of not coming with me."

"Perhaps forcing the young lady is not the wisest thing," Hobbs replied. "If she is not willing to go, you will find her a tedious passenger."

"When I want your opinion, I'll ask for it," Lord Richard said peevishly. "And

I daresay I shall have very great pleasure in subduing her."

"But is she not married, my lord?"

"She is, for the present. But, that is an obstacle that will soon be remedied. Either Sir Edward will divorce her in her disgrace, or I will make her a widow."

"I cannot think such things are right," Hobbs said.

"Well, discerning right from wrong is not your job, is it, Hobbs?" Lord Richard said. "Your job is to do as you're told."

"Quite right, sir," Hobbs said with a frown.

Hobbs began to think that his master had gone too far. He never really approved of Lord Richard's intrigues, but before it had been servants, tavern girls and the like, besides his near elopement with Miss Darnell and some minor flirtations with more fashionable ladies. Now Hobbs had just learned that Lord Richard had seduced his sister's maid, whom Hobbs had a great fondness for, and he was forcing a married woman against her will to run away with him. No, truly Lord Richard had never gone so far before.

Sir Edward came home, bringing with him his sister, who had been visiting her cousin. Sir Edward looked for Marian in the drawing room and did not see her, so he tried his wife's bedchamber. Still no one. The cook was still out shopping, the butler was seeing to his master's business and one of the maids was on holiday. Growing alarmed every moment, Sir Edward was greatly relieved when he came across Margaret. "Margaret," he said. "Where is Lady Sheffield?"

"She—she went out," Margaret said. She produced the note Lord Richard had given her. "She left you this letter." Sir Edward took it and read it eagerly. However, his eagerness did not last, for he soon sat down, quite dumbfounded. Catherine came in and asked what the matter was and Sir Edward showed her the letter.

"Well, I always thought she would find it a dull life," Catharine said. "I did not expect that she would do *this* however. What an undeserving little strumpet she is."

"Please do not say such things," Sir Edward said.

"Oh surely you're not defending her after this?" Catharine said. "You must see now she is a very wicked girl and has probably gone to one of Lord Richard's estates."

"Go away. I don't wish to speak to you right now." Catharine left the room indignantly. As Sir Edward sat in his wife's dressing room, wondering how he had failed her, he was informed there was a gentleman who wished to see him.

Supposing this man might have information concerning Marian, he agreed to see him. It was Lord Richard's valet.

"Sir Edward Sheffield," Mr. Hobbs said, after Sir Edward had greeted him. "I have come to advise you to go to my mater's house if you would see your wife again."

"What do you mean?" Sir Edward asked. "Is she there?"

"I cannot say more now," Mr. Hobbs replied. "His lordship does not know I am here. However, I advise you to come quickly."

"Very well," Sir Edward said. "I will come at once."

CHAPTER NINETEEN

Lord Richard was in the dining room with Mr. Wesley, Mr. George Wesley and John Amberly when Sir Edward arrived. Sir Edward noticed the men were all looking drowsy—in particular, the two Mr. Wesleys, who at this point were all but asleep.

"Sheffield!" Lord Richard exclaimed, looking a little apprehensive. "To what do I owe the pleasure?"

"Lord Richard, where is my wife?" Sir Edward demanded. Lord Richard gave a small laugh of derision.

"Do you mean to say you've lost her?" Lord Richard asked. "Why ask me?"

"You know very well why," Sir Edward replied in a menacing tone.

"I have no idea what you're talking about," Lord Richard said. "Mr. Hobbs, will you please show Sir Edward the door?" Mr. Hobbs led Sir Edward out of the room, but when they were in the hall, Mr. Hobbs gave Sir Edward a key and told him to go to the last room at the top of the stairs, for his wife was being kept there, quite against her will.

"But do not worry about Lord Richard, for I put opium in the wine, so he will be quite unfit to stop you." When Sir Edward heard that his wife was upstairs, he lost not a moment in rushing up to her.

He found the room she was supposed to be in and unlocked the door. Marian backed away when she heard the door opened until she realized it was her husband who had found her.

"Edward!" Marian exclaimed, throwing herself into his arms. "I was quite afraid I would never see you again!"

"Marian, what are you doing here?" Sir Edward asked her. "I thought you had left London."

"Lord Richard forced me to write that letter," Marian said, weeping. "He told me he was going to take me away to the continent tomorrow morning! I did not want to go, but he said he would kill you if I did not do as he said. I think he has gone quite mad. I could not bear to think that you would believe I deserted you. I begged Margaret to tell you what had happened but I was afraid she would not. I am very glad she did, however."

"What, did Margaret know about this?" Sir Edward asked.

"Of course," Marian said. "Is she not the one who told you?"

"No, Lord Richard's valet helped me find you," Sir Edward said. "Margaret told me only that you had gone out and left a letter for me."

"Vile girl!" Marian exclaimed. "Well, then she accepted Lord Richard's bribe, for he offered her any amount of money to do his bidding. But, Edward, you are not angry with me, are you? I tried to get away, truly I did."

"No, you are not to blame," Sir Edward said, embracing her. "I didn't know how to believe you had left me."

"I always knew Lord Richard had vices," Marian said, "But I confess I did not expect him to be such an abandoned wretch." Sir Edward took his wife back downstairs, taking, on his way, a sword that was mounted on the wall, which had belonged to Lord Richard's grandfather.

Lord Richard stood up, a little unsteadily, when Sir Edward returned to the dining room with Marian.

"What is this?" Lord Richard demanded angrily. "Hobbs, you idiot, what have you done? Did you not know this was the lady's husband?"

"I did indeed," Hobbs replied. "And I daresay he wanted her back."

"Well then," Lord Richard said, "You are dismissed from my service at once. And so," Lord Richard said to Sir Edward, coming around the table, and taking a poker from the fireplace. "You wish to fight me? With my own grandfather's sword, too. How noble of you." Lord Richard swung at Sir Edward with the poker, but Lord Richard's senses were so impaired by the wine and opium, that with very little effort, Sir Edward evaded the attack and pushed Lord Richard to the floor. Lord Richard at first seemed as though he would not get up and Sir Edward said, in a tone of great contempt,

"I shall not degrade myself by fighting with you in this state. But if you please, when you are yourself, you may name the day when we might recommence it." Sir Edward threw the sword down and turned to leave with his wife. Lord Richard got up and took out the pistol that was still in his waistcoat. As he aimed it at Sir Edward's back, Hobbs had grabbed the sword off the floor and now he ran it through Lord Richard's side and the pistol fired into the air. Lord Richard fell senseless to the ground.

Sir Edward and Marian instantly turned back to see what had happened, and Marian nearly fainted at the sight. Hobbs looked terrified at what he had done, and John, who had hitherto watched the scene in confusion and astonishment, began cursing.

"You've killed him!" John exclaimed. Hobbs knelt beside him.

"He's not dead," he said. "He's still breathing, though a little irregular. I shall go and fetch a surgeon."

"And what shall you tell him when he asks how it happened?" Sir Edward asked.

"I shall tell him Lord Richard was in a duel," Hobbs said. "Doctors see such cases often enough. He will ask no questions. This is not the first time his lordship's been in a duel."

"But you shall be found out when he becomes conscious," Sir Edward replied. "Things do not go well for servants who attack their masters, whatever the reason. Particularly someone of Lord Richard's influence."

"Well, I shall be gone by tomorrow," Hobbs replied. "Perhaps I shall take Lord Richard's passage to Calais, then make my way to the Indies. The passage included two gentlemen and a lady, for I was to go with him. I have a little money saved. Perhaps I can make my fortune in some other part of the world."

"Well, I shall give you a sum as well," Sir Edward said. "It is the least I can do after what you've done for us. And if there is anything else you wish, name it and it shall be done, if possible."

"But what are we to do with that confounded body on the floor?" John asked.

"Hobbs and I shall take care of this," Sir Edward replied. "John, if you please, take Marian to your house and I shall meet you there."

Hobbs left for Calais the next morning, taking with him Lady Emily's maid, for he intended to marry her. Lady Emily made a slight protest at being separated from her maid, particularly so soon, but she was soon made to see it was the best option, with the help of Marian, provided it was agreeable to Elizabeth. John and Marian left out some of the details as to why Hobbs needed to leave so quickly, namely that Lord Richard was the man Hobbs had wounded, and why Hobbs already had passage to Calais. As a parting gift, Lady Emily gave Elizabeth three hundred pounds. Sir Edward gave Mr. Hobbs a thousand pounds and offered to assist him in any profession he chose for himself.

The surgeon said that Lord Richard's situation was very serious, but it was not expected to be fatal. Rachel, of course, after hearing the account of Lord Richard's attempted abduction of Marian, realized he did not really love her and that she could not marry a man capable of such a thing. She was forced to acknowledge that Marian was right to discourage her from such a match. Sir Edward's maid, Margaret, was of course dismissed for her false dealing, but on account of her youth, they promised to speak no ill of her to any prospective employers.

Lord Richard recovered in due course, and was very angry that his assailant had been allowed, even assisted, to escape the country. Lady Emily had been chagrined to find that her brother had been the man nearly killed by Mr. Hobbs, but when Lord Richard was well enough recovered, Lady Emily realized how truly wicked her brother had been. The dowager, naturally, did not believe any part of the story and would discredit the whole of London before she ever admitted that her favorite grandson could behave so wickedly.

George Wesley was only sorry he had been asleep the whole time so that he could not have prevented anything that happened. John was very angry at Lord Richard for treating his sister in such a barbarous manner, but eventually forgave him.

A few days after Rachel had heard the story from Marian, she called William to come and see her. William, of course, could not resist the summons.

"William," she began. "I want to apologize for the way I spoke to you when I asked you to retract your challenge. I realize now that what you told me is true. I now know that Lord Richard is an absolute scoundrel and cannot imagine how I ever fancied myself in love with him."

"Then you do not love Lord Richard anymore?" William asked.

"How could I love him after what he has done?" Rachel replied. "He is clearly not the same person I thought I was in love with."

"Well, I am very glad that you have reconsidered throwing yourself away on him," William said. "I—I truly hope you might find a man who deserves you."

"I believe—I think I have," Rachel said, looking toward the ground. "But I rather wonder if I deserve him. I rejected him in a most ungrateful manner, you see. But I have thought of it often since then, and if it had not been for my blind infatuation with Lord Richard, I might have realized sooner what I had thrown away." Rachel looked up.

"What do you think, William? Do you think he will ever forgive me for my obstinacy?" William smiled.

"I think," he said, "That he would say there is nothing to forgive. And that he would be honored if you would reconsider his offer."

"Thank you," Rachel said. "I think I shall reconsider it. In fact, I believe I already have."

"So," William said, "Am I to understand that you agree to marry me?"

"Yes," Rachel replied, smiling. "I think you may understand it that way."

Lady Amberly accepted Rachel's engagement to William without much complaint. It was impossible that Rachel should marry Lord Richard after what had passed and Lady Amberly was comforted by the knowledge that William would inherit his own estate. And at least her third daughter, however underhanded it was accomplished, had married into the aristocracy.

About a month after the engagement between Rachel and William was announced, Catherine Sheffield came to her brother and informed him that she and Lord Richard had been privately married the previous morning. Sir Edward at first did not believe it, and even when he did, could not easily reconcile himself to the fact. Catharine, as usual, took great delight in astonishing everybody with what she had to say. When Sir Edward informed his wife of his sister's marriage, Marian herself could hardly believe it. But though she did not say so to Sir Edward, she could more easily forgive Lord Richard for marrying Catharine than if he had married Rachel, and secretly thought them perfectly well-suited to one another.

At the end of April, Lady Amberly returned to the country with William, Laura and Rachel. Mr. Carter and Laura were both regular visitors to Rosewood Manor and therefore were frequently in one another's company. It did not take Mr. Carter long to realize that Laura Forrester was much better suited to be the wife of a clergyman than Miss Anna Amberly was. And when, by Laura's smiles and blushes when he spoke to her, Mr. Carter discerned that his suit would not be altogether unwelcome, he made his proposals in due course and naturally they were accepted.

Mr. Forrester was pleased that the two young people he had so long felt were best suited for one another had come together at last. Besides Laura's dowry, which was now ten thousand pounds, her father granted Mr. Carter the living on his new estate. So Mr. Carter took the place of his new father-in-law in both of his parishes.

When William's engagement to Rachel was announced, it was not very long before Mrs. Forrester and her eldest daughter decided to retire to Bath, which was fashionable, but less expensive than London. Miss Diana Forrester, now Mrs. Harding, opened a small school with her husband in a nearby village. Miss Forrester, disappointed in her hopes of becoming mistress of her childhood home, eventually married Mr. Henderson, for they met frequently in Bath.

Captain Jennings never succeeded in his quest to marry a pretty young heiress. His hopes, therefore, rested on whatever his uncle would give him. His hopes of a large inheritance were sadly shaken when, after a girl, Mrs. Cox had a boy. Captain Jennings was by no means forgotten by his uncle in his will, but he did not benefit so much as he might have, had Mr. Cox never had any children of his own. Nor did Mr. Cox forget his wife's children, and he left them two thousand pounds apiece. Captain Jennings, in his despair, married a wealthy old widow, whose jealous temper, it might be said, was a just punishment for her husband's mercenary pursuits.

Late in the summer following their marriage, Lord Richard and Catharine moved to one of Lord Beauregard's estates, which was about twenty miles from Sheffield Park. Lord Richard wrote letters of apology, both to Sir Edward and to Marian, for his temporary madness and unforgivable actions.

After several months, Sir Edward and Lady Sheffield were prevailed on to forgive Lord Richard's past actions, well enough, at least, to admit them to Sheffield House, for the sake of Catharine.

The following fall, Marian invited Fanny Perdue to spend six or eight weeks at Sheffield Park. During this period, Lieutenant Darnell also came for a short visit. Since the resumption of hostilities between France and England, Lieutenant Darnell had risen rapidly in rank and thought it very likely he would soon be made a commander. Fanny was fascinated by his accounts of naval battles and foreign places and the young lieutenant was gratified by the sincere attention he received from his charming young listener.

Lieutenant Darnell was soon aware of Fanny's admiration for him, humble as he was, for Fanny had not yet reached the age where young ladies learn to conceal their enthusiasm for particular young men. He had, indeed, suspected it when they last met at his sister's house in Bath. He was not, however, so certain of his own worthiness, though he had risen somewhat in rank and fortune since his sister had encouraged him to court Marian.

"I'm very sorry that our conversations shall soon come to an end," Fanny said as they walked in the lane. "I shall miss hearing of all your adventures."

"My adventures," Lieutenant Darnell said with a smile. "Well, I suppose you might say I've had *some* adventures. Though most of the time it is a tedious life of keeping the sailors in order and keeping watch on deck."

"But still," Fanny said "I should like to see the world. I have always been fascinated with foreign places."

"During a war is, perhaps, not the best time to see it."

"And you shall soon be 'Captain Darnell,'" Fanny continued. "And then, perhaps, all the ladies will be madly in love with you."

"That I do not expect," he replied with a smile. "But I am most gratified that you would think so kindly of me."

"But I cannot help it," Fanny said. Her companion looked at her. Then she blushed and looked at the ground. "That is, you are a very good young man and deserve all the good opinions any person might have of you."

"I wish I deserved your good opinion."

"But you do. *I* think you do, at any rate. Is that not enough?"

"Miss Perdue, I think you are a very dear girl," Lieutenant Darnell said. "And if I were in a better situation, I might be at liberty to think of—" He paused.

"I think your situation is very sufficient for—well, for anything you might wish." Fanny blushed at what she had almost said.

"If I were post-captain and had a better fortune—but you see, I am only a lieutenant and my fortune is insufficient to offer to a young lady of your situation."

"But my fortune is sufficient enough, I should think, for my needs. Indeed, I think it would be more than enough for us both."

"But I don't want the world to suppose I would marry any lady for her fortune. And at present, the disparity of our fortunes might well cause some to think so."

"I don't care what everybody thinks," Fanny said obstinately. "It would be a pity if you, or I, or anyone, should let the opinion of the world cause us to be unhappy."

"Well there is nothing for it then," Lieutenant Darnell said, smiling. "I cannot argue with such reasonable arguments. But if you will consent to marry me, you must also consent to wait, at least, until I am made a commander. And, of course, for the consent of your father."

"Oh, yes," Fanny said. "Only I hope it will not be very long before you are promoted."

Fanny and Lieutenant Darnell both wrote separate applications for the consent of Mr. Perdue, and to these, Sir Edward added another on their behalf, commending the character, potential and good nature of his cousin, and Mr. Perdue held Sir Edward's opinion so highly, that his recommendation alone was almost enough to gain Mr. Perdue's consent.

Lord Richard and Catherine were perfectly suited to one another, and though he never really overcame his infatuation for Marian, he at least learned to conceal it better and never mentioned it again. Catharine did her duty by her husband by producing an heir in due course and, just for good measure, she also produced a second son and three daughters.

As for Sir Edward and Lady Sheffield, they were a perfect example to their peers of what conjugal felicity should be. To say that they never had any disagreements would be too much, but they never allowed these disagreements to injure their mutual respect for one another. Sir Edward continued to consult his wife on various matters and Marian always held proper deference for her husband's wishes. So it may be said that they lived as well and as happily as any real couple, in this real world, have ever lived.